SUMMER ROMANCE

It had been a wonderful evening. Fran Phillips and Myles Jaffray stayed on the dance floor until the last dance.

"You were meant for me," Myles sang softly to the music. "Are you, Fran? I think you are." She felt his lips against her golden hair.

Maybe I am meant for him, she thought. Why not let herself go and be his summer love? She'd be the only one to suffer when it was over.

Frightened, she pulled herself together. She knew what kind of man Myles Jaffray was. Was she going to give him the satisfaction of breaking another heart?

Bantam Books by Emilie Loring
Ask your bookseller for the books you have missed

EMILIE LORING

I Hear
Adventure Calling

HEAR ADVENTURE CALLING

*A Bantam Book / published by arrangement with
Little, Brown and Company, Inc.*

PRINTING HISTORY

Little, Brown edition published September 1948
2nd printing ... December 1948
3rd printing ... February 1949
Grosset & Dunlap edition published January 1950

Bantam edition / June 1964

2nd printing .... August 1964	6th printing .. November 1966
3rd printing ... February 1965	7th printing ..... March 1968
4th printing .... August 1965	8th printing .... June 1968
5th printing .... July 1966	9th printing .... May 1969
10th printing .... May 1970	
New Bantam edition / April 1975	
2nd printing .... July 1975	3rd printing .... May 1977

ISBN 0-553-11075-6

Published simultaneously in the United States and Canada

PRINTED IN THE UNITED STATES OF AMERICA

I

The door of the elevator closed with soundless speed. The sandy-haired operator in dark blue with an abundance of gold trimmings glanced inquiringly at the slim girl in a brown suit and matching beret.

"Grimes & Phillips." She answered his unspoken question. He touched a button and looked at the tall, dark-haired man in gray, the other occupant of the car.

"You said—"

"The roof," the man answered quickly.

"I thought you wanted—" The operator muttered the rest of the sentence and punched another button.

"Decided suddenly on the roof. Grand view of the city from there, I understand."

Nice voice, deep, rich and, boy, I'll bet he's used to getting what he wants, the girl thought. She stole a glance at him but the broad brim of his gray hat covered the upper part of his face as he looked down at the memoranda book he held. He had the just-out-of-uniform look. "Seeing Boston," she decided and watched the floor numbers as they lighted and blacked out.

"Seven." The door opened without benefit of human touch. As she stepped to the corridor she heard the operator say:

"Thought this was the floor you wanted, Mister."

She opened a door which proclaimed in conservative black letters that Grimes & Phillips pursued the practice of law within. The young woman with tightly curled brick-red hair at the switchboard in the office looked up and grinned.

"The Judge is waiting for you, Miss Phillips. Guess if it had been anyone else he'd have canceled the appointment, he's eating raw dog, these days, if a client is late. He sure has a case on Frances Phillips—Yes, *sir*," she spoke into an interoffice phone. "Yes, sir, I'll send her in." She snapped off the connection. "He's in the library. Better make it fast."

Fran paused at an open door. She had known the

1

man with a mane of white hair seated behind the flat desk since she was a small girl. His hair hadn't been white then, his shoulders hadn't sagged as they sagged now as if tired from carrying a load of responsibility. Not surprising when one remembered that the son who had planned to come into the office was now a white cross in a Belgian field and that her brother Ken, who had inherited the Phillips half of the partnership, was still in Germany.

"Come in, come in, Franny, what are you waiting for," The Judge rose and glared over his spectacles. "You're late, then you stand staring at me as if you were scared to death. Shut the door. Now sit down." As she perched on the edge of the chair across the desk from his, he asked:

"Did you bring the letter?" She nodded assent. "Read it to me again. I've had several communications from Ken and a long distance phone about how set you are against the change in trustee."

She drew two closely typewritten pages from her green shoulder bag.

"Remember, Judge, that this letter is dated one month before I received it." Her eyes followed the lines: "Ken writes that he intends to remain in Germany during this critical period as long as he is needed, which at present means indefinitely, that he has transferred the trusteeship of the property Aunt Rebecca left me to Myles Jaffray. Why, *why* did he pick on him?"

"What's the matter with Jaffray? Ever seen him?"

"No, and I never want to. Matilde, Gene Sargent's sister-in-law, went off her head about him—her husband Ben and he were training at the same airfield, they had grown up in the same summer resort. She was preparing to leave her husband and little girl—"

"For Jaffray?"

"It was the consensus of the woman's friends."

"That doesn't establish it as a fact. Who told you the gossip?"

"Gene Sargent, at the time we were in college together. She was so terribly upset that I suspected she was that way herself about him. The day he was coming to see her—he was home on a short leave—she told me the story, so I could keep out of the way and avoid meeting

2

him. I hadn't been mild in expressing my views about a home-smasher."

"Did the wife run away?"

"No. Ben crashed soon after the talk began and Matilde left the station with the child."

"So-o, she told you that you might keep out of the wolf's way? I don't see that the Sargent girl's yarn proves anything, except that the home-smasher—that's your word, not mine—may not have reciprocated her affection. Ken has lived and fought beside Jaffray for five years; since the end of the war they have been working together as administrators in the American Zone. Do you think he would have made him trustee of your property if he believed the Matilde story? How did your brother and he get together? Coincidental, as they say in the movies?"

"No. Gene told Myles Jaffray to look up Ken at the Officers' Training Camp. He did and they became friends."

"Something about the Matilde angle strikes me as phony. Your friend Gene doesn't happen to have green eyes?"

"No, they are almost black and very beautiful. What do green eyes have to do with my detestation of Myles Jaffray?"

He tapped on the desk with the tips of his fingers.

"Might have a lot to do with it, Franny," he said thoughtfully, with his eyes on the steel skeleton of a building rising against the sky beyond the window. "But that isn't what you are here to talk about. Read the letter. Stop giving me extracts." She picked up the two sheets.

"He writes that Myles is returning to this country, to New York, then goes on, 'No use fighting me about this, kiddo. You resented the fact that Aunt Becky tied up the estate she left you until you are twenty-five.'" She dropped the pages to the shining mahogany desk.

"Why did she, Judge? My home was with her from the time I was eleven, when Mother died. Father went a few years later. Because she was a partial invalid I wouldn't leave her while we were at war though I fairly ached to enlist. I selected a college near our home so that I could live with her. I doubled as her secretary, kept her

3

accounts, knew to a dot what she was spending. I loved her. I'm twenty-three. It hurts to know that she didn't trust me to take care of the estate she willed to me."

"It wasn't that she didn't trust you, Franny. Your mother was her young sister whom she adored and spoiled. When that same sister eloped with a stinker, in spite of the damning evidence Rebecca had dug up about his escapades, she was furiously angry. It didn't help that a few months later she could say, 'I told you so,' when the heel deserted his wife. Your mother divorced him and later married a fine man, your father. Rebecca liked him but she was haunted always with the fear that you might lose your head and heart over a no-good as your mother did, especially if you had money to tempt one."

"Even so, how could you, an up-to-the-minute person if ever I saw one, draw a will with the crazy clause that if I married without the consent of the trustee I lost the property? That belongs back in the days when fathers turned erring daughters out into the snowstorm. You have known me all my life. Do you think I have no common sense?"

"Sometimes when love comes in at the door common sense flies out of the window, Franny. I agree with you that what you call the crazy clause is early nineteenth-century stuff. I did my best to convince Rebecca that it might precipitate the very situation she dreaded. No use. It was her fortune, she had a right to dispose of it as she wished. I drew the will, heaving a sigh of relief when she made your brother Ken trustee, free to name his successor if it became necessary. Cheerio, in two years you can wave good-by to Jaffray. Now let's get on with the letter." She picked up the pages.

"Where was I? Here it is, 'Myles is the straightest, finest fella in the world—I know the truth about that Matilde episode—added to that he is an attorney who, in the few years between receiving his degree and enlistment, specialized in probate law. He drew the transfer of trustee papers, in consultation with an eminent Massachusetts lawyer at present on the staff of our general. They are fight-proof.'" She looked questioningly at the man across the desk. He nodded agreement.

"They are. The probate court has passed on them

4

though it hasn't allowed them yet. Go on with the letter. Keep your voice up. Can't hear myself think with that darn riveting going on outside."

"He goes on, 'Myles didn't want the responsibility, kicked like a steer against taking it when he read the clause that if you marry before you are twenty-five without the consent of the trustee—Aunt Becky figured that would be me—the bulk of the estate she left would be divided between certain charities.

"'Even when I explained to him how deeply hurt Aunt Becky had been by Mother's runaway marriage, he said, "Nothing doing. Why saddle me with the responsibility of saying you can or you can't to your sister Frances as to the man she wants to marry? From what you have told me about her—and boy, have you talked— sure as shootin' the kid will go haywire, plunge through hell and high water to marry the guy she thinks she wants to prove her independence."'" She looked up from the letter.

"You don't think I am idiot enough to do that fool thing, do you, Judge?"

"I don't know what I think, Franny, when you look at me with those enormous eyes which always remind me of brown velvet pansies. Go on with the letter."

"Let's see, here we are: He's still quoting Myles Jaffray. 'I've studied the photograph of your sister you carry round with you, enough to realize that.' He's referring to the plunge through hell and high water, Judge—'Pick another guy for the job. Fran would have her knife out for me and I had counted on our being friends.' Ken X-ed out the rest of the sentence before he went on:

"'Myles gave in finally when he realized what a load he would take from my shoulders by accepting the trustee appointment. I can't pay proper attention to the investments at this distance—said it would be his part in helping in my tremendously important job. It is important, Fran. Sometimes I wonder if I can swing it, then I hear Aunt Becky's voice, "Think defeat and you invite defeat. Think success and you invite success." Great old girl, Rebecca Harding, if she was nuts about early marriage.

"'I have sent the signed and properly sealed transfer

5

document to Judge Grimes. Be a good kid, don't get your dander up. I am doing what I know will be best for you.' "

She folded the letter and slipped it into her bag.

"Brother knows best. He still thinks of me as his kid sister. Can't you do anything about it, Judge?" He shook his leonine head.

"No, Franny. There is neither crack nor cranny in that document through which I can squeeze you free. If Jaffray drew it he can have anything he wants in this or in our New York office, even to a partnership eventually. See him before you are sure he is a calamity in your life." He tapped a slip of yellow paper on his desk.

"This cable came from him today: BOSTON NEXT WEEK. ARRANGE INTERVIEW WITH FRAN."

"With *Fran?*"

"Them's his very words." The Judge chuckled though his eyes under shaggy white brows were grave. "Cheerio, you may like him so much he will knock Blake Sinclair, your present heartbeat—that last lifted from my granddaughter's vocabulary—clear out of the showing. Could be that the boy next door was the lad of whom your aunt was afraid? He was a nice boy, until somewhere along the growing-up road he took a wrong turn."

Soft color rose to the uneven line of her bronze-gold hair. She crossed her arms on the desk and leaned toward him.

"Have you written Ken about Blake, Judge Grimes?"

"No, but your brother must have many correspondents who know you both. The gentleman referred to hasn't been hiding his high life under a bushel—to paraphrase a time-tested simile."

"He hasn't led a high life, as you call it, for months."

"Who says so?"

"I say so, and I ought to know. He says he never feels the temptation to gamble or drink when we are together."

"Great Scott, Franny, you're not considering marrying Sinclair to reform him, are you?"

"Sometimes I wonder if it is my duty"

"For crying out loud—lifted from my granddaughter—if you have that crazy bee in your bonnet I'm glad that marriage clause is in the will."

"Calm yourself, Your Honor." She laughed. "That was just to get your reaction. I don't intend to marry anybody for years, if then. I intend to be a career girl—and like it. To return to Myles Jaffray and his cable, I won't be here when he arrives."

"Where will you be?"

"Gene Sargent's father is the owner of the famous Sargent Galleries in New York City. He has a Gallery in the town on the coast of Maine where the family spends the summer. It is his pet and pride, Gene calls it Sargent Gallery, Jr. Paintings famous and not so famous, *objets d'art*, some of fabulous value, are on view and on sale. It's a Mecca for summer residents for miles away. He needs an assistant. I'm taking the job. I hear adventure calling."

"Franny, where did you pick up that gay little laugh? I'm glad to see your dimples flash again. You make me think of a gorgeous butterfly just out of its chrysalis, fanning its colorful wings for a take-off into freedom." He removed his spectacles and vigorously polished them with his handkerchief. She could see tears in his eyes before he replaced them. "You've been held in a strait jacket so long you rate adventure. Do you think you'll get much in the State of Maine? Why don't you go to Alaska or Hollywood or some place where things happen? Besides, with your training you could fill an important position, but, you don't need a job."

"You're making fun of me. Don't thrilling things happen wherever there are people? I'll take a chance on Maine. It is the first signpost I've seen since I fared forth to answer that clarion call. As for the job, I do need it, Judge. Not financially, but mentally and spiritually I need it terribly." She steadied her shaken voice. "I realize now what a tight little life I have lived these last years. You know, Aunt Becky didn't want guests. The Sargents are cultivated, delightful people, with a charming home; modern, the best modern, in their ideas; they attract others like themselves. It is only for the summer. When fall comes I will have a brand-new outlook, will have recovered my sense of direction, will know what I want to do with my life. I lived so close to Aunt Becky, followed her pattern of living so faithfully to keep the peace, that I feel like a jellyfish." The Judge chuckled.

7

"Even the jellyfish has a sense of direction, as you would know had you ever been lashed by one of the poisonous variety. How and where will you live? When do you go?"

"I am leaving tomorrow. The Gallery will open the first day of June. Mr. Sargent wants me there a few days before that I may learn the ropes. His wife has invited me to stay at their place, Rocky Point, but I will find a spot of my own. The Cambridge house is closed, with a caretaker engaged for the grounds. I splurged on a summer wardrobe, contributed to a couple of charities whose welfare I have at heart, and scraped the bottom of my bank account. Decided it would be interesting to live on my salary. The new trustee can't hold back my income due September fifth if I side-step meeting him, can he? That's a thought."

"Certainly not. Why would he want to?"

"You never can tell, authority does queer things to people. I'll bet Ken named him trustee of Rebecca Harding's estate to give him a financial boost on his return to practice, the fees will help with his expenses while he waits for clients. It would be so like that brother of mine. He's a push-over for lame ducks." The Judge frowned thoughtfully.

"I wouldn't exactly call Myles Jaffray a lame duck."

"Of course you wouldn't. You are sold on him, completely sold. I can see that with half an eye. Okay, if you won't fight for me at least promise you won't tell him where I am."

"How can he forward your income if he doesn't know where you are?"

"Through you, all communications through you."

"What will be your address?" She laid a card on the desk and a small dark blue envelope.

"Here it is, even to the phone number, also one of the keys to my safety-deposit box at the bank. My war bonds are there, also my pearls and jewelry; except for some small stuff and the large cluster diamond ring that was Aunt Becky's, I didn't want the care of it."

"Why leave the key with me?"

"If I want any of the things I thought you would get them for me, you have power of attorney for me, and

8

your signature is on a card at the bank which authorizes you to go to my box. You won't mind, will you?"

"No, but I hope you won't cash the bonds, Franny."

"Why should I, unless the new trustee goes berserk and refuses to give me money when I want it?" She shook her head to clear her eyes of the tears that suddenly blurred them. "I—I hate to leave you, Judge. I—I always feel that in a way I belong to you."

"You are not leaving me, child, I'll be right here whenever you need me. I am glad you are breaking away from old associations. You are right, you have lived a tight little life these last years in spite of war activities and college. Rebecca was a fine woman, but a born dictator. She had a yen to run the lives of others. Now she is trying to keep her dead hand on you, as shown in her will. Forget the past and make the present something vital and inspiring. Be sure and keep me posted."

"I will, you dear, I will." She kissed his cheek with impulsive tenderness, laughed and blinked away tears. "Exit the career woman."

"It's you, Miss," the operator greeted as she stepped into the passengerless car. "Remember the guy in gray who went up when you did, said he wanted to go to the roof?"

"I remember him. Good heavens, he didn't fall off, did he?"

"Naw, but he acted awful queer. Stopped at seventh twice, then came back. Perhaps he heard Judge Grimes shoutin'. When the old fella tries to talk above the rivetin' you could hear him at the State House. Anyhow he didn't seem certain where he wanted to go."

Fran thought of the deep authoritative voice.

"He seemed to me like a person who knew exactly where he wanted to go and would get there."

"Yeah, you said something. I guess he knows where he wants to go, all right. You can't tell nothin' about guys like him, though. He was so queer I reported him to the superintendent. He's going to have him watched if he's still in the building. There's been a lot of safebreaking in this neighborhood lately. Looks to me an' the superintendent as if this gent might be a finger man of a

9

gang—they dress snappy like him." The operator's voice
went flat.

"Street, Miss."

II

A breeze lightly scented with the salty tang of kelp,
murmurous with the lazy lap of the tide against rocks,
stirred the palm-designed chintz hangings at the long
open windows of the dining room in the Sargent home,
Rocky Point. It set a-flicker the tall tapers in the two
four-branch candelabra on the lace-covered table.

Delicate pink and violet tulips filled a pale green
Limoges bowl in the center; flat silver gleamed, crystal
goblets and wineglasses sparkled. The frock of the hostess was the shade of dark purple pansies, a color which
accentuated the silvery whiteness of her modishly high
coiffure; her brunette daughter, Gene, wore the filmy
pink of the tulips. The dinner coats of the host and the
men made a design of white between the pastel frocks of
the women guests.

Bare shoulders are in again for better or worse, large-
ly worse at this table, Fran Phillips decided. "Lucky I
wore my pale amber, more in harmony with the ensemble than the lettuce green taffeta I was tempted to wear.
If—"

"I take it you don't care for littleneck clams, Miss
Phillips," the man at her left commented in the hushed
voice of a conspirator. "That's the fourth you've
sneaked under the ice on which they are served."

Fran laughed as she met his amused dark eyes.

"Don't betray my guilty secret. I just can't swallow
them. It would be a social blunder to leave the six poor
little things untouched, so I give them decent burial. A
method distinctly my own. Rather original, what?"

"Do you apply the same deep-freeze method to persons you don't like?" Before she could answer he turned
to reply to a question of the hostess, at whose right he
sat.

Who is he, Fran asked herself, she must have been in
the throes of a mental blackout when they were introduced before dinner; perhaps they hadn't been intro-

10

duced—he wasn't the sort of person one forgot. Perhaps they hadn't met—the *apéritifs* were being served when she entered the library, she had been detained at the Gallery.

"You haven't heard a word I've said," accused the man at her right. "I don't believe you know my name."

"It is Morrison Grove, 'Morrie' to your hostess. When I refused a cocktail you brought me a glass of tomato juice with the lugubrious air of one offering a poison cup. We came in to dinner together and you asked if I had begun to feel at home in the State of Maine, an astonishing cliché coming from 'one of our rising men politically,' Mrs. Sargent speaking."

"One hundred per cent correct, even to that quote, if I say it who shouldn't." The slightly bald, slightly rubicund, slightly overweight old-young man beamed at her. "How do you do it? Apparently in spirit you were miles away from this room. What cataclysm of events landed you as assistant in the Sargent Gallery here?"

"Mr. Sargent needed an attractive, up-to-the-minute young woman to help—that's me, if I say it who shouldn't—I needed desperately an entire change of environment, Gene and I were classmates at college, she suggested that I come here for the summer. Here I am. Does that answer your question? It should. You now have the story of my life in tabloid."

"I'll bet I haven't. I'll bet a man was involved in that change of environment you needed so desperately. *Cherchez l'homme*. Take my bet?"

He turned to answer the question of a woman in pale blue at his right. The man at Fran's left, who had detected the hideaway of the clams, was listening intently to his hostess, who, Fran had discovered at their first meeting years ago, was a nonstop conversationalist.

"I'll bet a man was involved in that change of environment." The repetition of Morrison Grove's words in her memory sent her thoughts backtracking to the day in Judge Grimes's office three weeks ago. Since then he had written that the change of the trustee for Rebecca Harding's estate had been allowed by the court. In closing he added:

"I've had four conferences with Jaffray *re* your affairs.

11

Your brother showed good judgment in the selection of his successor. Glad to hear you like your job."

He had not mentioned Myles Jaffray's reaction to her refusal to meet him. Apparently it hadn't made the slightest dent in the life of the new trustee. She had expected he would write to her and demand a hearing, had mentally composed a courteous but frigid reply. It had been good. It would be a pity if she never had a chance to use the literary masterpiece.

"Did you mutter 'darn,' or was the sound something the breeze brought in?" Morrison Grove inquired. "What goes? Your cheeks are flaming, your eyes which I thought were the brown that goes with bronzy-gold hair are shooting sparks, and speaking of hair, I like it short like yours. Natural or permanent wave?"

"The fairy who attended my entrance into this world, it wasn't such a grim planet then, endowed me with a permanent."

"Hooray for the fairy. To return to those shooting sparks. Mad because I deserted you? Couldn't help it. The lady at my right is a political power—known as the Terrible Tassie—Miss Trent to you—originally an F.F.V. —she can influence a lot of votes in my direction—we both keep our legal residence in this county—I'm out for re-election to Congress. I had to listen to her, much as I prefer to look at and talk to you."

"Of course you had to listen and just to keep the record straight, my cheeks are not flaming, my eyes are not shooting sparks because of your neglect."

"Maybe not, but you are disturbed about something, can't fool your uncle Morrie. To proceed with my diagnosis, could it be that you have quarreled with the blond, screen-lover-good-looks lad directly across the table? His hair is as shining and smooth as the gold dome of your State House, his mustache resembles nothing so much as a third eyebrow. His gloomy gaze has been fixed on you in the intervals between turning his deadly charm on the gals each side of him."

The lad directly across the table was Blake Sinclair. She had felt his eyes on her and had carefully avoided meeting them. She had been amazed, then angry when he had spoken to her in the library before dinner. She had told him before she left home that she wanted

12

neither to see nor to hear from him until September. She had left unanswered his indignant, incredulous "Why?" She couldn't explain that she needed time and distance to get a perspective on that "deadly charm" to which she had not been unresponsive, while she kept him determinedly on the plane of friendship.

"Your expression gives you away. You have been thinking over my guess, haven't you? Right the first time, wasn't I?" Grove chuckled complacence.

"Is it part of your campaign program to probe for the secrets of a maiden's heart? Shame on you."

"Say, you know you've got what it takes. I didn't realize that girls would have your sparkle, charm and warm friendliness who were raised in the shadow of the Sacred Cod."

"Speak softly when you say that name, stranger. We can't until we meet a responsive spirit like you, then 'From the crown of her head to the sole of her foot, she is all mirth.' Adapted from *Much Ado about Nothing*. I hope you know your immortal William? It's a must when you play with one of us Sacred Cod girls." His shout of laughter drew startled eyes in their direction.

"Hold it. Having settled that question to our mutual satisfaction, what are you and gloomy Gus across the table fighting about? Confide. Me, I'm that congenial spirit, remember? I—" He turned to the woman at his right.

"Certainly I'm interested in what the women in the organization of which you are the head think of the Russian situation, Miss Tassie. It is of vital importance. The Bear is growling and—" Fran lost the rest of the sentence.

As the man at her left still was held on the conversational leash by his hostess her thoughts trekked back to Blake Sinclair and his presence at this table. She had introduced him to Gene when she was at college, the estate of his family adjoined Rebecca Harding's. Could she make him understand that it was useless to follow her? That she would not see him?

"Our hostess serves the most delectable salads in the state." Morrison Grove had broken away from his constituent. "I know. I get around. None of the jellied stuff I hate. This combination of chilled avocado, grapefruit

13

and fig bursting with cheese mixture is the berries. I'm something of a chef myself. Keep bachelor hall in ye old homestead. Like to pick up ideas. White wine in the dressing, what?"

"Could be. Ask Mrs. Sargent after dinner. She'll tell you."

"Not I. She would immediately embark on a lecture as to how and where the fruit is grown, whence the wine, and so forth. I admire the lady for her good looks, good works and expert housekeeping, but, I side-step her educational monologues."

Fran disciplined a smile. Criticizing one's hosts or their hospitality was a breach of courtesy she abhorred, but Morrison Grove was right, one couldn't comment on bird, beast or flower to Mrs. Sargent without precipitating a discourse on the subject.

"I see by your not too well controlled smirk that you get what I mean." She ignored his comment.

"While I was left high and dry like a boat on a beach at low tide with no one to talk to, did the lady at your right assure you that your re-election is in the bag?"

"No, quite the reverse." The question she had intended for a light touch clouded his face. "She says that her organization has been examining my records to see how I voted on foreign policy matters, it is not satisfied, and what the Terrible Tassie says, goes."

"Loud cheers for those women. Right on the job, aren't they? They know that the entire nation has foreign policy on the brain. Does it mean that you didn't go all out to help establish a lasting peace?" Her question added another layer of color to his face, she sensed his instant of defiance before he said smoothly.

"Perhaps I disagree with the plan to bring it about."

"You mean you think that our enormous productive capacity should not be used to overcome the chaos and suffering following this last tragic war?"

"What do you know about the plan being put before the country?"

"Not much, I am ashamed to admit, but from now on I'll be listening to the campaign speeches from the candidates themselves, if they are near, from radio if they are not. I'll form a policy of my own."

"You won't have to travel far to hear some of them.

14

Miss Trent gave me the jolt of my life when she told me that a returned serviceman was being proposed by the Good Government Association of this district as a candidate for my seat in the House."

"Being proposed doesn't necessarily mean he will be nominated, does it? Haven't you accomplishment enough on your record to offset your foreign policy bad mark?"

"I hope so, but there is more to it than that. His family has loads of the moolah, have been citizens here since the beginning of time—mine goes back only two generations—it produced a Colonial Governor. The house built on the land he acquired was the largest in the town, it's a knockout in architecture and grounds, is opened when a charity stages one of those Historic Landmarks shows. It was called Shore Acres then and the name has stuck. He's my friend, he's a grand guy, but he's had all the breaks."

"Ours is a democracy. A man doesn't need wealth and a social background even to become President. You'd better take a refresher course in American history."

"I get what you mean, but six years in the service added to what he had before will fire the imagination of the voting public."

"What were you doing through those same years?"

"Slaving at a desk in Washington for three of them. It wasn't my fault I didn't get into the fight. Had fifteen pounds sweated off me the day before I went up for examination, and say, is that something to do for one's country? But they wouldn't pass me."

"I'm sorry you were disappointed. You won't quit the Congressional fight because another candidate may be or has been proposed? You won't give up, will you? The easiest thing to do in the world is to give up."

"Not a chance. I'm right back in there pitching. Miss Trent's news knocked me out for a minute, that's all."

"Perhaps she is mistaken. Is she an authority on the political situation?"

"Authority! That woman is a law unto herself. She is the political arbiter of this county."

"Is your potential rival interesting? Having met you I would like to see him. Maybe I'm psychic, maybe I can see the winner in my crystal ball."

"Hey, soft-pedal. He's the man at your left. This dinner is a sort of Hail to the Hero welcome home to him."

Fran thought of the man's laughing eyes, of the richness of his voice even when hushed when he said, "I take it you don't care for littleneck clams, Miss Phillips." How had he known who she was? They hadn't met before dinner.

"What is our hero's name?" she whispered. "I'd like to know, I can't very well say 'you, there,' when I speak to him."

"Jeepers, do you have to ask? His service record has been front page stuff in the local news for two days. Airborne division. Made some spectacular jumps. He's been decorated and redecorated. He's Myles Jaffray, Major Myles Jaffray."

"Myles Jaffray?" Fran was unaware of her shocked repetition.

"Did I hear my name?" the man at her left inquired. He turned his back on his hostess as squarely as etiquette permitted. Not Ken's Myles Jaffray, she reassured herself while her eyes clung to his as if hypnotized. "If you don't like clams you do like raspberry mousse with marrons, don't you?"

His voice broke the spell of unbelief. Was he warning her that she was attracting attention?

"Mad about it." Would he notice the hint of vibrato in her voice? "I am a person of very strong likes and equally strong aversions."

"And loves and hates. You're telling me. You have stepped into the glacial age. You were gay, responsive and charming the first time I spoke to you. Didn't know who I was? Since then you have discovered?"

"I have. You know I didn't want to meet you. Why did you follow me?"

"Follow you." His low incredulous voice, his brows raised in surprise, sent a wave of color to her hair. Stupid, why had she given him that lead? "My dear Fran."

"Don't call me that."

"Dear or Fran?"

"Neither."

"Sorry, being with Ken so much I got the habit of

16

thinking of his kid sister as Fran. It won't happen again.
Get this. Personally you went out of my life when you
refused to meet me at Judge Grimes's office; nevertheless, I shall carry on my trustee duties in every detail.
Mrs. Sargent has given the high sign to her husband." As
he rose he drew out her chair and added close to her
ear.

"And I mean in every detail. That's a warning to
watch your step."

III

A voice singing, "You're So Sweet to Remember"
drifted from a concealed radio as hostess and women
guests entered the book-walled library where soft green
hangings were pushed back from the long open windows. I'll wager Myles Jaffray never will think that of
me, Fran decided as she dropped to a deep rose-color
pouf. I stepped off on the wrong foot with him.

"How come the shiver, Fran?" Gene Sargent's pale
pink skirt billowed as she seated herself behind the
coffee table. She dropped a cube of sugar on the saucer
of a Sèvres cup. "You can't be cold so near that gay
little fire behind you. Didn't pick up a bug today, did
you?"

"No, must be a reaction from the excitement of the
dinner party. I'm a temperamental person."

"I'll say you are, if you call this boring evening exciting." Her mouth, which nature had intended to be
lovely, had acquired a discontented droop at the corners. "You are wearing yourself to shreds at the Gallery.
You go into everything you do up to your elbows. That
suits Dad to a T. He's a slave driver. The New York
Galleries are a business, this summer project is an avocation, his pet and pride."

"It is fast getting to be mine. I'm thrilled over it. I
was late getting home tonight because I wanted to make
sure we were ready to receive the paintings tomorrow
for our—notice that *our*—one-man show the day after."

"That leads up to what I want to talk to you about,
this is my chance before the men come in. Mother and I
think you should be nearer the Gallery, you waste so

17

much strength getting back and forth." As she filled the gold-lined cups with dark, liquid amber the aroma of coffee fused with the scent of burning pine cones.

Surprise halted the raised cup on its way to Fran's mouth. When two weeks ago she had begun to look for a place to live—delightful as this home was, she wanted to be on her own—Gene and her mother had protested vehemently, had insisted that there was plenty of room at Rocky Point. What did this sudden change of front mean? The reason that it was to save her strength was a phony. The two places were but a ten-minute walk apart, she had her own car to use in bad weather.

"Your friend Gene doesn't happen to have green eyes, does she?" As clearly as if it had been spoken in her ear Judge Grimes's question echoed through her memory. They had been talking of Myles Jaffray and Gene's story about him and her sister-in-law. Myles was here now and—

"For Pete's sake, you look as if I had knocked you out, Fran. We don't want you to go, we are thinking of what is best for you."

What was the matter with her that someone was always deciding what was best for little Franny? First Aunt Becky, then Ken, Myles Jaffray, and now the Sargents. Did they think her a moron? She'd show them.

"If I looked stunned it is because you have divined what I have been thinking since your sister-in-law decided to visit you with her little girl. I have been scouting the surrounding country. The sixty-four-dollar question, in my life, is where can I go? Where find a spot of my own? I'm a career gal now, remember."

"I have the answer, the two room and bath apartment above the Gallery. It was planned for a second chauffeur before the species became extinct. With a record-breaking demand for accommodations in this summer resort, Mother decided to rent it and had the time of her life furnishing it like an illustration she saw in a magazine. It is really attractive, but Dad howled 'No.' He wouldn't have a stranger housed above his adored Sargent Gallery, Jr., so there it is, vacant."

"I took a look-see at it the other day when the door was open. It's adorable."

"If you want it, it's yours. The rent, as the living here,

18

is part of your salary. Lem Digby, the caretaker, and his wife live on the ground floor of the ell, and Si Pond, watchman, patrols the place at night, so you needn't be lonely or frightened. Betsy told Mother she would furnish your meals if you wanted her to."

"What a heavenly arrangement. As to being lonely, or frightened, I don't know the words."

Even as she made the smiling denial her heart did a cartwheel. Live alone over the treasures which could be stolen so easily? Henry Sargent had impressed on her the fact that many of them were of untold value. How much protection would the Digbys be in the ell? Silas Pond, the night watchman, was a gangling native who looked as if he had enough vitality to chew gum and no more. Could she do it? She could and would for the present. Suppose something exciting happened? Hadn't she told Judge Grimes that she was off for adventure? Nothing to prevent her moving to one of the resort hotels when there was a vacancy. She was not dependent on her salary for a living—her mistake, until September income date she was, and how. The change of view of Gene and her mother was still inexplicable. If it was because of Myles Jaffray it was the joke of the season.

"What's the verdict? I've given you time to think," Gene prodded.

"That the apartment suggestion is nothing short of inspired. There is room in the Gallery garage for my sedan. With that trusty steed at hand I can go out to dinner if Mrs. Betsy fails me. I'm all excited. May I move my bags in tomorrow?"

"Absolutely. You understand, don't you, Fran, that we hate to have you go, that it is for your good? I urged you to take the position and I never would forgive myself if you got overtired and broke down."

"Don't give it a thought. I'll have the time of my life."

"One thing more I want to warn you about, Fran. I saw you talking with Myles Jaffray at dinner. Beware the wolf, my child. Watch out for his 'You're the one woman in my life' line. He loves and leaves. To be frank I think you are too unsophisticated to attract him, but I felt it my duty to put you on guard."

"Thanks." It was a wonder Fran could get the word

on the air. Fury made her head spin. Once she had heard an angry man swear until the walls reverberated. If only she had as adequate a way of expressing her wrath! Myles Jaffray was "a wolf," she was "too unsophisticated to attract him." Was she? It would be exciting to make him aware of her.

"Friendly of you to flash the stop light, Gene. I'll heed the warning. Now that I have been put on guard, let's tune in on another station. How come that Blake Sinclair is here? I thought him miles away."

"He phoned this morning that he would be at the Inn for a month, intimated he was here for the tennis tournament. Invited me to dine and dance at the Country Club tonight. As one of Mother's guests had canceled I asked him to fill in at dinner. You haven't forgotten the rush he gave when I visited you, have you? I haven't, he almost turned my head. He has the profile of a Greek god, and that boy's got charm, he has. There's the explanation. Simple as that."

"Is anything simple in this cockeyed world, Gene?" Myles Jaffray inquired as he held a cup for her to fill.

Something in the bend of his head, a tone in his voice, struck a spark in Fran's memory. He was the man in gray who had been in the elevator the day of her conference with Judge Grimes. His cable had read "next week." Undoubtedly he had recognized her from her photograph and had been waiting for her to leave the building before he called on the Judge—the elevator man had said that he went to the seventh floor twice. Perhaps he had heard part of their conversation, she and the Judge had been shouting at one another to make themselves heard above the din of riveting. Apparently he hadn't wanted to see her any more than she wanted to see him. Suppose she told him that the operator had suspected him of being the finger man of a safe-cracking gang?

"What's the secret joke that is tilting up the corners of your mouth, Miss Phillips? Share it. This chaotic world needs laughter. No?" Jaffray set down the empty cup. "Gene, excuse us, I have a message from Ken Phillips for his sister. Finish your coffee, Fran, and we'll adjourn to the terrace."

"Is it so private you can't tell it here, Myles? I've hardly spoken to you tonight." Gene Sargent's tone was aggrieved.

"It is."

"I hope the message isn't as solemn as your voice. Run along, you two, make it snappy. We'll have some Oklahoma when the men come from the dining room. Don't look so scared, Fran, Myles won't eat you."

"Don't be too sure of that, Gene." He laughed and gnashed his strong white teeth. "I crunch the bones of bad little girls, me, I'm the demon trustee."

"What do you mean, 'trustee,' Myles?" The sharpness of Gene Sargent's eyes was repeated in her voice.

"Hasn't Fran told you that her brother appointed me trustee of Rebecca Harding's estate in his place?"

"She has not." Her face was white with anger. "Why the secrecy, Fran? Why didn't you tell me when I—I was advising you a few minutes ago?"

"Because, believe it or not, I kept pushing it out of my mind. I think the change unnecessary."

"And on that note we will adjourn for our talk fest," Jaffray declared smoothly. "Come on, Miss Phillips, unless you want to bring your objection to me out in the open and discuss it here. I can take it."

"That's noble of you. Let's get it over," Fran suggested crisply and sprang to her feet.

"Almost as light as day, thanks to daylight saving," Myles Jaffray observed, when they reached the terrace. "How about holding our conference on the rocks? Will it hurt that swanky yellow dress, can you make it in those high-heeled gold sandals?"

"No to the first question, and yes to the second. That flat boulder looks inviting."

They followed the path with its perennial borders of larkspur, dainty columbines, foxgloves, Canterbury bells, purple iris and a wealth of tall tulips that divided a lawn green as an emerald. Her sandals had not been designed for a trek like the present, Fran decided when they reached the rocks which jutted into the sea in a point, making a lovely cove on each side. She wasn't walking, she was toddling. She was aware of Jaffray's hand ready to steady her if she toppled but he did not touch her arm. She dropped to the broad, flat boulder.

21

Thank goodness she had made it. Seated beside her he frowned at her bare neck and arms.

"I was crazy to let you come without a wrap. You'll freeze. I'll sprint to the house and get one."

"I don't need it. We won't be here but a few minutes. The salty breeze is like warm velvet."

Now what, she wondered, what message had Ken sent that should be delivered in private? Spectacular night. The one burnished star visible was as bright as the revolving light on a rocky promontory down the coast. The tide lapped against the rocks and swished in recession. In the east where luminous sky and illimitable sea met, a crimson light heralded a rising moon. A boat with a mother-of-pearl sail drifted by slowly not far from shore. A salty breeze picked up the skipper's voice:

> Nita, Juanita,
> Ask thy soul if we should part.

"What a voice and what a song, perfect for this night," Myles Jaffray approved.

"Not such a cockeyed world when one sees it like this," Fran declared, then wished she had not shown she remembered his words in the library.

"Right. Smoke? No?"

He returned a silver case to the pocket of his white dinner jacket and clasped his hands about one knee. Fine hands, one with a dark seal ring; she liked them if she didn't like him. Why didn't he talk? She regarded him from the corners of her eyes. His profile was cut with cameo clearness against a sky turning from blue to violet. Perfect nose. Determined mouth and chin, she had recognized that characteristic the day she saw him in the elevator. Was he waiting for her to throw the opening conversational ball—controversial would doubtless prove to be the correct word. Better get the interview behind her, it was bound to be unpleasant. He had asked for it. "Here I go," she told herself, and plunged:

"What is Ken's message? If it is about his appointment of you as trustee under Aunt Becky's will, the subject is closed, definitely."

"You're the doctor, but before we close it *definitely*, I want it understood that your reaction doesn't make the

22

slightest difference to me. I have undertaken a job and I intend to put it through. As I told you earlier, you are quite outside my life except as a confounded responsibility."

"If you hate it why did you take the trusteeship?"

"To help your brother and incidentally this country." He rose, looked toward the house, and at the rocks sloping to the shore. Something about his narrowed eyes sent a chill, creepy, creepy, along Fran's veins. He had said he had something to tell her privately, did he suspect someone might be listening? Apparently satisfied that no one was near he sat beside her.

"Ken is fighting an unseen enemy now, an enemy determined to smash our plan for a united, independent Europe which is necessary for the survival of the civilized world," he confided in a low voice.

"There is something terrifying in the thought of an unseen enemy; it must be so much easier to fight face to face, if fighting is ever easy."

"That's right. We are fighting over there to make the purpose of the United States understood and appreciated, to prove that we are not in Europe for selfish gains, but to help people work together, to create conditions within which every individual may thrive without dragging down another. In short, opportunity for all. Having explained why I took on a job most distasteful to me, I'll close with the information that I am entitled to a vacation before I slip into harness. I shall spend it with my sister here. Don't let it worry you. You won't see me. Is that clear?"

"Crystal clear, especially about Ken's objective. Now that you have crunched the bad little girl to powder, let's proceed to the reason of this private interview, or have you already told all?"

"I have not. That preamble was to lay a foundation for the rest." He lighted a cigarette, tossed it impatiently into a tide pool and faced her. "Your brother has disappeared."

"Ken! Gone! How long have you known this? Why didn't you tell me before?"

"Sit down, please, or you'll lose your balance and hurtle down this cliff. That's better. You know, don't you, that there has been much un-American activity in the zone where Ken is stationed?" She nodded and clasped her hands together tightly in her lap.

"That activity has been driven underground. Ken had information as to the identity of the leader and decided to follow it up. The only way to avert suspicion from his purpose was to hint that he was being held somewhere as a prisoner. He asked me to tell you the truth the day before he was scheduled to disappear. No use for you to have it on your mind before, we both decided. 'Fran can take it, she's a good soldier,' Ken said."

"Now that I have it on my mind—" She choked back a sob of terror. "Is—is he in danger?"

"Yes."

"Did he have to be the one to go?"

"He and the higher-ups so decided."

"He is all the family I have in the world, I adore him. Why, why did you let him do it?" She was unashamedly aware that she was glaring at him through pools of tears.

"You overrate my influence with your brother. I volunteered to go in his place—my married sister is the only near relative I have, she doesn't need me, he had you. No dice. Ken had a source of information that would dry up if anyone but he tried to tap it. He declared that I could help more by taking the trusteeship, then he would be sure that no matter what happened to him you and your affairs would be taken care of."

"How can I live with this terrible anxiety? He may be tor—"

"Skip it. Keep your imagination on leash. When you begin to think of Ken's danger tune in on another station and quick. Each time you allow fear to get you it will be more difficult to keep the next crack under control. You lived through the war when Ken was in the thick of the fighting, didn't you? This is a different war which may prove quite as devastating. He told me you were valiant then and added:

" 'Tell Fran that the certainty that she is carrying on, chin up, will help me, tell her to believe that I will come through safely, to believe it hard.' "

"Oklahoma coming up!" The voice came from the

24

terrace. "Calling all players! Calling all play—" A door slammed on the last word.

"Come, Fran. We must go in."

"How can I with this horrible thing on my mind?"

"You haven't 'a horrible thing' on your mind, remember. You don't know what Ken is doing. No one here will know if the higher-ups succeed in keeping his disappearance hush-hush in this country, as they hope to do, a rumor will be started that he has been sent on a secret mission to a far country. No one must suspect what I have told you. Keep your mind shut tight against fear and your lips against confidences. Even in this small place there may be pricked ears. We have handed you a tough assignment, I know."

"I will do my best. Will you tell me if you hear *anything*, good or bad news?"

"I promise. Look up. How are your eyes? We don't want the people inside to suspect that I have been beating you. Okay. Not quite normal, but they'll pass. *En avant, soldat.*"

He caught her arm and steadied her as her heel turned on a jagged rock. She clutched his sleeve with her right hand and brushed the left across her eyes.

"Wait—a minute. I—I want to say that I'm sorry I was so hateful about the change of trustee. I didn't know—"

"That subject is definitely closed, remember. There you go again," he flared as she stumbled. "Why do you girls wear such fool heels?"

"I—couldn't see where—"

"Because of tears in your eyes? We'll fix that, pronto."

He swept her up into his arms and carried her to the lawn, looked down at her. The sailboat had come about and was nearer shore.

> Nita, Juanita,
> Be my own fair bride.

The breeze faithfully transcribed the passionate appeal in the singer's voice. Myles Jaffray's arms tightened.

"I haven't given you the whole of Ken's message, Fran. He sent you—this." He bent his head and kissed her lightly on the lips, then set her on her feet.

"Why did you do that?" Her voice was shaken by

25

anger. "I was just beginning to think perhaps you were not a detestable wolf, but if you kiss every girl the first time you meet her, Gene was right, you have—"

"Ssh." He placed his hand over her mouth and drew her close. "Don't move."

Her startled eyes followed his. Something was moving near the boulder on which they had been sitting. It looked like the figure of a person bent double, brown as the rocks, behind which it was scurrying. As if convinced he was safe from observation the man stood up and leaped to a rock below. Fran's heart was pounding, she could feel the hard beat of Myles Jaffray's against her shoulder. She opened her lips to whisper. He shook his head. His arm tightened. It seemed hours they stood motionless before they heard the scrape of a boat being drawn across a sandy beach.

"We can go, now," Myles whispered, and relaxed his hold.

"Who was it?" Her voice was as hushed as his.

"I don't know who the eavesdropper was, but something tells me that the song was a signal."

IV

An eighteenth-century oval mirror, its gilded rococo frame a mass of leaves, shells and scrolls, at one end of the small gallery reflected the slender girl in dark-amber crepe, gave back the broad gold girdle that cinched her waist, the glint of gold at throat and ears and in the waves of her short bronzy hair, the delicate color in her cheeks excitement had set there, the red of her lovely mouth, even the appraisal in her brown eyes as they regarded the lace-covered round table.

The silver bowl in the center filled with pink peonies and snapdragon, purple iris and pale yellow late tulips she had gathered from the flower border within the stone wall, was flanked by crystal plates of paper-thin sandwiches. Others displayed one-bite iced cakes. A tall silver urn, a large silver hot-kettle, were surrounded by gold-banded pink cups and saucers and the trimmings for coffee and tea.

Everything under control. Fran's ghost of a sigh expressed relief. She had been given full responsibility, plus a budget, to provide the social side of the preview of the one-man show. As a rule the Sargent Galleries didn't go in for teas. The artist who was exhibiting had asked for one and Henry Sargent, who was the Gallery, believing him to be a painter with a solid gold future, had consented.

The cloud of apprehension in which she had lived since she heard of her brother's dangerous mission, which had lifted while she was absorbed in preparations for the tea, settled down again over her spirit. How could she go on without betraying her fear for Ken's safety? It was harder to bear than the agonizing uncertainty of the war years. Then she could talk with others who were under the same strain, now, Myles Jaffray was the only person in the world to whom she could speak of it.

"You haven't had anything 'horrible' on your mind, remember." His warning echoed through her memory. "You don't know what he is doing. Keep your mind shut tight against fear." She thought of Ken's message, "Tell Fran to believe that I will come through safely, to believe it hard." She remembered Myles Jaffray's eyes as he had looked down into hers, the feel of his lips. Had her brother told him to kiss her? Suppose he had? How had Myles dared when he knew how she disliked him? No wonder Gene had warned her to beware of the wolf. The memory burned her cheeks. He had said she was out of his life, queer way of proving it.

She hadn't had a chance to finish her angry protest. The bent figure, brown as the rocks over which it was scrambling, the warning, "Ssh!" had contracted her throat. What had he meant by "Something tells me that song was a signal"? A signal for what? For whom? The memory of his whisper gave her the shivers. Were the words connected with Ken's mission?

Standing here reliving those tense moments wasn't playing the game as Ken wanted it played. She pushed "fear" into a safety-deposit box in her mind, turned the key on it and looked about the small gallery. She had been here three weeks. What had she learned? She checked: to recognize the style of the painters of the six small pictures by different artists hung against the soft-brown walls; that the Washington above the fern-

27

banked fireplace was a Gilbert Stuart, Vaughan-type portrait of the Father of his Country; that the marquetry cabinet was Louis XV and that the jewel-toned enamels on gold behind its glass doors were Byzantine, that the gilt-frame chairs and sofa were covered with Régence needlepoint.

The history of the inscrutable bronze Buddha seated cross-legged on the dark-red teakwood table and that of the Chinese mandarins on the English eighteenth-century *torchères* on each side of it still was to be acquired, but she was making progress. The work was intensely interesting, the contact with outstanding achievement stimulating. Keeping in step with this job would leave no time for fear.

"Here you are, dear."

Mrs. Sargent approached with her Queen Maryish air of invincible superiority, trailing the scent of choice perfume. Four strands of pearls encircled her throat, two gardenias gleamed high against the left shoulder of her black sheer frock, her matching turban revealed one side of her white hair, a faint suggestion of mascara on her long lashes intensified the clear blue of her eyes. A handsome woman *and* a determined one, Fran decided.

"You are looking very special, Mrs. Sargent," she complimented honestly. "Black is most becoming."

"Nice of you to tell me, dear. I never get a build-up from my family now that my son Ben is gone." The hard blue eyes misted. "I always wear black on the street in the city, as the socialite Spanish and French women do." She drew off immaculate white gloves from large capable hands glittering with diamonds and rearranged silver and cups and saucers that did not need rearranging.

"The table looks very nice. Gene was right when she told her father you were the perfect answer to his search for an assistant. I wish she would show as good judgment in her selection of the men with whom she plays. Sorry to criticize a friend of yours, dear, but I neither like nor trust that Blake Sinclair who has been her shadow for the last few days."

"I don't know why he came here, Mrs. Sargent. I told him before I left home that I wouldn't see him if he did come, and I won't, except as I meet him casually."

28

"That explanation encourages me. Perhaps he is working on Gene's sympathy to console him for your hardheartedness. I had hoped that she and Myles Jaffray—Oh, well, I can't live my daughter's life for her though I am sure I would make a better job of it than she is doing at present. She plays cards for large stakes and—Are you comfortable in the apartment upstairs?"

It took an instant for Fran to adjust her mind to Mrs. Sargent's lightning change of subject. She had been thinking of Gene's boast that her parents knew nothing of her card playing. Was Blake encouraging her? She had warned Gene that it was a pretty stupid parent who didn't know what its child was doing.

"Very comfortable, thank you. I have called it home for twenty-four hours only, but already I love it."

"Have we time to look at the exhibit before the guests arrive?" Mrs. Sargent consulted the jeweled watch on her wrist. "We have. The majority will stroll in late to make sure they are present when the society news photographers flash their bulbs. The art critics will appear after the crowd has thinned. Come with me, dear."

They entered the large gallery. A highly polished parquetry floor reflected the overhead light. The velvet covering of two long benches in the middle of the room repeated the shade of the soft sepia walls. The subjects of the twenty paintings hung with a generous amount of space between them were bits of shore or sea or country, rich with greens and blues, sharp thrusts and glowing patches of lemon and orange sunlight. Mrs. Sargent's eyes traveled from painting to painting and made the rounds a second time.

"Good. Very good, in fact remarkable. The man has what it takes. A miraculous achievement when one considers his background. He grew up in the poorer section of a large Western city, sold gasoline by day and attended school by night, managed two years abroad studying the great paintings of the world, before this last war, of course, and here he is hung in a Sargent Gallery, in itself an acknowledgment that he has arrived—all of which goes to prove my belief that you can accomplish anything you set your heart on—matrimony excepted—if you want it enough to work like—"

"Here you are, Mother," a voice boomed.

29

Henry Sargent charged toward them and interrupted what Fran knew would have developed into a discourse on will power. In the few weeks since her arrival she had learned that her employer moved always as if jet-propelled, and spoke as if megaphoning to a distant ship. The owner of the internationally respected Sargent Galleries was short and on the plump side. His face looked as if it had been shaved to the nap, his bullet-shaped head was covered with thick black hair slicked to a shine. Even on this warm June day he wore a wing collar, a lustrous pearl gleamed softly in the four-in-hand tie the exact shade of dark blue of his expertly tailored suit.

"Like the exhibit, Mother?" The tone of the question indicated a profound respect for the opinion of his wife.

"Yes. The canvases show up here. I'll confess that when we viewed them in the artist's slovenly studio I doubted if they warranted the expenditure of your time, Henry."

"He's good." Sargent rose on the tips of his brilliantly polished black shoes and settled back on his heels, a motion so habitual that now Fran rarely noticed it. "He's an accomplished draftsman who knows that good drawing is the base of all good work. He has imagination, a masterly grasp of color, also an inflated idea of the value of his work."

"Why not? He knows he has arrived or he wouldn't be here. I hope you sell a number of the pictures, Henry."

"The Sargent Gallery places pictures, it doesn't sell them, Mother," her husband instructed in the resigned tone of one who has made the correction many times. "You have the catalogue with prices, Miss Phillips?"

"Yes. In the Hepplewhite commode in the entresol. I shall be thrilled if I sell—place one, Mr. Sargent."

"Not so thrilled as the artist will be. Come along, Mother, I want your opinion on 'Country Lane.' Gene wants me to buy it for her. Who's prowling round the small gallery, Miss Phillips?"

"A man named Barth who was sent by the caterer to keep the tea table supplied."

"He looks as out of place in that swallowtail and trimmings in the Gallery as he would passing a collection plate in church. I don't like it. I don't want a person working here of whom I know nothing. There is a fortune here in *objets d'art* small enough to slip into a man's pocket. Keep an eye on him, Miss Phillips."

Fran had time only to wonder how she could keep an eye on the waiter and take orders for the paintings before he demanded:

"Where's Gene, Mother? Thought she was to pour tea this afternoon?"

"Here she comes. Oh, dear," Mrs. Sargent moaned, as her hatless, dark-haired daughter in a mist-gray chiffon afternoon frock with gleaming silver at her throat and ears entered with a man each side of her. "Oh, dear," she sighed again as she watched the three with harried eyes, "I wish she would shake that Sinclair smoothie. Thank goodness Myles is with them. I wonder which one sent her the bunch of violet sweet peas, stuck in her silver belt?"

Fran's face burned from embarrassment. Had Mrs. Sargent been correct when she suggested that Blake's attentions to Gene were a play for sympathy? She was responsible for his being here. Was it up to her to break her resolution not to see him and to tell him that he was *persona non grata* at Rocky Point?

"What's the matter with Sinclair, Mother?" At a warning "Hush-sh" from his wife Henry Sargent moderated the volume of his voice. "He's darned intelligent, the first man in our daughter's stag line who has known even the A B C of painting. Myles is a grand boy, but he wouldn't know a Gellée from a Claude Lorrain."

"But they were the same person, weren't they?" Fran knew from her employer's chuckle that she had walked into the trap he had set for her.

"Right. That was to test how much you remembered of what I explained to you yesterday, Miss Phillips. Mother, Sinclair told me that he had done more or less trading in paintings. He has picked up an item I want very much. That's off the record, Miss Phillips."

Fran nodded understanding. She returned to the small gallery in response to the waiter's beckoning finger. He was a good-looking man, one to be trusted not to slip *objets d'art* into his pocket, she thought as she joined him beside the table. His nose was modeled on

Napoleonic lines, his black eyes twinkled like beads in his long thin face, which, though lined, was youthful for his snow-white hair.

"Is everything O.K., Miss?" he inquired, in a hushed voice. "Mrs. Digby allowed me to use her kitchen for my supplies. There's a very fine woman, Miss. The boss said I was to ask if the cakes are small enough."

"Tell him they are perfect. I shall depend upon you to look after the table, Barth. I must be in the large gallery."

"You don't have to worry, Miss. For years I was head butler in a big house in Belgium—a palace almost—where there were more fine articles about than I see here. I know how tea parties should be done."

"In Belgium. You were lucky to get out. I had a friend, a U.S. captain, a flier, who was caught in the Battle of the Bulge."

"Had you really, Miss? I hope he came through all right?"

"Yes. Without a scratch. Captain Sinclair is here to-day. How does it happen that you are serving as a waiter after holding down such an interesting job in that palatial house?"

"The war, Miss. When the Krauts marched into Belgium I sneaked out. Got back to England—that's my country—and into the service in time for Dunkirk. That was hell, Miss, if you'll excuse my language. After that, I wasn't much good for hard work; I drifted to the U.S. I'd better fill the coffee urn and light the lamp under the hot water kettle, hadn't I, Miss?"

"Yes. Mrs. Sargent and her daughter are coming in now to pour."

She noticed the professionally appraising glance he cast over the table, her eyes followed him till he left the gallery. Had his story about serving in a big house in Belgium been true? Evidently he had looked over "the fine articles" here. The part about enlisting and Dunkirk was believable, his eyes were the eyes of one who had seen and experienced unforgettable horrors. His "That was hell, Miss" had been accompanied by an authentic shiver.

The galleries were filling. Large women in slim skirts, slim women in ballerina skirts or the melon type, women who knew the value of the paintings and *objets d'art* so advantageously displayed, women to whom they meant nothing but who knew to a breath the value of a soft, caressing voice, the upward sweep of long lashes, the touch of a hand on the sleeve of the man beside them, laughed and chatted their way through the crowd.

In their midst the artist, with bone-rimmed spectacles and crew cut of stiff iron-gray hair, in well-cut gray tweeds, appeared like a frightened boy who has set in motion a machine he couldn't stop. He clutched Fran's sleeve as she was passing.

"How's it going, Miss Phillips?" he demanded in a hoarse whisper. "You are Miss Phillips, aren't you? I met you when I came to look over the Gallery, didn't I?"

"I am and you did, Mr. Eckhard. The exhibition is going over the top. They like you. They are saying that you have force, taste, integrity and a lot of other nice things you will see in the write-ups tomorrow. The news cameramen are here. They want to snap you standing beside one of the pictures. Select 'Country Lane,' will you? I love it." Her warm approval lighted little lamps in his outsize eyes behind the owl-like lenses.

"No kidding? You have been so kind—making the tea so pretty—ever since I began to paint I have wanted a tea like the big shots have—I'll give it to you," he declared eagerly. Fran laughed and shook her head.

"No, you won't give it to me. I think I can sell it. Hurry, the cameramen are waiting."

"What do you think you can sell and what did he want to give you?" inquired Myles Jaffray behind her. She turned almost into his arms, drew back.

"Sorry to appear to crowd you, but the Gallery is so full one can't move without pushing someone," he explained. "Had tea? I'll bet you haven't. Beat it to your office, I understand you have one, and I'll bring you a cup. It is part of my trustee job, I suppose, to see that you don't kill yourself with overwork."

"Can't. I must stay here to answer questions about prices and take signatures on the dotted line."

"You won't succeed with that voice, no sales hypnotism in that. I intend to buy one of the paintings but not until you have had tea."

33

"Mean it?" she asked eagerly. She forgot who he was, forgot she disliked and distrusted him, remembered only that he was a possible prospect. "Buy it of me? No kidding?"

"No kidding. Go to your office and drink the tea I'll send you. In ten minutes I will knock on the door, you may return to the gallery and sell me a picture."

"Suppose Mr. Sargent misses me? He won't like it."

"I'll keep an eye on him. If he appears to be looking for you I will explain that I caught you as you were about to pass out from fatigue and hunger and persuaded you to stop for tea. Haven't had lunch, have you?"

"Now that you call it to my attention, I haven't."

"I thought you hadn't. Come on, I'll make sure you get to your office without being held up, then I'll go for the tea."

"Peace in our time, it's blissful," Fran confided to the room at large as she sank into the chair behind the flat desk in the small office Mr. Sargent called hers. A salty breeze stole in through the open window. A bee buzzed lazily against the screen. She had been on her feet since breakfast. Her sandals felt several sizes too small. She slipped them off. The relief, the unbelievable relief.

Someone was knocking on the door which opened into a cluttered room her boss called the repair shop, devoted to the removal of old varnish from paintings, repairing of frames, the storing of canvases which represented mistakes in judgment of their value, and wood for the fireplaces.

"Come in."

The waiter with the Napoleonic profile entered with a large tray.

"Your tea, Miss."

"How did you know I was here?"

"The tall gentleman in gray with the D. S. ribbon in his coat lapel said as how you would be in your office. Mrs. Digby showed me how to get here without going through where the company is. The door at the end of the clutter room, I'd call it, opens into the little hall opposite the door to her apartment, in case you'd like to know how I got here, Miss. Wouldn't you like me to draw up the small table in front of the easy chair, and set the tray on that? You'd be more comfortable, Miss."

"That is the chair Mr. Sargent occupies when he comes in to dictate. Set the tray on the desk in front of me. I'll pretend this light blue blotter is a lace cloth."

"I hope I have brought what you like, Miss."

"Tea, lemon, sugar, sandwiches and cakes. You have thought of everything, Barth."

"Thank you, Miss. Leave the tray on the desk and I'll come back for it. The gentleman said to tell you not to worry, he'd let you know when the rest time was up."

Fran unseeingly regarded the door he had closed behind him. Of course the gentleman who had sent him was Myles Jaffray. She had hoped he would bring the tea himself, it would have given her the chance to whisper, "Any news?"

Perhaps he had suspected the eager question and sidestepped because there was nothing to report. He had promised to tell her the moment he heard. She must trust to that and not pester him with questions. What was Ken doing at this moment? Was he safe or was he—

"Skip it. Keep your imagination on leash." Myles Jaffray's voice sounded off in her memory. "When you begin to think of Ken's danger force it from your mind. Each time you allow fear to get you it will be more difficult to keep the next crack under control."

He was right. She had this interesting job to help keep her imagination on lease, also her determination to make Myles Jaffray aware that she was in the world. He had known she had had no tea—was that a step toward her goal? Would he buy one of the paintings? Morrison Grove had said that his family had plenty of "the moolah" and she had believed that Ken had given him the trusteeship to tide him over until he had secured clients. Ouch! Suppose he heard of it.

She glanced at the banjo clock on the wall. In thirty seconds the ten minutes allowed her would be up. Amazing how refreshed she felt. He was knocking. On time to the minute. He would be like that. She slipped on her sandals, flinched at the first step and opened the door to the entresol. Blake Sinclair pushed by, closed the door and leaned against it.

"Run to earth. Now you'll listen." His voice was smug with satisfaction.

V

"How did you know where I was?"

Only half of Fran's mind was on the question. She didn't like being alone in this room with Blake Sinclair and she didn't intend to stay here while he aired his grievance against her. Would she find escape difficult? Was she afraid of this person she had known since he was a small boy?

"I've kept my eye on you. Saw you slip in here. As soon as I could decently shake old man Sargent, with whom I'm putting through a business deal, I followed. Smart fella, what?"

"Granted. I came here for a cup of tea and to rest my sandals for a few minutes. Now I feel like a million. I'll return to the scene of battle."

"Where's Jaffray?"

"Myles Jaffray? Not being omniscient I can't tell you."

"Didn't he come in here to have tea with you?"

"Regard the tray. One cup. You'd get a D minus in an observation and deduction test, Blake. Open the door. I must get back to work. I have three tentative offers for paintings. I want to clinch them before the maybe purchasers decide to—quote—think it over a little longer."

"Not a chance, you will stay here till you promise to go out with me."

"Don't be childish, Blake. I told you before I left home that I would not see you if you came. Circumstances have forced me to see you but I won't go out with you. Open the door."

"Not until you give me a date for this evening. I'll be darned if I know what all this is about, Fran. In spite of the fact that you never would let me kiss you, I know that you love me. Why play puss in the corner?"

Had she loved him or had her feeling been sisterly affection tinged with a sense of responsibility? He was extremely good-looking, had charm, fine manners—until now—was apparently successful in business, though he never had been definite in describing his job—had covered it with the word "investments"—they had been companions since they were children, had fought and made up through the years. She had been troubled by the stories of his "wildness," the neighbors called it.

"Do I get that date?"

His sharp question recalled her attention.

"You do not, period. I asked for time in which to think over your proposal of marriage—uninfluenced by your presence. You haven't given it to me, but you have settled the question in the last few minutes. Now—" A knock on the repair-shop door interrupted her low, contemptuous reply.

"Who's that?" Sinclair demanded.

"The waiter for the tray, I suppose."

"Did Jaffray slip out that way?"

"He did not, but it would be none of your business if he did, Blake." She opened the door.

"Here I am as per schedule," Myles Jaffray announced. He glanced at Sinclair, who was backed against the other door, his fair skin red from anger. "Sorry to interrupt a conference, Miss Phillips, but your boss is on the verge of a nervous breakdown because he can't locate his saleswoman. Come on."

"Fran! Stay—"

She slipped out.

Myles Jaffray shut the door hard on Sinclair's furious protest.

"Sorry, but we can't allow romance to interfere with your business career," he apologized.

In the stuffy, dusky repair shop he guided her between benches, stacked canvases, dismembered crates and a pile of firewood. She ignored his reference to romance though she could think of several telling retorts she would like to make.

"Why did you come this way? I expected you would appear at the entresol door."

"To avoid a one-man traffic jam. Sinclair saw me there when you went into the office. I knew he heard me say, 'In ten minutes.' He figured that he would get there first and did."

"Let's forget him and talk business." They entered the large gallery. "The crowd has thinned. Do you really intend to buy a picture?"

"I do. I will leave the selection to you and my sister,

Natalie Andrews. I will give it to her. Here she is, golly, with the Terrible Tassie in tow. Now I'm in for it. Miss Trent is determined that I step into the local political fight."

"Will you?"

"More about that later. Nat"—he touched a slender woman in black on the shoulder. "I want you to meet Frances Phillips. She has sold me the idea of buying one of these paintings for you. How are you, Miss Tassie?"

As Natalie turned to speak to her brother surprise blocked Fran's voice for an instant. Her hair was snowy white. She looked old enough to be Myles's mother. She smiled and youth returned to her face and with it sensitivity, tenderness and sympathetic understanding. "I could love you," Fran told herself.

"I am a little envious of you, Miss Phillips," Natalie Andrews confessed. "It must be exciting to be assistant in this gallery."

"If you wanted it, why didn't you make Henry Sargent give you the job?" Miss Trent demanded. Her heavy eyebrows jerked up and down when she spoke. Her dress was sapphire blue. Her height was increased by black hair piled on top of her head. All it needed was a few knitting needles stuck through it to be thoroughly Chinese in motif. No wonder she was hatless. Nothing would remain perched on top of that hair-do.

"I was talking for effect, Miss Tassie," Natalie Andrews confessed. "My days are filled to the brim now. You and Miss Phillips have met, haven't you?"

"Yes, at the Sargent dinner the other evening." Her eyebrows went into their act. "She monopolized Morrie Grove when I wanted to talk politics with him. The young people of today have no respect for their elders."

Fran's lips parted to record an astonished protest.

"Elders," Myles Jaffray repeated before she could speak. "*Elders.* I never expected to hear that word in regard to yourself from you, Miss Tassie. I thought you didn't believe in being age-conscious."

"I don't. I think it is stupid, particularly in this day and age when the scientists claim that a child born now may, with care, easily live to be a hundred. I will admit that some persons are older than others, though. I want to talk seriously with you, Myles."

"Not here, Miss Tassie. Invite me for tea. Once when I was dropping through space and my rip-cord release stuck, a vision of you pouring tea, in your stunning drawing room, flashed on the screen of my mind—you'd be amazed at the irrelevant things one thinks of at a time like that. 'Boy, keep your head,' I said aloud. 'You've got to get out of this. You want another go at Miss Tassie's fruit cake, don't you?' And believe it or not, that release came through with the works and the silk spread above me."

Miss Trent sniffed and patted his sleeve with an angular hand sparkling with diamonds in old fashioned settings.

"Myles, you're the light of my eyes. I'm a romantic ol—almost said old—woman, I love you. Where is the painting you are planning to buy? If I like it I will select one. Lead on, Miss Phillips. You appear to be the saleswoman."

"I won't have to lead far, Miss Trent. The picture is on the wall behind us."

For a few moments the four stood silently before the painting of a lane patterned in golden sunlight and soft green shadows cast by bordering trees.

"'Country Lane,' I love it," Natalie Andrews approved softly. "It is so heavenly peaceful. I knew a spot like that once. I can feel my problems folding their tents like the—"

"Is this the one you want, Matilde?" The man's voice behind her whitened Natalie Andrews's face. Myles Jaffray turned.

"How are you, Hal?" He spoke to the tall man, the classic perfection of whose face was marred by too high color, before he looked at the hatless woman in a beige frock beside him. Her rich auburn shoulder-length hair was alight with gold threads, her eyes were the green of emeralds as they defiantly met his. "I heard you were back again, Matilde. Miss Phillips, come to your desk and I'll write a check for 'Country Lane.'"

"Don't ignore me as if I were a returned bad penny, Myles." Matilde Sargent's red lips pouted, her very long, very black lashes swept up in pleading.

"Why not?" Miss Trent's question lashed. "You are, aren't you? Show me the picture you advise me to buy,

Miss Phillips." She maneuvered Natalie Andrews and Myles ahead of them, but not before the appraisal in Hal Andrews's eyes, as they regarded Fran, had changed to eager admiration. Because of the crowd moving up to view "Country Lane" they were held where they were.

"Myles has bought the picture I've set my heart on, Hal." Fran heard Matilde Sargent's impatient complaint behind her.

"That's just too bad. Let's get out of this. I've had enough."

"Poor little boy, wouldn't his ex-wife speak to him? Sometimes I suspect that you are still carrying a torch for her, Hal Andrews."

Fran's eyes were wide with surprise as they questioned those of the woman beside her.

"Miss Trent, was that—"

"You've guessed it, Natalie's divorced husband. I saw a movie, *The Men We Marry*; there ought to be one, *The Women Men Marry*—and in God's name—why? Ben Sargent was a gentleman in all that word connotes—why he picked that—"

"They are quite near us, Miss Trent," Fran reminded.

"What if they are, I'm stating facts." Her reply was truculent but in a lower key. "Watch out for him, Miss Phillips, I saw his eyes on you, saw two little devils spring up in them. He's what they call a wolf these days, my dear. If he prowls after you, as he will—I know the symptoms—be dull, talk about yourself, what *you* think, what *you* do, every minute, and he'll drop you like a hot coal. That is, unless you want him on your trail?"

"After that description, Miss Trent? Not I."

"That hussy, Matilde, is here to make trouble, I'll bet my diamonds."

"I'm sorry. I like Mrs. Andrews so much. I would hate to see her made unhappy."

"Unhappy? Why? She ought to be beating the tom-tom that she is legally rid of the man. He's rich as Croesus, handsome as a Greek god, but faithless as they come. I'm not worrying about her. It's Myles. If that predatory red-headed hellion tries to rope him in, I'll wring her neck, and I mean, wring her neck."

"She can't rope him in unless he wants to be roped, can she?"

"You look too intelligent to ask such a fool question, my girl. Push through the crowd. Show me the picture you advise me to buy. Introduce me to the artist. If I like him I'll take him home to dinner."

Two hours later Fran sank into a chintz-covered wing chair in the living room of her small apartment. She kicked off her high-heeled sandals. If she were to continue in this job—and she would—flat heels were indicated. Gorgeous sky to be seen through the open west window. A breeze drifting in brought the spicy scent of the pink geraniums in the window boxes.

She was in luck to find a place that was so attractive. If Mrs. Sargent had taken an illustration as a model for the furnishings, she had chosen a good one. Long hangings at the two large windows, one toward the east, one toward the west, matched the deep pink walls. Broad sofa and cushions were covered, like the wing chair, in chintz, a riot of pale pink, purples, and soft greens against a white background. The desk was a Governor Winthrop reproduction. Two tables held lamps with shades the exact tint of the large soft beige rug on the stained cypress floor. Two small chairs were done in vivid green. A low coffee table stood invitingly in front of the sofa.

Pictures of Blake, of her brother, her aunt, and a few of her college friends helped to make the room home for her. A crystal and gold clock she had brought from the Cambridge house was on the top of shelves which held her favorite books; they were the ones to which she had turned for refreshment and renewed courage when life had seemed so deadly monotonous. Each one of the silver boxes on the tables took her back to the place where she had acquired it. She could see the very spot in an Arts and Crafts Exhibit where she had bought the oval with the red carnelian set in the cover, could see Gene beside her—

"She plays for large stakes," Mrs. Sargent's voice cut into the colorful memory. Fran jumped to her feet and crossed to the east window from which she could see a broad expanse of ocean. "Large stakes." Was that why Gene had whispered to her, "I must see you, Fran. I'll drop in at your apartment after the show." She had helped her out before from the generous allowance Aunt Becky made her.

"What would you like for dinner, dearie?" Mrs. Digby, plump and smiling, stood in the open doorway, a white apron enveloped her peppermint striped dress like a ballerina skirt. Her round face shone with color and friendliness, her blue eyes were bright with interest.

"Come in, Mrs. Betsy. I don't really want anything. I had tea so late."

"Oh, but you must eat, child. You didn't touch the lunch I brought up for you. If you don't want dinner I could toss up a nice fruit salad, the caterer left a lot of sandwiches and cakes and—Lem brought some ice cream from the village for our supper."

"You're a darling, would you mind if I had it in about an hour? Leave things in the icebox where I can get them if you and Mr. Digby are going out. Miss Sargent said she would drop in after the picture show to see me on—business"—that was a guess—"and I would like to wait until after she has been here."

"Any time you say, dearie. Lem and I almost never go out in the evening, he don't like the movies, he sits and listens to the radio. Just ring your bell and I'll bring it up. 'Tisn't any trouble, I love to come into this room, it's so pretty since you fixed it up." A door closed below. "I guess that's Miss Gene now. I'll run down the back way."

As she crossed to a door at the rear of the room Gene Sargent called:

"Hi, there. I'm in a terrific jam, Fran."

"Come up, Gene."

"You've certainly made this room look like a million," Gene Sargent approved as she entered. Light from the crimson sky pouring through the west window turned her silver-gray frock to soft pink. She slumped into the wing chair, thrust her long legs straight out before her. Fran perched on the edge of the sofa.

"What's it all about, Gene?"

"Here's the awful truth. Luck has been against me. I owe money. Thought perhaps you could help me out with a loan till my next allowance day. Dad has theories as to the way to bring up a gal. He won't advance a cent until the date it is due."

"You couldn't have applied at a worse time, Gene. My bank balance is close to the vanishing stage. I plunged on clothes before I left home."

"I'll say you plunged. I'll bet you have the most colorful, the swankiest outfit on the coast of Maine this summer. You've earned it, you were an angel with that cranky aunt of yours. You didn't use all your money, did you, you who were taught thrift by Rebecca Harding?"

"I have seventy-five dollars in the bank. I counted on my pay here to carry me until next income day which will be the fifth of September. I will give you a check for fifty dollars and twenty-five in cash, if that will help."

"Seventy-five dollars! You're offering me a stone, gal, when I need bread. I'm in the red just one thousand dollars."

"*Gene!*"

"Ain't it awful, Mabel!" There was a quiver in her flippant quote. "That's how it is. I've got to get the money, somehow, somewhere. I thought first of you."

"I'd let you have it in a minute, Gene, if I had it. But seventy-five is the limit I can scrape together. I must leave something in the bank. I've spent most of my salary on one thing or another since I've been here."

"You'll have a fistful of the filthy lucre the fifth of September, won't you? Get an advance. Myles Jaffray is trustee of your property, isn't he? The gods are with us. He's here. Tell him you need money to pay for—for that antique diamond cluster ring you're wearing. It's bigger than a quarter, it looks like a thousand dollars."

"You know it was Aunt Becky's ring, Gene."

"Myles doesn't. You've got to help me. I'll do something desperate, if you don't."

"Don't talk like a nitwit. Why don't you go to your mother, tell her the story?"

"I can't. She's settled for me once, she said, 'Never again.'"

"Your father?"

"Dad's generous, but he wouldn't advance our allowances or increase them a penny were the alternative jail for Mother or me. He's of the 'This rock shall fly from its firm base as soon as I' school. Can you see him giving it to me for card debts?"

43

She couldn't, Fran assured herself; she had been here a little over three weeks but she had learned enough of Henry Sargent to know that if he once made up his mind no argument could change it.

"Come on, Franny, be a good sport. Ask Myles. After all, it's *your* money, nothing in his life."

"I can't ask him, Gene."

"I've got to have that money and you're the only person who can come across. If you don't—you'll be responsible for—" An automobile horn signifying impatience cut into the sentence.

"Who's waiting downstairs, Gene?"

"Blake Sinclair. We're on the way to—we're on the way to somewhere. He wanted to come up with me, but I told him you had asked me to stop and talk business."

"I? *I* asked you to come on business?"

"What difference does it make whose business it is? Darn him. Why doesn't he stop blowing that horn? I've got to go, Fran. Help me, won't you?"

"How soon must you have the money?"

"I ought to have it this minute, but if you'll promise to get it I'll get a reprieve."

"I can't promise, Gene."

"Will you try?"

"Yes. But don't count on it."

"I've got to have it—or else—" She dashed to the hall in answer to another furious summons.

Fran stood motionless in the middle of the room till she heard a car start. How could she get money for Gene? Asking Myles Jaffray for an advance on her allowance was out. Hadn't she told him that the subject of his trusteeship was definitely closed? Hadn't he told her that she was a confounded responsibility?

"I've got to have it—or else—" Gene's threat echoed through her memory. She shivered. What had she meant by "or else"?

VI

Myles Jaffray perched on the wall of the terrace of his home smoking. Far off between the spruce trees in the downhill garden he could see whitecaps rolling in

44

on a sandy beach. The world was so quiet that the rhythmic swish and ebb of the tide was faintly audible. A hazy violet dusk was settling down over beds and borders of late June flowers, muting them to the same soft neutral shade. Their scent and the night smell of damp earth were salted by a light breeze from the ocean.

Crocker, the gardener, was closing the gay umbrellas above the green iron tables in the garden, folding the awninged deck chairs as he had done in the days before the war. From daily repetition it had become something of a ritual. Myles thought of the many times when in the midst of flame, the shriek and crash of bombs, he had conjured the colorful memory—how he had visualized the trees his grandfather had set out on the land his great-grandfather had purchased; the flowers; women in lovely frocks having tea in the garden after a party; old Crocker, limping then as he limped now from table to table, closing the umbrellas. He remembered how his excursion into the past had refreshed and revitalized, had renewed and strengthened his belief that right would win the fight.

"Frances Phillips is beautiful and vital, Myles."

His sister's voice transported him from a world of battle and sudden death to the peace and fragrance of the present. He had forgotten she was at the coffee table on the terrace. A spoon tinkled as she set cup and saucer on the silver tray.

"Had you met her before she came here?"

"No."

That was the truth. He visualized the slim girl he had seen in the elevator the first time he had called on Judge Grimes, a full week before he was expected. He had recognized her from the photograph her brother carried, a photograph suddenly come vividly alive. One couldn't call that meeting her.

"Of course, it isn't my business," his sister's voice broke the photographic plate of memory, "equally of course you will consider my point of view dated when I say I think that a charming girl like her should not live alone." That brought him off the wall to his feet. He backed against a vine-covered pillar.

"What do you mean, 'live alone'? She's staying with the Sargents, isn't she?"

"She was. Yesterday she moved to the apartment above the Gallery."

"How do you know?"

"Mrs. Sargent told me at the preview this afternoon. She embarked on one of her lengthy explanations as to the whys and wherefores, in which I caught the word 'Matilde.' Of course she had no idea that the name was anathema to me. I had a feeling that she didn't approve of the transfer of her husband's assistant from Rocky Point to the apartment, but had been persuaded that the change was for the best. In short—if you can by any stretch of the imagination connect the word 'short' with Mrs. Sargent's conversation—I would say she was apologetic. The Gallery is full of valuable and salable stuff which could be picked up easily by a burglar. Even with Lem Digby there and Silas Pond, the night watchman, it is not a safe place for a girl alone."

"Safe? It's darned unsafe. Why wasn't I consulted?" His sister laughed.

"Why should you be, Major? You are out of the army now where your word was law in certain situations. Unless—unless you mean by being consulted that you—you are tied up with the Sargent family. It—it isn't Gene, is it?"

"It is not, accent on the not. The reason I should have been consulted—I had intended to tell you this evening—is that I am now trustee, succeeding her brother, of the estate Rebecca Harding left Fran Phillips."

"What has happened to Ken Phillips? I met him when he came to New York on leave. I liked him very much."

"Ken is okay." Is he? He pushed the perturbing question back into the shadows of his mind where fear belonged and slammed the door of imagination. It wasn't to be told that he had planned with Ken that he was to be near Fran this summer, until her brother had come safely through his mission. The arm of reprisal was long, her safety must be assured.

"He has decided to remain in Germany as long as he is needed, which anybody's guess will be for years." That statement was allowable. "He felt that the trusteeship should be handled by someone in this country and picked me. The Lord knows I didn't want it, but Ken is entitled to all the help I can give."

46

"Does the trusteeship give you the right to tell Miss Phillips what she can or cannot do?"

"No, except in one particular, a right which I will never exercise—but she doesn't know that. She resents my appointment, is hot about it, has taken a violent dislike to me. I don't get it. I'm no saint, but, by golly, I'm no sinner."

"Perhaps she has heard the gossip about you and Matilde and considers you a menace."

"That story went the rounds several years ago. How could she hear it?"

"Gene Sargent and she were at college together, weren't they? If Fran Phillips is being unjust to you because of that story I'll set her right, Myles."

"Let it go, let the situation straighten itself out. No use reviving tragic memories, Nat. Try not to look back on what is finished."

"Finished?" She rose impetuously. "Finished when Hal and Matilde appeared together this afternoon?"

There was light enough to see the glitter of tears in her eyes, abnormally large and dark in the pallor of her face. He laid his arm across her shoulders.

"Don't tear yourself to pieces over that heel, Nat."

She brushed her hand impatiently across her eyes.

"I won't, ever again. Did you notice his eyes when he saw Fran Phillips? I thought, 'There he goes again.' I hope she won't be fooled by him."

"Don't worry, Nat. I'll take care of that."

"I don't know why I cried. I stopped loving Hal years ago when he began trampling my heart, I can't love a person I don't respect. I'll try not to look back, but if ever the chance comes I will tell Frances Phillips that it was my husband, not my brother, with whom Matilde Sargent was planning to run away, that you answered 'No comment' when your friends told you that she declared she had lost her head over you."

"Her husband knew the truth—fiction to the contrary, you can't fool a man as to the identity of the person who is breaking up his home, not a keen guy like Ben Sargent. Why did she pick on me? Since college days when I played the field with no serious dents in the hearts of the girls or mine I have been too busy to cultivate a line that would interest the fair sex. I figured

47

that as I was heart-whole and fancy-free the gossip wouldn't hurt me, that I could save—"

"Your sister from being the subject of sensational headlines. I knew at the time that you were protecting Hal because of me but I was so stunned by surprise and grief that I let it go. This is different. I won't allow you to be misjudged any longer."

"Let it go now, Nat. Fighting a prejudice can be mighty stimulating—under some conditions. If I need your help I will ask for it."

"Is that a promise?"

"Sure. Let's tune in on another station." He had said that to Fran. No one watching her today would have suspected that her heart was anxious. Ken was right. She was a soldier.

"Thanks for 'Country Lane,' Myles. I love it. That artist is going places." She laughed. "He looked frightened stiff when Miss Tassie invited him to go home with her for dinner."

"Did he accept?"

"After he had glanced at Miss Phillips and caught her eager nod. Apparently he was leaning on her to steer him socially. His 'With pleasure, Miss Trent' was tinged with the deference that lady likes. I am glad he went. She can help him. One of his paintings in her charming house will make others want them. Speaking of houses, Myles, this place is yours. Do you want it?"

"Good Lord, no, not now."

"It would be an ideal summer home for children."

"That's right, but my children are still playing with the angels. I intend to settle in New York. I have had an offer to take over the probate work in an important firm there, which I shall do unless I am needed in the service."

"In the service? You are not expecting another war?"

"No, but it's a grim world just now, I think that our military forces should be kept up to war strength. Believing that, I'm ready to go if I am called."

"I hope that horror never will come again. There are fights nearer home. The Good Government Association wants you as its candidate for a seat in the House from this district. Will you try for it? You would make an ideal representative."

"No, I've threshed it out with the G.G.A. I'm not qualified to be a Representative. I have been out of this country for six years except for a few short leaves. I know nothing, really, of what people are thinking, of what they want. It will take me a few years to catch on. After that, I'll try for Congress. Morrison Grove is a good man. Slightly tarred with the isolationist brush, he'll outgrow that, in every other way sound. I have things on my mind I want to accomplish."

"Matrimony?"

"I don't know. I honestly don't know. Perhaps were I really in love I wouldn't stop, look, listen, until I was sure the girl could take the hard knocks of marriage without thinking herself a martyr and trekking to the divorce court. Someone said recently, 'You don't marry happiness, you make happiness after marriage.' The guy is right."

"It isn't always the woman who can't take the hard knocks, Myles."

"You've said something, it's fifty-fifty. If a couple goes into marriage knowing that adjustments are bound to be tough, that the going may be plenty rough in spots, yet, believing it to be the great adventure, that the rewards in companionship, in sunny stretches of road, in shared laughter, shared intimacies and interests will overbalance the hazards, such a marriage ought to result in a genuine till-death-do-us-part relationship and that is the only one I will settle for."

"You've given the subject a lot of thought."

"I have had plenty of time for thought during these last years. The experience I have been through has given me the long view, perspective, in one word. If I were building a house I would put into the planning all the wisdom and experience I had acquired on the subject. Why do less for the house of marriage?"

"Sound reasoning, Myles. I wonder if it will hold when you fall hard for a girl."

"Probably not, I have a feeling that sometime I will go haywire when I hear a voice singing:

Nita, Juanita,
Ask thy soul if we should part,

"Myles, I haven't heard you sing in years." Gene Sargent spoke from the embrasure of the long open window. The light from the room behind set the silver belt of her gray frock glistening. "Your voice would melt a heart of stone. That reminds me, I hope someone will be singing like that when your heart needs melting. I made Blake drive me here, Natalie, to see if I couldn't wangle 'Country Lane' from your brother. I want it." She perched on the terrace wall close to Myles. Sinclair declined a cigarette from the case he offered.

"Thanks, no, I smoke a special brand you can't get in this country."

"Too late for 'Country Lane,' Gene. I have presented the painting to my best girl." Myles crossed to the low table. "How about coffee?"

"No, thanks. Who is your best girl?" she demanded jealously.

"That's a closely guarded secret. Hush-hush."

"Perhaps I can guess, now that Matilde is back."

"Gene! You are—"

"Matilde?" Myles cut in on his sister's breathless voice. "Not for me. I've taken to heart old Weller's advice to his son—'Be werry careful o' vidders all your life.' . . . Now that you know where I stand, let's get back to the preview. Many pictures sold?"

"Four, and who do you think was one of the purchasers? Terrible Tassie. Fran sold them. She was so excited and exhausted from her first day of selling that she wouldn't come back to Rocky Point for dinner. She preferred to stay in her own attractive apartment, she said. But I think she was terribly upset about something else. She's scared to death of you, Myles."

"What do you mean by that?"

"Don't bite my head off, I'm just trying to make it easy for her."

"Make what easy?"

"If you must know, I didn't promise I wouldn't tell when she poured out her troubles to me, so here goes."

"For the love of Pete, what troubles?"

"Nothing you can't help, Myles, if you want to. Fran plunged on a diamond ring to the modest tune of one thousand dollars. Her bank balance is down to a new low, she is being dunned by the dealer and she swears

50

she won't ask you for an advance on her income. I'm doing a little spadework for her."

"Does she know that?"

"Of course not. I'm fond of her and I hate to see her worrying to death."

"If she is worried she ought not to be alone in that apartment"—Sinclair spoke for the first time since he had refused the cigarettes—"and I can't imagine a girl who had been raised under the iron rule of Rebecca Harding plunging into debt. Let's call for her, Gene, and take her to the Country Club for a little dancing and supper, help her forget her troubles."

"You know she won't go with you—why pester her, Blake? I like the Country Club idea, though, we'll go. Join us, Myles?"

"No" He glanced at his wrist watch. "Have a date with a man to talk politics."

"Morrie Grove, I'll bet. Fran gave him a pep talk the night of our dinner, now he is sure he will be nominated. She majored in political science in college, argued that as Democracy was being challenged every woman should be trained to understand something of politics and the state of the nation."

"Is she planning a political career, Gene? That's news to me."

"And from your shocked voice, unpleasant news, Blake. Don't be old-fashioned, only part time for the present, she won't let it interfere with marriage, she *claims*. Good night, Nat. Don't come in. I have no objection to having Myles see me to the car, though. I believe in encouraging good manners in the sterner sex."

He stood at the pillared entrance to the house watching the red taillight of the roadster blink out. How much truth had there been in Gene's yarn about Fran's debt for the ring? It hadn't rung true. Was she grinding an ax of her own? Was she trying to borrow money? Fran had refused to go out, he ought to find her at home. She had had no lunch and had declined the invitation to Rocky Point to dinner, she couldn't work as she had worked today on a cup of tea and a sliver of sandwich. Blake was 100 per cent right about her staying alone in the apartment over the Gallery. Gene's spadework had done its stuff, if not in the way she intended.

"I'm going out, Nat," he announced from the threshold of the living room. His sister, sitting near a lamp knitting, looked up and laughed.

"I'm glad. You really should do something about relieving Fran Phillips's mind about that debt."

"Do you believe that yarn of Gene's?"

"I do not. Before I met Miss Phillips today I heard quite a little about her background, and the sterling New England qualities of the aunt with whom she lived. I noticed her lovely ring. It is choice, but even as an antique I don't believe it cost a thousand dollars; if it did, she was horribly cheated. Whatever develops, remember that Gene Sargent doesn't know the first letter of the word 'loyalty.' How shall I explain your absence to that date you are expecting?"

"Entertain him yourself, you know more of Maine politics than I." He broke his own speed record to the garage, whistling thoughtfully,

Nita, Juanita,
Lean thou on my heart.

VII

Myles knocked on the door of the Gallery ell. A loud radioed voice inside stopped in the middle of a word. Through the window he saw the white Persian cat, Missy Snow, leap from Lemuel Digby's lap, saw him thrust his white stockinged feet into moccasins, saw his round-faced wife hold the navy-blue sock she was knitting suspended as her eyes followed the gangling figure of her husband shuffling across the room. A key clicked. The door opened a crack.

"Who is it?"

"Open up, Dig. I've come to say 'Hello.'"

The door was flung wide. Two gnarled, work-worn hands seized Myles's shoulders.

"It's the boy, Betsy," Digby called. "Come in. Come in, we heard you was home."

His wife jumped to her feet in such haste that the

52

chair in which she had been rocking lurched backward to the floor. Her crisp red and white striped cotton frock crackled with starch as she hurried forward.

"Myles, Myles, you're a sight for sore eyes, lad." He bent and kissed her rosy cheek down which a tear was rolling.

"Nothing sore about your eyes, Betsy Dig, they are sparkling like diamonds."

"Sure, an' you're the same lad, war hasn't changed you none." Her laugh was comfortably plump like her figure. "Always buttering me up when you came into the kitchen of Shore Acres for cookies. Those were the days. Sit down, Myles, sit down." He shook his head at the deep red plush-covered chair she patted invitingly.

"Not that one, you'd have to use a jack to get me out." He righted the overturned rocker before he pulled a golden oak chair from before the golden oak desk and straddled it. He folded his arms on top of its straight back. Lem Digby slipped his large feet out of his moccasins, sank into the chair Myles had rejected, lighted his pipe and rested his head with its sparse gray hair against the ornate tidy on the back. In one leap the white cat landed in his lap. His wife resumed rocking and knitting.

"Come back to stay, Myles?" she inquired.

"For a while. Then I'm off to work in New York—unless I'm needed in the service."

"By mighty, you don't think there's goin' to be another war, do you?"

"Not if this country pulls itself together to rebuild the American way of life and keeps in fighting trim, Dig."

"I look at you sittin' tall, 'bout six foot two, ain't you?—and powerful-lookin' for all you're lean as a racer, and it don't seem more'n a year or two since your father told me to take you shootin' for birds and teach you how to use a gun. You must have been about ten. That was all of twenty years ago."

"Just twenty-three, Lem. Time flies. I've kept count of his birthdays."

"Betsy's right, Myles. She keeps check on all the birthdays in town."

"Except my own." She chuckled. "Nat must be glad to have you back, Myles. She's been married a long time but I still can't think of her as Mrs. Andrews—Mrs. Jaffray Andrews she calls herself now. Lem and I were livin' at Shore Acres when she was born. She looks real peaked since she got her divorce. I suppose she still loves the skunk, some women are like that—as for me, I'd swish him in boilin' oil."

"By mighty, Betsy, you needn't fret. Life will take care of him, it has a way of givin' such fellas their comeuppance. We've read in the paper about your decorations and how you got 'em, Myles, and the wife an' me are terrible proud that we had a hand in raisin' you."

"You and the strap, Dig. Don't forget the strap. I won't if I live to be a hundred."

"The papers are sayin' that folks can live that long easy, Myles. You will, I—"

"Your father told me to make you mind, he hadn't the time," Lem Digby interrupted his wife's hopeful prophecy. "I guess the few whacks Betsy and I laid on helped you become what the papers say you are, 'a military genius come back to be a solid citizen.'"

"I hope the papers are right about the solid—" Was the sound he heard in the other part of the house Fran going out? He'd better wind up this visit. "Like this job, Dig?"

"It's all right, 'tain't like it was with your folks, though, but it's enough for us to handle. Your pa fixed it in his will so we don't need to work unless we want to, but the papers are saying that it's a dangerous thing for a man to retire an' have nothin' to do, with no interests he's apt to die, or have to reckon with senile dementia— I don't know what that is, but it sounds terrible. I take care of these grounds, watch out for trespassers here, an' on the beach—them Sargents like privacy. Silas Pond comes on at night; daytimes he's out in his fishin' boat with the phonograph goin', for company. Betsy takes care of the inside an' keeps it shinin'. She likes it fine."

"Sure, I like it." Mrs. Digby stopped rocking and knitting. She ran a long steel needle back and forth through her snow-white hair as she talked. "I like taking care of the pretty things, there are some real fine pieces of crockery. Now that you are back from the war whole, Myles, an' I have the girl to fuss over an' my flower border inside the stone wall is doin' fine, there isn't another thing in the world I want." She resumed knitting.

"What girl?"

"She means the assistant in the Gallery." Lem Digby paused to empty and refill his pipe. "You see, we never had children of our own. While Betsy had you and Nat to mother, it wasn't so bad; when you both went away for your education we was kinder lonesome."

"She's such a pretty girl," his wife contributed eagerly.

Myles thoughtfully drew a silver cigarette case from his pocket and as thoughtfully replaced it.

"Betsy, I'll lay my cards on the table. I'm interested in that girl."

Mrs. Digby's knitting dropped to her lap. She clasped her hands.

"Is she the girl you're going to marry, Myles? She's Miss Right for you."

"By mighty, Betsy, you're goin' fast. How do you know she's right for him? She ain't been living here for much over two days."

"Get along with you, Lem. Hasn't she been working at the Gallery for several weeks? And didn't she drop in here for tea with me some afternoons while she was livin' at Rocky Point? I read her cup for her once, she was real anxious. She asked, 'Do you see many tears for me?'"

"Did you?"

"You asked that as if you believed in them tea grounds fortunes, Myles."

"Some of the things Betsy has told me in the past came true, Dig. Did you see tears in her cup?"

"Not tears exactly, but trouble, and danger—there was a black cloud of danger." The last word was a hoarse whisper that Myles recognized as part of her fortunetelling technique, nonetheless it sent a shiver along his nerves.

"Did you tell her of the danger?"

"Sure, but I told her she'd come out of it all right and dandy."

"Of course there's danger living alone in that apartment above all those treasures." On his feet he swung the chair back to its place before the desk. "Is she there now?"

"Yes, but you needn't worry about her with Lem and me here, an' Silas Pond round nights. He isn't a fool if he does everlastingly chew gum."

"I want to see her. Show me the way."

"But Myles, she doesn't want callers. She told me that if any young man came to see her in the evening she wouldn't answer the bell, if he came around to this door I was to say she was out."

"But I'm not any young man, Betsy, I'm special." He laughed and linked his arm in hers. "Come on, show me the way. I want to take her out to supper."

"Her supper is here ready for her when she wants it, all she has to do is ring and I'll take it up. She didn't want it early because she said Miss Gene was comin' to talk business with her."

"Business? *Business?*"

"I guess 'twas pretty important. I heard Miss Gene say, 'I'm in a jam.' "

"A jam? Light breaks."

"Why didn't you phone her an' tell her you were goin' to take her to supper, Myles?"

"Because, like General Blood and Guts Patton, I believe in the value of a surprise attack. Come on, Betsy."

"Think I ought to do it, Lem? She said she didn't want to see callers."

"She was thinkin' of someone else, most probable. Myles ain't one of them wolves you read about in the papers. If she doesn't want to see him she'll get out of it someway. Can't lead that girl round by the ear, no sirree. I'm just waitin' to see the Sargents try, they've done it with each assistant so far."

"Lem says it's okay, Myles. We'll go through the small gallery, usually I run up the stairs that lead from the kitchen. There's a landing halfway that has a bay window with a seat where I can stop and get my breath. I'm not so spry on stairs as I was at Shore Acres."

Mrs. Digby rolled up her knitting and pulled herself out of the tight-fitting rocker. She led the way through a hall and touched a switch which flooded the small gallery with light. The oval mirror reflected the tall man in gray and the plump woman in the red and white striped dress. The eyes of Washington above the fireplace appeared to follow them as they crossed to the door which opened on the entresol. The Chinese mandarins and the bronze Buddha regarded them with expressionless faces. From the floor above came the music of a violin and a girl's voice:

My young and foolish heart.

"That's her singing," Mrs. Digby whispered as they started up the stairs. "She turns on the radio, then sings to the music. Her voice is real pretty. Here we go." Her raised hand stopped halfway to the brass knocker. "I hope I don't lose her trust for doin' this."

Song and violin stopped abruptly. The door opened in response to her hesitant knock.

"Mrs. Betsy, I was just coming down—" Fran saw Jaffray and put her hand to her throat. "Have you come to tell me—"

"I've come to save you from starvation." Her hand dropped in response to his steady, amused voice. "Mrs. Dig tells me you have not eaten since the sales marathon. Hop out of that orange-color lounge coat. Sports togs will do, I'm not dressed for a night spot. Make it quick."

"Won't you come into the living room?" He shook his head at the reluctant invitation.

"I'll stay here in the hall and smoke while Mrs. Dig helps you. I've got a lot to say. Speed, gal, speed."

She vanished. Betsy Digby rolled her eyes at him and giggled.

"I didn't think she'd go. You an' General Patton with your surprise attack," she whispered before she closed the door behind her.

Came the sound of a car stopping. Steps on the porch. A bell rang inside the apartment. Close to the door Myles heard Mrs. Digby's heavy tread cross the living room floor. Her voice, apparently at a speaking tube:

"She isn't home. No, I don't expect she'll be back till late. No, tell Miss Gene she didn't leave a message for her. Who's speaking? Mrs. Lem Digby, the caretaker. Yes, sir, I'll tell her to phone Miss Sargent soon's she comes in. Good night, sir."

He heard Betsy's diminishing tread; steps on the porch; the start of a car. Had Gene Sargent given up the plan to go to the Country Club? Why was she so anxious to contact Fran? Because of that "jam" Mrs. Betsy had heard mentioned? Had Blake Sinclair been with her? They'd gone. So far as they were concerned his evening with Fran was safe from interruption.

A great red moon was rising from the sea. It laid a glittering crimson path to the rocky shore. Myles stopped the open maroon convertible.

"Now, aren't you glad you came?"

"Yes. I've never seen a more perfect night."

"We do these things well in the State of Maine." He started the car. "Warm enough?"

"Yes, thanks. The salty breeze is like velvet against my face. My white pullover and cardigan are so warm I didn't need the top coat you insisted I take. I came with you because I suspected from your voice that you had something to tell your 'confounded responsibility.' "

"Right, but not about the subject uppermost in your thoughts. No news. As to the confounded responsibility, believe it or not, my shoulders are becoming used to the load. It doesn't seem so heavy. I'd miss it if I had to drop it. Gene told me that you sold four pictures this afternoon."

"Placed them, Major Jaffray, placed them. We don't sell pictures at the Sargent Gallery. Where and when did you see Gene? Sorry, I shouldn't have asked that."

"Why not? No secrets in my life—from you. She and Sinclair dropped in at Shore Acres after dinner on their way to the Country Club. While there she indicated that you were worried about your finances. What goes?"

"Nothing that you can help about."

"Haven't been getting into debt, have you?"

"I? Rebecca Harding's niece in debt? Pardon my surprise, I forgot that you never met the lady."

"I've not met her, but from Ken's account of his battles with her I feel that I know her from A to Z. A just, hard-boiled, extraordinarily successful career woman. Would you like an advance on your income? Is there a deadline you have to meet? It's a long way to September fifth." He had made it easy for her to tell him the truth about the ring on her finger which flashed in the light from the instrument board. She was silent so long

58

that he prompted, "How about it? Give me the bill and I will pay it."

"If you really mean that you want to help, advance me a thousand dollars. I prefer to pay my own bills."

Suspicion stiffened to conviction. She wanted the money to help Gene Sargent out of that jam. If rumor were true Gene was in a chronic state of jam. If Fran began to supply the funds to pay her debts, she would make it easy for her to continue gambling.

"Sorry, no can do right off the bat. A thousand dollars is a lot of money. I will have to check the accounts and see what I can do."

"I want it now, or not at all. So forget it. Where and when do we eat? I'm famished. You did invite me to supper, didn't you? I haven't made a social blunder in reminding you, have I?"

He loved her quick change from grave to gay, loved the challenging voice, the laughter in her eyes as they met his. What had caused the change? She was positively friendly. She couldn't have a thousand-dollar debt worrying her, she was asking for money to help Gene Sargent. There had been the suggestion of tears crowding behind her eyes when she said, "I came because I thought you had something to tell me." If only he had good news for her, but no report of Ken or his activities had come through the secret channel they had prepared.

"Certainly we eat. Too late for lobster?"

"Never too late for lobster in Maine."

"That goes double for me. See the rope of red, green and blue lights ahead? That's the pound."

The smell of the lobster house was a compound of not too fresh bait, wet hemp, the appetizing scent of clams steaming in seaweed and lobsters boiling. They selected two ugly, green clawing creatures with protruding black bead eyes from the tank. At a scrubbed pine table in a screened porch they waited for them to be boiled. The lash of the tide against the rocky shore, low voices from another table, the sound of a distant automobile horn occasionally broke the evening silence.

"This is a no-license county," Myles reminded. "What will you have to drink that you may have?"

"Hot coffee. License or no license means nothing in my young life. I don't drink."

59

"Aunt Becky again?"

"No. Frances Phillips this time. Believe it or not, I have done *some* thinking for myself and *considerable* observing." She shook her head at a menu presented by a waitress in the regalia of a bosun's mate. "Nothing but the lobster and a roll."

While they waited they weighed the qualifications for leadership of the presidential nominees; agreed that there was no corner of the world where the United States was not interested, where it could afford to be inactive; that foreign policy was the country's burning question; sympathized with England and France in their postwar struggles; deplored the pernicious effect of strikes and the more-pay-for-less work trend.

Conversation languished as they concentrated on the excavation of warm, pink meat from fire-truck-red lobsters to the accompaniment of " 'S-wonderful" from a juke box.

"It is wonderful, it's luscious." Fran dabbled her fingers in the water of a glass bowl and dried them. She smiled at the female bosun's mate who had cleared away the shell debris and was setting a pot of fresh coffee on the table. The waitress laid a check face down beside Myles, murmured "Thank you," and departed. Fran shook her head at the silver case he offered.

"I don't smoke. You may charge that up to Aunt Becky. Early in my career she said 'No.' I meekly conformed."

"She isn't here to say 'No' now."

"Now I don't care to. Perhaps that is the advantage of not commencing young."

"You don't impress me as being a meek person. Quite the contrary. You didn't hesitate to tell me where I got off."

"I said I was sorry I had been so waspish, didn't I?" She remembered that she had decided to make him aware of her and smiled, engagingly, she hoped.

"You did. My apologies. I was meanly trying to get even for that 'confounded responsibility' crack a while ago. Now that the subject that was 'definitely closed' has been reopened, give me a break. Tell me why you are—I hope it is *were*, now, though I don't quite trust that last smile of yours—so dead set against me."

"It is still *are*." She abandoned the role of Circe. It wasn't her line. Her eyes were on the fragments of the roll she was crumbling.

"You *mean* that? Why? If you dislike me so much why did you come out with me?"

"I hoped you had news—"

"I thought it was you." Gene Sargent greeted them gaily. Myles rose and frowned at the man beside her whose eyes were on the girl seated at the table.

"Did you and Sinclair come up through the floor? I neither saw nor heard you till you spoke. Thought you two were going to the Country Club."

"We went. No one there, all gone to the square-dance party in the Town Hall, to benefit the firehouse. Blake suggested we try to get Fran to go with us so we broke the speed law getting to the Gallery, only to discover that she was out. Passing this point we saw you through the screen and decided we would try to round up two more patrons for the dance as our good deed for the day. Join us, please, Myles."

"Sure, I'm all for it. I'll take Fran back and then meet you at Town Hall."

"Why not give her a chance to say she'll come along?" Sinclair demanded belligerently.

"No square dance for me after the day I've put in," Fran declined emphatically. "Why don't you drive me home, Blake, then Mr. Jaffray will be free to go with Gene? You can join them later."

"Boy, that's the thought of the day. Mean it, sweetheart? I—"

"Nothing doing," Myles cut in on Sinclair's jubilant voice. "When I start out with a lady I see her home. Come on, Fran."

As the two girls preceded the men Myles heard Gene's tense whisper:

"Did you get it, Fran? I'm desperate, remember."

VIII

On the beach below the rocky cliff in front of the Gallery Fran stretched at full length to dry her wet swim suit. Elbows in the sand, chin in her hands, through dark glasses she could see the golden beach opposite the cove, the two large resort hotels on the slope above it. It was splotched with the colors of gay umbrellas, crowded with bathers, wading, sitting, lying down, hoping for relief from the intense heat. A dark spot offshore was the boat of the life-guard. Far beyond loomed the lighthouse, gleaming with a mother-of-pearl luster.

The sky was cloudless blue. Her eyes followed the swoop of a foraging, screaming gull to the top of a jade-green wave before they closed in lazy content. Lucky her day off had followed the work and excitement of the preview of the Eckhard paintings. Gene was right, she did plunge into whatever she undertook up to her elbows. Why couldn't she take things calmly? " 'Tisn't your nature, kid," Ken had answered when she had asked him the question. She was going into her first field-hockey game at college and had been shaking with excitement. Even so, she had made three goals, she remembered.

Ken. Where was he? If she could only know he was safe. She must not think of him. If she did she might show her anxiety and betray his mission. Myles Jaffray had said, "Even in this small place there may be pricked ears." That settled it. Exit Ken from her thoughts.

She pulled off her sunglasses and rested her cheek against folded, sandy arms. This must be the way a cat or dog felt when stretched in the sunlight, utterly relaxed. Nothing was expected of her. Gene had taken over the Gallery for the working day. Lunch, packed by Mrs. Betsy in a basket, flanked by a book and magazine, was parked on a near-by rock. Nothing to do till she dressed for the matinee at The Theater.

The faint moan of the bell buoy offshore, the lazy, languorous lap, lap, of the tide would lull her to sleep if she didn't watch out. The salty ocean breeze would apply an extra coat of tan, her skin was sufficiently brown now. Thank goodness she didn't burn to lobster red.

Lobster! The word set off a flashback. Last evening when Myles Jaffray had left her at the door with a curt "Good night," she had raced up the stairs, snapped on the light in her living room, flung her coat on a chair and herself on the broad couch. She heard a car start. Why had he waited all this time? What could she do about the thousand dollars Gene needed? Sell some bonds? Judge Grimes could get them from her deposit box if she sent an order. She couldn't betray Gene's need to Myles Jaffray, he might be in love with her, perhaps he had decided to stop "loving and leaving" to marry and settle down, it was evident that she was crazy about him. Had he heard the whispered "Did you get it, Fran? I'm desperate—"

When she opened her eyes the room was bright with daylight. The lamp was burning. Outside the door Mrs. Betsy called:

"Ready for your breakfast, dearie?"

Her thoughts reverted to last evening. Why had Myles insisted on bringing her home if he did not intend to speak to her on the way? Had he been angry when she declared that she still disliked him? Naturally. How would she feel if the same thing had been said to her? She had racked her brain for a contribution of small talk to break the silence but nothing came. He must think her dull. Miss Tassie had said that was a sure-kill for a man's interest—maybe so, but she had not talked about herself.

The conclusion brought her up sitting. The abrupt movement sent the two white gulls who were rocking placidly on a blue-green wavelet into the air mewing shrilly. She brushed sand from her bare legs and the ballerina skirt of her amber satin swim suit. Thank goodness skirts were top fashion again.

She played jackstones with five pebbles as her thoughts returned to Myles Jaffray. Had he brought her home last evening because he realized that the moment she had suggested Blake Sinclair as his substitute she had regretted it? So far he had shown an uncanny knowledge of what she was thinking. Why had he been so sure she wouldn't go to the dance in aid of the firehouse? That answer was easy. He didn't want her. When it came to that, why would he? She had been consistently disagreeable to him.

A kingfisher flashed by, a streak of brilliant blue. Five gulls floating on the water rose with shrill cries and flew out to sea. What had frightened them? Someone on the cliff? Right. Men's voices. She hitched back nearer the rocks where she couldn't be seen from above and threw a Chinese beach coat, the shadowy brown of dark amber, across her shoulders.

A small piece of rock bounded down and landed on the sand beside her. The speakers must be on the bench near the edge of the cliff directly overhead. The land and beach were the property of the Sargents. Were the persons above trespassers or members of the family?

"You may leave it for me to inspect." She would recognize Henry Sargent's booming voice were it broadcast from one of the recently discovered magnetic poles.

"I know that you have proof that it is genuine." The loud impatient response evidently was in reply to a comment too low for her to hear. "I haven't forgotten you discovered it in the attic of a Southern plantation, that it had been in the family for generations, but I want time in which to examine it myself."

A murmured protest?

"Of course it will be safe. It is fully insured from fire or theft the moment it enters the building behind us. If I decide it is a Constable, as you claim—there aren't many of them—one sold in England recently for £5650 —I'll hand over a check—it's a cracking big sum to pay."

A mumbled interlude.

"Of course I won't mention it till the deal is completed. Do you think I'm a rookie in this business, that I don't know there are other galleries that—"

Fran clapped her hands over her ears. She had been listening to what was not intended for her to hear, and how she had listened! Her ears had been stretched to bursting point. It was up to her to forget that a priceless painting was to be delivered to the Gallery, forget what she had heard, and—quick.

She waited for what seemed hours before she uncovered her ears and listened. No sound of voices. The men on the cliff above had gone. One by one gray gulls and white gulls returned, dived, settled down to ride the sparkling, restless sea. Henry Sargent must have been speaking of the painting that Blake Sinclair had "picked up, an item he wanted very much." Doubtless Blake had been the mumbler—

"Excuse me, Miss." The apologetic voice brought

64

Fran to her feet and entirely into the dark amber beach coat.

"What are you doing here, Barth? This is a private beach," she reminded the man who stood, feet apart, hands thrust deep into the pockets of dark brown dungarees. The sleeves of his matching shirt, which, obviously, had seen better days and many of them, were rolled above arms dark and hairy as a gorilla's. A Napoleonic lock of white hair dangled above his Napoleonic nose.

"I'm sorry I startled you, Miss. I walked from the village along the rocks—no parties today, I'm not working—back there I saw a crab in a tide pool, I'm much interested in crustaceans, crawled down to look at it and lost my direction. Like to see it, Miss?" He drew a reddish object from his right pocket and dropped it on the sand.

Fran's eyes were on the grotesque thing backing toward the water, but not her mind. Why should imagination tie his sudden appearance to the conversation she had heard above? Had he been crouched near listening? In his brown outfit he would have been undistinguishable from the rocks. That was a crazy suspicion. Why would a man, late head butler in a "near palace" in Belgium, now accommodating as a waiter, be interested in the sale of a painting?

"Perhaps you'll be good enough to set me straight, Miss."

"Where do you want to go?"

"To where the artists hang out. I hear there's quite a bunch of them."

"Follow this sandy beach till you come to steps cut in the rocks. Mount those and you'll see a path that leads along the top of the cliffs to the Inlet, the artists' colony." Her suspicion nerve tingled again. Had he been eavesdropping for a purpose? Was he a scout for another gallery? "Are you interested in painting, Barth?"

"Only because there were many famous paintings in the house where I was butler, Miss. I don't claim to know one artist from another. I like pictures but I can't understand surrealist stuff. That was a pretty exhibition in the Sargent Gallery yesterday, I took a look at it after I cleared up. Had a little talk with the artist. I'd say the paintings had a lot of what my Belgian employer called 'atmosphere.' I'll be moving on. Thank you for directing me, Miss."

Fran's eyes followed him as he picked his way along the sand, his large shoes leaving miniature pools in their wake. Who was he? What was he doing in this small town? Henry Sargent hadn't liked having a strange man serving as a waiter yesterday.

"I don't like it," he had scolded. "I don't like having a person working here of whom I know nothing. There's a fortune in *objets d'art* small enough to be slipped into a man's pocket, to be picked up."

She remembered what the elevator boy had said about the man in gray the day she had called on Judge Grimes, "Looks to me and the super as if he might be the finger man of a gang."

Myles hadn't been, but this one-time butler, Dunkirk casualty, accommodator, might be here to collect data as to the value and location of marketable treasures. That was a cheery thought when she was often alone in the Gallery for hours at a time.

"Hi!"

Fran looked up in answer to the hail. A small, black-haired girl in a checked pink and white gingham play-suit was hopping from rock to rock down the cliff. She held her breath. Suppose the child fell and hurt herself? How would she get her up? She didn't fall. She was as sure-footed as a chamois. In a final leap she landed on the sandy beach.

"Hi!" she said again. Standing with feet spread far apart she stared at Fran.

"Hi, yourself. Where did you come from?" It wasn't necessary to ask. She was a small edition of Gene Sargent, the same dark hair, the same dark eyes, the tipped-down corners of what otherwise would be a lovely mouth. She was Matilde's and Ben Sargent's child. Mrs. Betsy had said she was the spittin' image of her aunt.

"I live at Rocky Point. Like to have me keep you company?" Her eyes strayed to the basket before they resumed their staring regard of the girl on the sand.

"Yes, sit down, won't you?" Fran slipped out of the beach coat.

"Jeepers, you're a honey in that swim suit. Got what it takes, haven't you? Shall I get the lunch?"

"How do you know there is a lunch?"

"Do I look like a dumb bunny? I'm 'most eight and in the fourth grade. Awful smart for a kid who's been dragged from school to school, my teacher said. You wouldn't have knitting in a basket covered with a white cloth, would you?"

"Right. Get the basket and we'll see what Mrs. Betsy packed for us."

"Okay, sister."

She had the basket on the sand before a diving gull reached the water. On her knees she watched eagerly as Fran spread a large white napkin.

"Is there enough for three?" she inquired anxiously.

"Three? Where do you get three?" Fran stopped in the process of filling a paper plate with wax-paper packages of sandwiches. "You haven't a twin up your sleeve, have you?"

"No, don't be gooshy, it's Tweedledee, remember him in *Alice*, don't you? Hi, Tweed, you can come."

In response to the hail a nose, beadlike black eyes and twitching black and white ears appeared above a rock, another authoritative "Hi!" and a fox terrier landed in one leap on the sand, barely escaping the spread napkin. He squatted beside the little girl and looked up at her as if for further orders.

"Cute, isn't he?" She tweaked his ears till he yelped. "He goes everywhere with me, for protection. Hal Andrews says he'll be darned—he said damned, but Grandmama says I mustn't use the word—if he can understand why anyone would kidnap me; he doesn't like me and I hate him. There's lots of sandwiches. I guess Mrs. Betsy suspected you'd have company."

She sat with her feet tucked under her. The dog licked his chops and hitched toward the white napkin. She slapped him.

"Mind your manners, Tweed. Hal hates my dog, too, but, gee, you should see Tweed bare his teeth and hear him snarl when he comes into the room. My nurse says the dog has more sense than some humans she knows. I guess she means Mother."

"Divide this package of sandwiches with Tweedles. I know his name but I don't know yours." Fran successfully switched the subject.

67

"I'm Pat Sargent my real name is Patricia but we don't use it. I know who you are. You're the new salesgirl at the Gallery."

She hadn't thought of herself as being a salesgirl, but perhaps she was just that.

"In case you care, I am Frances Phillips, Fran to my friends. Now that we have been properly introduced will you have a drink of milk?"

"Sure. There are two paper cups. I guess you were expecting a beau." She held a fragment of sandwich high above the dog's head. "Speak for it, Tweed." The terrier's ear-piercing yelp set the gulls a-wing.

"Mummy told Aunt Gene that Mr. Sinclair was nuts about you." The little girl's eyes and voice were sly. "She said she'd better help him get you or you'd snitch Myles Jaffray from right under her nose. I kept quiet as a mouse in the corner, they didn't know I was in the room. Aunt Gene was mad, she turned red as a boiled lobster, she said, 'Something tells me if Hal doesn't come across quick, you'll make a play for Myles yourself, Matilde. When I want your advice, I'll ask for it. Till then—'"

"Let's talk about you, Pat. Like school?"

"Sure. That's a dumb question. How could I be head of my class if I didn't like it? My God, this little cake—"

"*Pat!* You shouldn't use that word like that."

"What word?"

"God. Haven't you learned the Ten Commandments in Sunday School? Remember the Fourth, 'Thou shalt not take the name of the Lord thy God in vain'?"

"Jeepers, Mummy's always saying it, especially when she breaks a fingernail. I guess you're what nurse would call spinsterish prim, like Miss Tassie, but I like you a lot. You're kind of warming, make me feel cosy inside, if you get what I mean. Everyone else thinks I'm a problem child, but you don't seem to. If you say I shouldn't say—my—the devil, here comes that fat Morrie Grove to spoil our picnic."

Fran looked up. Morrison Grove in white slacks, crimson jersey and sunburned face of equally high visibility was descending the cliff on low.

"Mind if I join you?" he called. "Saw you from the water." He puffed slightly as he jumped to the beach.

The dog accompanied his every move with a shrill bark. "Thought perhaps you'd like to go for a spin and stop for lunch somewhere, Miss Phillips. For Pete's sake, shut up that pooch, kid."

"Thanks for the invitation, Mr. Grove, but I have a ticket for the matinee. Mr. Morrison Grove, Miss Patricia Sargent."

"You don't have to be so polite, introducing us. I know him." Pat bit into a cake. "I guess he's the beau you were expecting, Miss Fran. I know when I'm not wanted. I'll shoot along. Mummy says the girl who gets Morrie Grove has her sympathy. He's a tightwad. Better watch your step. Come on, Tweed." From halfway up the cliff she called:

"Thanks for the lunch. I'll be seeing you."

The two on the beach watched the girl and dog leap from rock to rock with the agility of goats and disappear. Morrison Grove flexed his fingers.

"I'm a man of peace—usually—but there are times when I am sorely tempted to wring that brat's neck, and this is one of them."

"Come back here against the cliff in the shadow out of that blazing sun and your blood pressure will return to normal. Sit down and finish the sandwiches. There is one package left and two cakes—Pat majored on the cakes—and eggs stuffed with anchovy in the bottom of the basket which, meanly, I had not produced."

"Did you get anything to eat?"

"I did. I will now share the eggs with you. That child made my heart ache. I got the impression that she isn't wanted and knows it."

He settled back against the cliff and accepted the sandwiches she offered.

"This sure is heaven. Don't worry about the kid, her grandparents adore her, they'll straighten out life for her. A little bird is whispering that Hal Andrews has declared he won't marry the mother if the child is included in the transaction."

If that happened, would Matilde keep the child or was Gene right, would she let Hal Andrews go and try for Myles Jaffray, Fran wondered before she observed, "That doesn't sound as if he cared much for the mother."

"He cares for no one but himself. He had the loveliest wife in the world, and he—" Grove cleared his husky voice. "Better for Pat if she isn't dragged into that setup, the two will lead a fighting cat and dog life. While we are still on the subject of Matilde and her affairs, I am not a tightwad. Once in her youth—her family lived here—I took out Matilde. She indicated orchids. I hadn't the money to buy them and refused to take the hint. That kayoed me with her. What Ben Sargent, the grand fella, saw in her stymied me. She was pretty but what else?"

"Let's not spend time on this perfect day thinking of unpleasant persons and events. Was that your launch that whizzed by a while ago?"

"Yes. Recognized you through binoculars and decided to ask you to come for a spin. Landed at Rocky Point pier. Sinclair had parked his snappy blue roadster and was just setting out in a dinghy. He had the nerve to ask if I were looking for you and before I could reply 'What business is it of yours?' he volunteered:

" 'If it is Miss Phillips you're looking for she left town in a bus this morning for parts unknown—to her land-lady.' I knew better because I had seen you here. I didn't let on to him, though."

"Mrs. Betsy is an accomplished but harmless prevaricator, I've discovered. I told her that if anyone called for me to tell them that I was incommunicado for twenty-four hours. The word not being in her vocabulary she translated it to suit herself."

"Now I've butted in and spoiled your day."

"I am glad you came. I mean it. Look at the gulls. They scent a picnic. They are settling down like a white and gray cloud on the blue water. I adore this place."

"It suits you. You're a dish in that swim suit."

"Suppose we cut out personal remarks, Mr. Grove."

"For the love of Mike, what's in that to turn you to ice? Haven't you been told before you're a knockout in that rig?" His honest incredulity made her protest seem silly.

"Just between you and me this is the first time I have worn it. I've been wearing an old one—so characteristically New Englandish to save something for 'best.' "

"The dimples are flashing again. That takes a load

70

from these old shoulders. Thought for a minute you were mad at me. My remark was respectful admiration. Modern version."

"We'll settle for respectful admiration. How's the political campaign going?"

"Swell. Jaffray came out flat that he is not a candidate and the G.G.A. swung to me."

"I'm glad. If you are re-elected it will mean Washington again. Won't your business, profession, or what have you, suffer while you are away?"

"Haven't either. Was a newspaperman for a while, then inherited just enough money to spoil me for a settled job. If I'm elected I'll do my darnedest to make good. Elected or not, I intend to take a course my Alma Mater thought up, 'Great Issues.' It is required work for seniors, designed to send them out into the world equipped with an idea, if no more, of the big problems to be met and solved in this critical decade. I can use a little such information."

"You and the rest of us. It sounds like a divinely inspired idea. Listen. Isn't that the puff-puff of a motor coming this way?"

"Yes. On order." He struggled to his feet. "You wouldn't think from my stiffness now that I was a relay runner champion once, would you? Can I take you anywhere?" he asked as a tender with outboard motor slid smoothly onto the beach.

"N-o-o, no thanks. Is that your man at the wheel?"

"No. Picked up the guy at the Rocky Point pier. He was helping Sinclair put off. I asked him if he knew anything about boats. He allowed he did, having just finished three years in the navy as lieutenant (j.g.). I hired him to bring the tender round. Couldn't see myself scrambling up these rocks. Sure you won't come along?"

"No. I'll repack the basket, throw the scraps, if any, to the gulls and do the scrambling act myself."

"You're the doctor. Bye-bye till we meet again."

Her eyes followed him as he crossed the beach. The man in brown shirt and dungarees standing back to the cliff steadied the boat as he stepped in, pushed it off and swung aboard expertly. She watched till it rounded the point and was out of sight.

"First a butler in Belgium, next a casualty of Dunkirk, now a lieutenant (j.g.) in our navy," she reflected aloud. "I wonder in what guise you will appear next, Mister—Barth?"

IX

The play was well written, well acted and staged with professional skill, but the wooden building of the summer theater was unbearably hot. When, just before the final curtain, the coatless leading man in a shirt visibly wet with perspiration clasped to his manly, if damp, bosom the woman in his life, whose honey of a white evening frock looked as if it had stepped from a page of *Vogue*, the female portion of the audience shuddered audibly. It was nothing short of sacrilege.

Fran made her way through the crowded aisle to the exit. The heat was terrific. If only she had come in her sedan. The plan to walk home for exercise had died on its feet. Was the overhead rumble a plane or the prelude to an approaching storm? Above the highest peak in the line of coastal hills a descending red sun shone through a haze. The heat rated a sharp thundershower to cool the air. Let it come if only it would hold off till she reached home.

Outside The Theater she waited for a chance to cross to the highway. Car after car drew up, filled with laughing passengers and drove away. The gay comedy had left the audience refreshed and rested, its problems pushed into the background. Brightly painted taxis and shabby taxis crowded shining touring cars and luxurious limousines toward the waiting crowd. Symphony afternoon at home had nothing on this for the variety and number of automobiles that had come from miles up and down the coast.

Had she better wait for a taxi to return or walk? The black cloud rising above the top of a gigantic pine had a wicked look. She glanced at her short-sleeved white shark-skin frock with a cummerbund of turquoise and coral, the spectator-sports supreme of her summer wardrobe. It was a beauty. Waiting was indicated. Thank goodness she had no hat to consider.

"Miss Phillips." Natalie Andrews spoke behind her. "I was afraid I would lose you in the crowd. Is your car here or did you come with someone?"

"I walked. I'm a lone ranger. I was thinking when you spoke that if my sedan were parked here it would take an hour or two to reach it."

"We've just missed my chauffeur. He'll come around again. I hope that angry cloud is a heat-breaker. Drive home with me for tea. I promise that you will be delivered at the Gallery later dry and safe."

"I can't think of anything I would rather do. I am a lady of leisure. Gene has taken over my job for the day."

Even in the curious red light Natalie Andrews looked younger than she had yesterday afternoon, not more than thirty-five. Her short white hair was youthfully cut and waved close to her head. The lustrous pearls at ears and throat and her fair skin reflected the tint of her soft pink cotton frock. The play had left the brilliance of laughter in her deep blue eyes, she was chic from head to pink sandals.

"Hi, Nat!" a voice called as she followed Fran into the back of an open green covertible. "Give me a lift. I'm stranded."

"Sorry, Matilde, but I haven't room for another passenger. Drive on, Gus."

Her face was deeply flushed. Did she believe that her brother had been horribly hurt by the woman who had hailed her? Miss Tassie had gone on record as fearing that "the red-headed hellion" might try to "rope him." Perhaps the refusal was not on his account, perhaps she resented her ex-husband's attention to Matilde Sargent at the preview of Eckhard's paintings. Pat's confidences this morning confirmed later by Morrison Grove had been revealing. How could a woman trust a man with eyes like his? Wicked eyes. She hadn't had a lot of experience, but enough to recognize invitation in them when they met hers.

"It was a good show, wasn't it?" With the question Natalie Andrews's tension eased. She settled back in the seat and unclenched the hands in her lap.

Fran agreed that it was. The car smoothly sped along a road bordered and scented by pines and balsams.

Spaces between their branches afforded glimpses of sky, beach and a distant sea. They passed a high, ornate iron fence behind which one caught glimpses of a brick house, with corner towers and long windows.

"How charming," Fran exclaimed.

"That is Sunnyside, Miss Trent's home. There is a gate in the hedge between her garden and ours. She and my mother were devoted friends; when Mother married and came north to live, Miss Tassie bought acres of land adjoining ours, moved her house here, bricks, carvings, even windows. It is a museum piece. She is devoted to Myles and me, too devoted at times, it is difficult for her to keep hands off our lives."

They discussed the actors, commended their sporting spirit in carrying on while heat streaked their make-up; kept the conversational ball in air till the chauffeur opened the door of the roadster in front of a beautiful old red brick house whose white pillars rose to the second story, whose wings were widespread.

Natalie Andrews led the way through a broad hall carpeted with jewel-tone Persian rugs from which spiraled a staircase perfect in design and detail.

"The Jaffray ancestors."

She indicated the portraits hung against the ivory-tinted walls. There were men in blue coats and high white stocks; men in naval and army uniforms of a much older day; one wore the black robe of a judge, his fine hand rested on a book. She opened the door of a small room. Mirrored walls gave back the deep rose color of bench and hangings, the sheen of silver toilet appointments.

"In here if you want to restore your make-up, and who doesn't after broiling in The Theater. The door at the end of the hall opens on the terrace. Join me there."

Aunt Rebecca's garden had been something to write home about, but it couldn't touch this for charm and color and fragrance, Fran thought, as she stood on the top step of the broad terrace. Pink peonies, gigantic spikes of heavenly blue anchusa, foxgloves and Canterbury bells, stately Madonna lilies and Shasta daisies for a white touch, day lilies for yellow, tall, late purple tulips, against a background of dark rhododendrons. Paths in a velvety green lawn led to the central point, an old-fashioned pool in the center of which a bronze boy blew a horn from which liquid diamonds rose high in the air to tinkle back with the sound of broken glass into water where goldfish flashed like living flames. A pair of yellow summer birds bathed daintily in the shallows. Gay umbrellas shaded green iron tables. Striped awnings topped deck chairs.

"Will you have your tea iced or hot, Miss Phillips?" inquired Natalie Andrews. She seated herself at a table equipped with choice old Georgian silver, pale yellow china of paper-thin delicacy, and a tall frosted-glass pitcher and glasses.

"Hot, thank you. Somewhere I read that the hotter the day the hotter the tea should be for refreshment. Please call me Fran, not Miss Phillips. I have been loving the garden. Many of the plants would be past their prime at home."

"Flowers and fruits are about two weeks later in Maine."

"This breeze is a lifesaver." Fran sank into a white wicker chair near the tea table with a sigh of relief.

"I suspect it is the van of a storm. Look between those two towering pines. You can see the surf rolling in on the beach. It is some surf." She offered a cup on a doily-covered plate. "Trim the tea to your taste. Help yourself to cinnamon toast, sandwiches and cakes."

"Thank you. I don't need to eat. I have been feasting on your garden. Color is food and drink to me."

"I will pass your praise on to Crocker, our gardener. He is the magician who makes it grow. It is not my garden. I inherited the New York house. This place belongs to Myles. It should. It has descended from Jaffray to Jaffray and, I hope, will go that way for generations to come. Do you enjoy your work?"

It took a split second for Fran to reorient herself. She had been visualizing the Jaffray men who peopled the hall.

"Very much, it is so varied. The number of visitors who come to the Gallery never ceases to amaze me. When I came up from the beach this noon and dodged into the Digbys' entrance, cars were parked in the drive and I caught the hum of many voices within the building. I felt guilty to leave Gene to carry on alone, but I have learned not to upset Mr. Sargent's schedule. Visitors come from miles away. Neither distance nor our prices faze them. They spend like drunken sailors."

"Most persons like an objective when they drive in summer and love to buy. There is something about a vacation that spreads one's spending wings. That crash of thunder was nearer."

"On the terrace? I know the way, Susie. You're right, I ought to. I've been coming here for years." The voice came from inside the house.

"Oh, dear, that's Morrie, and I thought we two were all set for a get-acquainted party," Natalie Andrews had time to murmur before Grove appeared in the doorway.

"Greetings again, Miss Phillips. How goes the battle, Nat?" His round, smiling face reminded Fran of the red moon that had poked above the horizon last night. It was redder, if that were possible, than when she had seen him on the beach at noon. His all-white costume accentuated his color.

"I assume that you mean by 'battle' my daily life, Morrie. It is going extremely well at the moment. I had the good luck to kidnap Fran at The Theater."

"Boy, weren't the players up against it? It makes me hot to think of them." A wicker chair registered a creak of protest as he sank into it heavily. "I went backstage and they were limp from the heat. What a crack of thunder! Smell sulphur?"

"I hope the storm won't pass us by. We need it to clear the air. Did the girl who played the ingénue lure you behind the scenes, Morrie? She was charming, so unspoiled."

"She is all that but a trifle young to interest your Uncle Morrison, Nat. It takes a woman of your poise and beauty to shoot up my blood pressure."

The tender meaning in his words dyed her face a soft pink. Fran remembered the huskiness of his voice when this noon he had said, "He had the loveliest wife in the world." She had the embarrassed feeling that she had opened a door without knocking. As if he realized he had spoken out of turn Grove said lightly:

"In case you are interested, I am reporting this summer experiment for the paper I once honored with my presence. Its success is news. I don't want sugar or cream in my tea, Nat. How come you have forgotten? I haven't thrown sand in the works by my honest, if clumsy, tribute to your charm, have I?"

"Take this cup and stop your nonsense, Morrie," Natalie Andrews protested, but his words had brought youth and laughter to her face. "What news from the political front? Speaking of battles, how goes your campaign?"

"Fair blows the wind. Quite poetic, what? Getting backstage again perked up my yen for drama. Hear the news about Miss Tassie?"

"No. What sensational thing has she done now?"

"Not sensational this time. She has invited the artist of yesterday's one-man show to be her guest at Sunnyside while he paints the surrounding country."

"How like her, she can be so kind. Did he accept? Does he think we are paintable? How did you hear?"

"I'll answer your questions in reverse, Nat. I was included in the invitation to dinner after the preview; he thinks this country paintable and he accepted for the one-guest house party. He's quite a guy, if you ask me. Speaking of guys, remember the man who brought round my tender, Miss Phillips? Shucks—why be so formal? Why not Fran?"

"No reason in the world, make it Fran. I remember the man. This morning he told you he had been a lieutenant (j.g.) in our navy, yesterday he told me he was a casualty of Dunkirk."

Morrison Grove's whistle was long and low.

"What do you know about that!"

"Nothing but what he told me. If you believe him, before Dunkirk he was a butler in an 'almost palace' in Belgium. Also, he was the waiter at the preview yesterday."

"You're kidding."

"I'm not, but apparently someone is."

"Something tells me that fella will bear watching."

"Who'll bear watching, Morrie?" Myles Jaffray, who had taken the terrace steps two at a time, waited for an ominous rumble to die away before he added, "This storm will. It promises to be a corker." He was wearing light gray slacks and a matching sports coat. His powder-blue shirt with turned-back collar made his eyes and hair seem darker. He perched on the terrace wall and lighted a cigarette.

"Where did you come from, Fran? No tea, Nat. I'm waiting for an answer to my first question, my second was by way of greeting."

"I'll answer the first, Myles." Morrison Grove paused to shake his head when Natalie in pantomime offered to refill his cup. "We were talking about the waiter who assisted at the preview tea, yesterday." He repeated the story the man had told Fran and the quite different scrap of personal history he had given him. "Perhaps Dunkirk or a like experience has affected his mind. Sounds like the hallucinations of a psycho to me."

"Our visiting fireman also is interested in crustaceans, he confided when he appeared on the Sargent beach this morning," Fran contributed. "His brown outfit was so like the color of the rocks that I didn't see him until he spoke."

"Brown? The color of the rocks? Sure about that?" Myles inquired.

"Very sure. Perhaps he is a spy, I understand they are still operating all over the world. Perhaps Barth is his cover-name. Don't members of the Stragetic Service use a cover-name? I believe he is in the village for a purpose."

"Your guess is as good as mine." Should she tell them she suspected he might be a finger man sent to collect data about the Gallery treasures? No, better keep that figment of imagination to herself for the present.

"I rather liked the man when I asked him to take a tray to your office yesterday, Fran. He didn't seem crazy to me, he appeared to know the butling job from A to Z."

"Did he seem curious about anyone or about anything, Myles?"

"No-o-o, Nat—hold on a minute, he did say he thought that the paintings on exhibition were exceptionally good. Which comment from a man in his line of work surprised me; he added that he had served as a guard in a National Gallery in Brussels."

"Still another job. I bet next he'll claim to have been secretary to one of the big shots in Washington. I have a hunch that our mysterious stranger—"

78

"Hail, hail, the gang's all here," Blake Sinclair interrupted as he stepped from the doorway to the terrace. His smooth blond hair shone like gold, his white costume was the latest word in sports clothes. He bent over Natalie Andrews's welcoming hand with his top-drawer air of devotion.

"You told me I might drop in for tea, didn't you, Mrs. Andrews? I couldn't resist the pull of this lovely home—and you."

The lowered tone of the last two words emphasized the hint of I've-been-living-for-this-moment in his voice. Fran recognized the act. It was one of his specialities, done with a touch of gaiety which kept it from being saccharine. Was Natalie impressed? She was smiling, taking the tribute as it was intended.

"The leading man in the play this afternoon said something like that, but not nearly so well. Were you at The Theater, Mr. Sinclair?"

"No. Matilde Sargent deserted Gene, who was on duty at the Gallery, to go to the matinee, so I stayed to help, and believe me, we had a hectic afternoon. The place was crowded."

"How will you have your tea, Mr. Sinclair?"

"As it comes. Thank you." He helped himself to a sandwich and with plate and cup balanced on the arm of a large chair beside Fran.

"What made this day particularly hectic, Blake?" she asked.

"Eckhard appeared. He insisted upon changing one of his paintings for one he had brought from his Inn room. Gene protested. She knew that her father had had them hung as he wanted them. The artist was determined to have his way and got it. Didn't have another frame so changed the canvas in the repair shop. I heard that Miss Tassie Trent has taken him up. The attention has gone to his head. That's the way with these people who learn just enough—"

"Just enough!" Morrison Grove echoed. "That guy knows more than enough. He spent several years abroad studying the old masters. I understand he is one of the experts in the country on the authenticity of paintings."

"What?" Sinclair steadied his cup which his sudden

movement had tilted, and waited for a thunderous rumble to die away. He laughed. "I was about to ask, 'What is your authority for that?' when that awful crash startled me. Boy, I'm glad to know that about Eckhard. I can use him sometime." He looked at Fran. "I see that you have returned from parts unknown, sweetheart. Quick trip, wasn't it?"

"Quick! It was sensational. I took off in a rocket ship for a junket to the moon and back. It's being done, you know." His eyes narrowed in annoyance. He liked the conversational light touch for himself but objected to it in others. She recognized the symptoms of rising anger.

"That's a gag, all right. Okay, if you want to be mysterious, I can take it. That word 'mystery' reminds me, as I came in Grove was prophesying in a spine-chilling whisper, 'I have a hunch our mysterious stranger—' Sounds exciting. Who's our mysterious stranger, Senator?"

"Your mistake, Sinclair. I'm a candidate for re-election to the House, not the Senate. I appreciate your tact, though. Who is 'our mysterious stranger'? I've completely forgotten about whom we were talking when you made your theatrical entrance. Thanks for the tea, Nat. I'll get going before the deluge comes. I planned to call on a few of my constituents. Likely to find the man of the house at home this time of day. That crash sounded as might an atomic bomb with variations." At the door he stopped.

"That was a queer chap we ran into on the moon, Fran. We'll have a heart-to-heart about him later, strictly *entre nous*, remember. That's my exit line."

The silence which followed his departure was broken first by the distant sound of a car starting, then by Blake Sinclair.

"What the devil did he mean by meeting a chap on the moon, Fran? Have you spent the day with him?"

"I take off my hat to your courage—or is it nerve, Sinclair?" Myles Jaffray declared before she could answer. "In a way I'm Fran's guardian, but I wouldn't dare ask her to account for her day."

"You may be her guardian—in a way—Jaffray. I understand that Ken Phillips turned over the large Harding

80

estate to you to handle—some gravy—but Fran and I have been practically engaged since dancing school days, naturally I am concerned as to the way and with whom she junkets to the moon—or anywhere else."

"I wonder what privileges being 'practically engaged' covers?" Myles's ruminative voice turned Sinclair white with anger. He rose, set plate and cup on the table with a small crash and squared his shoulders.

"I'll tell you and—"

"Where do you get that 'practically,' Blake?" Fran's question interrupted his furious protest. "We never have been engaged. My apologies, Mrs. Andrews, for airing a perennial quarrel here. Is my face red. Thanks for the transportation and tea. I loved both. I'm off to the Gallery before the storm drenches me." A blinding flash of lightning was followed by a detonation that rattled the tea equipment.

"My car is in the drive. I'll agree to get you home before the rain comes, Fran," Sinclair proposed eagerly.

"She can't go," Myles Jaffray answered for her. "I have papers for her to sign. Come into my workroom, Fran."

"I'm taking her home and—" Blake Sinclair cleared his hoarse voice. "I bow to the high hand of the law," he admitted suavely. "Who am I to interfere between guardian and ward? Something tells me that Aunt Becky was a piker as a dictator in comparison with the one Ken wished on you, sweetheart. Thanks for the tea, Mrs. Andrews."

No sound save a roll of thunder. Then a car door was slammed, a clutch viciously let in.

"Myles," Natalie's voice and eyes were troubled, "was it necessary to make him angry? Blake Sinclair is better as a friend than an enemy."

"I'll take a chance at his enmity. I could break his neck for that crack about 'gravy.' Come on, Fran, let's get at the papers."

"I'm not coming anywhere, Major Jaffray. I'm going home, I'm going alone and I'm going now. My apologies for this outrageous burst of temperament, Mrs.—" A resounding crash and thunderous rumble froze the words in her throat.

"Don't be absurd, Fran. You can't go into this storm

81

in that white frock and those white sandals. Myles, stop her." He shook his head.

"I am amazed at you, Nat, urging a guest to stay when she wants to go." Fran heard him say as she dashed into the house. In the living room she hesitated. She was an idiot to buck this storm. She would go back—Myles Jaffray's voice stopped her.

"Don't you realize that she wants to go with Sinclair? He's probably waiting for her." That settled it. She would go on and take what was coming. Was this the terrible danger ahead that Mrs. Betsy had seen in her teacup?

X

Thank goodness Blake Sinclair's car was out of sight, he drove like a madman when angry, he probably was at the Inn by this time. No chance of being forced by the storm to ride with him, Fran rejoiced, as keeping close to bordering shrubs whose leaves rattled in the rising wind she ran along the drive of Shore Acres to the highway. No chance either that Myles Jaffray would follow her. His closing remark she had overheard had period at the end of it, a large and definite period. That was the way it was and that was the way she wanted it, wasn't it?

A zigzag streak of fire cracked open the sky directly above her head and closed with a deafening crash. Ooch! It stopped her flight and shut her eyes. She huddled against a towering rhododendron. She would try to thumb a ride when she reached the road. Flash! Crash! Better go back? No. She had made a spectacle of herself on the terrace by her refusal to wait till the storm had passed. Adolescent stuff and how. Myles's "She can't go" had goaded her to furious protest. For years Aunt Becky had dominated her life, Blake's jibe that she had exchanged one dictator for another was true. It was the new trustee who now said, "Come," "Go." The fact that he had no legal right to dictate didn't help.

The highway at last. No wonder it had taken time to reach it. She had stopped at each crash. Not a car in sight. A big drop of rain struck the macadam with a resounding "ping." The only shelter visible was a mammoth oak across the road. Its lower branches spread invitingly like a tent. It appeared friendly and protective, but "Never stand under a tree in a thunderstorm" had been among the first rules for safety she had learned.

Ping! Another drop struck and bounced like a bullet. Ping! Ping! Ping! The staccato sounds united in a patter, changed to a steady beat. Rain swirled in white sheets driven by the wind. The storm was making such a fiendish racket, the rain was so heavy she wouldn't see a car till it ran her down. Had she better walk along—

What had thrown her to the ground? A hit-and-run? She shook her head to clear it. Had lightning struck her? Her eyes cleared. She could see, she could hear, thank heaven. She struggled to her feet. Across the road the great oak sprawled in the field behind her. The massive trunk, white and splintered, stuck up above the lowest branches like huge, ghostly claws pawing the air. Her arms and legs moved normally. Nothing had happened to her but shock and a ruined frock.

"The high price of pride," reminded a voice from behind a sheet of rain. Headlights like outsize misty opals blinded her, beyond them was the dark blotch of a car and the sound of a door being opened.

"You look like a crumpled bird hunched up against that shrub. You've ruined your snappy costume. Dislike me too much to hop in, or shall I drive on?" Myles Jaffray's voice was hoarse. Had he just escaped the crashing tree?

In the instant she hesitated came a flash and horrific crash. She made the seat of his roadster in a split second. He reached across her and banged the door shut.

"Where do you want to go?"

"Anywhere out of this storm. Home, please."

"Yours? Mine is nearer."

"Mine. I just couldn't face your sister." She drew a soggy handkerchief from her more soggy bag and sopped at the rivulets running down her face from her hair.

"Hold on, that damp rag won't help." He drew to the side of the road and produced a large white handkerchief from an inner pocket of his gray sports coat. "Use

this—no, on second thought I can do it better. Chin up."
He carefully dried her face. Her eyes met his. He
laughed.

"This is nothing to laugh about."

"Boy, you're telling me. If you had lived through the
hell of fear I lived through—when I saw that tree crash—
knowing you were on this road— We'll let the rest go for
the present. Aren't you ashamed of yourself for staging
that burst of temper on the terrace?"

"Yes. Didn't I admit that I wouldn't go back and face
your sister?"

"Okay so far. Two dollars says it won't be the last
time. I realize I have a problem child on my hands."

"You may drop the responsibility like a hot cake
without a yip of protest from the aforementioned problem child."

"Mighty noble of you to offer, but when I tackle a
stiff proposition—and, is this a stiff one—I see it through
for better or for worse. Something familiar about the
last five words. Feeling drier? Are you chilly? There is a
rug—"

"I am feeling drier, not chilly, and about six years
old. I hope *sometime* to meet *someone* who realizes that
I am grownup. Is it your intention to park here for
what is left of the day? If so, I'll walk. I can't possibly get
wetter." A flash and following detonation rattled the
windshield. It short-circuited her flare of independence.
Suppose he opened the door and ordered, "Okay. Out."

He sent the car ahead, bent forward as he drove.
Squeegee, squeegee, went the wipers, powerless to clear
the windshield of the pelting drops that clouded it.
Rain sparkled like a sheet of diamonds in the long rays
of the headlights. The black road glistened. The storm
flashed with blinding light, plunged the world into
Stygian darkness, crashed with deafening roar. She
caught a corner of his coat and held fast.

"How many dec-i-bels in that—that last blowout?" she
asked when she could be heard; then, to drive home the
impression that she was impervious to fear, answered
her own question with unsteady gaiety.

"If you ask me, almost one hundred and thirty, which
number sound-engineers call 'the threshold of pain,' the

point at which human eardrums begin to tear apart. I hope my chatter doesn't disturb you."

"Not a bit. I'd a whole lot rather you would chatter than cry. I'm impressed by your knowledge. 'And still the wonder grew, that one small head could carry all she knew.' Adapted to suit the occasion."

"There's more in that same head than meets the eye," she countered. "I'm an ace secretary, if I say it—" A crash froze the next word on her lips. She shivered.

"If anything should happen to you your sister never, *never*, will forgive me for taking you out in this storm."

"Nothing will happen to me or you." Was he aware of the fingers clutching his coat? "In practically nothing flat we will be at the Gallery. It is so pitch-black that I can't see the outlines of the building but between crashes I heard the lash of waves against the rocks in front of it and the bell buoy tolling furiously. Tomorrow the cliff walk will be swarming with visitors to see the surf.

"Here we are. I can just make out the road in. That dark hulk is the ell. Thought I saw a flash of light in the kitchen window. My mistake. Must have been the reflection of the headlights. Dark as Erebus. Has the storm put the electric current out of business? That would be the last perfect touch. You'd better go in through the Digby entrance. Betsy will help you peel off those wet clothes. Stay here till I come back." He was a running shadow, then came a violent pounding, the return of the shadow.

"Nothing doing." He slipped behind the wheel. His hair shone in the light from the instrument board like the wet head of a seal. "It was so dark I almost broke my neck over that wood box beside the door. Fool place to keep it. Couldn't rouse anyone. Dig and his wife must be held up somewhere waiting for the storm to pass. Cheerio, Fran, it always does pass. We'll go round to the front entrance, or will you come home with me?"

"You don't think I'll take you through this storm again, do you? I will be perfectly safe here. Silas Pond must be somewhere on the place, he has a room in the basement, the Digbys would make sure of that before they left."

"Good old Si. Years ago the boys nicknamed him

'Nosey.' His sense of smell is uncommonly keen. One day he smelled smoke in a barn where hay was smoldering, and saved the whole village, his cronies contended. This was your day off. Didn't you say Gene Sargent was to take over? Where is she?"

"The Gallery closes at five-thirty. I hope she reached home before the storm broke. She wouldn't have left the place without someone here." The headlights shed a dim light on steps and porch. Myles tried to clear the windshield.

"I can't see a glimmer in the building. What goes? Have the valuable things inside been left unguarded? Incredible. I'll bet the artist who exhibited yesterday would be in for a nervous breakdown if he knew."

"Blake said he was here this afternoon, remember? He's good, but I doubt if he is important enough to be stolen. A burglar would be looking for a master—" Stolen! "Good heavens!"

"What's the matter? You sound frightened."

It wouldn't do to tell him that the word "stolen" had brought the remembrance of the Constable that Blake Sinclair had left at the Gallery surging to the top of her mind. No one was to know that Henry Sargent had it. He didn't suspect she knew. Had he told Gene where it was, warned her of its value and importance?

"I—I was thinking of the Digbys, that the ell might have been struck, that they were lying inside unconscious."

"That's a cheery thought, improvised to answer my question, wasn't it? Stop imagining horrors and hop out. Give me the key."

He followed as she sprinted up the steps. The key stuck. He rattled it in the lock.

"The perversity of inanimate things," he growled before it turned and the door opened. Crossing the entresol they stopped suddenly. Their eyes met.

"Did a door close?" Fran whispered. "Perhaps you did see a light in the kitchen. Perhaps it wasn't our headlights."

"Don't talk. Listen."

He gripped her arm and held her motionless beside him. No sound within the building save the splash of rain against the windows and the soft drip, drip of water

86

on the parquetry floor from her drenched frock. From without between rumbles of thunder came the lash and beat of waves, the mournful toll of the buoy.

"Try for a light. Where's the switch?" Myles inquired close to her ear. She pressed a button in the wall. Light flooded galleries and entresol.

"The Lord be thanked the powerhouse is still on the job." His voice was low but fervent. "Perhaps we didn't hear that spooky sound as of a door being cautiously closed, perhaps our jitter-nerves faked it. Perhaps the Digbys left a note. Come on, let's investigate."

"Not in this wet frock. I would ruin the polish of the floors. That would be curtains for me as career woman here. Wait till I change. I won't be long."

"You're not going alone."

"Now you are being foolish. I'll be perfectly—"

"Stop arguing. Give me the key to your apartment, I hope you left it locked. Up we go."

He led the way. Opened the door of her living room.

"Don't worry, I'm not coming in. Wanted to make sure no one pounced when you entered. I'll wait downstairs. Leave this door open. If you hear any kind of sound, yell."

In her bedroom she peeled off the wet white frock, streaked with blue and coral from the cummerbund, paid the tribute of a sigh to its former just-rightness as she hung it above the tub to drip. The storm must have poured gallons of water over her, her sandals were mud-color, she was drenched to the skin. She'd better hurry or Myles would think her a quitter afraid to come down. There had been the sound of a door closing, he knew that as well as she, if he were accrediting it to the jitters.

Five minutes later, breathless from haste, she pelted down the stairs buckling the broad gold belt of a four-toned amber plaid wool skirt around the waist of a crepe blouse of the darkest shade. She hadn't stopped to dry her hair, which lay in little tight curls over her head. Myles was standing before the Louis XV cabinet in the small gallery. The door was open. He caught her hand as she reached to close it.

"Don't touch. There may be fingerprints. I found it this way. I'm not so sure now that the sound of the closing door should be laid to the jitters." Though he spoke in a low tone his voice echoed in the still room. He seemed to think it unnecessary to whisper but she did.

"Hear or see anything while I was upstairs?"

"No. I would be willing to swear, though, that when I first stepped into this gallery the cabinet was closed. I went to the kitchen door of the Digbys' apartment and stood in the dark listening. Except for the fury of the storm outside I heard nothing stirring, not even the white cat. This door may have been slightly ajar when I first saw it and the impact of my feet on the floor swung it open. The enamels on the shelves look as if they might be worth their weight in gold, figuratively speaking."

"Figuratively speaking, they are."

"Isn't the cabinet kept locked?"

"Yes. Here's the key to it and the catalogue of its contents. Before I left for my swim this morning I gave them to Gene in case anyone showed a purchasing interest in the enamels. She was to return them to my desk before she left, a duplicate key to the apartment is in my desk in my office. It was there."

"Check your list."

Back and forth from jewel-toned enamels to the catalogue traveled her eyes. She checked again, whispered:

"The most valuable piece is missing."

"Sure?" She nodded. "Any chance that Gene would take it out to show to a customer and forget to put it back? Customer. That's a thought. She may have sold it."

"She wouldn't do that without leaving a memorandum. She knows to a cent the value of each article in the Gallery, if she had sold it she wouldn't leave the door of the cabinet open." She glanced around the gallery. "Nothing else seems to be miss— Look!" She pointed to the fireplace above which hung Stuart's Washington— "The wood was laid ready for lighting. It has been disturbed." It had. It was scattered as if a piece had been hastily seized.

"What do you make of that?" she whispered.

"Can't figure it out; if the glass in the cabinet door had been smashed it would be evident that a stick from the fireplace had been used on it. It wasn't. It—"

88

"There's the phone! Gene calling, probably. Maybe you are right. Maybe she did sell the enamel. I'm so relieved at the possibility, my heart has spread wings."

Myles stood close behind her, as seated in an English Regency painted armchair at an Empire card table in the entresol she answered the call.

"The Sargent Galleries."

"That you, dearie?"

"It's Mrs. Betsy on the verge of tears," Fran whispered over her shoulder. "Fran Phillips speaking, Mrs. Digby."

"The Lord be praised you're home, dearie. We got word that Lem's mother was having one of her spells and we must come at once. We left at about two in a hurry. Miss Gene was there and her sister-in-law, the widow, when the call came an' she said for us to beat it an' they would look after everything. I felt kind of uneasy because there was a strange young man with them, you know how girls are these days—"

"What young man?" Fran listened. Myles whispered:

"What goes that has whitened your face?"

"Just a minute, Mrs. Betsy." She covered the receiver and spoke over her shoulder. "She doesn't know who the man was with the girls but just as she and Lem were leaving, Barth, the waiter, who helped with the tea, appeared. When they told him why and where they were going, he asked if he couldn't stay and help at the Gallery."

"Ask if he did. Quick. I can hear everything she says."

"Did he stay, Mrs. Betsy?"

"I can't say, dearie. We were so anxious to get away we didn't stop to find out. Autos were coming and going when we left. Lots of folks to see the new picture, I guess. An' what d'you know, when we got to Lem's mother's, there she was, merry as a grig, surprised enough to see us, said nobody had sent for us."

"What did you make of that?"

"We didn't stop to make anything of it, dearie, we lit out for home. Suspicioned some deviltry was afoot, the papers are full of such tricks. We got on a rough road detour, our gas tank sprang a leak and before you could say Jack Robinson every drop was gone. I sat in the car while Lem walked three miles to a filling station. Are you there, dearie?"

"Yes. Go on."

Fran listened with an undercurrent of speculation running through her mind. Barth, waiter, ex-butler, perhaps finger man, had appeared as the Digbys were leaving—in response to a faked call—where was the £5650 painting—had he been after that? Was the missing enamel a red herring drawn across the trail? If only she knew where the Constable was and could check—

"The gas fellas wouldn't drive Lem back and he had to foot it against the storm," Mrs. Betsy was continuing her saga. "He was all in when he reached me. I got him to my sister's. The doctor says if he keeps quiet tonight he'll be fine in the morning, but, oh dear—"

"Stop and get your breath, Mrs. Betsy. He will come through all right."

"Sure, 'tisn't him I'm worrying about, there's two things. I'm whispering, I don't want Lem to hear, he'd be mad as hops. I was so upset I left the key in the outside of the kitchen door. Get it quick. And the other thing is, you shouldn't be alone in that place all night with all the valuables, not after that fake call that came for us."

Myles seized the phone.

"She isn't alone, Betsy, and she won't stay here tonight. We're getting out as soon as this storm lets up." The wire faithfully transmitted her croon of satisfaction.

"I'm that thankful you're there, Myles, I could cry. Get supper in our place. There's cold chicken in the icebox and—" He cradled the telephone.

"They've shut her off. The Digbys are out of this picture tonight. You'd better phone your boss. Tell him what has happened, and that Silas hasn't reported yet. He'll carry on from there."

After a lengthy conversation she rose from the table.

"Mr. Sargent was annoyed almost to inarticulateness. I could hear his gasp of agony when I reported that the enamel was missing. He is furious that Silas Pond hasn't shown up. He roared that a watchman shouldn't let a little blow like this stop him. He is coming himself to take over, will bring the deputy sheriff and it may take time to get him. Ordered me to remain on duty till he arrived. Said I'd better go to Rocky Point for the night. I shan't go."

"You'll go there or home with me. Nat would love to have you."

"I'm not leaving. I'll lock myself in upstairs—"

"Remember we found the door of the cabinet swinging?" She nodded. "Remember that the ex-butler arrived just as the Digbys were leaving in reply to a faked message? I see by your eyes that you get me. I heard Betsy say she left the key in the outside of the kitchen door. Someone came in that way. Someone opened the Louis XV cabinet and stole an enamel. Who? If after those reminders you still intend to spend the night here, I stay too."

"Don't be absurd. You couldn't."

"Couldn't I? Want to be shown? Will you go or stay?"

"I'll go to the Sargents'. You are something of a dictator, aren't you?"

"So Sinclair, to whom you are 'practically engaged,' implied. I've gained my point. I usually get what I start for. Remember that. We'll have time to raid the icebox before your boss comes and when he does come, watch out. Don't lead with your chin. Wait for him to ask questions. After which warning, *en avant, soldat.*"

"I keep wondering why that man Barth appeared just as he did," Fran said as they reached the threshold of the Digby kitchen. Myles snapped on the light. "We know that the young man whom Betsy said came with Gene and Matilde Sargent was Blake, so that mystery—"

"I'll be darned. Look!" The last word was a whisper. Myles pointed to the floor. Muddy footprints crossed the marbleized black and white linoleum from pantry to window, from window to the entrance door upon which he had pounded for admittance not so long before.

"They are still very wet." Fran's whisper matched his for eeriness. "This proves that a door did close, we didn't imagine it. The key is on the inside, Mrs. Betsy said she left it in the lock outside. Remember the glint of light you saw in the kitchen when we stopped the car?"

"Right. Whoever it was must have slipped out when we came in the front door. That stuck key made noise enough to warn anyone in the building. We needn't whisper. He's gone." He went from window to window, carefully avoiding the footprints, and drew the shades, then to the entrance door, which opened easily. He closed it and turned the key.

"Whoever it was went out this way. If we could get an impression of the footprints—"

"The situation has 'The Face on the Barroom Floor' touch, hasn't it?"

"Stop giggling, or you'll have hysterics. About those footprints. I have an idea. Is there a sheet of blotting paper in the house?"

"There are two, large blue ones, on the desk in my office. I'll get them."

"Nothing doing. That's my job. Wait in the small gallery."

It seemed hours that she stood near the swinging door of the cabinet. It set her imagination galloping. Suppose the person who had opened it hadn't left the house? Suppose he had hidden in her office or the repair shop? He might spring out at Myles. She shouldn't have let him go alone. Perhaps at this very moment he was lying gagged and helpless—

She dashed from the gallery through the entresol to her office. The room was lighted. Myles stood motionless in the middle of it apparently concentrating on the door of the repair shop. Two sheets of light blue blotting paper dangled from his left hand. She breathed a little "Oh" of relief. He turned his head, placed his right forefinger against his lips, and resumed what appeared to be watchful waiting.

He had cautioned her to silence. Why? Had he trapped the thief? A sound the other side of the door. He tensed. She stiffened in sympathy. There it was again. Someone moving cautiously? Icy chills crawled up her spine and coasted down. Her teeth chattered. The key was on this side. Had Myles locked a person in? *Why* stand there like a bronze sentinel? Why didn't he *do* something?

He shook his head in response to her clutch on his sleeve. A sound in the repair shop as if a picture frame had been knocked over set her heart thumping in her throat. Was the thief who had stolen the enamel box trying to escape through the rear door? Was it Barth? Could be. He had come that way yesterday. They must stop him. Another cautious sound. Myles bent his head, whispered close to her ear.

"The big ruler on your desk. Quick! Quiet."

She thrust it into his hand.

"Okay. Beat it upstairs. Lock yourself in. I'll open that door."

XI

She didn't go. He crossed the room too intent on his plan to know that she followed. She might be able to help if he—

"Hey! Let me out!" The drawling voice was hoarse, weak, the accompanying thump on the door feeble. "Hey! Let me out!" The last word was little more than a sob.

"Si-las!" Excitement cracked Fran's whisper in the middle.

Myles turned the key and yanked open the door. He caught and steadied the tall man in blue and white striped shirt and navy dungarees who tumbled forward, carefully lowered him into the deep chair Fran pushed behind him. To the accompaniment of guttural sounds in his throat, Silas Pond planted elbows on his knees and lowered his head into bony red hands as if it were too heavy for his scrawny neck to uphold.

"Take it easy, Si," Myles counseled. "Don't try to talk yet. Bring water, Fran. Even if I knew where to find it I wouldn't dare give him anything else till I know what happened to him."

She broke her own speed record, which was among the higher brackets, to the Digby kitchen and back. Silas still sat with his head down. He raised it and seized the glass she offered.

"Go slow, sip it, Si. If you drink too fast it may make you sick."

He ignored Myles's warning, downed the water in one gulp, winced and cautiously turned his head from side to side.

"Guess my neck ain't broke," he admitted weakly. "Cricky, but it hurts. Did I swallow my gum? N-o-o, I got it." He leaned his head against the back of the chair,

93

closed his eyes and began to chew, his prominent Adam's apple going up, going down, with each movement of his jaws. Perched on the broad desk Fran watched it with fascinated eyes and with difficulty restrained her excited urge to ask him questions. Time was flying. Why didn't Myles begin? As if he sensed her impatience he said in a low voice:

"Give him time to pull himself together." Silas roused. His pale blue eyes were dazed but his voice was stronger.

"I'm comin' to fast, Myles. Cricky, it must have been an all-fired crack."

"What happened to you, Nosey? Tell us as quickly as you can."

"Shucks, seems like the time when you was a boy, fer you to be callin' me Nosey, Myles. Tell you what happened is just what I can't do. I don't know."

"What can you remember, Mr. Si?" Fran prompted.

He closed his eyes and chewed ruminatively as if the movement of his jaws might stimulate memory.

"Lemme see." Considering what had happened, his drawl was maddening. "I remember I came earlier than usual because I see the storm comin'—my head hurts fierce." He groaned.

"Go on, please, Mr. Si," Fran urged.

"I left my bike in the garage. Miss Gene hurried off as soon's I appeared. I knew the Digbys would be here so I went back to the garage to sharpen the lawn mower. When I got back to the house the hell-raisin' storm was on."

"Then what happened?" Myles prodded.

"Left my sou'wester an' oilskins in my room in the basement." He closed his eyes, twisted his neck experimentally and groaned.

"Okay, you left your oilskins in your room, Si. What next?"

"Gimme a minute to think, Myles. I come upstairs to start my rounds. Stepped into what Mr. Sargent calls the entrysol, thought I heard a sound here, the door was open."

"By 'here' do you mean my office?"

"Yes, Miss Phillips." He shook his head as if to clear his eyes. "First I thought 'twas the storm makin' it. I heard it again. Stepped in cautious like. Black as pitch."

94

He clutched his head with his hands. "It hurts gosh-awful. S'pose my neck's broke?"

Myles, standing beside him, gently parted the thick straw-color hair on the flat top of his head.

"There's a lump big as a duck's egg here, it's a humdinger, but the skin isn't even scratched. If you'd broken your neck, Nosey, you couldn't move it. Pull yourself together. Go on. We must find out what happened. Every minute counts. You'd just stepped in cautious like, black as pitch," he reminded.

"It's comin' back. I stood there a minute and sniffed. Someone'd been smokin'. It warn't a pipe nor a seegar, 'twas cigarettes, kinder sickish smell. Says I to myself, 'The old man'd have a fit if he gets onto it, he don't 'low smokin' on the premises, even Miss Gene, who smoked every minute, don't do it here. Beats me how that girl—"

"You sniffed. Then what?" Myles switched him from the detour to the main line of his story.

"After I sniffed I says to myself, 'Better see what's been goin' on', an reached for the light button side the door. Come a terrible crash of thunder, I remember thinkin', 'Cricky, I been struck,' an' that's the last I knew till in a kind of dream I thought a car stopped. A long time after I heard the light button snap in this room—my head began to hurt like thunder, I got to my knees, knocked over something, that roused me enough to yell an' pound."

"Sure you didn't hear a movement in this room when you came to the door?"

"Nope. You don't mean someone bopped me, that 'twasn't the lightning?"

"Lightning has strange tricks, but it couldn't shoot you through that door and lock it on this side. Someone took a crack at you. Who?"

Silas Pond struggled to his feet.

"That makes me feel kinder sick, I guess I better—" Myles caught his arm and steadied him.

"Go ahead, Fran, turn on the light on the stairs. Hurry. I'll get him down before anything happens—with luck."

Ten minutes later he joined her in her office.

"Nosey's lying down. I promised him that you and I

would play watchdogs till he feels better. Where's that blotting paper? I hope those footprints haven't dried up."

They hadn't. The light blue blotters faithfully soaked up the moisture. Myles regarded four muddy patterns, two rights, two lefts, with satisfaction.

"Aren't they the berries? Boy, are we the smart dicks."

"Will you show them to Mr. Sargent?"

"Not yet. Didn't try to get all. There are several left on the floor for him to discover. I'd like to solve this mystery myself—ourselves, if you are with me."

"I—a dick. And Judge Grimes said there was no adventure to be expected—by me—in the State of Maine."

"What do you mean by that?"

"Sometime I'll tell you, meanwhile if you don't want Mr. Sargent to see those prints, better hide them. You can't stand there holding them."

"I can, but as you suggest, I'd better not. Can't take them to my car now, might run into your boss."

"Hide them here. Be careful you don't smooch them, they are still damp." She lifted the cover of the cabinet in which the flour barrel stood. "It is almost empty. It may not improve the flour, but this is an emergency. Quick." She shivered. "These walls may have eyes." He carefully fitted the two sheets around the inside of the barrel. She adjusted the cover.

"So far so good. It will take some doing to get those out again without being seen, but we'll meet that problem when we get to it. Listen."

Rain beat against the windows. Thunder rolled. A loosened vine tapped eerily on the glass like the fingers of a wraith of the night begging for shelter from the storm. Fran had read of blood turning to ice, now she knew it could. Hers had congealed.

"What—what did you hear?" she whispered.

"A key in the lock."

"Miss Phillips!" The booming call was followed by a flash and crash which shook the building.

"Enter your boss to the sizzle of lightning and the ruffle of thunder." Myles's excited whisper thawed her heart and set it beating like a tom-tom. "It's our cue for an entrance, Fran, the show is on."

The next hour was hectic. Henry Sargent, accompanied step by step by Howlett, the lanky, lugubrious deputy sheriff, went over the ground she and Myles had covered. To his credit he showed concern about Silas Pond's injury, spared a few moments to check on him, and returned to his cross-examination of Fran. She remembered Myles's warning to wait for his questions. When they came she answered as fully as possible. Worn-out by the repetition she protested.

"I have told you twice that I don't know *why* the cabinet door was open, Mr. Sargent; Gene was in charge until five-thirty, presumably, she ought to know, perhaps wind down the chimney could have scattered the wood in the fireplace, but I doubt it." At Shore Acres Blake Sinclair had said he stayed with Gene till closing time. Let her tell her father that, why implicate Blake?

Henry Sargent cross-examined Myles as to his reason for being on the premises, why he went into Fran's office. Was he sure he had seen a light in the kitchen when he stopped his car outside? What did he make of the footprints on the kitchen floor? Sure they weren't his own? The one-time major answered questions, until Henry Sargent began to repeat, then blew up.

"Hold everything, sir. Fran and I have told you all we know about the situation we found here when we came in out of the storm. Now, for Pete's sake, let up on her."

"I guess you're right," Henry Sargent admitted. "Sure the enamel is all that is missing?" He wasn't inquiring about the painting Blake had left because he didn't know that she knew he had it, she reasoned. He was standing near the Hepplewhite commode when he asked the question. "Have you looked in here?" He opened the door.

"The Henry VIII apostle spoons are gone. Did you know that, Miss Phillips?"

"I didn't think of looking there, Mr. Sargent. Everything happened so fast—"

"Don't apologize."

"I'm *not* apologizing." Indignation kept her from tears. "I'm trying to explain—"

"Only set of the kind," Henry Sargent interrupted. "The burglar was a good picker. Must have had a preview."

Barth?

The name flashed through Fran's mind. Had she been right in her suspicion that he was a finger man?

"Don't mention what has happened here to anyone," Henry Sargent warned. "To *anyone*, uderstand? You two, Howlett and I are the only persons, beside the thief, or thieves, who know of the burglary. Si Pond does not suspect the enamel has been stolen. I'll tell him when his brain clears, he may remember some clue to the theft. If the news of the break can be kept hush-hush we'll have the guilty party on the anxious seat, if he is still in the neighborhood, and I believe he is."

"Do you think it may have been a villager?" Fran whispered as if the suspect might be within hearing. Henry Sargent rose on his toes and settled back on his heels.

"My thoughts are not for publication—yet. Myles, drive Miss Phillips to Rocky Point. The storm has blown out to sea. The moon is breaking through. Howlett and I will stay through the night, look after Silas and examine every crack and cranny that might reveal a clue."

"I don't want to go, Mr. Sargent. If I stay I may be able to ferret out something."

"You've told all you know about it, Miss Phillips. When you see Gene ask if she made a sale this afternoon, conversationally, you understand, don't tell her of the theft. Run along. Mother knows you are coming."

In her room she hurriedly packed an overnight bag. Looked back before she closed the door, with the key on the outside. Mr. Sargent and the deputy might want to search here. Was he anxious to have her go that he might have a clear field?

Myles stopped the roadster at the Digby entrance. The doorway was dark. Moonlight had not yet filtered through the overhanging branches of trees.

"I have a hunch I may find a clue here," he whispered. "Won't take but a minute. If you see anything move scream your head off."

She heard him running along the path to the door. Held her breath, it helped her to listen more intently. He was coming back. He opened the trunk of the car and closed it softly. When they were again in motion she inquired:

"Did you find a clue?"

"Almost broke my neck stepping on a short length of cordwood. I'll bet it is the piece from the fireplace with which Nosey was knocked out. He was lucky it didn't kill him. The assailant must have escaped by way of the kitchen door."

They maintained a thoughtful silence as the roadster covered the short distance under a sky now pricked through and through with stars in an enchanted world silvered with moonlight, shaken at intervals by faint rumbles; far off over the water the heavens flickered and flashed. Myles stopped the car before the door of Rocky Point.

"Sit here for a minute, I've been doing some tall thinking. I'll bet you have, you've been so quiet. I didn't like the tone in which Henry Sargent declared he would examine every crack and cranny that might reveal a clue. Made me wonder if he believes it was an inside job, if he suspects the Digbys? If he does he's gone haywire."

"How can he suspect them? They were not there. That duck's egg on top of Silas Pond's head is evidence that someone hit him after the storm had commenced. He couldn't very well crack his own head, lock himself into the repair shop and return the key to the office, could he? Suppose they investigate the Digby kitchen and find the blotting paper with the footprints in the flour barrel? That's something real to worry about."

"They won't. I moved them."

"Smart fella. Where to?"

"Smart fellas don't tell all they know."

"If not where, perhaps you'll tell me when?"

"Remember your boss's attack of coughing after he strained his voice yelling questions at you? Remember that I went to the kitchen for water? That was when."

"I wondered why you were gone so long. There was a moment when I suspected that Henry Sargent also was wondering. Tell me where you put the blotting paper. I ought to know. I'm in this up to my neck, remember."

"What you don't know can't be third-degreed out of you. Forget it." He came round the car and opened the door. "Be sure and get hold of Gene, diplomatically inquire if she sold anything this afternoon. Her father has put the nix on letting her know what happened."

"No light in her room. She is probably at the Country Club. It isn't late, though I feel as if I had lived through a century or two since I fared forth for The Theater this afternoon."

"She may be in the library, you and I know that Sinclair was with her after Matilde left. I noticed you didn't mention that fact to your boss. We know that the artist was there fussing about changing his pictures, we forgot to mention that. I suppose asking Gene if she sold anything is a fool question, if she pinch-hits for you on the job she would have enough business sense to leave a memorandum. How will you get in?"

She drew a key from her pocket.

"Mrs. Sargent told me to keep it so I wouldn't have to ring." He followed her into the hall.

"I want to be sure you are safe inside before I leave. Quiet as a tomb, isn't it? Feeling more— That's a second fool question. Don't worry about anything. I'll be at the Gallery early. Good night."

What was the second "fool question" that had roughened his voice, Fran wondered as he closed the heavy door softly behind him. She walked along the hall looking into the different rooms. All lighted. No one visible. Music was coming from above. She ran upstairs and knocked on the door of Mrs. Sargent's room. There was a moment's pause before a voice called, "Come in."

Mrs. Sargent in a purple crepe housecoat was reclining on a chaise longue. She looked up from a book and turned down the radio.

"It's you, dear. Henry told me to expect you. Frightful storm, wasn't it? Thunderstorms upset me." Her colorless face and troubled eyes confirmed the words. "He said the Digbys had been called away, that you must not stay there without them. He's right. He's always right; once, just once I wish he could be proved wrong."

"Where is Gene?"

"Gone to spend the night with Kitty Saunders. Cards, I suspect. Oh, dear, that girl is a bad influence. How was the theater?"

Over the air came the music of a band playing, "Come to the Mardi Gras." The leader was giving out with the trumpet. The gay accompaniment lilted and danced through Fran's thoughts as she told of the success of the comedy; of the devastation the heat had wrought on make-ups; of tea at Shore Acres. She concluded:

"I don't wonder the storm upset you. Lightning laid low that historic oak on the highway."

"What a pity. It is centuries old. How was Natalie?"

"Looking wonderful and apparently on top of the world."

"Poor child, she had a mean break. I wish Matilde would give Nat's ex-husband his walking ticket—perhaps he will give her up. It seems to me the older children grow the more worry they are. Nat may have her troubles, but she doesn't have to make a 1939 allowance cover this year's increased outgo. Henry doesn't or won't realize how much more living costs." She opened her book, tuned up the radio.

"Sorry, I shouldn't depress you with my problems. Nice to have you back, dear. Good night."

Before Fran closed her door she heard Mrs. Sargent say softly:

"Come out. She's gone."

Fran opened the window of her room and looked out to sea. Waves were rolling toward shore, each crest silver-plated with moonlight. Far out an occasional flash ripped open the sky. Who had been hiding in Mrs. Sargent's room and why? Did Myles get away without trouble? After what had happened at the Gallery anything was possible. She leaned out. No one in sight.

"Ka-chew!" The shattering sneeze rose from the shrubs that bordered the turn-around. She listened. "Kach—" A second sneeze broke in the middle. Her heart zoomed to her throat. Was the strangled sound tied up with the theft at the Gallery? Had the thief followed the roadster from there?

At that very moment in the garage at Shore Acres, Myles Jaffray opened the trunk of his car to remove the sheets of blotting paper and the wood he had put there when he had stopped at the Digby entrance. He stared unbelievingly. Drew an electric torch from his pocket and flashed it round the interior. Gone!

101

XII

On the porch of the Gallery Fran gazed at the limitless horizon of sky and sea. It was incredible that this sunny, brilliant morning was in the same world that had staged yesterday's torrid heat, furious wind, rain, lightning and thunder of last night's storm.

The air was cool and crystal clear, with a hint of the clarity of early autumn. Flowers in the border within the stone wall were lifting drenched heads, were scenting the light breeze with fragrance. Giant zinnias in every tint and shade of their color chart were coming into bloom, Lemon Queen and Orange King calendulas added the glow of gold. The beautiful roof lines of Rocky Point on the next promontory stood out in sharp relief against the cloudless turquoise of the sky. Rocks glistened with wet seaweed, against them mountainous waves broke into geysers of sparkling spray to the accompaniment of the frantic toll of the buoy. Gulls wheeled and dived. The cliff walk was dotted with early visitors to view the surf. In the west the coastal hills loomed like dark cutouts against the blue.

The mournful warning of the bell brought the events of the evening before surging to the top of her mind. They could easily qualify as nightmare. The arrival of Henry Sargent and Howlett, the deputy sheriff, and their countless questions. After Myles and she had left had they worked out an explanation of the footprints in the kitchen left for their inspection?

Would Henry Sargent be successful in keeping the burglary a secret? If his wife had known of it she had given no sign last evening. She had been pale, her eyes troubled when she referred to the increased cost of living. The domestic wheels at Rocky Point ran with soundless perfection. Was the upkeep worrying her? She had settled her daughter's debts once. Had she taken the money from her household expense budget, was she afraid that her husband would find out? Gene had said:

"Dad is generous but he wouldn't advance our allowances or increase them a penny were the alternative jail for Mother or me."

That was exaggeration, of course, but after the ruthless cross-examination he had put her through last night, she could believe it.

To whom had Mrs. Sargent softly called, "Come out. She's gone"? Was it tied up in any way with the person in the border of shrubs who had sneezed? What would Myles say when she told him— A door opened behind her.

"It's my guess you were up with the birds, Miss Phillips."

Howlett's nasal voice brought her face to face with the present, plus his abnormally tall, abnormally lank person, and the blinding brilliance of his plaid shirt. A fringe of sandy hair surrounded a shining oasis on top of his dome-shaped head. His large mouth spread to his enormous ears when he opened it to poke with a straw at the interstices of his horse-like teeth. She had been too absorbed in Henry Sargent's reactions last night to pay much attention to the deputy sheriff.

"I didn't wait for breakfast, Mr. Howlett, I was so anxious to know if you discovered a clue to the theft of the enamel and spoons. Was anything else missing? Did Mr. Sargent say he was looking for a picture, for instance? Where is he?"

"Went home to breakfast. Took Si along to the Doc's, got kinder worried about his head. He was a pretty sick fella this mornin'. Whoever hit him'll have something to pay—jail, most probable. You know your boss don't want a hint of what happened to git out. It's my guess he's right. Said I wasn't to tell nobody nothing till he come back."

"How soon will that be, Sheriff?" Myles Jaffray inquired from the drive at the foot of the porch steps.

Fran hadn't realized she was tense till she relaxed with a suddenness that left her knees wobbly. Now there was someone to share with her the responsibility of answering questions; someone with whom to talk over the startling events of the night before. Howlett's "Said I wasn't to tell nobody nothin' till he came back" had been packed with ominous suggestion. Had Myles been right? Had they searched the Digby apartment? If the missing articles were found there they had been planted by the person who had left muddy prints on the kitchen floor. Lucky that Myles had changed the hiding place of the sheets of blotting paper, lucky there was a lump on top of Si Pond's head—though he might not think so—to prove that someone had been in the building with malicious intent.

"Search me, how soon he'll be back, Myles." Howlett shook his head and poked with the straw simultaneously. "He said he was goin' to phone the County Court House to send along a fingerprint expert. It's my guess he'll have to wait. It's too early for the place to be open for business."

"We'll hang round till he comes. Had your breakfast, Fran?"

"No. I was too anxious to get here to wait for it at Rocky Point."

"Same here. I was awake at the crack of dawn. We'll take over Betsy's kitchen. Know how to make coffee?"

"You forget you are speaking to a girl trained by Rebecca Harding."

"Like heck, I do. Glad you can get a laugh out of this mix-up. I'll bet before we get through there will be some astounding crossing of wires. We'll go through the small gallery. Come on." He grinned. "I'm always saying, 'Come on,' to you, Fran, and you always bristle with resentment."

Howlett blocked the doorway.

"Don't suppose I ought to let you in, Myles. Mr. Sargent said—"

"Forget it, Sheriff, you wouldn't let a lady starve, would you? Be a sport, move."

"This town'd get the moon for you, if you wanted it, Myles, but you'll have to take the blame if Mr. Sargent rows." Howlett registered the protest as he stepped aside to let them pass. "It's my guess I may lose the deputy job for letting you in. Mr. S. is a heavy taxpayer. He's got influence."

"I'm a heavy taxpayer. I've got influence. If he makes trouble, I'll see you through, Sheriff. Come on, Fran. There I go again." They crossed the entresol to the accompaniment of a mumble of protest behind them.

"The door of the cabinet is still open."

"What's the idea of whispering and tiptoeing, woman?" Myles inquired in a loud voice. "It gives me the

104

willies. Probably left open for the fingerprint expert to examine." On the threshold of the sunny blue and white kitchen he stopped.

"Gone!"

"Who's whispering now? What's gone?"

"The footprints." He crossed the room slowly, peering intently at the marbleized linoleum. "Not so much as a smooch left."

"Mr. Sargent and Howlett must have wiped them up." She turned from the open door of the icebox. "How about bacon and eggs—Major?"

"Sounds like the beginning of a perfect day. This is as good a time as any to remind you that I am no longer a major. If it would not be too much of a strain, how about using my first name?"

"Address the trustee of Rebecca Harding's estate so familiarly? I wouldn't dare."

"I hate sarcasm in women."

"So do I, I hate it in anyone. I'm sorry. I seem always to be saying, 'I'm sorry,' to you, Mr. Jaffray."

"Now that is nicely washed up, let's proceed with breakfast. How can I help?"

"Find the silver and set the table. Know how?"

"You forget you are speaking to a boy partially raised by Betsy Digby, the prize housekeeper of the village."

His part of the preparations completed, he stood watching her at the electric range.

"Like to cook?"

"When I have to. I wouldn't select it as a career. Why do you ask?"

"You are forking those eggs in the double boiler as if your life depended on a successful scramble, as if you are tremendously interested in what you are doing."

"I am. To do a job as well as one can takes the drudgery out of it. 'The Voice of Experience,' speaking. Breakfast is ready, sir."

"This is the life," he approved as they faced each other across the table in the sunny breakfast nook. The canary in the gilded cage in the sitting room threatened to split its yellow throat in song. Missy Snow, the white Persian, appeared suddenly on the sill outside the window and stared in at them with secretive, amber eyes.

"Great morning after the storm," Myles approved. "Reminds me of those lines, let's see, how do they go? I've got 'em,

> Every day is a fresh beginning,
> Every morn is the world made new.

Said first by one Susan Coolidge, in case you're interested, Miss Phillips."

"You shouldn't be wasting your time in this Maine village, Mr. Jaffray, you belong on 'The Invitation to Learning' program."

"Glad you appreciate my hard-earned erudition. Boy, these eggs look like fluffed gold. Any day you need a reference I'll swear that Rebecca Harding's niece is a swell cook and makes delicious coffee. More and more I am being convinced that if I had a daughter I'd like to have her brought up by Aunt Becky."

"I'll wager the daughter will object. 'Advice from one who knows.' I'm so full of inhibitions—"

"Your aunt and her generation had another name for them—principles."

"Maybe. Suppose we stop giving Fran Phillips featured billing and talk about something else." She leaned toward him, whispered, "Did you get a clue from the footprints on the blotters?" He shook his head. "Had they dried and left no trace? I was afraid of it."

"Worse than that. Hold onto your chair—tight. This will set the room spinning. They've disappeared."

"Disappeared? *Gone?*"

"Softly, softly. These walls may have ears as well as eyes. I wouldn't put it past them. Listen, my child, and you shall hear—"

He explained that the night before when he had come to the kitchen for a glass of water for Henry Sargent he had managed to drop the sheets of blotting paper into the woodbox outside the door; reminded her that he had stopped there for a moment on their way to Rocky Point; that he did pick up a piece of wood which he put in the trunk of the car with the blotted footprints, that when he checked at Shore Acres garage, blotters and wood were missing.

"Who could have taken them?"

"Only one answer to that, the person who saw me put them in the roadster last night, the guy who conked Si Pond—that piece of wood might prove evidence against him. I figure that when the marauder sneaked out of the kitchen, he hung around waiting developments, that he saw us when we discovered the muddy footprints, before I drew the shades. Doubtless he was hidden in the shrubs—when I slipped the blotters into the wood box outside the door."

"He must have been soaked to the skin. Why not get a search warrant and go through every kitchen in the village looking for a wet suit of clothes drying? It couldn't possibly be dry by this time."

"How explain the search warrant? Your boss doesn't want publicity, remember."

"Right. Your reminder brought down the suggestion like a spent rocket. I got the search warrant idea from whodunits, learned from them also that a man's house is his castle till the law says 'Open.' Even if our burglar saw you put the sheets of blotting paper into the wood box, when could he have taken them out of the roadster?"

"Only chance would have been when I went into the Sargent house with you. Perhaps he hung on the back of the car from the Digbys'. Sounds corny as the dickens, but I can think of no other explanation. No sign of him when I drove into my garage."

"Perhaps—perhaps it was the sneezer."

"What sneezer? Expound your theory, woman. What are you talking about?"

She told of the sneeze which had risen from the shrubs, of its strangled successor, of Mrs. Sargent's low, "Come out. She's gone."

"Now what do you think?"

"Too complicated. Can't think so soon after breakfast."

Of course he could, equally of course he was evading answering her, she decided.

"What do we do next?"

"Await developments while we give an imitation of two persons who are at peace with the world. Meanwhile, Fran, your suggestion that we snoop around for a wet suit of clothes is getting my intensive consideration."

"You might also watch out for a person with a head cold."

"Miss Phillips!" The summons boomed from the small gallery. Fran sprang to her feet.

"The voice of authority. I'm all gooseflesh. Something is about to break."

"Take it easy. Remember I stand between you and your boss in this."

"That gives me more shivers. It suggests that he may suspect me, that I may be the fall guy." His quick laugh was infectious. She smiled in sympathy. "What's so funny about that?"

"The ease with which you, with your Rebecca Harding training, get off a slang phrase. Where do you pick them up?"

" 'I see by the papers—' "

"You and the Digs. That 'fall guy' is a cockeyed thought. Isn't it time for you to report on your job, to open the Gallery?"

"It is. I didn't think of that simple explanation of his summons. I hope I'll get a chance to wash these dishes before Mrs. Betsy returns, I don't want her to find an untidy kitchen. Yes, Mr. Sargent," she called in reply to another booming "Miss Phillips," and followed his voice.

He was pacing the floor of her office. Stopped abruptly and faced her. Now what? Her heart did a cartwheel and came right side up again to resume its hard beating. He teetered, removed his eyeglasses and tapped the left lens against his right thumb.

"How long have you been working for me, Miss Phillips?"

Here's where I get my pay check and am eased out, Fran decided. Her lips parted to reply.

"You needn't answer, I know. You have been here long enough for me to trust you implicitly. I hope you have the same feeling toward me."

Amazement tightened her throat, tears of relief blurred her eyes at the unexpected tribute.

"I have, Mr. Sargent. Thank you."

"Don't thank me. Thank yourself that you have chosen to be the sort of person who inspires trust. Close the door."

With the feeling of faring forth on an uncharted sea without compass and rudder, she shut out the reassuring sound of Myles's voice talking to the sheriff on the porch. Wonderful voice, a voice you would grope your way toward were you lost in the dark, sure of finding a helping hand.

"Sit down, Miss Phillips," Henry Sargent's command interrupted her reflections. "You appear as if poised to take off in a relay race." After she was seated he faced her from the other side of the desk.

"I understand Sinclair came to this town to see you."

Surprise widened her eyes. Blake had been as far from her thoughts as the humanitarian use of atomic energy.

"I thought from what you said the day of the preview of Mr. Eckhard's pictures that he came to sell you a painting, Mr. Sargent, an item you wanted very much."

"That was another reason for his coming. He offered me a Constable. Do you know where it is?"

"*I? No*, sir. I wouldn't know a Constable if I saw it."

"Study Eckhard's work, notice the bold use of sharp lights, they are put in with a palette knife. Constable used that method in his later years as he became increasingly occupied with the expression of light, air and movement."

"How large is the canvas?"

"Thirty-one by thirty-eight. It follows his style of the early thirties, when his skies are masses of soft, warm gray color, the edges touched with liquid silver. Sinclair delivered the painting yesterday morning, brought it in his car. A Constable sold the other day in England for £5650. I was so sure the one he offered was genuine that I made him a down payment on it."

"Isn't it the real thing? Blake wouldn't cheat—"

"Sit down again, Miss Phillips. Don't get excited. I don't know whether or not it is a genuine Constable. It's gone."

"*Gone!* Was the burglar after *that*, last night?"

"I can't figure it out. If the person who stole it is planning to sell the canvas, he's crazy. The news of the theft will spread through the artistic world, the thief would be apprehended promptly."

"Are you sure you remember where you put the painting?"

"Yes."

"Blake said there was a crowd in the Gallery all the afternoon."

"He was here?"

"Yes, Mr. Sargent, helping Gene. He stayed till closing time. Have you thought that the Constable might have been carried off by a visitor at the Gallery who figured that he, or she, would be supposed to be a purchaser of one of the Eckhard paintings?"

"That doesn't hold water because it is well known that no picture may be taken away while the exhibit is on. I was convinced that the person who took the Constable swiped the Byzantine enamel and the Apostle spoons. Couldn't have happened while Gene was here. Someone broke and entered, was hunting up the painting, or already had found it, when Si arrived, someone who had prepared the way by the faked call to the Digbys. The muddy prints on the kitchen floor and the lump on Si's head prove it."

That statement ruled out suspicion of the Digbys, Allah be praised. The thief hadn't had to do much breaking and entering with a key on the outside of the kitchen door. Neither she nor Myles had told of Mrs. Betsy's forgetfulness. Why drag her into the line-up? What would be Mr. Sargent's reaction if he knew that prints taken of the muddy tracks had been stolen? What was the object of this interview behind a closed door? Gave her a creepy feeling that a trap was about to spring. She had told all she knew about the theft last night. He had stopped his restless pacing to come to anchor before her desk. Now what?

"As I told you and Myles Jaffray, I don't want a hint of what happened here yesterday to get on the air. With the exception of the thief, you and he, Howlett and I, are the only persons who know. Si still thinks he was struck by lightning, just as well to let him believe that for the present. You'll have reason to agree with me when I tell you what we found in the repair shop."

Fran's heart took off to her throat and as speedily grounded. She'd had a premonition that she would be mixed up in this and here it was. Indignation ousted fear.

"Please stop dramatizing, Mr. Sargent. Tell me right off quick what you found in the repair shop—which it is very evident you believe will affect me."

In answer he drew from his coat pocket something covered with soft white paper, carefully unwrapped it. With his hand thrust into the toe, he set a high-heeled gold sandal with ankle strap on the desk. It looked like one of the pair she had worn the evening she and Myles Jaffray had sat on the rocks and heard the song coming from the boat.

"Yours, Miss Phillips?"

"It looks like mine but there must be other gold sandals in this community. Where did you get it?"

"In your apartment upstairs."

"In my apartment?" Eyes wide with unbelief she stared at him. "Why did you go there? Did you think you would find the enamel box and the spoons?"

"I did not. I told you we would search every crack and cranny, didn't I? We found the prints of a woman's slipper on the dusty floor in the back of the repair shop. Then we looked for a shoe that fitted them and found this."

"You are on an entirely wrong track, Mr. Sargent. I wasn't in the repair shop yesterday. I left here at two o'clock for The Theater, had been back here about fifteen minutes when I telephoned you what Myles and I found on our return."

"I know all that, I've figured it out. Had you loaned the gold shoes?"

"No, sir."

"I am trusting you to tell me whatever you discover about this, no matter where or *to whom*—remember that, *to whom*—the trail leads. The sandal prints in the dust led to a lot of old frames leaning against the wall. Behind the junk we found—"

"The missing Constable?" she supplied jubilantly, forgetting for the moment that her gold sandal was under suspicion.

"No."

He tapped his eyeglass against his thumb with maddening deliberation, cleared his throat.

"The Apostle spoons."

XIII

At the white sink in the sunny kitchen Myles Jaffray attacked the used breakfast dishes. Fran had planned to restore the room to order before the return of the Digbys, but two cars filled with potential customers had driven in while he was talking with the sheriff, which meant that her work for the day in the Gallery had begun. It was up to him to take over.

He thought back over the many times when, as a boy, he had washed and dried dishes for the comfort of being near heart-warming Betsy. A motherless kid had moments of loneliness that a child with two parents never experienced. As he dipped cups and saucers into an iridescent, sparkling mountain of suds—she'd give him the dickens for being so lavish with soap flakes—he thought of some of the tragic moments in the last six years when, had he been told that he would again return to the town of his birth, he would have rated the prophecy dream stuff.

A plane roared above the house. His eyes followed its flight over the top of the highest hill until it disappeared. He thought of the day he had jumped into a dense forest on a mountainside to take relief to the crew of a wrecked Flying Fortress that had started for a tough target without benefit of fighter protection. Others had volunteered for the rescue, but he wouldn't send one of his men. He had been trained to give more than basic first aid. Added to that, there was one chance in ten that the paratrooper who went would come through. It was his job. A miss in landing, even a half mile from the crashed plane, might mean hours of wandering through impenetrable forest, if he lasted that long, and death to those to be rescued.

He impatiently mopped his forehead. Could memory start sweat? He hadn't missed. One of his decorations was proof of that. His arrival had saved three lives, the others— Good Lord, why look back on the horrors that were finished? Were they finished or was it all to do over again?

That sort of thinking didn't help the present tense

world situation, the fact that the outlook was grim. As soon as this vacation was over he would get into something constructive. The G.G.A. had assured him that it would be a cinch for him to secure Grove's seat in the House. In the first place he wouldn't campaign against his friend who was doing a good job, in the second he wasn't ready for it. How about concentrating on the present? He was committed to remaining here as long as Fran stayed, or until a report came through of her brother's safety. There was a spicy incident right here in his home town to be accounted for. Who had broken into the Gallery yesterday and why? It was Henry Sargent's problem, but because it was Fran's also he had made it his.

Fran. He and Ken had talked of her and planned so much for her that he had felt she belonged to him. Cup in one hand, dish towel in the other, he gazed unseeingly at the blue and gold world outside the window. Fran. So that was how it was. Whatever touched her was his concern. He nodded, admitted under his breath:

"That's the way it has been and I didn't know it, that's the way it is, and that is the way it will be—forever." He added aloud, "You've made a quick switch from the past to the future, Mr. Jaffray."

There was enough in the immediate present that needed his entire attention; funny, though, what a glow that possible future had left in his heart. Was the sneeze Fran had heard tied up with the disappearance of the sheets of blotting paper? Could be that a person watching the ell had been soaked to the skin and chilled to the bone, though that wasn't the modern explanation of the reason for a cold.

If the sneezer had seen him shift the blotters from the wood box to his roadster, there was something to Fran's suggestion that a search through the village for a wet suit of clothing might bring results. Why not try it out?

He opened the door in response to the "Miew" of the white Persian on the sill outside the window. Missy Snow stalked in with the air of a queen approaching her throne, or a woman certain of the perfection of her ensemble, jumped to the seat of the rocker in the corner and blinked amber eyes at the man who was rinsing dish towels.

113

He laughed as he carefully spread them on the rack to dry as he had been taught by Mrs. Betsy. Suppose the troopers he had commanded could see their "jump-or-be-damned Major," as they called him, he hoped affectionately, at his present job? Didn't take much imagination to line up their colorful comments. There had been men from the State of Maine in his outfit, before he left for New York he would look them up. He slipped on his coat.

"Oh, you've done them," Fran exclaimed from the doorway. She had changed from the plaid wool in which she had arrived at the Gallery to a cool-looking green linen the shade of the large peridot in the ring on the little finger of her right hand. Pat Sargent in a blue and white checked play suit, beside her, hailed him.

"Hi, Myles!" Tweed, the fox terrier, sat on his haunches, wary, beady eyes on the hunched-back white Persian who was emitting threatening warnings.

"What are you doing out so early in the morning, Miss Sargent?" Myles inquired.

"I'm 'sistant to Miss Phillips. She said I might stay." Patricia clutched Fran's skirt as if she feared forcible separation from her.

"She's my number one helper," Fran answered the question in his eyes. "I saw a few minutes of leisure ahead and dashed here to clear up—with Pat's assistance—and I find the dishes done."

"And well done, if you ask me. I'm good. While on the subject I will observe that I am a matrimonial prize; expert dishwasher, as a cook I have a few specialties, and note this, I have never acquired the newspaper-at-breakfast habit. How's that?"

"Sensational. An A-1 reference. Modest about your attainments, aren't you?"

"Jeepers, aren't you two having fun." Patricia's eyes and voice were wistful. "I didn't know anyone laughed or was pleasant in the morning. All the people in our house are cross as two sticks—gee, you should hear Gene—I beat it."

"Tuck this into your thought-box, Pat." Fran caught the child's hand in hers. "I love life, but when I get up in the morning feeling so sour that I take the sunshine out of the day for everyone I meet I hope the good Lord

114

will remove me from this earthly scene." Vivid color surged to the soft line of her hair as she met Myles's eyes.

"I'm sorry I let myself go. It is a subject upon which I have definite views."

"I'll say they are definite. They burned the wires. Just for the record, if that was aimed at me, I fairly radiate good nature in the morning. Add that to my A-1 reference."

"It wasn't aimed at anyone. It was a long-repressed conviction blowing its top."

He wouldn't tell her now that he understood why, that Ken had confided that until about 11 A.M. Rebecca Harding had made life hell for each person with whom she came in contact. He drew a pipe from his pocket.

"Boy, no matches. Find some for me, will you, Miss Sargent?"

"Look on the desk in my office, Patricia."

"Okay, boss."

Myles waited until the little girl with the dog at her heels was out of sight.

"What did Henry Sargent have on his mind that he couldn't impart with your office door open, Fran?"

"N-nothing of importance."

"Then why be afraid to look at me when you answer?"

"Who is third-degreeing now? Afraid of you? Don't be absurd."

"Uh, huh, you're not afraid. We'll leave it there for the present." With the recently realized knowledge of his love for her setting his pulses quick-stepping, he was tempted to catch her in his arms and hold her close till she told him. That would wreck the comradely response she was beginning to show. Just in time last night he had broken off the question, "Feeling more friendly toward me?" To have asked it would have been crowding his luck.

"Any new developments of the late unpleasantness?" he inquired. "Did you get the impression during the aforementioned closed-door interview that your boss had rooted out even one clue?"

"Y-yes. But, I have been ordered not to—"

"Miss Phillips!"

"There he is again. He said he would call me when the fingerprint expert arrives. I must go. Why don't you ask him what he discovered?"

"I don't want to meet him yet. I'm off by way of the kitchen door. If you discover anything, remember we are in this mess together. Keep me posted. He's yelling for you again. Beat it. I'll be seeing you."

Where start the quest for the wet clothing, he ruminated when he reached the highway. A plane from the near-by airport roared overhead. Cars of every description swarmed up and down the main street of the village. A low truck with THE THEATER in large letters on the side was filled with a heterogeneous collection of furniture. Borrowing stage settings? Nat had loaned some from Shore Acres.

It was vacation season and the town was a paradise for vacationists who liked the sea. They were sprinkled over boardinghouse lawns, perched on boardinghouse porch rails, crowded the street in every variety of sports clothing. Fat men and thin men in swim trunks revealed by flapping beach robes; women and children in play suits, halters and shorts—minus beach robes—hurried, strolled, window-shopped. A few smartly dressed women with canes passed. A beauty shop snuggled close to the movie theater, a chain store on the left, a bakery on the right flanked the dingy post office from the cupola of which floated the Stars and Stripes. A group buying postcards surrounded a magazine stand.

"Myles!"

From the curb of the sidewalk hatless Tassie Trent in a purple and white striped cotton morning frock hailed him and waved a stout stick.

"Give me a lift?"

Without waiting for his answer she stepped into the street, and with imperious, uplifted hand stopped traffic moving forward after a long wait in response to the signal of an officer ahead. Myles helped her into the open convertible to the accompaniment of angry toots.

"How come you are caught in this crowd, Miss Tassie?" he inquired when the car was once more in motion and his face, reddened by the protesting horns, had cooled. "You shouldn't have stepped into the street like that, you might have been knocked down. Where do you want to go?"

"Sunnyside. You don't have to bawl me out, Myles. I've learned my lesson, I'll never do this again."

"Are you tired?"

"Tired? My eye, I'm sight-sick. But it's given me an idea. I'll introduce a bill in our legislature requiring every landlord to install a full-length mirror in each room he rents."

"What's the big idea?"

"See that woman on the sidewalk with that harsh hennaed hair, in bright blue halter and shorts?" She pointed with her cane. "If she had had a full-length view of those fat, bare legs, that spare tire of flesh around her middle—"

"For the love of *Pete*, Miss Tassie, soft pedal. She heard you. She's—"

He took advantage of an opening in traffic to shoot ahead. The woman in blue had stepped into the street with every indication that she was about to advance belligerently on her critic with a beach umbrella.

"I hope she did hear me." Tassie Trent's voice was full of fight, but an octave lower. "It may make her think after she cools down. It's disgraceful the way these vacationists, some of them, dress or undress when they come to this beautiful village; they ought to have more respect for the residents. Bermuda has the right idea. Beach clothes for the beach and nowhere else. Did last night's storm do much damage at Shore Acres?"

"A few trees down. How did Sunnyside fare?"

"No casualties unless you count John's drenched suit."

"John? Who's John?"

"Why does that name startle you? A ghost from your guilty past?"

"No ghosts in my past. It wasn't the name that caused the outburst. Didn't you see the man ahead stop short without putting out his hand? For a second I had a vision of this car piling up on him." That would take care of his exclamation. Was he on the trail of the drenched suit worn by the person who had seen him hide the blotters in the wood box?

"Now that explanation is out of the way, Miss Tassie,

117

who is John? A new butler? You haven't lost your spectacular superefficient black, Caesar, have you? He is magnificent and I mean magnificent."

"Certainly not. I am speaking of John Eckhard, the artist. He's staying with me. You haven't forgotten so soon that you bought his 'Country Lane,' have you?"

Eckhard. Eckhard came home with drenched clothes last night. Had the footprints in the Digby kitchen been his? Had he seen the blotters placed in the wood box? He had been at the Gallery in the afternoon. Had he hidden in the building until Gene had left and then— Fool idea. What would be his object? Not to steal an enamel box and a set of spoons. If he had been inside all the time he wouldn't have left muddy footprints on the floor, would he?

"And the Senator was paying about as much attention to my voice as you are to what I am telling you now." The caustic statement brought him smack up against the present.

"I was listening, Miss Tassie, you said you were planning a party for the artists and some of your neighbors to meet Eckhard. I'll confess, though, that at the same time I was wondering why he was at the Sargent Gallery yesterday afternoon, fussing, that was the word used, about changing one of his pictures."

"Fiddlesticks, that was an excuse, he was there hoping to see that girl. He's nuts about her. Told me she was the loveliest person in looks and manners he had ever met."

"What girl?"

"There you go again. Where did you pick up this explosive way of speaking, Myles?"

"Sorry, must be the effect of the war, it is being blamed for every change. Has Eckhard gone overboard for Gene or the widow Sargent? Come to think of it, it would be a slick move for him to marry the boss's daughter, even daughter-in-law, he would be sure his pictures would be exhibited and how."

"Who said anything about Gene Sargent or that poisonous Matilde? I didn't. Do you think a sane man would be fooled into thinking either one the loveliest person he ever had met? I hope you don't. I was referring to Frances Phillips, the girl for whom Morrie

Grove has gone overboard. You knew that, didn't you? Says when or if he goes to Washington he'll try to persuade her to come along as his secretary."

"I'm beginning to think I don't know anything that is going on. Me, I'm old Rip van Winkle rousing from a twenty years' sleep. Here we are. Sunnyside is a beautiful home. You're a lucky gal, Miss Tassie Trent."

She sat in the car looking at the brick house with its towers, vines and background of shrubs.

"It's all right. I had every bit of brick and wood brought from the family plantation house in Virginia, but it remains a house, it takes children to make a home." She stepped to the drive, held tight to the hand he stretched to steady her.

"Don't wait too long before you marry, Myles. I want to leave this estate to a child of yours. My eye, I've turned sob-sister. Forget it." She shrugged. "Don't hurry about settling down. Better to wait too long than to marry the wrong person, boy."

"You've said it, but how can one tell who is the right person?"

"One can't, till after the first fifty years, I reckon. Come in and have lunch with me. Eckhard will be back. I'd like you to meet him and size him up. I think he's a genius."

Is he a genius, Myles pondered as after luncheon Miss Tassie, Eckhard and he sat smoking on the terrace above the garden from which came the tinkle of water in the fountain pool and the fragrance of roses. The artist wore white slacks and open-neck shirt topped by a sports coat of broad navy and white stripes. In the early fifties, perhaps. Not a person whose thoughts one could gauge from his large eyes behind thick lenses, couldn't get much from what he said, either, he had talked little through luncheon. That wasn't his fault. Miss Tassie had kept up a constant barrage of "Do you remembers" about past years to him. Must have been boring to the guy.

"Did you find a spot to paint which set genius burning this morning, John?" she inquired and lighted a fresh cigarette from a stub she held between her lips.

"No. I'll poke round a few days before I start work. I did close a deal for a studio at the Inlet."

"That was unnecessary. There are plenty of vacant rooms in this great house for you to use. Select any one of them and it is yours."

"That's kind of you, Miss Trent, and a terrible temptation, but I know yours truly, I've lived with him a long time, and I know that I will do better work away from this luxury—not that I don't enjoy it—I'm fairly eating it up—but I would get soft here, and I must work. I have a number of unfinished canvases in my room at the Inn. I begin to feel the urge to get at them."

"Sinclair reported that you substituted one painting for another at the Gallery yesterday, Eckhard. I hope it wasn't my 'Country Lane.'" Had the man's eyes narrowed at mention of the change of pictures? That was imagination, he decided, as Eckhard laughed.

"'Country Lane' is no longer mine. It is yours. Sinclair and Miss Sargent thought me fussy, but, after all, why shouldn't I make a change? They are my pictures. I took down one, carried it to what they call the repair shop, removed it from the frame and substituted one I had brought from the Inn which I fancied might be more salable. It was a good hunch. I found this telephone message when I came in to lunch." He drew a slip of paper from his coat pocket, read:

"'"Romance in Stone" sold this morning. Congratulations. Fran Phillips.' That's the story of yesterday afternoon."

"Sounds as if you knew your stuff."

"Of course he knows his stuff, Myles. Do you think he would be hung in a Sargent Gallery, in a one man exhibition, if he didn't?" Miss Tassie was quite breathless in defense of her protégé. "A success story, I'd call it. What is the subject of the picture just sold, John?"

"A Belgian castle, enough of it standing to show its one-time grandeur, to suggest its romantic past, in contrast to the rest of it, a heap of rubble, overrun with vines. I developed the painting from a sketch I made while I was in the army in that country."

A ruined palace. Belgium. Barth, the waiter, had told Fran he had been a butler in a "near palace" there. Could it be mere coincidence that the two men had arrived in

120

this village at the same time? Back up on that trail. The mystery at the Gallery was giving him crazy notions. Dollars to dimes the ex-butler never had seen a palace in Belgium any more than he had been wounded at Dunkirk. Hadn't he told Morrie Grove he had served in the U.S. Navy four years? Undoubtedly he was a psychopathic case, harmless, one not to be taken seriously.

"The storm gave the Inlet the works, yesterday." Eckhard stopped to light a coffee-colored meerschaum representing the head of a leering satyr. "I went there in the late afternoon to look over the studio that was to rent. Stayed for an alfresco supper in the midst of which the heavens opened, we rushed for the house. That wasn't a protection, for the roof leaked. I haven't done so much bailing out since I was an amateur yachtsman. The village tailor wasn't hopeful that he could restore my suit to its original freshness, which after all wasn't so fresh, as it was of before-the-war vintage."

Exit one wet suit as a clue to the Gallery mystery; added to that, the man hadn't a sign of a cold. He could cross off Eckhard from the list of suspects, Myles decided as he rose.

"It has been like old times to drop in for lunch with you, Miss Tassie. My regards to Susanna, tell her there is no cook in the world who can touch her lobster thermidor. Glad to have had this chance to get acquainted, Eckhard. I'm not an art critic, but I know what I like and I like your work immensely."

Color deepened the violent sunburn of the artist's face to the edge of his still iron-gray hair. The prominent eyes behind the owl-like lenses misted as he clasped the hand Myles extended.

"You're mighty friendly, Major Jaffray, to a stranger. You and Congressman Grove sure have put out the Welcome mat for me. I met him at the village tailor's. He was caught in the storm last night. His suit, if one is to believe the tailor, is in a more hopeless condition than mine. Looked as if he had been standing under a tree or among bushes that had stained them."

"Standing among bushes that had stained them." The words rotated in Myles's mind in unison with the wheels of the car as he drove along the main street. Could Morrison Grove be the person who had left muddy footprints on the kitchen floor, who had discovered the hideout of the blue blotting paper? A crazy suspicion. Morrie had left Shore Acres in his sedan before the storm broke, he had said he was about to make calls on constituents. What possible reason could he have to hang around the Gallery, to conk Silas Pond?

Was he in love with Fran? Suppose he were, suppose he had given up hope of getting Nat, gone all out for another woman? That wouldn't take him to the Gallery. She was at Shore Acres when he drove away. Common sense would suggest that she would remain there through the storm. Could be, though, that a man in love had no common sense. Nevertheless there was a wet suit stained by the drip from tree or shrubs to be accounted for. Slight as it was, incredible as it was, he'd better not pass up the chance that it was a clue. Morrie Grove was his dish for the present. He'd drop in on him.

The dapper white-coated Filipino who opened the door of the buff Colonial house where Morrison Grove kept bachelor hall shook his head in response to Myles's inquiry.

"No, sir, the boss not home. He telephoned from the tailor's, where he took his suit, that he was going out of town for a few days. Very sudden, sir, he didn't take a bag."

"Did Mr. Grove have a cold when he left?"

"Not a real cold, sir. He sneezed once this morning, but that was all I heard."

"Very sudden, sir, he didn't take a bag. . . . He sneezed once." Myles turned over the words mentally as he drove through the main street. Yesterday afternoon on the terrace at Shore Acres Morrie had exclaimed:

"Something tells me that fella will bear watching."

Had he seen Barth steal away from the ell? Was he on the trail of the man's past? He shot the roadster forward, muttering to himself:

"I'll be darned! It's possible."

XIV

"Quite a crowd tonight, Caesar," Myles greeted the very tall, very black, very straight butler at the door of Sunnyside.

"Yes, sir, Mr. Myles. Seems like the good old days befo' the war when Miss Tassie had parties an' you was always on han'. She receivin' in the drawin' room, sir."

Having paid his respects to hostess and guest of honor, Myles stood in the doorway of the dining room with its beautiful woodwork, carved shutters and high cornices which were the envy of every antiquarian in the country. From the broad hall drifted the music of woodwinds and strings playing, "The Night Was Made for Love."

The music provided a running accompaniment to his thoughts. Three days ago he had had luncheon here with Miss Tassie and Eckhard, now the great room was filled with guests in gala attire invited to meet the artist. Was pink the top fashion for women's frocks this summer? Those in view ran the gamut of tints and shades from flesh color to American Beauty. There was a sprinkling of black among the white dinner jackets.

He responded to friendly waves and affectionate hails while his thoughts and the music traveled on together. Three days gone and he had made no progress in getting at the truth of the theft at the Gallery. Had anyone? Fran had been incommunicado, he had been unable to reach her. Did it mean that for one reason or another her dislike of him had been given fresh impetus or that a clue to the break had been unearthed and she had been forbidden by her boss to talk with him?

Morrison Grove also had been elusive. He had followed up his call at the house with telephone inquiries. "Out of town," each time a voice had replied. Too late now to check on the clue of the wet suit, it would be bone dry by this time. The more he thought of it the more he believed it to be coincidental, like the arrival in the same town of the artist who had painted the ruins of a Belgian castle and the butler who had served in one, if you could believe the man's story.

"Can I get you something, sir?"

Barth, ex-butler, ex-Dunkirk, ex-what-have-you, appeared as if conjured into being by his thoughts. The lock of hair dangling on his high forehead was as white as his immaculate shirt front.

For no apparent reason Myles's memory televised a figure skulking among rocks, sound tracks broadcast a song:

Nita, Juanita,
Ask thy soul if we should part,

and the scrape of a boat across a beach.

At the time he had suspected that the song had been a signal; for a hectic instant had thought it might be connected with news of Ken, had dismissed the idea as impossible. Man and girl rendezvous, doubtless.

"His brown outfit was so like the color of the rocks," Fran had said on the terrace of Shore Acres. Perhaps she was right, perhaps the man was a spy, they were operating on both sides of the Atlantic.

"Miss Trent engaged me to help out the servants," Barth added as if his presence rated explanation, as if he had read Myles's mind.

"Thanks, but I'll look after myself."

"Quite a crowd around the table, sir. I can bring something from the pantry."

Darn the guy's persistence. Myles opened his lips to assure the waiter that a crowd didn't fill him with terror, closed them as he met the man's steady eyes. "What goes? What goes?" he asked himself. More behind this than meets the ear?

"Something tells me you're right, Barth. If Susanna's chicken salad, plus pecans, is on the menu I'd like that with anything else you recommend."

"Very good, sir. There is a table at the right end of the terrace, quite secluded in case you prefer to eat alone. If agreeable to you I'll bring a tray there in about ten minutes, in *ten minutes*, if that will suit you, sir."

He didn't wait to learn if it would, which made the statement more of an order than a suggestion. Myles's eyes followed his black shoulders and white head as he edged his way toward the pantry door between laughing, chatting, eating groups. What in thunder had he

124

meant by steering him to a certain table? Why assume that he wanted to eat solo? Morrie Grove had the man tagged as a psycho, that didn't seem the right answer to this episode. If he were a spy, for whom was he working? Had he a secret message to deliver? Ken? The possibility sent his heart to his throat. Reason dropped it back into place. There was only one channel through which news of Ken Phillips could come and it was not through a person.

"*Ten minutes,*" the man who called himself Barth had emphasized. He checked by his watch. Battles had been won and lost in less time than that. What would the next ten minutes disclose?

He returned to the drawing room with its soft gray walls and tourmaline pink hangings at long, open windows. Niches each side of the marble fireplace held a collection of Royal Doulton figurines whose costumes matched in color the hangings; above the mantel hung a Manet, of a girl in a field, which had the color, vivacity, and sparkle of the artist's later work. The furniture had been taken out. Which fact meant dancing till dawn, undoubtedly. Miss Tassie was a night owl and assumed that her guests were also.

Tonight she was resplendent in light blue net with silver sequins which glinted with each motion of her restless body. A narrow coronet of diamonds encircled her mountainous black hair-do. Eckhard, in white dinner clothes, and a state of pride and excitement, was beside her. Would she have worn that huge brooch and the broad bracelets of aquamarines and diamonds had she known of the theft at the Gallery? Had Henry Sargent the right to keep under cover the fact that his property had been stolen?

"Hi, Myles!" Morrison Grove stopped beside him, his sunburn brought into high relief by his white coat. "Hear you've been trying to contact me. Anything important?"

"Thought it was at the time, but it's blown over." Too late to bring up the question, "How account for your drenched suit the night of the storm?"

"This is strictly off the record." Grove moved a step nearer and spoke in a low voice. "When I was on the newspaper I helped the FBI with a little information.

Thought they might be able to reciprocate. I got darned uneasy about our mystery man, have been trying to check on him."

"Mystery man?" Myles's eyes and voice registered bewilderment though he knew quite well of whom Grove was speaking.

"You haven't forgotten Fran's visiting fireman, with his assortment of jobs, have you?"

"Oh, that guy. Thought you had him filed as a psychopathic case. He's here tonight."

"You're telling me, and Miss Tassie plastered with diamonds. I have a hunch we may need a couple of strong boys before the evening is through."

"Did you get the goods on—" Myles left the sentence unfinished as a man and girl stopped near them.

"Eckhard is the white-haired boy tonight," Grove asserted jovially as if unaware that Myles had ceased speaking abruptly. "Quite a party. Miss Tassie is the top patron of the arts in this community, always giving a hand up to strugglers on the ladder of fame. Eckhard's no longer a struggler, though. He's quite a guy if he can't talk without a pipe in his hand. He's giving the works of art in this house the once-over. Queer specialty, running down art fakers."

"He appears to have a lot on the ball. I was here for lunch the day after the record-breaking storm. He told me he was drenched in the downpour, said you had been too."

"Did he? How did he know that my car had a blowout and I changed a tire near a hedge?" Grove's question was low and eager. The couple near moved on. "Did he tell you he was huddled beside the shrubs outside the Digbys' door at the Gallery during that same storm? I'd give dollars—"

"Major Jaffray, at long last. Why so late arriving, Myles?" Gene Sargent tucked her hand under his arm and regarded Grove with unfriendly eyes. "I've seen you before this evening, Morrie."

" 'Sdeath, I'm going, lady. Your suggestion was so subtly phrased you rate the diplomatic service." He resettled the bachelor's-buttons in the lapel of Myles's white dinner jacket.

"My boy, all in good time will be given to you the

knowledge about to be passed on when so rudely interrupted, but, to one who shall be nameless there shall be no enlightenment. Selah."

The corners of Gene Sargent's lovely mouth tipped down, two sharp lines cut between her black brows.

"What did he mean by that rigmarole, Myles?"

"Search me, I can't follow Morrie when he talks in parables."

"Who can? Miss Tassie was threatened with a nervous breakdown when you didn't appear." Her hand tightened on his arm. "I suspect you are the heir apparent of Sunnyside. You're the hottest thing in popularity in this house."

"And you are something to write home about in that deep rose color frock, Gene. It does a lot for your dark eyes and hair which need nothing in the way of charm that nature has not already provided. After which exchange of courtesies I will explain that I had to wait at home for a long-distance call. Lucky I didn't have far to come, I cut through the gate in the hedge between the two places. What a crowd. Looks as if all the world and his wife of this community had turned out to give Eckhard the glad hand."

"And incidentally gorge on one of Miss Tassie's out-of-this-world suppers. Everyone is here but Fran Phillips and Blake Sinclair."

Myles swallowed an emphatic, "You're telling me," and substituted what he hoped was a surprised, "Weren't they invited?"

"Of course. I don't know what to make of Fran. She was such a mouse when her aunt was alive, now instead of being a negative person she's positive—and how. When Blake came she declared she wouldn't go out with him, via grapevine, I hear that they play tennis together every afternoon when she is through work. Perhaps you can explain her change of heart. I can't."

Had Fran discovered that she loved Sinclair? Was that why he had been unable to reach her or was the reason tied up with the theft at the Gallery?

"He is an old friend," he commented casually. "Maybe she is worried about that thousand dollar debt? Perhaps she is confiding in him."

"That's taken care of." Her voice had the buoyancy of

a balloon released from captivity. "Fran phoned me this morning that she wouldn't have to lie awake worrying any more. The money is in sight with which to pay it, without benefit of her trustee, I gathered."

He ignored the thrust. He'd bet Fran wasn't the person who could stop worrying, it was Gene. Judge Grimes had phoned him this evening that he had sold bonds on Fran's order and suggested that he find out why. He suspected she was helping Sinclair.

"I'm glad she has the payment for that stunning ring off her conscience. Now she can enjoy it. Unpaid-for possessions are not much fun. If she worried enough it may be a lesson to her not to get into debt. As Ken isn't here perhaps I'd better speak to her—"

"No, Myles, no. She told me she never wanted to think of it again. Speak of the angels, here they come." She clasped her free hand over the other in his arm. Her raised face almost touched his bent to hear her whisper.

"That intense blue-with-green chiffon she is wearing would be a lot more becoming to a girl more blond, don't you think?"

He looked up and met Fran's eyes. He didn't like the little contemptuous line of her lips. He didn't like the way she looked up at Sinclair and asked a question. Neither did he like the hands on his arm. He gently but firmly shook them off.

"I took a good look as she passed. Seems all right to me, stands out in this sea of pink. The shimmer of silver each time she moves gets me. I'm a push-over for glitter. Not that I'm a judge, but I'd say it was perfect for her."

"One can't expect a man to appreciate the fine nuances of dressing. She is wearing her luscious double string of pearls. How did she get them? She told me she left them in her depos—" Had memory flashed a red stop signal? "Morrie Grove is making a dash for her as usual. I hope he gets her permanently. She could be of enormous help to him with her money and social background. I wonder how Nat likes his defection?"

"She seems to be bearing up under the blow, she doesn't look disturbed." He smilingly regarded his sister, who, in an off-the-shoulder black tulle frock, was talking animatedly with a portly Senator for whose election she had worked.

"Disturbed. She is radiant. Why not? She is one of the richest—and one of the most admired women in the state. Could a woman wearing those sensational diamond clips look disturbed? My money says she couldn't."

"Nat had a tough break, Gene. Wealth and diamonds do not necessarily spell happiness."

"No? I've heard that one before. You've had money all your life, everything you've wanted has been handed you on a silver platter. Try being held down to a measly allowance and you'd change your ideas, Myles."

"Why remain held down? You are an exceptionally intelligent girl. Made the honor list at college, didn't you? Break away. Make a career for yourself. It's being done every day. Isn't that the major reason why girls leave home?"

"This girl would leave her happy home and quick if she had the cash. Lately Dad has been as jumpy as a jack rabbit, Mother is worrying herself to a frazzle trying to beat the H.C.L., and Matilde is wearing her nerves on the outside, your ex-brother-in-law is showing signs of gnawing his rope. So far my attempts to increase my income have landed me in the red, a deep-dyed crimson, but, if at first you don't succeed, you know that one. Morrie Grove has walked off with Fran and Blake Sinclair is coming this way. I have something of importance to tell him. Just for once I would rather talk with him than you, Myles. Would you mind—"she suggested eagerly.

"That is the most direct 'Here's your hat' I have ever received. I'm off."

Even as he chatted with friends Gene's words kept intruding in his mind: "So far my attempts to increase my income have landed me in the red." It tied in with his suspicion that the bonds had been sold to pay her debts. Had she lost at cards to Blake Sinclair? Her eagerness to talk with him followed close on Judge Grimes's telephoned message that a check had been sent special delivery to Fran. Months ago in Germany when they had been discussing the change of trustee of Rebecca Harding's estate Ken Phillips had warned:

"If you take over, Myles, watch out for Blake Sinclair. He's a congenital gambler. Not only in cards, he's been

129

involved in several fly-by-night concerns. Nothing dishonest proved, just reckless, eager to take a chance. Don't misunderstand me, I'm not afraid that Fran will pick up the gambling bug, she's immune to that sort of thing, but Blake might promise to quit if she will marry him—I believe the guy loves her as much as he can love anyone but himself—and she has 'my-brother's-keeper' complex developed to the nth degree. Don't let her. The clause in Aunt Becky's will gives you authority to stop it, to try, at least. I have a hunch that if Master Blake knew she would lose her money if she married him he would take a cooling-off period."

"She'll marry him only over my dead body, Ken," he mentally assured his absent friend. "Neither will she go to Washington as Morrie Grove's secretary."

"I Still Get Jealous When They Look at You," one of the musicians was singing. Myles met his own frowning eyes in a hall mirror, and grinned at his reflection. There was something in what the man was saying.

When by a circuitous route he reached the table in the vine-shaded end of the terrace the musicians were back to "The Night Was Made for Love." The soft notes drifted from the hall. They were 100 per cent right, it was a night of enchantment. A low laugh floated up from the fragrant garden to the accompaniment of the soft rustle of leaves and the plash of a fountain. From the other end of the terrace came a murmur of voices, broken by an impassioned, "Dearest, I love—"

Myles moved deeper into the shadow. Was he spoiling sport by his presence? Could he be seen? Why had the man who called himself Barth selected this particular spot? Barth. Who was he?

"And Miss Tassie fairly plastered with diamonds."

As if in answer to his question Grove's words flashed on the screen of memory. Had Morrie reason to be worried? He had been checking on "the mystery man." Had he discovered that he was involved in the theft at the Gallery? No soap. Unless Henry Sargent had confided in him—and dollars to dimes he hadn't—Morrie didn't know there had been a theft. He glanced at the illuminated dial of his watch. One minute to go. Some-one coming. On time to the—

130

Nita, Juanita,
Ask thy soul if we should part.

Clear and loud the whistled tune came from the garden. Curious that only a few moments ago he had thought of the song. Would it be answered this time? He retreated into deeper shadow. He would watch the effect on the waiter when he discovered that there was no one at the table.

A girl stopped in the doorway, looked right and left before in a flash of green and blue and silver she darted to the shadows in which he stood. "Oh," she breathed when she realized she was not alone.

"It's Myles, Fran. Why the 'villain still pursued her' act?" She shook her head and laid her fingers on her lips as a man crossed the terrace to the steps.

"I'm thankful it is you, Myles. He mustn't see me. You are the only one who can understand. Mr. Sargent won't let me talk—" Excitement tightened her throat and shut off her whisper.

With an arm across her shoulders he drew her close, so close he could feel the hard beat of her heart. Suppose he pressed his lips to her soft hair on a level with his chin? Now he was crazy. Was she in terror of the man standing at the head of the steps looking up at the star-riddled sky? Was he there in answer to the whistle in the garden? Was he waiting for a repetition of the signal, always supposing that it had been a signal? Now he was going back to the house. Light from the hall shone on his face.

Eckhard. *Eckhard.* Morrie had said he had been huddled under the shrubs near the Gallery ell during the storm. Had he conked Si Pond? Was he following Fran because he suspected she had seen him?

"What's it all about?" he asked softly. "Are you afraid of Eckhard?" She shook her head against his shoulder.

"No. *No.* When he came out I thought he was the person who has been watching me."

"Let's go to the garden where we can talk without the possibility of being overheard."

"No. If I stay here, he can't see me."

"Who can't see you?"

131

"The waiter who calls himself Barth. I felt his eyes on me every minute I was in the supper room."

Should he tell her that the man was due to arrive with a tray at any moment? No. Surprised, Barth might reveal his reason for watching her when he saw her here with him.

"You've got that waiter wrong, darling. Why should he—"

"You here, Mr. Myles?"

Myles released Fran as the butler peered into the shadow.

"Yes, Caesar. What goes?"

"It's that waiter Miss Tassie hired to help tonight. He tol' me he promised to bring a tray here for you, an' to tell you he was called away sudden like, an' he was sorry to disappoint you because you had been mighty kind to him."

"Any idea what took him off so suddenly?"

Caesar stepped nearer and lowered his voice. "I heard some sort of a row at the back door, guess he'd got in trouble. I think they took him off. Good thing. I told Miss Tassie she shouldn't be hiring strangers here she didn't know nothing about, when all our family silver is here. What'd she know 'bout this man? I wish you'd speak to her, Mr. Myles, she won't listen to me. She don't mind who she takes in. She just met this artist man once, an' asked him to visit us. It's dangerous, that's what it is. Would you like me to bring a tray here for you and the young lady, sir?"

"No, we'll come to the supper room, Caesar."

He watched the tall straight back until the butler entered the house. "Heard some sort of a row at the back door, guess he'd got in trouble," Caesar had said. Had Morrie's FBI caught up with "the mystery man"?

XV

"What does it mean, Myles?"

He shook his head in answer to Fran's whispered question.

"You know as much as I do. For one thing it means that the man Barth, who, you said, had been watching

132

you, has made a quick getaway himself, or has been forcibly removed. Anyway, he's gone. Come into the garden where we can talk without whispering, and you can tell me what it's all about. There is a seat this side of the rocks where we will not be overheard, if someone hasn't thought of it first."

Through the soft summer night, under a sky gold-plated with stars, they walked down the garden path between flowers bowing in obeisance as her bouffant skirt of blue and green and silver brushed them; past the pool tinkling with crystal drippings from the marble finger tips of a Psyche, kneeling, the better to see her lovely reflected face in the water mirror; past an old-time summerhouse with lacelike white trellises from which stole the sound of a woman's soft, excited laughter; round a group of ghostly birches to a lawn that edged the rocky shore against which beat dark indigo billows topped with silver snow.

"Eureka, no one on the iron seat," Myles exulted. "Quick before someone beats us to it. Warm enough?" he asked when they were seated.

"As toast."

"Must be cold toast, else why the shivers?"

"The ocean is so dark, so illimitable, it stopped my heart for a second. In daylight it is glorious, at night it suggests lurking danger."

"See the white hulk against the horizon, where sea mist and star shine mingle in a glow? That's a ship plowing forward gallantly without fear of the mighty forces beneath it."

"Without fear. Gallantly. That's a design for living. If one had the will power always to slam the door hard against fear life would be a different proposition, wouldn't it?"

"It would. Now that we are on the subject of fear, what gave you the jitters tonight, what about the man, Barth, watching you?"

"The moment Blake and I entered the supper room, my attention was drawn to him like a pin to a magnet. Because his eyes were on me, I suppose. Perhaps he has added hypnosis to his long list of vocations."

"Sure he was looking at you, not at Sinclair?"

"Yes."

"How long were you in the room?"

"Long enough to have something to eat, and coffee."

"Did Barth serve you?"

"Serve us? He hovered. He kept offering things."

"Did Sinclair comment on his superattention?"

"No. Blake gave his entire attention to the eats. He said he'd never expected to taste such salads and feather rolls this side of Paradise."

"You arrived late. Did you come with Sinclair?"

"Yes. He was late calling for me. He dined at Rocky Point. I was invited but refused because I expected a special-delivery registered letter and package and had to be at home when it came."

"Did it come?"

"Yes. I signed for it, so that's off my mind."

"A little bird whispered that you refused to see Sinclair when he struck town. Why the change of heart?"

"Perhaps the Fates took a hand. Who knows? To return to Morrie Grove's mystery man. Now that he has departed I begin to think that the uneasy sense that he was watching me was a product of my overworked imagination. I have had the theft at the Gallery on my mind every waking minute and a good many sleeping ones."

"Has Henry Sargent been needling you?"

"No, on the contrary he told me he trusted me 'implicitly.' He gave me permission to tell you, under oath of secrecy, of his discovery in the repair shop the night of the burglary after we left. He declared that a man who had accomplished what you had in a military way should be able to solve the problem. There's an orchid for you, and a rare one, considering the source from which it came."

"Hope I live up to my reputation—which, however, was not gained in the whodunit field. About that discovery? Give. Don't keep me in suspense."

She told him, told of the still missing Constable.

" 'Sdeath! Borrowed from our Congressman. A £5650 painting, roughly twenty-three thousand in our money. Now we are getting somewhere. That makes the enamel box and Apostle spoons look like chicken feed. Herring dragged across the trail, of course. Do you know where your boss put the picture after Sinclair left it with him?"

"No. I asked him if he were sure he remembered where he had placed it. He said, 'Very sure,' period."

"He claims that your gold sandal made the prints in the dust. Did you check on it?"

"Yes. It was a perfect fit."

"What report did the fingerprint expert make on the sandal?"

"No marks, not even Mr. Sargent's, he had slipped his hand into the shoe when he picked it up. It had been wiped clean."

"The guy who borrowed it was thorough, wasn't he? How come these people could get into your apartment, first the thief, then your boss? It was locked when I opened it for you when we came in from the storm."

"I left it unlocked when you and I went to Rocky Point that night. I thought Mr. Sargent might want to investigate. Added to that, there is a duplicate key in my desk, both Gene and he know where it is kept."

"Add the thief, that makes three. Let's get back to the footprints in the dust—they make our kitchen discovery look like thirty cents—the Apostle spoons were found at the end of the trail. It was a plant, of course. Whoever put them there expected them to be found. Any clue to the whereabouts of the enamel box?"

"If one has been discovered it is being kept off the record."

"Looks to me as if the person who snitched the painting is trying to throw suspicion on you."

"That's a masterpiece of understatement. Suspicion? They were trying to nail the theft on me. But, why? Why? Did he know that I needed—"

"Go on. Why the gasp?"

"I had a perfectly crazy answer to my own question."

"And that is?"

"No, it is too improbable."

Had the same thought crossed her mind which had flashed through his with the speed of summer lightning?

Had Gene taken the box to sell to pay her debt—always supposing she was in debt—and throw suspicion on Fran? Why do it when she knew that Fran was trying to raise money for her? Whoever took the box apparently lit out with the valuable painting—hold on, though, the theft of the box and the Constable could have been independent jobs. Was that a flash of intuition or plain hokum?

"Two thieves keep not their motion in one sphere."

"What do you mean by that adaptation from William Shakespeare, Mr. Jaffray?"

"Telling myself that a hunch I had wasn't so hot." As impossible as my idea that Gene would try to double-cross her friend, he added to himself.

"Whatever develops remember that Gene Sargent doesn't know the first letter of the word 'loyalty.' She would sacrifice her best friend if it would serve her purpose." Natalie's reminder rang through his memory. Could it be true? Was Gene like that?

"Has my story thrown you into the silence? You don't believe I took that box, do you?"

"Of course I don't, darling." He cleared his voice of gruffness. If he didn't watch out he'd be kissing her lovely unsteady mouth. Where would that get him? Answer, in the doghouse—for good. This was a crisis and it behooved him to tread softly. "I have been trying to earn Henry Sargent's orchid, to figure why your sandal was used. Anyone who knows you must know that you don't need money—you don't, do you?"

"You as the trustee of Rebecca Harding's estate are better qualified to answer than I."

"Stop fencing. Let's get down to facts. It wasn't so long ago you asked me to advance a thousand dollars with which to pay a bill. Remember?"

"I remember that you refused to give it to me."

"That's right. Now you have the money, haven't you?"

"What do you mean? You are not implying that I sold that enamel box, are you?" He caught her bare arm and drew her back to the seat.

"Sit down again, Franny, let's thresh out this thing. I know you didn't sell the enamel box, but I suspect you have sold a thousand dollars' worth of bonds. Come clean. Why?"

"If I did—I'm not saying I did—it is none of your business, they were not part of the trust, they were mine."

" 'Were mine'. Then you have sold them. Are you financing that double-crosser, Blake Sinclair?"

136

"Financing *Blake*?" Unless she was a superb actress her incredulous voice proved that his question was not the solution. "Blake is not a double-crosser and I don't intend to sit here another minute to hear my oldest friend maligned."

"Wait. Have you told the truth?" He caught her hand, bent his head the better to see her eyes in the dim light. She drew as far away as his arm permitted.

"Don't kiss me and then say Ken sent it," she flared. He laughed.

"In case you are interested, the next time I kiss you won't be for your brother, Miss Phillips. Now you may go."

She went on the run.

Why had he made the break of accusing Sinclair? That was a sure-fire way of sending her straight into the arms of her "oldest friend." He followed her slowly, followed the silver glint of her blue-and-green frock, round the ghostly clump of birches; past the white trellised summerhouse—silent now; past the marble Psyche forever bending in quest of assurance of her beauty; up the flower-bordered path to the accompaniment of "I Wonder Who's Kissing Her Now."

She was dancing with Sinclair when he reached the drawing room. He didn't like the way she was smiling up at her partner, as if he were the one man of importance in her life. She was doing it to show him, she had known when he appeared in the door, for a fleeting instant their eyes had met. He had himself to thank for it, he should have known better than to let himself go on the guy.

"How about a little stepping for the sake of old times, Myles?" Matilde Sargent suggested. She slipped a bare arm about his neck. "Why miss this divine music?"

He let her sentimental "for the sake of old times" pass without comment. There had never been "old times" between them. No one knew better than she that he had refused to be drawn into her net. As they danced they passed Natalie talking and laughing with her ex-husband.

"Looks as if that was on again," Matilde commented bitterly. "I'll bet he still loves her."

"Does he? I wouldn't know." Morrison Grove tapped his shoulder.

"Your hostess wants you, Major. Sorry to substitute a tightwad for a Congressional Medal man, Matilde, but that's the way it's got to be, when Miss Tassie speaks."

"Who told you I called you—" They danced away before Myles heard the completion of the honeyed sentence. Was Matilde making a bid for Morrie now that Hal was cooling? Life in Washington would be her meat.

"There is more than one woman in this room, Myles," Tassie Trent suggested dryly when he reached her.

"You said something then, Miss Tassie. May I have the pleasure?" Before she could reply he swept her into the "How Lucky You Are" waltz.

"You dance like a dream," he declared after they had circled the room. "Like it, don't you?"

"Love it. Always have. Always will. Those women seated against the wall with 'Too old to dance' plastered all over them give me a pain in the neck, but so many things give me a pain in the neck, now, Myles. I'm terrified. The world is in such a mess." Her troubled eyes met his; unbelievable as it was, he would swear that her grim mouth quivered.

"You may be mistaken as to their expression, Miss Tassie. Could be it means, 'I wish I'd be invited to dance.' I'll ask one of them later. I bet I'll prove I'm right." He stopped at the door and led her to the terrace.

"Sit here, we'll have the place to ourselves, everyone is inside dancing." He drew a chair near the one into which she sank with an exhausted sigh.

"You're tired, it isn't like you to be low in your mind, Miss Tassie. I'll bet you played eighteen holes of golf today. Right?"

"Right, Myles, but that didn't make me low in my mind."

"Perhaps not, but fatigue made you a fair target for the depression bug. You know, Miss Tassie, that a U.S. golf champion can't remain a U.S. golf champion forever."

"Telling me diplomatically that I'm too old to play, Myles?"

"I am not. I am suggesting that being hostess to a

party like this on top of eighteen holes of golf would be a strain on anyone."

"My trouble isn't physical. When I saw Nat smiling at that faithless ex of hers—"

"If Nat was smiling why were you worried? Looks to me as if she didn't care a rap."

"I'm afraid she'll take him back."

"Take him back? Your imagination has seized the bit in its teeth and is running away with you."

"Maybe that isn't the real trouble. When Matilde put her arm around your neck a little ripple of sound ran round the room, and I knew that the old story that you had broken up Ben Sargent's home had reared its snaky head."

"You know there was not a word of truth in that, Miss Tassie."

"Of course I know, know that Hal Andrews was the man. Now I've spoiled your evening by conjuring up that ghost."

"Don't worry, there isn't enough of that lie left in my memory to make even an emaciated ghost. Is that all you have on your mind? If not, speak now and forever after hold your peace."

"Thank God, you can joke about it, I can't. I saw Gene Sargent hanging on your arm when you first came in, you were looking down at her as if she were a little bit of heaven."

"You're getting mixed up with a song, Miss Tassie."

"I'm not getting mixed up with a song, that expresses the way you looked, anyone seeing you would have thought you'd gone off the deep end about her. I just can't take it."

His shout of laughter gave pause to a couple stealing across the terrace. They stopped for a startled instant, then hand in hand ran down the steps to the garden.

"Now, we've discovered the cause of your descent into Avernus, Miss Tassie, the nigger in the woodpile to change the simile, you're jealous. You know you've been my number one girl and—"

"Don't try to be funny," she snapped. "I'm not jealous, you flatter yourself, but I love you and Nat as I would the children I never had." The vibrato was back in her voice. "If you marry either of those Sargent creatures I'll die, I'll just die. I want you to be happy, Myles."

"In my way or yours, Miss Tassie?"

"I guess you're right." She sniffed. "You needn't be so stern about it. The dancers are coming out, flocking to the garden. I must return to my older guests. Here comes the Phillips girl—she has a flair for the right clothes—and that Blake Sinclair. Don't like him." Fran stopped beside her.

"It has been a perfect party, Miss Trent. Thanks for my share of it."

"Glad you enjoyed it." Before Fran was out of hearing she added in a voice that carried:

"Nice of you to tell me your heart's secret, Myles. Who wouldn't love Gene?"

Had Fran paused long enough to hear that or had he imagined it? Miss Trent slipped her hand under his arm.

"Escort your number one girl into the house, Myles." He looked down at her sternly.

"I don't know whether I will or not. You may have done me great harm by that last broadcast, Miss Tassie. You intended Fran Phillips to hear it, didn't you?"

"Sure, it was what the economists call a calculated risk. It worked. I found out something I have suspected. The musicians are playing 'I'm Falling in Love with Someone.'" She chuckled. "A perfect note on which to make our entrance."

XVI

"Sinclair is good but not so good as Jaffray," John Eckhard declared as he dropped into a seat beside Fran in the well-filled bleachers outside the tennis court at the Country Club. "Hi, Pat," he hailed the small girl the other side of her. With a wave of his pipe he indicated the two tall, white-clad contestants. "Jaffray has endurance. Sinclair started off like a bunch of firecrackers, all snap and sparkle but he won't last."

In silence they watched the players, listened to the score announced by the umpire on his high seat in line with the net at the side of the court, and the pad of balls against rackets. The players changed sides.

"Jaffray will have the sun in his eyes now," Eckhard commented. "What a perfect day. Too bright for me to paint this morning. Sinclair is letting his temper get a little out of hand, isn't he?"

A little out of hand, he was furious. Fran recognized the symptoms, the characteristic jerk of his head, the impatient bang of the racket against his knee. It was so like him, he was a bad loser.

"They appeared evenly matched when they started. Now the late Major is gaining." She felt his quick look at her.

"Why don't you like Jaffray, Miss Phillips? I think he's a prince."

The unexpected question set the blood burning in her cheeks. She couldn't very well explain that Miss Tassie's congratulations on his heart interest in Gene Sargent she had overheard on the terrace had rekindled the distrust of him she had had for years. Hadn't he called her "darling" only a short time before? It wasn't the "darling" that was bandied about casually among the men and girls she knew, there had been a timbre in his voice which had set her heart knocking. Hadn't he said that the next time he kissed her—something in his voice had intimated there would be a next time—would be for himself? It was his line, of course, just as making each girl he met think she had completely bowled him over was Blake Sinclair's. Blake's was less dangerous, because it was so apparently a line. Myles Jaffray was more subtle.

"Are you practicing mind reading, Mr. Eckhard? Why assume that I don't like the returned hero?"

"The barb in 'the returned hero' would confirm my suspicion if the twist in 'the late Major' hadn't. I don't like to hear a man who accomplished the heroic work Jaffray accomplished in the war spoken of with scorn. However, it is not for me to probe your mental or—heart reactions. Jaffray will win, all right, he'll get what he wants in this world and what he wants will be grade A. A contest like this is as good as an X-ray for charting the sort of life a man has lived."

"You terrify me with your conclusions," she declared

141

gaily, though her conscience smarted from his reproach. "Are you a psychoanalyst, as well as an artist?"

"You're ribbing me. I don't mind, I know I hurt you by my criticism of your jabs at Jaffray, but it won't do you any harm. My ambition is to paint portraits. To make a success in that field, artistic, not merely financial, one must be able to discover the real person behind a face, to detect spiritual values often obscured by material commitments."

Fran squeezed the hand of the eagerly listening small girl beside her.

"We'd hate to have him see the real person behind our faces, wouldn't we, Patricia?"

"I wouldn't say that. I'm not so bad and you must be sweet all through, Fran, or I wouldn't feel so warm and cozy when I'm with you. Jeepers. He ought to see behind Mummy's and Gene's make-ups. I bet he'd paint 'em bright green and red with big yellow polka dots." Eckhard chuckled.

"There speaks a surrealist in embryo. I can't imagine a more adequate color palette for the portrayal of jangled lives. To turn to a subject more in keeping with this perfect, sea-scented afternoon, I'd like to paint you in that white dress, Miss Fran."

"In *this* spectator sports frock? Don't you want something more glamorous?"

"It's perfect with the sunlight bringing out the gold in your hair, the touch of jade green in your beads and ring. Sit for me, will you?"

"Gee, don't cry about it."

Patricia's curt suggestion sent a tide of dark red to the edge of his iron-gray hair and lighted a murderous gleam in the eyes behind the owl-like lenses. Before he could verbally express his reaction she added:

"I guess you're nuts about Fran, but it's peanuts to what a lot of others are. Hal Andrews is the latest. He was at the Gallery two mornings looking at your pictures, Mr. Eckhard, then he didn't come. I overheard him tell Mother you were a dumb Dora, Fran. What did you say to him?"

A smile twitched at Fran's lips. She had tried Miss Tassie's prescription for getting rid of a wolf. The second morning he appeared, she had kept up a nonstop

142

monologue about herself, had even dragged in an ancient experience of Aunt Becky's. Apparently it had worked.

"Why are you smiling, Fran?"

"What is the joke, Miss Phillips?" Eckhard supplemented.

"Game, set, match to Myles Jaffray."

The announcement from the umpire was followed by prolonged applause. It relieved Fran of the necessity of explaining her smile.

"Mr. Sinclair just banged a ball into the net," Pat shrilled. She was on her toes craning her neck. "Now, they're shaking hands. I'll bet Blake is hopping 'cause Myles gave him the old heave-ho. I heard him tell Gene he could lick Jaffray with one hand tied behind him."

"Perhaps he lost because he had two to use," Eckhard suggested dryly. "Now that the contest is over have tea with me, will you, Miss Fran?" He bowed ceremoniously to Patricia. "Your charming friend is included in the invitation."

"Huh, I guess I know when I'd be the spare tire. I'll have tea with my grandmother. You'd better be nice to me, Mr. Eckhard, or my grandfather will fire your old pictures out of his gallery." She descended the fast-emptying stand in a series of leaps.

"I didn't know a little girl could be such a tough brat," Eckhard confided as he and Fran followed slowly.

"Pat's all right at heart, she hasn't yet learned not to say what comes to the top in that active brain of hers."

"Have you?"

"Yes and no. Aunt Becky used to say, 'I have but one lamp by which my feet are guided, the lamp of experience.' I think my lamp is better, the Golden Rule. Often the light is tragically obscured by my disagreeable self, but it isn't the fault of the lamp that I don't follow the gleam. It is there always. That sounds terribly preachy, my apologies. Thanks for the invitation to tea, but I promised to meet Blake Sinclair at the Club after—"

"His victory?"

"Who's 'jabbing' now?"

"Right. Will you have tea with me tomorrow? I'd like to talk over the portrait."

"Not tomorrow, this is my day off. I won't have another for a week. I would love to have tea with you then."

"It's a date. I see Miss Tassie ahead. She will have views on the tournament I would like to hear. She doesn't pull her punches. After I leave her I think of the many brilliant cracks I might have made in rebuttal of her views but it is always after. Where are you to meet Sinclair?"

"On the terrace. He has a table engaged. He'll have to shower and dress. Run along, don't have me on your mind."

Why, why had Blake behaved like a silly boy about his defeat—come to think of it, a modern boy wouldn't have shown his feelings like that. They were trained to be good sports in games, she thought, as she passed between the tables toward the corner of the terrace where she had been told to meet him. Why should she feel embarrassed, as if she were responsible for his burst of temper?

"Fran, sit here with us. We have two extra seats, one for you, one for Myles."

The eager hail, the hand on her arm, dispelled the fog of regret. Her eyes smiled response to the smiling eyes of Natalie Andrews. Miss Tassie was seated beside her, John Eckhard had risen and was standing behind the chair at her left.

"Thanks a million, but I promised to have tea with Blake."

Here he comes, looking as if he could bite the prong from an iron anchor, she deplored as she hastened toward him with the foolish thought that if she didn't hurry the storm of his anger might break.

"You played a grand game, Blake," she approved after they had ordered.

"I'm overtrained. I was at my peak three days ago. If the finals had been reached then I would have had Jaffray eating out of my hand."

Would he? Myles must have played as many sets as he to reach the finals.

"Why aren't you playing in the women's doubles, Fran?"

"Who, me? You forget I am now a working woman with a job. I can't get off for an afternoon. You've been an angel to play with me after office hours, that I may keep in practice."

"Like your job?"

He was crumbling a sandwich. Fran had a premonition that the indifferent question was introductory. What was coming?

"Love it. I grew up in an atmosphere of books and more books, and music. I'm learning a lot about the world of art and the idiosyncrasies of human nature."

"Where does that last come in?"

"My boss—customers—my boss."

"What do you think of him?"

"I think he's a grand person."

"Keep your voice low when you answer this question. Has he spoken to you of a painting I left with him for approval?"

Henry Sargent had forbidden her to speak of the theft at the Gallery, but if she encouraged Blake to talk she might root out some sort of clue to the disappearance of the Constable.

"He didn't tell me at the time you left it, Blake"—so much was true—"I'll confess something that Mr. Sargent doesn't know; remember the morning you and he talked about it on the cliff?"

"I left the painting with him a short time after. Go on."

"I was on the beach below. I didn't hear a word of what you said but I couldn't miss a word of my boss's bellow. When I realized that I was listening to a confidential conversation, I covered my ears and shut out his voice and your murmurs. When I uncovered them the voices above had ceased."

"He didn't tell you that I delivered the painting?"

"I didn't see him that day before I left for The Theater." It was getting increasingly difficult to keep faith with Henry Sargent and tell the truth.

"I turned the picture over to him five minutes after we left the cliff, it was the day of the terrific thunderstorm, remember?"

She nodded. As if she ever would forget that storm and what followed.

"I can't get an answer out of the old man. I'm losing

145

time. I've a lot of money locked up in it. I want to pass it on to someone else if he turns thumbs down."

Not until this minute had she realized that subconsciously she had felt that Blake Sinclair was in some way involved in the disappearance of the Constable.

"Why that funny little gasp? I'll bet you know where it is," he accused suspiciously.

His eyes burned with intensity. She couldn't tell him that "the funny little gasp" had been caused by relief, that she felt like a person who had come to the surface after being held under water.

"I do *not* know where it is. That 'gasp' was pure excitement, you were so dramatic. You had me going right along with you."

"I believe the old guy has lost it."

"*Lost* it? How could he lose it, Blake? He was so anxious to have it. I can tell you this. The afternoon of the preview of Eckhard's paintings, Mr. Sargent told me that you had picked up an 'item' he wanted very much, then swore me to secrecy. I was surprised. I didn't know you dealt in old masters."

"Don't as a rule. When I find something it's on the q.t. Remember that, and *don't talk*, Fran."

"Good heavens, that warning was Humphrey Bogart at his most villainous. Why should I talk? I'm only what Pat Sargent calls a salesgirl. Relax, you're white under your tan. You are asking a lot of money for the painting, aren't you?"

"Not more than it's worth."

"I wouldn't know about that, but Henry Sargent didn't climb to the ownership of the Sargent Galleries and a position of superior authority in the world of art without taking every precaution to be sure that what he buys and places is genuine."

"What the devil do you mean by that? Has he insinuated that the one I submitted isn't?"

"Sit down, Blake, please, you are attracting attention. That's better. Now smile as if I were irresistibly fascinating."

"You are, dream girl. When I get this mix-up straightened out—"

"Remember your promise, that you would cut out sentiment if I consented to go out with you. To return

146

to the missing painting, why don't you ask Henry Sargent to speed up his decision?"

"Bad business to have him think I am anxious."

"In that case all you can do is wait and—"

"Blake, I've been looking everywhere for you." Gene Sargent in a dark red cotton frock sank into a chair at the table. "Bring me coffee and plain toast," she said to the blue-liveried boy who had appeared with the speed of a rabbit from a magician's hat. "Don't glower at me, Fran. Dad let me leave the Gallery at five to come here, ten minutes after the man who is pinch-hitting for Si Pond appeared. Who won the tournament? Didn't stop to ask."

"Your little tin god, Jaffray."

"Why the venom, Mr. Sinclair? I told you he would."

"Any sales today?" Fran inquired eagerly to avert the storm gathering in Blake's eyes.

"Another Eckhard. That man's going places."

"Going places, Gene, he's there. He'll be famous. He wants to paint my portrait, and am I proud," Fran announced grandiloquently, then wished she had bitten off her tongue before speaking.

"He does? Don't let him."

"Why are you dictating to Miss Phillips, Blake?" Gene demanded.

"Why shouldn't I? We are practically—"

Fran rose.

"Thanks for the tea party, Blake. I must pick up Pat and take her home. Want a ride, Gene?"

"No, thank you. I'll stick to the runner-up. I can see he needs a little cheerful company. Stay while I drink my coffee, Blake, I have a plan for this evening that will soothe your battered ego."

Before Fran reached her parked sedan she saw Pat in a car with her grandmother.

"Granny wouldn't let me wait for you," she shouted. "See you tomor—" Her voice diminished in the distance.

All right with me, Fran thought. Pat's nice, but she has been with me all day and so much of her company is like living exclusively in a child's world.

"Took you a whale of a time to get here," Myles Jaffray commented from behind the wheel of her sedan. "Hop in."

"When *you* hop out." Had he forgotten she had been furiously angry when she left him in Miss Tassie's garden?

"For the love of Pete, don't be difficult, Fran. Get in, please. I'm giving good manners the go-by not getting out to open the door for you. But this parking place is filling and I'm side-stepping congratulations. I have something—"

"Ken?" she interrupted breathlessly, and was in the seat beside him in a flash. She watched his face as he concentrated on maneuvering the sedan between closely parked cars. Two little lines cut deep between his dark brows. His lips clamped tight to suppress a sharp exclamation as a bobby-soxer learning to drive a large open car backed into the sedan.

"Okay, go ahead, kid. Go ahead!" he called impatiently as the badly scared youngster stopped and looked back. It wasn't like him to be so impatient, Fran thought, then reminded herself that she hadn't known him long enough to know whether it was like him or not. Had he bad news from Ken to tell her, or had something happened at the tournament to set him on edge? He had changed from tennis clothes. His maize Daks were topped by a tropical sports shirt in chamois and tan design, his wool coat matched his trousers in color.

"Considering awarding me an Oscar?" he inquired when they reached the highway. "Thank the Lord that kid's out of the picture." Evidently he had felt her eyes on him. She had supposed him to be too intent on their perilous exit—with the bobby-soxer still at the wheel of the car ahead—to notice her inspection.

"I was merely admiring the well-dressed man, a cat may look at a king, sirrah. You don't need an Oscar. You won the championship cup, one trophy a day is enough." How could her voice sound so flippant when, "Any news of Ken?" was tugging at the end of her tongue? "Why did you kidnap me?" she substituted.

"The first and outstanding reason I can't disclose yet—it's too personal." The windshield mirror gave back his smile and something in his eyes that sent hers glancing off to sea.

148

"The fishing boat is coming in. The flag is up. That means there's a tuna aboard, doesn't it?"

"Right the first time. This is your day off. Let's drive up the coast for dinner. Any evening commitments?"

"No-o-o, but I—"

"Then here we go. I have much to tell you that needs your undivided attention."

"About?"

"No, Franny." He laid his hand over hers in her lap and as quickly removed it. "No news from Ken. It's about that orchid I'm out to earn. I've been trying to get in touch with you for days—you're pretty smart at dodging, aren't you—since Miss Tassie's blowout to tell you—"

She stiffened. Was he about to confide his love for Gene? For a few minutes she had forgotten that.

"Relax, Fran, it isn't what you think it is. We'll take up that subject later, not too much later, when I have time to go into it and all its ramifications. The night of the party in honor of our visiting celebrity, Morrie told me—"

He repeated Grove's story of Eckhard's presence outside the Digbys' door the night of the storm.

"Why was Morrie at that same door?" she inquired.

"Trying to make a political call on Betsy and Dig."

"Did John Eckhard see *him*?"

"If he did Morrie doesn't know it."

"Did he find out why our artist celebrity was huddling there in the rain?"

"No, he's stumped as to the reason. I want you to do that."

"Me? Why? What he does is nothing to me."

"I must be sure of that. If he was outside the door when I removed the sheets of blotting paper from the wood box, he was the guy who snitched them later; added to that, it is more than one chance in ten that the muddy tracks on the kitchen floor were his. Remember a key had been left in the door, an invitation to enter, if ever there were one. He may know something about your gold sandal. That's why what he does may mean something to you."

"It gives me the creeps to think of it. Of course I'll try to find out. I won't be underhanded about it, though.

He wants to paint my portrait. We may become such friends that he will tell me."

"He told us at tea that he would try to persuade you to sit for him. He'd like to paint you in our garden."

"Why in yours?"

"Who can explain the artistic mind? Consider it, will you?"

"That can wait. I'd like to get Eckhard and the footprints and his motive for hanging round the Digby door straightened out. He must have had one."

"You've said it. I can't believe that it was the possession of an enamel box. It might have been the Constable. In spite of the evidence piling up against him, I can't believe him to be the sort of person who would steal or hit Si Pond over the head—we've lost sight of that angle."

"Blake is on the verge of a nervous breakdown over the painting. It's a relief that you know about it, Myles, I must talk with someone."

"Does Sinclair know that the Constable has disappeared?"

"Not a suspicion that it has been stolen—if it has been, I still have hope that my boss will find it—but he has a lot of money tied up in it and thinks that Henry Sargent should take it or leave it and give him a chance to dispose of it somewhere else."

"Sounds reasonable. When did you hear all this?"

"At the Club while we were having tea. I tried to calm him by suggesting that Henry Sargent hadn't risen to his present eminence in the art world by buying faked paintings, that he wanted to make sure it was genuine."

"That's right. What did he say?"

"Went into the air, he was so white I was frightened. 'What the devil do you mean by that?' he exploded. 'Has he insinuated that the picture I submitted is a fake?'

"Good heavens, I thought for a minute we were headed for the ditch. I could see glaring headlines, *'Trustee and Charming Ward in Smash-up.'* Perhaps ward isn't the right word?" She hoped he hadn't noticed the quaver in the voice she had tried to make gay. For a moment she had been frightened.

"Ward will serve—for the present. Sorry I frightened you. An idea burst in my head like a light bulb and—"

"Don't have another like it while you are driving, please. To return to the lost painting. I'll confess that until Blake went into the air, I had had a mean suspicion that he knew something about its disappearance. Now, I am sure he doesn't."

"So am I, darn sure. That washes up the subject for the present. Where would you like to eat, Miss Phillips?"

XVII

In a cotton frock as softly pink as the Perfection rose she had tucked in her hair, Fran sat on the stone wall in front of the Gallery watching Betsy Digby weed the flower border.

Zinnias in pastel shades of yellow, salmon and mauve towered; giant asters were bursting into bloom; gladiolus in heavenly shades held proud heads high; regal lilies nodded pearly petals above the patchwork of gold, yellow, purple, white, light blue, dark blue, violet, reds of all shades and the green foliage of annuals.

"Smell the petunias. See that beauty."

Fran gently touched an outsize violet specimen with the tip of her putter.

"Aren't they fragrant this morning?" Her enthusiasm was addressed to the top of an enormous hat in the hayfield tradition.

Betsy Digby's blue and white striped cotton dress ballooned as she sank back on her heels, no mean accomplishment for one of her plump proportions. She tossed a tall weed with big roots into a small yellow wheelbarrow beside her, pushed back the big hat till it made a halo for her round, red face and drew off white cotton gloves.

"They smell real nice, dearie. Handsome now, aren't they, so big and ruffled. Time was when I wouldn't grow petunias, they were so unint'r'sting." She chuckled. "Like some folks I know, only the flowers have improved and the humans haven't. Comin' on to be a terrible hot day. I don't see how you can sit there without a hat. I'd be afraid of a sunstroke. Good you got in your puttin' an' I started weedin' early." She wiped her face with her sleeve. "Guess there won't be many visitors to the Gallery today." Fran glanced at the watch on her wrist.

"Too early to tell yet. We do not open till nine-thirty. 'Not snow, nor rain, nor heat, nor gloom of night stays our patrons from the swift completion of their appointed rounds.'"

"Pity sake, dearie, what you runnin' on about?"

"I was adapting the inscription on the New York Post Office, which applies to mail carriers, to our clientele."

"You mentioned snow, rain, heat an' gloom of night—that was New York, guess if'd had been New England, they'd have to reckon with fog."

"Do you have much here?"

"Haven't you ever summered in Maine?"

"It just happens that this is my first season here."

"Then you haven't seen anything. Some years when fog rolls in it gets into the house and everything you touch is wet; it drips from eaves like rain; you can't see a house from the road even if 'tis lighted; an' the foghorn keeps up a terrible muffled blaring, an' the bell buoy off in front here keeps a-tollin'."

"What a visitation! Does the fog demon give warning of his approach?"

Mrs. Betsy frowned at the horizon.

"Sure, when it's coming you can see a purplish bank off there. Sometimes it's a false alarm, it drifts out to sea without landing. I've known summers when we haven't had a wisp of it. Must be terrible for the airplanes when it comes, though."

"They've found something to beat it that was used in wartime in England when airfields were fogged in. FIDO it is called."

"That's a dog's name."

"It stands for Fog—Intensive—Dispersal—Of."

"Does it, now. Something to beat the fog, you said? Now I think of it, Myles and Nat gave the airfield some sort of equipment for fightin' fog as a memorial to the boys of our county who didn't come back. Amazing what folks are learnin' all the time. Instead of squattin' here moralizing I'd better pay attention to my knittin'."

Fran glanced at her watch again. She had ten minutes before it would be time to open the galleries. She could see the entrance and would dash for the house the moment she heard Henry Sargent's car—he had been on the job early and late since the break-in. This was the first chance she had had to really talk with Mrs. Betsy since the terrific thunderstorm, days ago. When she had served the meals she had appeared to be in a hurry. Was she avoiding the subject? Did she know more of what had happened that day than Mr. Sargent suspected?

"How is Si Pond?"

Fran's question set Mrs. Betsy back on her heels. She pushed up the hat, started to wipe her hot face with her sleeve, substituted a large bandana handkerchief she drew from the capacious pocket of her striped dress.

"This sure is goin' to be a sizzler. You askin' about Si Pond? Dearie, he's got us guessin'. Beats all how he keeps kinder peaked when he eats like a horse, his wife, Marthy, says. Won't see nobody, won't talk with nobody, an' him always talkin' his head off with folks—just sits chewin' gum. Don't seem's though a bump could change him like that."

Had Henry Sargent imposed silence for fear of reprisal if a certain person—or persons—knew Si was talking of his accident?

"Have you heard how he acquired the bump, Mrs. Betsy?"

"Folks say a branch must have broken in the storm and knocked him off his bike when he was on his way here; he don't remember what happened."

"Could be. The wind was fierce enough to blow down a whole tree, to say nothing of a branch. You and Mr. Dig had your troubles that same day, hadn't you? Have you discovered who sent the faked message that your mother-in-law was ill?"

"Not for certain, but we have our suspicions, Lem's havin' that call traced. I've been wanting to talk it over with Myles, but Lem said, 'Not yet. Wait till we're sure. We might be haled into court, if we're wrong.' He's been reading in the papers 'bout folks being sued for libel. We don't want to be defendants in that sort of mess."

"Have you thought of any reason *why* the person you suspect would try to get you away from the Gallery?"

"That's what stumps us. We came home the next noon expecting to find the place looted. Nothing gone, we could see. Do you know anything about it?"

There was a flash in the keen blue eyes after the quick question. Fran felt her cheeks redden.

"I see you do, dearie," Mrs. Betsy answered herself and resumed weeding. "Lem and I aren't so dumb as Mr. Sargent thinks."

What do I say next, Fran wondered. Go all out for the name of the suspect?

"Who do you think sent the message that Mr. Lem's mother was having one of her spells, please tell me, Mrs. Betsy?" she wheedled.

Mrs. Digby viciously plunged her trowel around a stubborn root and considered.

"Don't know why I shouldn't," she conceded. "You look as if you could keep a secret—keeping one of your own, so close you don't know it yourself—aren't you?" Laughter twinkled in her eyes as she looked up. "I don't mean by that you can't tell Myles what I'm going to say, I want you to, then we'll know if he thinks Lem and I are crazy. Lean down. This breeze isn't strong but it could carry. We're sure it was—"

"Miss Phillips! Miss Phillips!"

The shout snapped Betsy Digby's lips shut with the name she had been about to whisper behind them.

"Mercy on us, what's happened? Fire?"

"No, the call to duty. I was so interested in what you were saying I forgot to watch the time—and the door; that will mean trouble and plenty. Tell me the rest when you bring up my dinner, Mrs. Betsy. Don't let Lem frighten you dumb."

She dashed across the lawn, up the steps, dropped the putter on the porch, and arrived a trifle breathless in the small gallery beside Henry Sargent, who in a Chinese-gray seersucker with dark red cummerbund and matching bow tie was standing before the Louis XV cabinet.

"Loo—" His voice failed him. He pointed.

Fran's eyes followed his index finger, widened incredulously, came back to him.

154

"The missing enamel box," she said softly, "or am I just seeing things?"

He nodded, pulled at the soft collar of his white shirt as if that were cutting off his voice and nodded again.

"When did you discover it?" she whispered.

"When I came in five minutes ago." The answer was hoarse from excitement.

"I didn't hear you come."

"I know that. You and Betsy were gossiping by the stone wall." His voice increased in volume with his grievance. "I'm surprised that you would leave this place unguarded after what happened."

"Sorry, Mr. Sargent. From where I was sitting I could see and hear anyone approaching the Gallery."

"Didn't see or hear me, did you?"

"No."

She couldn't tell him she had forgotten to look or listen in her eagerness to hear the name of the person the Digbys suspected had sent the faked message.

"Not that I think it was returned this morning, must have been in the night." To Fran's relief he had abandoned the subject of her neglect. "Except for time out to go home for lunch yesterday, I was here all day. I let Gene off a little before five, she was anxious to hear about the tennis at the Club; I stayed until six and locked up."

"Did Gene go to Rocky Point with you at noon?"

"No. Betsy Digby served a lunch for her in your office."

"Does she know the box has been returned?"

"You forget that Gene didn't know it was missing. She wouldn't take time to check on the contents of the cabinet. She doesn't care what happens to my treasures. You'd think she would take more interest in what provides her bread and butter."

"This gallery takes care of the frills like marmalade and jam, and—plenty of each, doesn't it, not the bread and butter?" In spite of being puzzled and disturbed Fran managed to keep her voice light in the hope of lifting the cloud of bitterness from his spirit. Gene's lack of interest in his pet project was an oft-told tale. She made no attempt to disguise her boredom at being obliged to spend summer after summer at the same place because of what she called her father's senseless devotion to Sargent Gallery, Jr.

His stern mouth softened as a parent's might at mention of a favorite son.

"If patrons continue this summer to buy as they have to date there will be marmalade and jam—" Memory sharpened the voice in which he went on, "not unless the Constable is found, though, the insurance won't be paid till the company is sure the painting was stolen, long before that Sinclair will be clamoring for my decision."

The evening of the burglary he had said:

"We'll have the guilty party on the anxious seat."

Should she tell him that already Blake was anxious and suspicious?

"To get back to the enamel." He gave her no time to decide. "The cabinet is locked. Where is your key?"

"Upstairs. I didn't give it to Gene as I do usually because I knew you would have yours. After what happened the other day I thought one key to the cabinet at large was enough. I change the hiding place each week just in case one of our patrons should be curious and wander through my apartment. I don't lock it when I am on duty."

"You don't think a patron—"

She ran upstairs in the midst of his roar. The pink walls of the living room gave out a rosy glow where morning sunlight touched them. "Nice," she said aloud as she said each time she entered the attractive room which had become home to her.

In the act of reaching for the small golden box on top of the gilt and crystal clock, her arm dropped. The hands still pointed to eight o'clock. Never had she known it to stop. It was as faithful as the sun. Had she upset its balance yesterday when she checked on the key inside the box before starting for lunch at the Country Club? Unlikely. She had left just after noon and she would take her oath that it had musically chimed twelve before she closed the door. Perhaps she hadn't heard it, perhaps she was remembering another day? She was so accustomed to its chime that for hours she didn't notice it. Suppose someone had been hunting for the key and—

In frantic haste she seized the box. It was empty.

She catapulted down the stairs. Henry Sargent was teetering in front of the cabinet.

"Look! *Look!*" She whispered. "It's gone."

"What's gone?"

"The key. Gone from this box. It's stopped."

"Take your time, Miss Phillips. Take your time. Cut out whispering. You have me doing it. What's gone? What's stopped?"

She told him.

"The clock stopped at eight? Didn't you notice it when you got up this morning?"

"No, sir. I glanced at the clock, saw it was eight. I hail the rising morn at seven, and believe me from that moment on I hustled to get in a swim before it was time for Mrs. Betsy to serve my breakfast on the porch. I remember now, she said I was early. After breakfast, I did my stint on the putting green, talked with her and then—you know the rest."

"Where were you at eight o'clock last night?"

"Driving home from the lobster pound."

"Sure of that?"

"Yes, Mr. Sargent."

Never would she be more sure of anything. When she refused to go to a movie after dinner with the excuse she had work to do, Myles had demanded:

"Why are you slaving over this job when you don't need it?"

"Because I like it. Why do you slave at law? I understand you don't need the money."

"The *work* you have to do this evening is an excuse for not going with me. I'm wise to *that*." His answer had put a full stop to the conversation, except for a stiff "Good night."

"Um-m, it stopped at eight o'clock." Henry Sargent's voice recalled her to the present.

"What stopped at eight o'clock, Mr. Sargent?" inquired a voice behind them. "Someone's heart? At about that time mine was chilled to a standstill. The top of the morning to you, Fran."

"Come in, Myles. Perhaps you can help us. Take him into your office, Miss Phillips, and tell him what happened. I'll carry on here." Henry Sargent settled his tie, wriggled his coat into place on his shoulders and assumed his professional suavity. "I hear a car. Patrons. Go along. Quick."

"Now what's the excitement?" Myles inquired of Fran, who from force of habit had stepped behind her desk in the office. "Sit down." She shook her head.

"Can't. Too excited. This mystery is getting to be like a tangle of yarn with no loose end with which one can start to untangle."

"There's a loose end in every tangle, two of them. Remember, I don't know what you're talking about. I swore last night I wouldn't come near you again, you make no bones of your dislike, and here I am, a glutton for punishment."

"You've evidently forgotten that the first evening on the rocks you declared that though you would spend your vacation with your sister, I wouldn't see you. I have seen you almost every day since." His amused eyes sent color to her face.

"Nice of you to have kept count. I didn't know then that we would be co-dicks. It's the lure of the mystery in which we're mixed up, not your charm, that's the answer. Now that is nicely taken care of, sit down, bring me up to date on our burglary. Why get het up this hot day? Betsy Dig speaking."

"You look as cool as a cucumber in that linen suit," she commented resentfully. "Perhaps you'd be het up if you'd had the shock I had."

"What was the shock? Let's have it."

He perched on the corner of her desk as she began the recital with her talk with Betsy Digby, included the report on Si Pond and ended with Henry Sargent's, "It stopped at eight o'clock."

"That is where I came in." Myles produced a cigarette.

"No smoking in this building."

"That's right. Your reminder reminds me that Si Pond had smelled cigarette smoke before he passed out from a crack on his head. We've lost sight of that angle in our case. I'd like to get Betsy's interrupted confidential information straight. She had just said, 'We're sure it was—' when Henry Sargent's call clamped her lips shut."

"Correct. A few moments before she had told me that Mr. Digby was tracing the call."

158

"Surprising as it may seem I thought of that and checked the next day. No record of a call from the town in which Dig's mother lives."

"Whoever sent the message would figure on that and would send it from another place, wouldn't he? I say 'he' because I can't argue myself out of the feeling that the man Barth had something to do with it. Otherwise, why should he appear here almost at the moment they were leaving? Have you heard what happened to him the night of Miss Tassie's party?"

"No. To return to the clock, where is it?"

"In my living room."

"Let's take a look-see."

Side by side they stood before the gilt and crystal clock flanked by photographs in silver frames.

"It says eight-fifteen now. It's ticking."

"Thank goodness. I must have started it when I lifted off the box in which I had hidden the key to the cabinet. Am I pleased? It is like a member of the family, it would hurt to have it stop, 'never to go again,' like Grandfather's clock."

"It strikes the hour?"

"Yes, and one stroke on the half."

"Didn't you hear it last evening? You were home early enough. Perhaps you kept another date after you turned me down. I wouldn't know."

"I didn't look at it. It was so hot I undressed in the dark."

He wouldn't know, either, that she had cut their evening together short because she was becoming afraid of his attraction for her, afraid of her sense of utter content when she was with him, afraid she would forget the little hum that ran around the room when Matilde Sargent put her arm about his neck and they had danced; forget that he had told Miss Tassie of his love for Gene, that he had taken over the trusteeship of the estate to help Ken, that she was "a confounded responsibility." Of course she shouldn't have gone to dinner with him, distrusting him as she did, but she had thought he might have news of Ken and—why fool herself? Had she gone on Ken's account or because—

"Listen. This will tell the story." While she had been thinking Myles had been studying the clock. He carefully moved the hour hand to nine and the minute hand to twelve. The clock struck "One."

"One? Isn't it going on?" Fran whispered as if afraid that a louder tone would upset the mechanism for good.

"That's all. We've got something! At last we've *got* something! Between twelve-thirty and one yesterday someone ran this clock round to eight without giving it a chance to strike. The next hour chime had to be one. Who was here between twelve-thirty and one o'clock?"

Gene? Had she had the enamel box all this time? As a last resort had she planned to sell it toward paying her debt? The day after Miss Tassie's party she had been given one thousand dollars realized from the sale of bonds. Yesterday had been the first time she had been on duty at the Gallery since. Had she returned the box then? Should she tell Myles what she suspected? She looked up and met his eyes. He shook his head.

"You needn't answer my question, Fran, I'll work it out myself." He was standing before the clock running the hands round and waiting for the hour and half-hour to chime. "Lots of pictures you have here. Mighty good ones of Ken and 'your oldest friend.' Sinclair is photogenic and—does he know it. What's this behind the clock?" He held up a small key that looked like a choice example of gold filigree.

"That's it. Loud cheers. The key to the Louis XV cabinet."

"We're getting on. Now if we knew—"

"Here you are, dearie." Mrs. Betsy puffed from the haste in which she had mounted the back stairs. "I run up to ask if you'd be here for dinner. I'm going to the village, I'll get anything—" She stepped into the room. "Myles, where'd you come from, I didn't see you?"

"Didn't know I was a clock expert, either, did you, Betsy? This one went on a sit-down strike. Must have stopped yesterday at about one. I'm getting it on the beam again."

"About one. Pity sake, I bet he stopped it?"

"He? Was Mr. Sargent in this room yesterday?" For one hectic second Fran wondered if Henry Sargent had worked up the mystery of the theft of the enamel box to protect the Constable.

"The boss? No, dearie, no. It was that young man

who comes here with Miss Gene, I'm no good remembering names. I was puffing up the front stairs to water your window boxes and I met him coming out of your living room. I guess I looked like a meat ax, because he laughed and said:

" 'Keep your shirt on, Mrs. Betsy!'—which I didn't think was a proper thing for him to say to a lady if I am only the caretaker—'Miss Phillips sent me for her dark glasses, she'll need them when she watches me win the tournament, I'm such a brilliant player.' At that he laughed again and ran down the stairs. You have photographs of him all around this room, so I thought 'twas all right." She looked from the girl to Myles and back to the girl.

"You look kinder funny, dearie. Didn't I do right to let him take them?"

"Sure, Betsy." Myles covered Fran's silence, she was having trouble with her voice. "When a girl keeps so many pictures of a man in her room, he must be a dear friend, practically engaged, I'd say. The clock seems to be on the job again and—"

"Miss Phillips! Miss Phillips!" The roar came from below.

"There goes the public address system. Down we go, Fran. By the way, did you get those dark glasses? No answer? 'Nuff said. Come on, we'd better face the firing squad pronto and find out what your boss has on his mind."

XVIII

What Henry Sargent had on his mind had no connection with the discovery of the returned enamel box, but with a phone call from a gilt-edge patron who was considering the purchase of the Chinese mandarins plus the eighteenth-century English *torchères*. He wanted Fran's suggestion as to a more advantageous way of showing them.

Myles left them discussing a different light and a black velvet background and drove away. Fran was right, the mystery was tangling into a knot and a tight one at that. Of course there was a loose end, where to find it was the riddle of the month. Was it the name of the person who had sent the phony telephone message? She was sure that Barth was responsible. He didn't agree with her. Suppose she were right? Would the man have made the curious appointment to meet him at the table at the end of the terrace at Miss Tassie's party? It was more probable that he had information to impart about the break-in.

Flash. Wouldn't that account for his sudden disappearance? Had the whistle in the garden been a warning to him to make his getaway? Caesar had reported a row at the back door. Perhaps the thief or thieves had discovered that he knew too much for their safety and had forcibly removed him. Now that the enamel box and Apostle spoons had been returned, there could be no doubt that their objective had been the Constable.

Confidence in the honesty of the ex-butler didn't mean that he hadn't been trying to find him. In between practice for the tournament, business of the estate, conferring with the G.G.A. as to election proceedings, correspondence and a round of social affairs, he had followed innumerable clues to come up against a dead end each time. He couldn't enlist Morrie Grove as assistant without explaining why he wanted to find the guy; his promise to Henry Sargent prohibited that.

The fragrance of balsam and pine baked from the trees by the sun mingled with the smell of the sea. A cicada shrilled. What a hot sound. Apples in an orchard showed a tinge of red, the year was ripening. The back country road patterned with sunlight and shadow was deserted as he had hoped it would be, hails from friends and acquaintances passing would wreck his train of thought. So far as he was concerned Barth was eliminated from his list of suspects. Had he a list of suspects? A list? He had the fraction of one. He'd better push that one out of his mind for the present, thoughts had an unbelievable way of getting on the air.

Yesterday Sinclair had stepped into the picture. Why had he been in Fran's apartment? His explanation that she had sent him for her dark glasses was phony. Had he been putting back the key to the Louis XV cabinet after returning the box he had stolen the night of the storm? That didn't hold water. There was not the slightest indication that he had been in the vicinity of the Gallery after Gene and he left; besides, if he had been hard up enough to snitch the enamel to sell he would have kept it. Perhaps he had been looking through her rooms in search of the Constable, Fran had said he was on the verge of a nervous breakdown because Henry Sargent had made no report on it.

Why her apartment? Could he have been hunting for the painting the night of the storm with no thought or even knowledge of the value of the enamel box or the Apostle spoons? It might have been he who, surprised while searching, had knocked out Si Pond—

Si, old Nosey, who wasn't talking, had been allowed to slip into the background of his thoughts while he had been speculating as to why Eckhard had been huddled against the shrubs outside the Digby kitchen that same night. Si was his hot tip for the present.

He returned to the village. In the pharmacy, bursting at the seams with merchandise of infinite variety, smelling of a blend of roasting peanuts and fly exterminator, he bought half a dozen packages of each variety of gum—he hadn't known there were so many makes in the world. The outsize proprietor in a white jacket pulled down his steel-rimmed spectacles till they rested on the tip of his stubby nose and regarded Myles over the top of the lenses with curiosity not unmixed with mirth as he tied up the package.

"Pick up the gum-chewin' habit in the army, Major, or are you calculatin' to sign up for a baseball team?"

"Wrong station, Tiny. I heard that Si Pond was laid up. Decided to drop in on him and implement the stimulation of my presence with a gift of gum."

"Tiny" Carter, so nicknamed because of his abnormal girth, glanced to right and left before he leaned across the counter.

"Something queer about Si, he isn't talking, just sits and rocks and chews, you know, 'tisn't like him not to talk," he confided in a wheezy whisper. "He claims a fallin' branch knocked him off his bicycle and most cracked his skull. There's a whisper going round that he hasn't seen hide nor hair of that bike since, if he knows what become of it he's a good actor. Don't seem as if the busted branch could have rode off on it, does it?"

"Stranger things have happened."

"You're telling me. I guess even Marthy is stumped, she's the live wire in that house. Don't like her. Haven't any use for a wife that brags she's smarter than the man she married. All the womenfolks in the neighborhood are tickled pink that the roomer walked out on her."

"What roomer?"

"Gee whiz, Myles, don't snap my head off, I was only passin' on a little gossip. She let a room and Si rented his fishin' boat, complete with phonograph, to a fella who got a job as waiter for the caterer who supplies the food for some of the parties the summer big shots give. Funny, how we never count you and Nat among them—though you top 'em all in importance—you're like town folks."

"Sure we are. Where is the roomer now?"

"Suddenly lit out. Left what few clothes he had. Marthy didn't lose, she'd made him pay in advance, trust her for that. I'll admit she's smart as a steel trap, if I don't like her." He turned to a painfully sunburned customer whose tattoo on the counter was increasing in speed and volume.

"Yes, sir? Can I help you? Hot isn't it, sir? This isn't real Maine weather, no, *sir*."

Si Pond's bike had disappeared, Myles ruminated as he waited at the crossroads for the light to change. Barth, no doubt that the roomer was Barth, had "lit out." Not probable that he had taken the bicycle, he had been at Miss Tassie's party days after it disappeared. Si had been struck down inside the Gallery. Had he parked the bike as usual in the garage? Quite a yarn he had made up about having been struck by a falling branch. Was Henry Sargent the inventor of it?

He turned into a road at the end of which he could see a white cottage snuggled close to the ground as if it feared that the tide rolling in from a vast expanse of ocean might wrest it from its position near the edge of the cliff. Just off shore a boat rocked at its mooring. He drove slowly, checking the information he had gathered.

"A bike missing," he repeated softly. A man on a bicycle could have followed my roadster to Rocky Point that night and snitched the blotting paper with the muddy footprints while I was in the house. Something

164

told me that my hunch he had hung on the back was too cockeyed to be probable.

"Hi, Si!"

The tall man in a chair on the porch ablaze with nasturtiums in boxes on the rail stood up so quickly that a gull which had been perched on a near-by boulder rose in the air with a scream. He waved a bony hand.

"Come up, come up, Myles. Cricky, where did you drop from? Set here." He drew forward a green-cushioned white rocker and sank into its mate. "What brought you this hot day?" His voice had sharpened, narrowed lids partly obscured his pale eyes. With difficulty Myles shook off the hypnotic effect of the rise and fall of his prominent Adam's apple as he chewed.

"I heard you were still a little balmy from the knock-out the tree branch gave you, Nosey, so thought I'd drop in and give you the once-over. Brought this."

Si opened the package.

"Cricky, that's somethin'." He spit the gum in his mouth over the top of the nasturtiums and substituted a fresh stick. He glanced at the screened door to the house.

"Did Mr. Sargent send you? Jest nod or shake your head. I don't want Marthy to know I'm talkin'. He didn't. Has he found out who broke in that night? He ain't. He told me things was missin' when he brought me home the next mornin', told me I wasn't to know it, not to talk. I haven't. Hasn't found anything, I take it?" He accepted Myles's motionless head as a token of agreement. "Cricky, it's getting kind of serious. If that thief's still at large he might bust into your house, everybody knows about the Jaffray emeralds, or Miss Tassie's, and get something valuable, aren't you fearin' that?"

"No." Myles leaned close and whispered. "Found your bike?" Si answered with a negative shake which set every straw-colored hair in motion till his head looked like a dish mop in action. "Okay, write the make, size, number of the wheel on this."

Si scowled at the memorandum book and pencil which had been pressed into his hand and scratched his big left ear.

"Cricky, don't know's I can remember."

"Sure, you can remember. You've *got* to remember.

165

A lot hangs on where that bike was taken after it was snitched from the garage. If we can locate it—don't be afraid to tell me, I'm doing this for Mr. Sargent, he has practically"—hang it, was he picking up Sinclair's word —"engaged me to solve the mystery."

"If that's so—guess I can remember." He wrote. Myles returned the book quickly to his pocket and lighted a cigarette.

"By the way, Nosey, after you came to the other night in Miss Phillips's office, you said that before you passed out you smelled cigarette smoke. Was it like this?" He blew a few rings.

"Cricky, I—"

"Si." Gray-haired, sharp-featured Martha Pond followed her impatient voice to the porch. "Were you *talking*? Why, Myles Jaffray." As he rose she wiped a floury hand on a flowery apron and extended it, twinkled birdlike eyes at him. "How's Natalie, Myles?"

"Fine, thank you. Sorry to hear that Si had an accident. I was told in the village that besides his getting a crack on the head his bike disappeared. Sit down, Mrs. Pond." She perched on the edge of a chair he drew forward.

"I can't stay but a minute, I'm rollin' out pastry. I don't like it here anyway, those pesky gulls diving and flying and screaming get on my nerves. Hear 'em now. Ain't it the limit about the bike? I bought it with money I earned doing laundry for the summer folks, and—"

"Not all of it you didn't, Marthy," her husband corrected mildly. "You bought the bell and the headlight." His tone of indulgent amusement set her bright eyes snapping.

"If you'd waited till after the storm that night like I told you to, you wouldn't have got that crack on the head from the falling branch or lost your bicycle. You remember that artist man was here the next day and—"

"You mean Mr. Eckhard?" Myles interrupted. Si's eyes signaled a watch-your-step warning.

"Surprising the number of folks been interested in that missin' bike," he drawled. "There was all the neighbors askin' questions and Congressman Grove drove out to say he was sorry I lost it and had I any idea when it was taken."

166

"You wouldn't open your mouth to one of them," his wife reminded acidly. "I was so ashamed thought I'd sink through the floor. Now you've commenced talking like a house afire and—"

"Too much, Marthy, too much. Quit now, you've set my brain spinnin' again." Si rested his elbows on his knees and sunk his head into his hands. "You'd better go, Myles. I can't talk any more, feel as if I was goin' to have one of my sinkin' spells."

"First, let me give you an arm into the house, Nosey."

"No, no. I'm better off out here in the air."

"Think I should leave him while he's like this, Mrs. Pond?"

"Sure, Myles." She threw a look of disdain at the straw-color hair, all she could see of her husband's head. "This is the first I ever heard of a sinking spell. Goodby, give my love to Nat."

As he drove toward the highway, Myles checked the information he had gathered. The missing bike was a new angle to the mystery. Where and how did it figure? Why had Eckhard called to inquire about it? Did Si know where it was? If he did he was putting on a convincing act of ignorance.

Now that he had the number and make of the bicycle why not advertise its loss in the local paper? He would sign the ad XYZ, and have the answers sent to him at Shore Acres. How ought he to word it? He pulled up by the side of the road and wrote out an ad on a page of his notebook.

At the newspaper office a perspiring man in a collarless striped shirt in charge of advertising read through the copy Myles handed him, pulled a pencil from behind his ear, made a correction, and raised his voice to make it heard above the distant rumble of presses.

"One insertion will be seventy-five cents. Three for two dollars."

"Make it three." Myles laid down the money.

"Okay, seems like a lost-bicycle epidemic has struck town. This is the third this morning. Hot, ain't it? First we have a winter that breaks the snow record, now heat's trying to bust the thermometer. What a climate. What can I do for you, Madam?"

Myles lingered a moment hoping for a chance to ask

"Who are the other two advertisers?" but the gray-haired woman had a long grievance to relate, and he moved on.

It didn't necessarily follow that the other ads were for Si's bike, he tried to reassure himself as he started his roadster, there must be several hundred in the town. Now what? He resisted the almost irresistible tug to return to the Gallery and tell Fran of his latest discoveries. That was out. Lord, how he loved her, besides liking her, a liking that had begun long ago in Germany when he had listened to Ken's stories about her. It was slightly encouraging that she realized he had seen her almost every day since they met at the Sargent dinner. It wasn't his fault that it hadn't been every day.

He glanced at the clock on the instrument board. Twelve-thirty. She might be having luncheon and would have time to talk with him. Nothing doing. If he saw her now he would have no excuse to lure her out with him tonight. *Twelve-thirty.* At about this time yesterday Sinclair was snooping through Fran's apartment. Where was he today? Lunching at the Country Club, probably. He practically—darn that word—lived there. This was the day of the mixed doubles. Not a bad idea to follow him up.

Each table on the terrace was occupied, but each table had one empty chair, he concluded as he smilingly declined to accept those offered, till he reached the group for which he was looking. Gene Sargent and Matilde, Sinclair and John Eckhard. All in white.

"Myles, sit with us," Gene invited eagerly. "We've been holding this chair against all comers for you."

"You shouldn't flatter me, Gene, I can't take it. What are you eating?"

"Lobster cocktails. They are out of this world."

"Sounds all right to me." He gave an order to the boy. "That takes care of that. Are you playing this afternoon, Matilde?"

"Yes, at three. Hal Andrews and I battle for the silver cups Miss Tassie presented this year, cups that will *belong* to the victors. It will be poison to her if we win." Myles ignored her bitter comment.

"Are you playing in the women's doubles, Gene?"

"I am. I wanted Fran as a partner but she is so

infatuated with her job that she wouldn't ask Dad for time off, not that I think he would have given it to her, he's tense about Sargent Gallery, Jr., at present."

"That reminds me, I saw her for a minute when I stopped to give Betsy Dig a message from Nat. She said if I came to the Club would I inquire if her dark goggles had been found. She thinks she may have left them on the bleachers yesterday."

"She wasn't wearing them when I was with her, Jaffray," Eckhard declared. "We were watching you and Sinclair in your finals."

"She's forgotten that she gave them to me to keep for her at tea after the game," Sinclair explained smoothly. "They are in my coat pocket at the Inn. We have a date tonight. I'll return them then. Glad you reminded me, Jaffray."

You liar, you darned liar, I don't believe Fran is going out with you tonight, any more than I believe you have her goggles in your pocket at the Inn. I'll smoke you—

"Blake, you can't have a date with Fran tonight." Gene's impatient reminder collided head on with his train of thought. "We've promised to play poker with Kitty Saunders to give her a chance to recoup last night's—"

"I'll take that up with you later, Gene," Sinclair interrupted hastily. "Fran and I are cooking up a scheme to combine our two estates and build small houses. You look startled, Jaffray. Have you forgotten that Rebecca Harding's real estate was not included in the trust?"

"Forgotten? Do you think I could forget that I haven't that headache to contend with? I called on Si Pond this morning, Gene, he's been having a tough time—as if a crack on the head wasn't trouble enough his bike has been stolen."

"Stolen!" A small cracker John Eckhard had intended for the sauce in the lobster cocktail slipped from his fingers to the floor. He laughed. "I echoed that word as intensely as if Si were a dear and valued friend. The only time I've spoken to him was the day of the preview of my paintings."

Why is he lying, Myles wondered. He called on Si. Just where does that get us?

"Not that I care particularly, but why is Si—was that

the name—having a tough time?" Blake Sinclair inquired.

"Remember the record-breaking thunderstorm we
had—it was one of the matinee days, to be exact—the day
you dropped in for tea at Shore Acres, Sinclair? On his
way to report for duty at the Gallery the wind wrenched
a branch from a tree and knocked him unconscious.
That's the story, but—"

Aware of the tense attention of the two men, Myles
leaned forward and lowered his voice.

"There is a whisper going the rounds that it wasn't a
branch, that he was conked as he left the Gallery garage
after stabling his bicycle."

"Conked," Gene echoed. "Can you tell me why anyone would be sufficiently afraid of Si Pond to conk him?
He wouldn't hurt a fly."

"I can't, I'm just reporting the whisper that's going
the rounds, and believe me, a whispering campaign can
get results. I saw it work on the black market racket in
Germany. This morning I took a look at what remained
of the bump on Si's head, in its original size it must
have been a piperoo. If a man did it and he is caught, it
will rate a nice long jail sentence, with a fine added for
full measure."

"Let's hope the brute will be caught," Eckhard declared. "Are you with me, Sinclair?"

"Sure, sure, this Si person is nothing in my young life,
but I'm always on the side of justice. Boy, why are we
spending so much time talking about a guy we don't any
of us know?"

"Myles and I know him and like him," Gene defend-
ed. "There's something in your suggestion of a whispering campaign that gives me the jitters, Myles." Her face
had grown curiously white under the tan.

"It shouldn't bother you, you didn't bop Si, Gene;
perhaps after all the gossips are wrong, perhaps he was
floored by a branch, but if he wasn't, a whisper-wave,
and that is what has started in this town, is a sure-fire
weapon—like the Northwest Mounty, it never fails to get
its man. I believe—"

"For you, Major Jaffray." A boy in blue livery with
freckles thick as stars in the Milky Way on his round

170

face offered a note. "Gentleman waiting in the lobby for an answer, sir."

"Myles, come back, won't you?" Gene pleaded as he rose.

"Sure. I'll meet you at the tennis court if not here."

Just inside the window that opened on the terrace he read the note.

I'm not waiting in the lobby. If you want to know what became of the bike be in the summerhouse in Miss Trent's garden at midnight.

XIX

Myles hunted up the boy who had delivered the note. "You said that the man who sent this was waiting in the lobby? No one there. How come?"

"Gee, Major Jaffray, don't get sore at me. Bill Duffy, the bell captain, gave me the message and the note to be delivered as soon as you came in." Anxiety whitened his face till the freckles looked like a sprinkling of chocolate chips.

"All right, I'll go for Duffy."

But the bell captain was off duty. For the present that ended the attempt to discover who had sent the note.

Gene had saved a seat for him in the crowded bleachers. His sister and Tassie Trent were directly in front of them. How did Nat feel when she saw the man whose wife she had been devoting himself to another woman? Could a law dissolve a marriage? Could she see him without remembering the days when he had been passionately in love with her and she with him? Would her love have gone out the window had it been founded on respect? One should be implicit in the other for a successful marriage.

"What are you thinking of, Myles?" Gene slipped her hand under his arm. "Whatever it is has slashed two deep lines between your eyes and clamped your lips in a hard line."

"That's a tough-looking face you've described. I was watching the two boys on the high-diving platform at

171

the pool and thinking they should be ordered off. When the game starts half this audience will be holding its breath watching them instead of paying attention to the players."

"Someone else had the same idea, they're coming down. Relax. Not that I believe that concern for those boys has turned your face to a granite mask. Join us for sunset supper some Sunday on top of the mountain, Myles. We're waiting until Kitty Saunders's friend arrives to set the date."

"Isn't it a jungle now?" He could see a glint of gold where sunlight struck a window of the building on top. "How's the road up?"

"Jungle is right, the underbrush has grown so in the last three years that it's a trackless wilderness; as for the road, it's full of shell holes and dark as Hades from overgrown trees."

"Won't that make it bad coming down? Why wait for sunset? Why not lunch?"

"We'll start earlier but Blake won't go unless Fran will and she won't side-step the morning service. You know she sings in the Episcopal Church choir."

"Yes. I've heard her."

"I wonder what Aunt Rebecca would say, she was a stanch Presbyterian. Fran says, 'What difference does creed make?' "

"She's right, isn't she? Will she join the picnic supper?"

"She's for it, insists that she will drive up in her own car, doesn't want anyone to wait for her and lose the sunset, she may be late."

"Why should she be late?"

"Page her for the answer. She says she has an important date for each Sunday afternoon. I suspect she devotes that time to cramming on the lives and loves, dates and style of painting of famous artists. Dad says she has them at her tongue's end. It's so like her to put all there is in her into what she undertakes. Hal and Matilde are entering the court. Does the sight of my one-time sister-in-law shoot up your blood pressure?"

"Not a shoot. Why should it?"

"Ooooch, there goes my head into the guillotine bas-

172

ket. Your years in the army have made you terribly grim, Myles."

"Could be, it wasn't all joy ride. Here come the opponents. Let's give the contestants a hand."

Myles's eyes were on the players but the disk jockey of memory put on a record. Miss Tassie's voice:

"When Matilde put her arm around your neck a little ripple of sound ran around the room and I knew the story that you had broken up Ben Sargent's home had reared its snaky head."

Had Fran heard the revival? Nat would straighten it out and quick, but it was such a damn lie, fashioned by Matilde out of whole cloth to protect Andrews and herself, no one who knew him should believe it. Fran wouldn't if she loved him. That was a joke. Was it? Why should it be? He would make her trust him without proving to her that the gossip was a lie. Right off, quick.

"Where are you going, Myles?"

"Going? What·do you mean? I'm here."

"You started as if you were about to jump up and run to a fire."

"Did I? Must have been a jab from my conscience when I remembered I had forgotten an important date for this afternoon. What is the score?"

As he watched the games, he saw Matilde and Hal Andrews lose by a few points; later on the Clubhouse-terrace cooling off with soda, lemon and limeades, in tall frosted glasses tinkling with ice, his mind was busy with the significance of the note from the mysterious sender. Sure, he wanted to know what had become of the bike, sure, he would be in the summerhouse in Miss Trent's garden at midnight, he answered the questions.

That last wouldn't be easy of accomplishment. The garden had a Cerberus, a colored watchman, Augustus, who guarded it as jealously as the three-headed dog guards the entrance to the infernal regions. The person who had suggested the rendezvous must be a stranger in the village. Every resident, summer or permanent, knew of Tassie Trent's precaution to protect her property.

Before he had solved the problem of how to keep the date without taking anyone into his confidence or raising a riot in the garden, Fran appeared in a white tennis frock with a racket under her arm.

"Nothing to drink, now, thanks," she answered the chorus of suggestions for her refreshment. "You all look so warm and lazy I've lost the courage to suggest a game."

"Say no more, lady, I'm your man." Myles commandeered her racket.

"Fran always plays with me at this time of day, Jaffray," Sinclair reminded acidly.

"Make it 'practically' always, right, Fran?" Boy, but he had taken a chance to ask. She nodded and his heart picked up its beat. "Why not make it doubles, Gene? Sargent and Sinclair versus Phillips and Jaffray."

"That's the thought for the day. Come to the locker room while I pick up my racket, Fran. We'll meet you boys at the court."

They played until it was difficult to see the balls.

"That was fun," Fran declared as she and Myles lowered the net while Gene and Sinclair were arguing heatedly at one end of the court. "We had to keep on our toes to win, though."

"That's the most worth-while victory, to win after a hard fight." That was a shot in the arm for himself. "Did you come in your car?"

"No, I walked."

"I'll drive you to the Gallery to change; then we'll go somewhere for dinner."

"I can't. I have—"

"You must. I need your advice. I've had a mysterious letter. Not Ken, darling. Gene and Sinclair are coming this way. He said he had a date with you. Quick, tell him you are not going."

"I didn't have a date with him."

"Oh, Fran," Blake Sinclair interrupted. "I'll have to renege on our plan for this evening. Gene reminded me that I had promised to join a party at Kitty Saunders's."

"Don't give it a thought. I didn't know we had one. I told the Major I would dine with him."

Had she agreed to his proposition because she was hurt by Sinclair's defection, or because his hint of a mysterious note intrigued her or because she wanted to go with him? He would like to believe the last, Myles told himself, but common sense said "No."

"Let's go somewhere to dance," Fran proposed. "I

sold—my mistake—placed another Eckhard today, that rates a celebration; besides I've heard that your dancing is out of this world, Myles." Her smile did not warm him, he knew it was for the purpose of turning a knife in Sinclair's self-esteem if not his heart.

He left her at the Gallery to dress and returned to Shore Acres to shower and change.

"Myles!" Natalie called as he entered the hall. He terminated his sprint for the stairs and stopped at the living-room door.

"What's up?"

Her hair looked very white in contrast to the dark amethysts with crimson lights at her ears and around her throat, several shades deeper than her filmy frock. As she came near he could see that her eyes had known tears recently.

"What's happened to make you cry, Nat?" he asked tenderly.

"Tears that have parked behind my eyes for the last few years put on their act at the slightest opportunity." Her smile was tremulous. "Morrie Grove came back from the tournament with me. He was convinced that seeing Hal and Matilde playing together hurt me horribly—it didn't—asked me again to marry him. I hope this time I made him understand that it is impossible."

"Was that why you cried?"

"Not while he was here, after he left. I hated to hurt him, hated to see him lavishing love hopelessly."

"Is it hopeless? He's a right guy, Nat."

"I know he is, know that he will make some woman happy, but I can't marry him. I can't marry anyone. In spite of the divorce I still feel that I have a husband living. If opportunity presents try to convince Morrie that I mean what I say, Myles. But I didn't stop you to sob out my reactions on your shoulder. He left this note for you. Said to be sure you had it the moment you came in, it was important." He took the envelope she offered.

"Any idea what's in it?"

"No. He tried to find you after the tournament but you had disappeared. That's all. Run along, you were charging for the stairs when I stopped you."

"I'm taking a lady out to dinner."

"Fran? Is she the answer to your prayer?"

"Yes. It will always be Fran, Natalie, has been for several years, I discovered suddenly. She doesn't know it yet, though. Suppose I bring her back here after we have dined and danced for a game of Oklahoma?"

"It would be perfect."

He thought of his date in Miss Tassie's garden at midnight, of what had happened to Si Pond, of the mystery of the Gallery. Was Fran safe there at night with only the Digbys and the new watchman? He stopped on the lowest stair.

"Telephone her while I am dressing, ask her to spend the night here, will you, Nat?"

"With pleasure, but I doubt if she will come."

"Try. I want to get her away from the Gallery."

"Is your reason connected with the mystery?"

"What mystery?"

"Your astonishment is well done, but it is an act, isn't it? A whisper was going the rounds at the Club this afternoon that the night of the storm Si Pond was not knocked out by a branch but was attacked by someone in the house."

"That really is something." He grinned. "As I mentioned earlier, I have a date to take a lady to dinner, if I don't appear soon she will walk out on me." Halfway up the stairs he stopped and looked down at his sister looking up at him.

"Telephone at once, will you, Nat? Make her come. Tell her you are low in your mind and need cheerful company."

"I will not. I won't play Aunty Doleful for anyone, even for you who are the biggest thing in my life, Myles. I'll tell her we had the family jewels sent from the bank today, to catalogue them, that I think she may get a thrill out of seeing the Jaffray emeralds before they go back tomorrow. If she can resist that lure she's no woman."

In his room Myles opened the note from Morrison Grove and frowned over its contents.

I'll be away for a few days. Got a line on you know who. Stand by for a crash. M.G.

Slowly he tore the note to shreds. Did that information tie in with the appointment in Miss Tassie's garden? He would know at midnight, not so long to wait with Fran for company. Would she resist the lure of the emeralds?

He was reassured when he entered the Gallery. She hadn't resisted. She was waiting in the entresol in a white eyelet frock with a bouffant skirt, pearls about her throat, a long green wool coat over her arm, an overnight case at her feet.

"I suppose you know your sister invited me to spend the night at Shore Acres?" she greeted him. "It was your idea, wasn't it? Something tells me it is tied up with our mystery."

"You're psychic." He picked up the bag. "Have you told Betsy Dig you will be away tonight?"

"Yes, and Lem and the new watchman. I even phoned Henry Sargent—may his tribe increase—for permission to leave."

"Feeling on top of the world, aren't you? What was his reaction?"

"Go to it, or words to that effect, but he warned me to be sure and lock the door of my apartment. That deed is done."

"Then we are on our way. Just a minute, have you had a chance to sound out Betsy about the fake phone call, has she told you the name of her suspect?"

"I asked her. She wouldn't tell me, and Lem warned her again that they could get into a heap of trouble if they talked. You might try, you are perfection in her eyes."

"Too bad I can't acquire top rating with another person—who shall be nameless for the present. Hang it, there's the phone. Don't answer, Fran, or we may be held up."

"It could be your sister trying to reach you." Seated in the English Regency armchair at the Empire card table she answered the ring.

"Sargent Gallery. Yes, he is. Just a minute." She passed the receiver to Myles standing behind her. "It's for you."

"Jaffray speaking." He could see the anxiety in her eyes looking up at him. Always she had the hope of a

177

word from Ken, the fear of bad news with her. It was a tough break. "What's that?"

"Keep away from the Trent place tonight," a low voice from somewhere repeated. A click and the line was silent.

"What was it, Major? You look as I imagine you might when about to drop from a plane. Anything to change our plans?"

"Change them, woman? Not a chance. Come on, the night is young and I'll tell you the rest later."

XX

They dined and danced at a newly, lavishly decorated night spot a few miles north on the coast. The walls were delicate lemon-color, softly lighted from behind the cornice. One was covered by a ceiling-to-floor mirror which reflected the lime-green hangings at long windows which opened on the terrace where shadowy figures danced to the music of a dreamy Viennese waltz, charming frocks on lovely women and white dinner clothes on good-looking men. Chairs were covered with lime-color leather, huge vases of garden flowers on pedestals at each end of the dais gave a perfect accent or color contrast—light blue, dark blue plumes of late larkspur, pink lilies, yellow snapdragons, spikes of glads in pastel coloring with a sharp accent of scarlet and crimson.

Dark-skinned musicians in white with lemon- or lime-color cummerbunds were giving out with brass and strings, "You Were Meant for Me," tenderness, love and longing in every note.

"You said you would explain why you needed my advice and about what later," Fran reminded. "Isn't this late enough?"

"Not quite. I'm saving the story for a conversation piece on the way home so you won't be bored. One more dance. Then we'll go."

"You were meant for me," Myles repeated softly. "Are you? I think you are," he added as he put his arm about her.

Was she? Why not let herself go and really like him? Suppose he did "love and leave"? She'd have fun while

178

with him, wouldn't she? She would be the only one to suffer when it was over. Crazy thought. She pushed it from her mind and concentrated on the faces of the girls who passed. Behind one she sensed the glow of victory; the next was marred by angry defiance; one showed desperate hunger for love as she looked up into the face bent close to hers; there was fright behind the eyes of another—no wonder, the expression of the man with whom she was dancing was loathsomely gloating.

"I'm still here"—Myles's voice in her ear, Myles's arm tightening in reminder.

"I'm sorry. I was absorbed in watching—"

"Absorbed, you're telling me. Let's go."

In the parking place made brilliant as day by floodlights he held her long green wool coat. "Better put this on. You are warm after dancing and there's a bit of breeze."

"Look! Quick. Front seat of the limousine just pulling out. The black one. Did you see him?"

"*Him?* Who?"

"Our ex-butler, ex-Dunkirk, in chauffeur's livery."

"Boy, did he see you?"

"I think not. He had all he could do to get out without hitting a car."

"Hop in. We're following."

He kept a discreet distance behind the large black car, its taillight a red polka dot ahead.

"I'd give a hundred dollars if the top of this convertible were up," he declared. "We are as conspicuous as two gulls perched on the bell buoy."

"May be, but the top down makes deliciously cool driving. It was hot inside. What a sky, bespangled with stars. There goes a shoot—" The windshield mirror reflected his grin.

"Remembered the penalty that goes with the mention of a shooting star just in time, didn't you, Miss Phillips?"

"I'm really a *very* quick thinker," she appraised herself with exaggerated modesty.

"I'll say you are. I'm pretty quick myself as I would prove if I didn't have to keep my eyes on that light ahead."

"Can you talk as you drive," she chanted in waltz

time, "because if you can now is the time for the conversation piece you were saving."

"Don't tell me you are bored so soon."

"I'm not bored. I'm curious, no, intensely interested is better."

"Wait till we see where the limousine ahead is going. If you are right and the man Barth is driving, I'm all at sea about what is scheduled to take place at midnight." She sat up straight and expectant.

"Midnight. Myles, what do you *mean?*"

"I like the feel of your hand on my arm, Fran." She snatched it back and clasped it hard with the other in her lap. "But, don't do it so suddenly. It started the car on a slight detour. Steady again. Put it back. Golly, I looked at you for a split second and lost the light."

"The moral of that is, don't look at me. What do we do now that we've lost it?"

"Go on until, or if, we come to a crossroad. The black limousine must have turned off."

"And if there isn't one?"

"Go back. This highway leads to Canada and way stations. Too late to start for that."

"Canada. Our man Barth would be safe across the border, wouldn't he?"

"Safe from what?"

"Arrest."

"Do you still believe he is responsible for the break at the Gallery?"

"I have done a lot of thinking about him and have concluded that he is a D. P."

"A Displaced Person? That's a new angle. I don't get it. What object would he have in telling so many contradictory stories about himself?"

"He may have slipped into the country without credentials, it's being done. With his free-wheeling mind—if free-wheeling is what I think it is—he could— Look! At the right. A road?"

"It is. Some way back I noticed the break in the treetops. Shall we follow? Are you game?"

"I wouldn't miss seeing the elusive Mr. Barth's face when we catch up with him for the choicest Byzantine enamel in the Gallery."

"I still wish we had the top up." He turned the

roadster into the side road. "You may bet your last dollar I wouldn't take you into this if I thought there was danger, D.P. or Dunkirk. I'm sure Barth is not a criminal."

"This road can't have been used much, it is so narrow. Ooch!"

"What happened?"

"Don't stop, nothing, really. A branch brushed my shoulder, gave me the jitters, imagined the man we are after had grabbed me."

"Is that all, thought for a minute you'd been hurt." He drove forward slowly, looking to the right and left.

It wasn't "*all*," but this was not the moment to tell him that it had been her cheek, not her shoulder, the branch had grabbed and grabbed hard. Ooch, how it smarted. Felt moist. Bleeding? She didn't dare touch it for fear he would see her. He mustn't suspect. Nothing must interfere, surely not this little scratch, with his pursuit of the man whom she believed to be guilty if he didn't.

"Fireflies are out with their lanterns, swarms of them. See something shining?" she whispered.

He nodded, drove on slowly. Stopped when a large black limousine blocked the road perhaps twenty feet ahead. The lights of the convertible illumined the license plate.

"New York," Myles said softly. "Stay here. I'm going to investigate."

"I'll come with you."

"No." He held the door he had partially opened. "Stay where you are, Fran. I may have to dodge back. If you are with me I'll be handicapped."

"Do you mean that I would be excess baggage?"

"That's just what I mean, Franny. Many a man in a dangerous situation has lost his life because he had to look out for a person who through the mistaken idea that he or she could help had come along, while had he only himself to look out for, he would have pulled through. Understand?"

"Yes, sir. After that, nothing would tempt me to leave this seat, sir." It was a wonder she could speak so lightly when her smarting cheek was flooding her eyes with tears. He was too absorbed now to notice what she did. She touched it. Sticky. With blood?

"Now you are off my mind. Listen. Hear anything?"

Nothing but the hard beat of her heart at first, then the cautious rustle of unseen living things on the ground, the crack of a twig; the distant barking of a dog, the faraway wail of the siren of a police car, the whisper of leaves as a light breeze stirred them.

"Nothing human," she whispered.

"Then here I go. Move into my seat. I'll leave the lights on and the engine running. If you see me hotfooting in this direction back out, I'll catch up with you. We can't turn here."

She nodded, her voice wouldn't come through her tight throat. It looked as if an evening of dining and dancing might turn into a breath-snatching adventure. Adventure? Too bad Judge Grimes was not here. He had derided the idea of adventure in the State of Maine. She touched her smarting cheek, held her fingers near the light on the instrument board. Blood on them. She could do nothing now to stop the ooze. It would dry in a few minutes. Better forget it and concentrate on the present not-too-safe situation.

She watched tensely as Myles walked forward, his white clothes turned to gold color in the beams of light. He was making no secret of his approach, he was whistling softly, "You Were Meant for Me."

Was the man, Barth, hidden in the shrubs lying in wait for him? Had her blood turned to ice? If not why would she shiver this hot night? She shouldn't have let him go alone, she might be of some assistance if the situation got rough.

She swung open the door, thrust out her foot, withdrew it slowly. Myles had said that many a man had lost his life trying to save a person who had come along thinking he might help. Her place was at the wheel of the roadster ready to move it at the first signal from him. The stillness, broken only by the muted purr of the engine, was weird, the incessant flash of fireflies added to the eerie effect. If only Myles would call, make some sound. He had stopped whistling. If she could hear that, it wouldn't be so—

182

"What's going on?" A gruff voice in the dark behind her set her heart beating like a tom-tom.

If a start of surprise were proof of a guilty conscience the man beside the roadster staring at her across the empty seat would justly rate her a criminal of the deepest dye, she had almost jumped out of her skin when he spoke. He snapped on an electric torch. A State Police officer. The last perfect touch to this nightmarish situation.

"Why are you parked here? Why don't you answer?" He leaned over the door and focused the beam of light on her face. "Holy smoke, did he beat you up before he left you?"

"*Beat me up?* What do you mean, er—Captain?" He was a sergeant, but promotion might help. Was there a law or rule against parking on a side road like this one? What explanation could she offer that he would accept?

"Are you dumb? Why don't you answer a civil question? 'Twon't be so civil if you don't get a move on." A firefly putting on its act on the front of his cap made her think of a miner's light.

"I've been wondering just how I could explain so you would understand, Captain. My—my husband heard a motor horn in this road, thought it might be an SOS and drove in. See that shining black car ahead? He went to inquire if there was trouble, if he could help."

"Glib little storyteller, aren't you? I'll find out now what gave you a bloody face. Thought at first it was smeared lip-stick, it's been done before, but I can see it isn't. What scratched you up like that?"

"It's a secret, Captain, and—"

"Cut out the old oil. You *know* I'm not a captain. Tell the truth, if you can. Did he play rough? It's my meat to pick up a guy like that."

"My—my husband did not play rough. You came through this road. You know how narrow it is and—" Indignation choked off her voice.

"Stop and get your breath, lady. Keep your hand away from your cheek. Each time you touch it you add a bloody smooch. I'm staying here till the guy comes back. Take your time."

"I don'* need time to tell you that a branch caught my cheek and gave it a vicious dig. If you don't believe

183

it, look." She released the wheel she had been clutching, slid into the other seat and offered her cheek for inspection. "I—I didn't tell my husband because it would worry him and he was anxious to see if the driver in front needed help." He focused his light on her face and bent his head the better to see.

"Holy smoke, that was a rip-snorter. Looks to me as if a big thorn did it. Right, I can see the black thing—"

"What goes? What goes?" inquired a grim voice. Myles. The headlights of the roadster played up the hard white line about his mouth. Fran slipped back into the driver's seat. The free hand of the policeman slid to his holster, the other leveled his torch.

"'Bout time you ap-pear—the Lord love me if it isn't our jump-and-be-damned Major." He saluted before he grasped the hand extended. "What in hell are you doing in this back road, sir?"

"Following the limousine ahead, Sergeant Bothwell."

"Your wife told me you thought you heard an SOS." For an instant Fran's apologetic eyes met Myles's. "Now that you have come I'll investigate the car. Was it a smash-up? Anyone hurt?"

"Not a sign of a person, not even a bag. Sergeant, if you need me to testify as to what you find, drop in at Shore Acres, see me anyway. If that's all, we'll be on our way."

"Okay, Major. Tell my man in the car at the entrance to this road to drive in, will you? It's been great to see you again, and to meet the missus." He saluted. "Good night, Mrs. Jaffray. Better take care of—our Major," he substituted in response to the warning shake of her head.

"Need our lights, Sergeant?"

"No. I have this powerful torch. Back out. My man can't get in until you do. I'll be seeing you."

"You sure will, Sergeant, and soon now that I know where to find you. Slide into the other seat, Fran."

He delivered the sergeant's message to the driver of the police car parked near the entrance to the road, waited till the red taillight had disappeared before he announced:

"The sergeant was my prize jumper, but before he gets too far away to receive the beating up of his life, there are a few things I'd like straightened out. Was he trying to kiss you?"

"Good heavens, *no*."

"He was suspiciously near. Why were you in that seat when I told you to stay at the wheel?"

"I—I would like to explain why I told him we were married—Myles. It seemed the simplest explanation of my presence on that back road."

"I can't think of a better one. Now that you have that off your mind, answer my question. Why was he bending over you?"

"I suggest that we start for home or we'll be late for Oklahoma with Natalie."

"We stay right here till my question is answered. Why was Bothwell's face so close to yours?"

"You are not intimating that I was tempting him, are you?"

"I am not. I'm after the truth."

"You are a determined person, aren't you?"

"Lady, you ain't seen nothing yet. Go on. Tell all."

"If I want to get home I suppose I'll have to." She was in luck that he had already forgotten that she had told the sergeant he was her husband. "If you must know, he saw my cheek and jumped to the conclusion that either I had been beaten up or—"

"What's the matter with your cheek?" Hand under her chin he turned her face toward him. "Good Lord, what happened, Franny? Did you get out to follow me? Did you fall, darling?"

"No, I obeyed orders. Remember that on the way in I said a branch grabbed my shoulder? I knew you would stop if I told you it had gouged my face."

"Missed your eye, thank God. Hurts like the devil, doesn't it? Don't shake your head or you will spill the tears in your eyes. If one rolls down your cheek I won't be responsible for my reactions." He shot the car ahead. "Here we go."

"You'd better drive me to the Gallery. Mrs. Betsy will take care of my face. The sergeant said the thorn that tore it was still there."

"I'll take care of it. I saw the thorn. I don't want to touch it till we get home. I had to know first aid and a

185

lot more than first in my job. You have a date with the Jaffray emeralds. Haven't forgotten, have you?"

"As if I could. I adore jewels. Have they a history?" If he would talk it would take her mind off the throb and smart of her cheek—perhaps. For a few minutes during the police interview she had forgotten it; now it was aching on all cylinders.

"Yes. Jaffray, an English baronet, brought some of them with him when he fled to this country after an altercation with his king. He was the first of his name to come. His descendants have added to them until now there is a sizable collection, rings, necklaces, bracelets, a tiara, small but effective, also topaz, sapphires, and rubies. They are all set in diamonds, by the way. Warm enough, Franny?"

"Warm enough?" She marshaled a laugh to combat her crumply surrender to his tender inquiry. Her defense mechanism had let her down. "Warm enough in a top coat this almost breathless night? Even the little breeze has gone. The air may be breathless but it's sweet. What is the spicy smell?"

"Wild mint in the field we are passing."

"Passing! We're not just passing, we're jet-bombing. Hasn't the State of Maine speed laws? Next time you are held up you may not meet an ex-buddy to smooth your path."

"And that of my wife. I'm not breaking the speed law. Bothwell was one of my best men. There were several from this state. I have hoped I would run into them again. Remember that I have something to tell you?"

"I do. I've been living for this moment."

"Rest your good cheek against my sleeve, it may ease the ache in the other. It is a purely platonic suggestion, I'm taking Ken's place—besides, it will be easier for you to hear what I say. I must keep my voice low. Remember we thought someone had hung onto the back of the roadster the night we lost the blotters. Comfy?" She nodded and laughed.

"A revival of horse-and-buggy days."

"I understand that the custom moved along with the automobile. Here's the story."

He told of the missing bicycle; of the note delivered to him at the Country Club; of Morrie Grove's message that he was off on the trail of the mysterious stranger; of the telephoned warning before they left the Gallery.

"Myles! You won't go to the summerhouse after *that?*"

"Put your head back. I can't talk when you sit up straight and tense. It cramps my narrative style. That's better. There's a sequel. On the seat of the limousine we followed I found a paper on which had been scribbled—"

"What, Myles? *What?*"

" 'Don't follow. Stop. Think. Where would you hide—' "

"Myles. Go on!"

" '—what you had stolen?' "

XXI

Fran snapped on the bedside light. The result was like switching on the sun—the soft yellow walls glowed, the rich mahogany furniture gleamed. No use trying to sleep while her bruised cheek smarted and burned. Much better this hot night to sit on the balcony of the room than twist and turn in bed, even if the sheets were of coolest, finest linen, lavender-scented.

She thrust her feet into silver mules, belted a hyacinth lounge coat over her turquoise crepe pajamas and stole across the velvet rug, green as the foliage of jonquils. She resisted the urge to glance in the mirror at the scratch on her cheek Myles had protected by gauze. The sight of the disfiguration wouldn't help her relax.

The long window was open but the click of the screen latch set her heart quick-stepping. Had the sound been heard? Don't be gooshy, she scolded herself. Pat's word seemed to fit the situation. Why feel guilty? Were Natalie Andrews to hear or see her she would understand. She must have prowled through countless sleepless nights herself.

In a gaily cushioned wicker chair she folded her arms on the top of the ornate wrought-iron grille which framed the balcony and looked down into the dusky garden. The air was sweet with the scent of drowsy flowers, and so still that the ebb and flow of the tide on the beach was like a silken orchestral accompaniment to

187

the tinkle of water in the fountain pool and the occasional chirp of a cricket. Branches of tall trees stretched skyward as if trying to contact the stars that blossomed thick as dandelions in a neglected lawn.

She rested her unscratched cheek against her bare arm. Not that she was sleepy, just unaccountably weary. The dressing of the ugly gouge had been painful but Myles had been so tender, so solicitous that she had clenched her teeth to keep back any expression of discomfort.

Tenderness appeared to be an outstanding characteristic of Natalie and her brother, a characteristic defined as one of the "sympathetic affections," an affection which had been lacking in her life since the loss of her parents. Aunt Becky had loved her but believed in repressing all expression of her love. Ken had brought her up in the Sure-I-love-you-why-talk-about-it school. Perhaps one reason she had considered marrying Blake was because he noticed what she was wearing, was ready with, "You're out of sight in that hat, sweetheart," or, "You'll have the stags queuing for a dance and how, tonight, dream girl." A slight and shaky plank in the platform of matrimony. Matrimony with him? Thank goodness, that crazy possibility had been wiped out completely.

If she hadn't just naturally lost her taste for him and his line his mysterious behavior yesterday would have put her on guard. Why had he gone to her apartment? His explanation to Betsy Digby that she had sent him for her dark glasses was a lie. Had he stopped the clock? Had he slipped the key to the Louis XV cabinet behind it after returning the enamel box?

The box. The night of Miss Tassie's party, while she and Myles had been talking on the seat above the cliff, she had demanded:

"They were trying to nail the theft on me. Why? Why?" Before she had finished the question a voice within her had interrupted, "Gene took the box to sell in case I couldn't get the thousand dollars for her."

It looked now as if the voice had the right idea for, soon after Gene had received the money from the bonds Judge Grimes had sold, the enamel box had appeared in the cabinet. It was incredible that she would steal from her father, more unbelievable that she would use the gold sandal to point suspicion at her friend, but that was the way it seemed to be.

The knowledge must be pushed into the back of her mind and kept there until after September when she would be through at the Gallery. Could she do it? Go on day after day without letting Gene suspect that she was aware of her treachery? She must or life here would be unendurable. "Make the present something vital and inspiring," Judge Grimes had said. She wouldn't let this get her down. She would finish the job. She had had a secret yearning to try out on the stage or in the movies. This was her chance to prove that she could act.

How deeply had Blake Sinclair been involved in Gene's financial quagmire? Had she needed the money to pay a gaming debt to him? Had he threatened to go to her father if she didn't come across? Not a pretty suspicion of the boy next door. How responsible was Fran Phillips for his presence in the village? If months ago she had given a final and irrevocable *No* to his proposal of marriage would he have followed her here? Why shoulder all the blame? He had come also to sell a choice painting to Henry Sargent, hadn't he? Which question brought her spang against the Gallery mystery and the message Myles had found on the seat of the black limousine.

Don't follow. Stop. Think. Where would you hide what you had stolen?

Stolen. Had the note referred to the Constable? The question banished weariness, brought her to her feet. She leaned against the lacy wrought-iron panel that framed the balcony, tipped back her head to watch a meteor whizz its way across the field of gold. Eyes on the starry heavens she searched her memory for one loose end which, if followed, would untangle the mystery. "Where would you hide what you had stolen?" she repeated softly.

Presumably the man Barth whom she had seen driving the limousine from the parking place at the night club had written the message. Did he know where the painting was? Had he been trying to get the knowledge across to her the night of Miss Tassie's party when he had hovered about Blake and herself? She had felt there was method in his attention. But Myles had said that the waiter had made a quick getaway from the house—that suggested guilt.

Suppose I had stolen the painting, she asked herself—this was a good time to work out the problem—never would she have a quieter—suppose after I had stolen it I decided that it should be hidden until the excitement of the theft had cooled off, what would I do with it? No use trying to smuggle a 31 x 38 canvas out of the town. Henry Sargent would have agents on the lookout for that. The only clue to the person who had taken it was that Si's bike had been stolen the same night. So far, that information hadn't cut much ice.

"Where would you hide what you had stolen?"

She repeated the words hoping they would serve as a springboard for an answer to the question. Was Myles thinking along the same line? Was the message which had been left on the seat of the limousine tied up with the mysterious note he had received at the Club advising him to be in the summerhouse at Sunnyside at midnight? Who had phoned, "Keep away from the Trent place tonight?"

If he had been disturbed by the two messages it was not apparent. Even after he had cleansed and dressed her cheek in his workroom, he had returned with Natalie and herself to the living room with the chest of jewels he had taken from his safe. He opened it and sat on the arm of his sister's chair telling bits of the history of different pieces.

The tiara of emeralds set in flashing diamonds had been worn by his great-grandmother, also his grandmother when presented at the Court of St. James's. His mother had worn it at an Ambassador's dinner, he hoped his wife—if ever he had a wife—would wear it in Washington if not in England. That remark suggested that he was considering abandoning his flitting from flower to flower program to settle down. Was Gene the girl? Why think of what pricked like a splinter deep in her heart each time her mind touched on it?

He had waited while she and Nat cooed over the colorful collection, declared their preferences as to

190

stones and settings, then had locked the chest and started for his workroom. In the doorway he stopped to advise:

"Send our patient to bed, Nat, she has had a tough evening. Happy dreams, Fran."

This night was so quiet it seemed to belong to another and unfamiliar world. At this very moment he might be stepping into the summerhouse in Miss Tassie's garden. What would he find? Over the telephone he had been warned to keep away from the place. As he had stood on the threshold of the living room advising Nat to send her to bed she had been tempted to beg him not to go, then had remembered that his sister knew nothing of the meeting, that probably he didn't want her to know and had snapped her lips shut on the protest.

Was the summerhouse in Miss Tassie's garden visible from here? She leaned forward. No, but she could see the dark hedge between the two places and a blur of white that might be the gate of which Natalie had spoken. She brushed her hand across her eyes to clear them. Something dark was moving cautiously toward the white blur. Was it Myles?

She watched, barely breathing, till the moving shadow vanished. Had it slipped through the gateway into the Sunnyside garden? Myles shouldn't have gone. Someone had written him to come, another had warned him to keep away. Too tricky. Why hadn't she made him promise not to go? She might have capitalized on her wounded cheek—no, she couldn't tell a man who had been through what Myles had experienced what to do.

Another shadow moving along the hedge. Perhaps the second was Myles. Perhaps the first she had seen was the person who had sent him the note, perhaps she could catch up with him—phooey about not giving him advice, why not try? Why not beg him to stay away from the summerhouse?

She kicked off silver mules, pulled on white wedgies she had brought for the morning, rolled the legs of her blue pajamas above her knees and twisted them tight to hold them up; slipped the lavender cotton frock, also provided to wear to the Gallery, over her head and belted it, thrust her arms into the long green coat and an electric torch into the deep pocket. She caught a

191

glimpse of herself as she passed the pier mirror. She was a sight with the patch on her face. Why worry over that minor detail, if the legs of her pajamas stayed up? A vision of herself with a pantalette effect, if they didn't, induced a nervous chuckle.

In the hall outside her bedroom door she held her breath and listened. A stair creaking. Someone coming? One! The boom came from the stair landing.

"Relax, foolish," she jeered at herself. The first sound she had heard had been the old clock catching its breath before striking. She counted the strokes. Twelve. Was the mysterious rendezvous on? Had she lost Myles by waiting for the house to become still? She had seen two persons on their way to the midnight meeting. Why give up? "Don't wobble" had been one of Aunt Becky's major rules for living. No knowing what help she might be if she could get to the summerhouse; even at the risk of being "excess baggage" she would go.

She crept down the spiral staircase. The hall was softly lighted, not so softly that she couldn't see the stern eyes of the Jaffray men who lined the walls; their expression wouldn't be a patch on the eyes of their heir if he could see her now. Were the curious little ghostly sounds their whispers? It was abundantly evident they didn't approve of her. Why should they approve of a guest who gumshoe'd down the ancestral stairs at midnight? Something wrong with that picture. Perhaps they thought she was a thief after the jewels.

"The jewels." Good heavens, what a night to creep through the house, the one night in the year when the Jaffray emeralds were here. Even Natalie, friendly as she was, might wonder, if she saw her. She couldn't allow that possibility to hold her up. Having started she must go forward gallantly, without fear. Myles had said that about the ship on the horizon. After all, she wasn't doing this for pleasure, but in the hope of preventing trouble.

Safely past the front living-room door on her right, the powder room on her left, one more to pass, that of the back living room, before she reached the end of the hall. The terrace at last. Down the steps, around the fountain. Darn! The patch of lawn she would have to cross to reach the gate in the hedge was quite light. Could she make it without being seen? Someone coming.

The faint thud of feet on turf. She flung herself flat on the ground behind a stone bench near the fountain.

He—it must be a man, no woman would be wandering around the garden at midnight. Wouldn't she? What about a gal named Fran Phillips? He was coming nearer. Now he was visible. It was light enough to see a dark figure swathed in what appeared to be a topcoat this breathless night. A hat brim was drawn low. He had stopped at the pool. Why?

What was that shining against the hedge? Looked like the glint of nickel. Nickel? A bicycle! Could it be Si's? If it were, was she on the trail of the person who had broken into the Gallery? The bike had disappeared then. Would an honest man be prowling round this garden at midnight? Never mind what happened, she'd stop him. At last had she found an end of the tangled skein?

She raised herself cautiously to her feet. Splash. Something had been flung into the pool. A revolver? *Revolver!* This might be the person who had sent the mysterious summons for a meeting at the summerhouse. Had he shot Myles? Was he drowning the evidence? He shouldn't escape. She stole up behind the dark figure, thrust the end of her electric torch into his back.

"Hands up! And I mean, hands up." The man whirled in response to her hoarse command.

"What the devil—*Fran!*"

The hand that held the torch dropped. She stared unbelievingly up at the man staring back at her.

"You?" she demanded in a strangled whisper. *"You?"*

XXII

Had his watch stopped? Battle-scarred as it was it had kept on the job faithfully through years of conflict. More than five minutes must have passed since the hands pointed to ten before twelve. Myles held it to his ear. It was ticking. It wouldn't do to pace off his restlessness even if Miss Tassie's summerhouse provided sufficient space, which it didn't.

Five minutes since he had arrived, most of the time spent thinking of the meaning of the scribbled words on the slip of paper he had found on the seat of the black limousine a few hours before.

Don't follow. Stop. Think. Where would you hide what you had stolen?

No signature to provide a clue to the writer. Had it been the man who called himself Barth? Sounded like the advice of one who had had experience, not such bad advice, either. Someone had phoned, "Keep away from the Trent place tonight." Who but the person who had made the appointment knew that he was expected here?

Corking night for a rendezvous if only he and Fran could enjoy it together. The lacelike iron trellises that framed the entrance made a pattern against her "bespangled sky" which spread like a glowing canopy above the ghostly clump of birches beyond which the lawn stretched to the edge of the rocky cliff. Flashing fireflies were almost as thick as the stars, the chirp of crickets was superimposed on the soft splash of the tide. The air was heavy with the scent of flowers and warm earth.

Lucky he had taken time to change to dark clothes. As he slipped along the border of shrubs and through the gateway between the two places his white suit would have presented an excellent target had there been a person near who was target-minded. It seemed as if he had been waiting hours but his watch said ten minutes. He had intended to be earlier to check on the approaches to the place, but dressing Fran's cheek had detained him, he wouldn't have hurried that had he never reported for this interview, if interview was what he was up against. It was a wicked gouge, but not so deep as he had feared. It would leave no scar. He would have the doctor check on it tomorrow. She had been a soldier. After it was over she had been eager to see the jewels.

The jewels. For the love of Pete! Suppose someone was hep to the fact that they were at Shore Acres? Suppose he had been enticed here by a hint of mystery to get him away from home when they were snitched? Old Crocker was the only man on the place at night, hot lot of protection he would be. Might be the same gang that was mixed up with the Gallery theft. Si Pond had suggested that possibility. Boy, but he had been an easy mark. He would beat it back—

A rustle? Someone moving or had he imagined the sound? He held his breath. Listened.

"Hello, there."

A whisper. His pulses broke into quickstep. Now what? The soft lap, lap of the tide, the monotonous chirp of crickets—pierced by the sharp call of a bird roused in its nest. Silence. A weird silence which anything might break.

"Are you inside, Jaffray?"

Jaffray. Something familiar in the low voice, something friendly that wiped out the suspicion that the theft of the jewels was tied up with this meeting.

"Yes."

The walls of the summerhouse seemed to throw back his hushed response like a shuttlecock. Yes! Yes! Yes!

"Righto. I'm coming in. If you have a light don't show it."

A figure blotted out the star shine for an instant, the smell of tobacco plowed under the fragrance from the garden. Eckhard needed no other identification. The artist was the last person he had expected to see.

"Step into the shadow. You're an easy target where you are."

"For whom?" John Eckhard's chuckle was low, but he moved quickly. "Augustus is off on a celebration, I've taken over as the sunnyside watchdog tonight by arrangement with him. We have the place to ourselves."

"Then why the necessity of this clandestine appointment?"

"It does seem nutty, Major, but what I have to tell you is strictly hush-hush. Were we seen talking together as if in confidence for five minutes, there is a chance the person we are after would get wise."

"We? Why imply that I am after someone?"

"Aren't you? If not why did you secrete these in the wood box at the Digbys' door?" He moved a roll into the faint light and quickly drew it back. Myles recognized the sheets of blotting paper with the muddy footprints—that is, it looked like them. His bump of caution buzzed a warning.

"Where's your evidence to prove I have seen that

before? Don't light your pipe. You may have been trailed by the very person you claim would be interested in your reason for being here. It would betray your presence. I'll bet there isn't another in the world that smells like it."

"Is it as bad as that? Relax, the pipe is back in my pocket. We are wasting a lot of time."

"You are, I didn't make this appointment."

"That's right. To get down to cases, you know I'm a painter, what you don't know is that I am an expert on faked art."

"That's not a secret. Morrie Grove announced it on our terrace the afternoon of the big storm."

"He did? Not so good. I told Miss Tassie in confidence, she must have passed it on to him. Who heard it?"

"My sister Natalie, Miss Phillips, Blake Sinclair and I."

"Sinclair? Not a very large company, it won't matter. This is something I am sure you do not know, that my exhibition was staged here because someone high in the world of art had been informed that several paintings attributed to old masters but painted by someone unknown had been sent to this country to be sold as genuine examples."

"Here? To this small place? To the Sargent Gallery?"

"Don't belittle the Sargent Gallery. Even this branch of the main concern is internationally famous. We have no information that the attempt to place one was to be made here, but the high-ups are taking no chances. An expert has been stationed—not to be known as an expert —in the vicinity of every art dealer along the eastern seaboard to stop the imitations before they get west of the Mississippi where disposing of them at a spectacular price would be a cinch. That's why I am here."

"Does Henry Sargent know why your pictures are in his gallery?"

"He does not. Only one person in this place knows it, besides you. After all, I have made good as a painter. I had to take a chance he would accept my work. He did."

"Let's get back to the blotters. Do they fit into your detection scheme?"

"You know more about that than I. I'm relying on you to fill in the chinks."

"There has to be a story before the chinks can be filled. Shoot."

Seated beside Myles on the bench at one side of the summerhouse Eckhard went back to the afternoon before the storm when he had angered Gene Sargent by changing the hanging of his pictures in the large gallery. Sinclair, who was present, had ribbed her about her short temper. In the repair shop he had taken one canvas from its frame and substituted another he had brought from his room at the Inn. Later, thinking over the change, he had decided that he could have hung "Romance in Stone" in a better light. After he finished the business of hiring the studio he hiked back to the Gallery hoping to contact Si Pond, the watchman, with whom he had become friendly, who would let him in. Earlier Miss Sargent had told him that the Digbys had been called away suddenly.

"Then you weren't at the Inlet when the storm started as you told Miss Trent you were?"

"I shifted the time a little, Major. Let's say I indulged in fiction license. It seemed expedient. No watchman was visible on the place when I arrived. I hoped there might be a window unlatched in the Digby apartment. I was determined to check on the lighting of my picture—many a painting has lost out because of poor hanging. I'm a stubborn cuss when I get an idea. Just as I reached the path to the ell came a blinding flash, a shattering crash and the heavens opened. I crouched among the shrubs near the kitchen door as a protection against the deluge, figured it was bound to let up in a few minutes.

"The world was black as pitch. I was wondering what move to make when I heard feet splashing along the path, then a figure muffled in an auto robe, I couldn't make out whether male or female, fumbled at the door. Lightning split the sky. Whoever it was slipped inside the house. I heard a key turn."

"Why didn't you grab that chance to get in out of the rain?"

"It was so sudden surprise knocked me for a loop. Then I began to think, and it didn't look good. The Digbys were away. I thought of the treasures in the Gallery, of my paintings which represented the work of years, and dashed into the path intending to investigate the mysterious entrance. Headlights blinded me. I jumped back, a fool thing to do, made me appear guilty as hell."

"You've said it. Morrison Grove recognized you."

"Why was he there?"

"To call on the Digbys, his constituents. You are out of luck, Eckhard. It isn't publicly known yet, but that same afternoon, we assume it must have been late, because it couldn't have happened when Gene was on the job, a valuable enamel box and a set of Apostle spoons disappeared from the Gallery."

Not necessary to mention the fact that they had been found later, or that the Constable—the *Constable!* Was the painting a fake? Was that the explanation of its disappearance? Blake Sinclair had offered it for sale, secretly. When, on the terrace at Shore Acres, he had discovered that Eckhard was an expert on old masters had he dashed for the Gallery to find and hide it? Wrong number. Fran had said, "Blake is on the verge of a nervous breakdown about the painting, he can't understand why Mr. Sargent is holding up his decision. I had a mean suspicion that he knew something about its disappearance. Now I am sure he doesn't." That let Sinclair out.

"What do you make of the theft, Major? You've been silent so long I thought you were working out a solution. I bet the person I saw slip in made off with the treasures."

"I haven't a solution to offer—yet. What became of Morrie Grove?"

"He didn't get out of the car, if it was Grove—I couldn't see, I'm taking your word for it. As the house was dark naturally he would conclude that the Digbys were away and back out. I hung around getting wetter and wetter, hoping to see the person who went in forcibly ejected. I told you I was stubborn. No light. No sound inside. I figured that Si Pond must be on the job by this time, perhaps he had caught the intruder and fired him out the front way. Came the headlights of another car—the yarn has the movie touch, hasn't it—another dark figure dashed along the path to the door, pounded, rushed back, drove away."

That was my entrance into the scenario, Myles thought. "Go on," he prodded.

"I waited hunched against the shrubs, drenched to the skin. I couldn't be any wetter than I was, why not see the situation through? The light in the small gallery went on. The second car had brought someone who belonged, I deduced. Now for the showdown. If there was a yell for help I was Johnny on the spot. I huddled deeper into the bushes with each flash, knowing that if I were discovered I would lose a dramatic denouement."

"You were taking chances. You might have been accused of theft."

"That's right, but remember I didn't know there had been a theft. Not long after, the light in the kitchen came on. I saw you and Miss Fran in a doorway looking at the floor. 'Aha,' I told myself, 'that first visitor left a trail.' I'm a mystery story addict. I was raised on the Sherlock Holmes formula, observation and deduction. Then you pulled down the shades, opened the outside door, closed and locked it."

"Play by play account so far; you missed a lead, though. You didn't know that Betsy Digby left a key in the lock outside that very door before she hurried away, which fact made it a cinch for the first person to enter and lock it after him on the inside. Did waiting pay a dividend? Did you see the mysterious him or her come out?"

"No. By that time I was so stiff, chilled and almost deaf from the crashes of thunder I decided to move to make sure I could. I stole around the ell to the garage, hoping that because of the storm Si Pond would be late in arriving and I might contact him."

"Why not contact me inside the house?"

"Wet and bedraggled as I was you would have thought me crazy, besides, apparently you were getting along all right, no one had molested you. I didn't see Si, but I saw his bike."

"So, that is where it went?"

"Temporarily. Chills set my teeth chattering. I was

fed up with my man hunt, decided to borrow the bike and beat it to Sunnyside, I would return it in the morning before Si missed it. As you and he were on the premises to keep order, I wasn't needed. Cautiously I pushed the wheel back to the shrubs to make my start from there. I could see two cars at the front entrance, no use mixing up with them."

"And while you were at the garage, the party of the first part made his escape?"

"That's what I thought then, wait till you hear the rest. I was mounting the bike when the kitchen door opened. Someone reached out, thrust something into the wood box and withdrew. The door closed soundlessly. Excitement ousted chills."

"Why didn't you grab him—or her? Couldn't you see who it was?"

"It was done so quickly that I saw nothing but a dark figure against the light. My move was to stay put. If something had been hidden surreptitiously it was bound to be retrieved. I waited and shivered and shook till headlights again illuminated the ell. The car didn't come within sight. Someone ran to the wood box—I heard the creak of the cover—took out what looked like a roll of dark paper, picked up something in the path and ran back. The car started. So did I. I tailed it on the bike."

"And stole the blotters when I was in the house at Rocky Point?"

"I didn't get to Rocky Point. I hadn't gone a hundred feet when the front wheel hit something or something hit the wheel. I crashed. When I came to the bike was gone."

"After that, what?"

"Decided to call it a day, hiked back to Sunnyside. It wasn't too late to ask Caesar to mix me a hot toddy which I drained to the last drop—and then to bed."

"Any aftereffects from the chill?"

"No. After that drenching I was entitled to double pneumonia, but I didn't even sneeze, which backs up the modern contention that colds come from germs, not from exposure to the elements."

He didn't even sneeze. Myles weighed the statement against Fran's report of the sound she had heard rising from the shrubs at Rocky Point. It cleared Eckhard of

200

the theft of the blotters—or did it? There were a lot of holes in his story.

"The afternoon you were changing the paintings, do you remember seeing the man Barth about the place?"

"Barth? I don't place the name. What would he be doing—Barth? Oh, *Barth*. That's funny."

He might not recognize a faked painting but he knew a faked laugh when he heard it, Myles assured himself.

"Now I know whom you mean, the waiter who served at the tea at the opening of my one-man show. After he cleared up he came into the gallery, I hung around till everyone had gone. He talked most intelligently of the exhibit. Said he had taken a fling at painting before the war."

"Another avocation? To hear him tell it that man has as many facets of accomplishment as a multifacet diamond. Now that you have placed him, was he at the Gallery the afternoon of the storm?"

"Could be, even if I didn't see him. Where does he come in?"

"As the Digbys were about to leave he appeared and asked if he could help them get away."

"That must have been before I arrived, I didn't show up until about three. He wasn't round then—at least, I didn't see him."

"Si's bike is still missing. In the note you sent asking me to come here—you did send it, didn't you?"

"Right as rain."

"You wrote, 'If you want to know what became of the bike—' I do want to know. Come across with the information."

"I haven't it, Major. I used that as bait to get you here. I felt we must talk this out."

"Who knew you sent the note?" He told of the telephone warning. "Is this a double cross?"

"Keep away from the Trent place tonight!" Eckhard whispered the repetition. "I'd be willing to swear that I wasn't seen when I gave the note to the bell captain."

"Where did you write it?"

"In the Club smoking room."

"Did you seal it at once?"

"Come to think of it, I didn't. No one in the room. I

left it open on the desk while I answered the phone in the booth. No one came in, I'm sure."

"The mystery grows. At the Club today you volunteered the information that the only time you had met Si Pond was the day of the preview. He says you called on him to inquire if the bike had been found."

"Thought he wasn't talking?"

"He isn't. It was his wife who said you had been there, also that Congressman Grove had appeared quite concerned about its disappearance."

"Grove?"

"Soft-pedal that whistle. It doesn't go with a secret conclave."

"Surprise got the better of caution. Do you think *Grove* knocked me from the bike?"

"I do not and I suspect you *know* he didn't. He knows nothing of the theft at the Gallery the night of the storm. He's on a man hunt of his own."

"Man hunt? What do you mean? What man is he hunting?"

If there wasn't troubled concern in that question Myles never had heard it.

"You'll have to ask him. He has FBI affiliations." That ought to be a jolt. "To return to your story. Where did you get the idea I would be interested in these sheets of blotting paper?"

"I didn't suspect you until I started after the roadster driven, I figured, by the person who had picked them up from the wood box. I didn't know then it was blotting paper. I saw only a dark roll. I nearly took a header when I made out the license number and realized to whom the car belonged."

"So far you're right. I did soak up the muddy footprints on the kitchen floor, did drop the blotters into the wood box, did retrieve them later and put them in the trunk of my car. When I reached my garage I looked for them. Gone. You said that after you were knocked off the bike you returned to Sunnyside. How come you have them now?"

"Found them."

"Found them?" Myles lowered his voice in response to a warning thump on his knee. "Where?"

"You couldn't guess if I gave you a million chances. They were—"

A blinding light cut off his sentence. A black-gloved hand seized the roll of blotting paper.

"You'll never find them again, you—"

Myles sprang in the direction of the growl. The powerful light which had blinded him was snapped off, leaving him in darkness shot through and through with darting meteors. He shook his head to clear his eyes, rubbed them.

"Eckhard, Eckhard, where are you?" he whispered. No sound save the distant murmur of the tide, even the crickets were silent.

"Eckhard," he whispered again. No answer. Now that his sight was coming back, he could see the dim interior of the summerhouse. No one here. Had that blinding light been part of the artist's plan? It had come just as he was about to reveal where the blotters had been found. Why stand here trying to figure the thing out when two men were making their getaway?

Outside the summerhouse he stopped to listen. No sound but the lap of the tide and the cricket chorus. He crossed the garden on the turf borders. The gate between the two places was open as he had left it. Cautiously he passed through. Stopped. Voices? Two figures standing by the fountain. They heard him, and turned.

"Fran! *Sinclair!*"

He stared as he would at visitors from another world. Fran meeting Sinclair here at midnight. It was incredible. It—

"Don't look so horrified, Myles." She took a step toward him. "Meeting Blake was an accident and—" The apology in her voice, her patched cheek, drove him to fury. Why was she here with that heel? He looked her over from her head to her feet.

"Next time you plan a rendezvous, Fran, you'd better dress for the part. Is that a pajama leg I see dangling below your coat?" He cleared his hoarse voice. "Go back to the house and quick."

"What business is it of yours, Jaffray, what Fran does? We are prac—"

"Shut up, Sinclair. Get out of this garden. On second

203

thought I'll take you into the house myself, Miss Phillips. Come on."

"You've said 'come on' to me for the last time, Mr. Jaffray. I'm fed-up with your master-minding. I'll go by myself. Blake, you'd better go, the gentleman seems edgy."

If she hadn't been so furiously angry Myles would have sworn that she intended his eyes to follow hers to the hedge. A bicycle. In the instant that he looked she dashed toward the house.

"That your bike, Sinclair?" he demanded.

"Where? Oh, that? Never saw it before. I don't ride a wheel. Now if you are through your third degree, tough guy, I'll mosey along."

"I'm not through. What are you doing in this garden at midnight?"

Sinclair's mouth widened in a suggestive smile.

"When a lady invites me to meet her I don't tell, Major."

"You liar. Implying that—" The garden was flooded with light.

"Myles! Myles!" his sister called. "Come quickly."

XXIII

There was just enough salty breeze to keep the jade-green sea astir with turbulence. Brasses on the power-boat blazed in the noon sunlight. Two gulls flying above the white wake gave out with raucous screams. As he stood at the wheel Myles Jaffray's eyes followed the distant coast line with the background of purple-blue hills. The blur of warm color was the Inlet; Rocky Point and the Gallery had shrunk to the proportions of doll houses; the dark spot among the treetops was the tip of a Sunnyside tower and further on a chimney top indicated Shore Acres.

At sight of the rosy brick memory flashed a close-up with sound effects of the midnight meeting with Fran a week ago, of the sudden illumination of the garden, of Nat's frightened call, "Myles! Myles!" When he reached her she had breathlessly explained that, fearing Fran was being kept awake by her bruised cheek, she had gone to her room only to find it unoccupied. Thinking that pain might have made the girl lightheaded, she had run through the house, then to the terrace, had heard his angry voice, snapped on the powerful garden light and called.

He had begged her not to ask for an explanation, to trust him when he said that everything was all right, that she would find Fran in her room. He had waited on the stairs while Nat tapped at her door, whispered, "she's here," and disappeared within the room. What had Fran told her? Nat had not mentioned the incident to him since.

He had made a record-breaking return to the garden. Sinclair had gone but the bicycle still leaned around the hedge. Two sheets of soggy blotting paper which once might have been light blue were partially submerged in the fountain pool. He had fished them out and had carefully dried them in his room. Not the trace of a footprint was visible, that evidence of the mysterious visitor to the Gallery was washed up. Undoubtedly Sinclair had flung them into the water, which must mean that the muddy spots on the kitchen floor had been made by his feet, otherwise what motive would he have to destroy the blotters?

Had Fran met him intentionally or had she surprised him there? That first question was an insult to her. Why had she been in the garden? He hadn't spoken to her since that night. She had hung up when she recognized his voice on the telephone, had been absorbed in conversation with patrons when he had dropped in at the Gallery. Granted that he had been raw when he called attention to her pajamas and ordered her into the house, she might have answered his note telling her that he had important news—honesty had compelled him to admit that it was not about Ken—that was tied up with their mystery.

He had seen her at the Club yesterday; a long scratch showed that her cheek was healing normally. What had he accomplished by his outburst of fury—was anything ever accomplished but a crash by letting the brake off one's temper? Nothing this time but to drive her to Sinclair for companionship. They were motoring, sailing, playing tennis together after her work was done.

205

Gene had said, "Everything you've wanted has been handed you on a silver platter." Lot she knew about it. His rise from private to major had been earned the hard way. Looked as if winning Fran were in the same category. So what, obstacles to be hurdled never had stopped him from working for what he wanted, he wouldn't change when it came to the greatest objective in his life.

Had Fran seen the bicycle against the hedge whose number and make checked with Si's figures? It had been tested for fingerprints before it was returned to its owner. Not a betraying mark. It had been wiped clean. Sinclair had declared he had never seen it before. Why was he in the Shore Acres garden at midnight? His insinuation that Fran had sent for him was unbelievable. If Nat's frightened summons had not come when it did he would have a true explanation—and quick. Had he flashed the light in Miss Tassie's summerhouse? Looked like it, who else would have flung the seized blotters into the pool? Why had Eckhard disappeared?

During the past week he had avoided the artist while he analyzed his story. Had he found a loose end from which to untangle the mystery of the Gallery theft? Dollars to dimes he had. Slow going, but it was a start. Eckhard had admitted that he had been prowling round the Digbys' ell the late afternoon of the storm to check on the hanging of his painting. Something fishy about that. Why was it necessary to check that night? Business was through for the day, why not wait until morning? The important loot, the Constable, had not been mentioned at the midnight meeting. Was it probable that he, in the neighborhood to check on the arrival of bogus old masters, wouldn't have been tipped off that the painting, authentic or fake, was in Sinclair's possession?

The blotters that showed the muddy outlines of feet, supposedly those of the person whom Eckhard had seen enter the ell, had been snitched just as the artist was about to tell where he had found them—had he been about to tell or had the flashed light been prearranged? Had Sinclair grabbed them? Fran would know if he had anything in his hand when first she saw him in the garden. She couldn't dodge a show-down forever, he would talk with her. He'd hang around the Gallery until

206

he wore her out. Having decided that, he would go on to the second item. Nothing so restful as a decision, it cleared the way for the next move; conversely, nothing was so upsetting as vacillation, it played hob with one's judgment. The next item on his agenda was consideration of the newspaper clipping he had received in the morning mail.

He glanced at the lighthouse that loomed ahead, snowy white against the clear blue sky, blue except for a violet haze on the horizon which might mean that the fog genie was preparing to drop in on the village. One huge lens gleamed like a Gargantuan eye. Too near. He brought the boat about quickly. The rocky promontory on which the light perched sheered off in a treacherous ledge. Twice in college vacations he and his boat had been left high and dry on it for hours.

He was far enough away now to drift while he read the clipping. He stretched out on the tan leather seat—oops, hot as blazes—drew a cigarette case and a slip of paper from the pocket of his open-neck blue shirt, adjusted the brim of a soft hat to shade his eyes and concentrated on the printed lines.

A picture from the exhibition of —————— was stolen here today.

He glanced at the heading—the date also had been blacked out.

It is one of several hundred that have been gathered in —————— for a six-week exhibition. The pictures were lent by —————— museums and private galleries. The theft took place in midafternoon while hundreds of visitors crowded the halls.

Myles squinted unseeingly at a trimming on the wheel the sun had set ablaze. "While hundreds of visitors crowded the halls," he repeated softly. Was it possible that the Constable had been stolen while Gene was busy with patrons—there had been many that afternoon, Sinclair had reported when he dropped in at Shore Acres. He read on:

The thief succeeded in taking the painting out of its frame. The stolen picture was one of ——————— which belongs in a private gallery whose owner's name has not been revealed.

Why had the names of the museum where the show was held, of the painting, the artist, the nationality of the private gallery, the date of the article, been blacked out? Why send the deleted clipping to him? It didn't make sense. The fact that stuck in his mind was that the thief had succeeded in taking the painting out of the fr—

Good Lord, a scrape! He thrust the clipping into the pocket of his tan slacks, sprang to his feet and seized an oar. Mightily he pushed against a hidden rock. A seal, dark and wet and shining, sunning on the lighthouse ledge, slipped into the water with a splash, Myles's silver cigarette case slid from his shirt pocket and followed suit. Boy, two minutes more and he would have been marooned for hours. He had figured that the breeze would keep the boat away from the ledge, he had forgotten the tide.

Seated at the wheel with the boat bucking the outgoing tide and the breeze flapping his soft shirt, he picked up the course of reflection interrupted by the warning scrape on the ledge. The stolen painting had been removed from its frame. Couldn't be much of a job. Eckhard had said he had changed one picture for another in the repair shop—but this other guy had accomplished it in a hall crowded with visitors. Must have been a prestidigitator. While Eckhard was on the job had he swapped one of his for the Constable? How would he know where to find the masterpiece? Fran had said that no one but Henry Sargent knew where it had been placed. That missing canvas measured 31 × 38. How large were Eckhard's?

Smart fella. The question would provide his excuse for visiting the Gallery. He would say that Nat wanted him to measure "Country Lane" that she might plan where to hang it in the New York house. He would bring down two birds with one stone—make Fran listen to him and at the same time find out if Eckhard could have changed the Constable to one of his frames.

The artist had confided that only one person in the place beside himself knew the underlying reason his work had been hung in the Sargent Gallery. Was the owner that person? Not likely, he was too explosive to be trusted with a secret. Was he? He had managed to keep the theft at the Gallery under cover for days, even now the rumor that Silas Pond had been struck by a thief who wanted his bike, not by a broken branch, was little more than a whisper.

Silas. He was forever discounting Si in his summing up. Si had smelled "sort of sickish" cigarette smoke before the blow had floored him. That let out Eckhard as his assailant, no one could mistake the smell of his pipe. Looked as if the next move was to collect a few cigarettes and try them out on Si. Perhaps Fate had chucked his silver case overboard to give him an excuse.

If the owner of the Sargent Gallery had the low-down as to why Eckhard's paintings were on exhibition there, why hadn't the clipping been sent to him rather than to a person like himself who knew only that he liked work of certain artists without being able to explain technically why? Was it because someone knew that the painting which Sinclair had delivered to Henry Sargent was the stolen masterpiece? If it were true no wonder Fran's "oldest friend" was threatened with a nervous breakdown.

Cross off Henry Sargent as the person who knew all, who was the next most likely to be taken into Eckhard's confidence? Morrie Grove and he appeared to hit it off well, but Morrie was keen on the trail of the "mysterious stranger." Barth. Barth! Why was he working as an accommodating waiter if he had money enough to live at Si Pond's and hire his boat, complete with phonograph? Was it possible that he was the artist's side-kick? Apparently he had had something of importance to impart the night at Miss Tassie's! Had he left the message on the seat of the limousine?

The scribbled note had suggested:

Don't follow. Stop. Think. Where would you hide what you had stolen?

Proof enough that the man knew the Constable was missing. How did he know? He had been on hand to speed the Digbys on their way the afternoon they had received the fake message. Lem and his wife were sure they knew who had sent it. He'd drop in at the Gallery this very afternoon, and get that bit of information from Betsy. Had Barth sent it to get them off the premises while he took the painting? How could he get away with a 31×38 piece of canvas? If he had, why advise him, Myles Jaffray, who had no connection with the Gallery, to think where he would hide what he had stolen?

Okay, he'd bite, working on the premise that Barth had stolen a picture from its frame at a crowded exhibition, that he had smuggled it to this country—he was assuming that the exhibition had been held overseas—had offered it for sale to Henry Sargent, why would he steal it again? Because someone was on his trail, of course, a sleuth who had ferreted him out. Having discovered he was being watched, where would he hide what he had stolen?

Somewhere near. There was a theory that a person who had committed a crime was safest from detection when walking the streets of a crowded city. Recently the papers had headlined the story of a man who had kidnaped a farmer's daughter; woods and towns for hundreds of miles around were combed for the missing couple, but no one thought of looking in an empty bungalow not five hundred feet from the girl's home in which she was kept a prisoner until her kidnaper was caught.

If he followed that line of reasoning where was the nearest hiding place to the Gallery? Rocky Point on one side. Miss Tassie's home on the other. Sunnyside? Eckhard had been a guest there at the time of the theft at the Gallery. Caesar had said:

"What does she know 'bout this artist man? She don't mind who she takes in. She just met him once an' asked him to visit us. It's dangerous, that's what it is."

Curious how all clues led to Eckhard. Why would he steal the masterpiece? Could be he was a sleuth on the trail of the thief. Perhaps that yarn he had told the other night about being here as a fake expert was a lie, maybe he was the thief. If he wasn't, who was? Sinclair?

He had brought the Constable to Henry Sargent. Ken had warned that the guy would bear watching, that he would take chances. From now on he would concentrate on Sinclair and Eckhard—

"Hi! Myles!" He stood up to locate the hail.

"Cla-m—b-a-k-e!" The voice came from the beach at Rocky Point. He could make out a figure waving a megaphone. "Join us! Make it fa-st!"

Two dollars said it was Morrison Grove who had broadcast the invitation. A week had passed since he had sent the note:

> Got a line on you know who.
> Stand by for a crash.

Did his return mean that the information he had been after was in the bag? "Stand by for a crash," he had said. Was it imminent? Why not show the clipping and the note he had found in the limousine to him? It might tie in with the information—always supposing he had some—about Barth.

"Where would you hide what you had stolen?" The question popped up in his mind with the celerity of a jack-in-the-box.

"Where would I?" he repeated aloud. The flap of the colors at the stern, the swish at the bow of the boat bucking the outgoing tide, were the only answer to his question.

When he reached the Sargent beach the aroma of steaming clams and roasting lobsters rose from a pile of rocks. The fox terrier lying on a boulder was sniffling and drooling expectantly. Gene in white swim suit, Matilde in brilliant green splashed with silver, Pat in light blue were unpacking cups and plates, spoons and forks from a hamper, placing them on a white cloth on the beach. Mrs. Sargent, in a violet cotton frock and a matching skimmer, was stirring chowder, redolent of clams and onions, with a long ladle in an aluminum kettle over a low fire.

You always remind me of a piece of furniture, perfectly upholstered, padded, slimmed and restrained in just the right places—Myles was ashamed of the thought as she greeted him with affectionate cordiality. Morrison

Grove in dirty white slacks and bright red jersey, Hal Andrews in T shirt printed in Mexican design and tan slacks, Blake Sinclair in blue denim, all wearing chef's huge aprons, were poking in the wet seaweed in the rock oven. Gene dropped a handful of spoons on the cloth and hurdled a pile of plates to welcome him.

"Myles. At last. I phoned Shore Acres twice to tell you the bake was on. No one knew where you were."

"I told Nat I was going out in the boat."

"She wasn't at home, Susie, your antediluvian maid, reported."

"Next time I'll publicize my activities on a bulletin board. How come you are here, Gene, isn't this Fran's day off?"

"Dad has taken over at the Gallery, he is breaking in a new assistant to spell Fran. I've struck. I'm fed up substituting for her. I always want to do something special on her day off."

"You should be glad to help your father, Gene, he does so much for you," Mrs. Sargent reproved. "The chowder is ready."

They sat on the sand around the white cloth, all except Patricia—who perched on the boulder beside the sniffing, whining terrier.

"I'll say this chow is delicious—in fact, delectable." She turned her cup upside down to prove its emptiness and pounded deafeningly on it with a spoon. "Service! Service! Ready for the next course."

"You'll have to wait for the rest of us to catch up, Patricia," her grandmother reproved. "How does it happen that you have deserted your adored Fran for your family, ducky?"

"I got her settled—this is the day she sits for the portrait. Not much fun hanging round while John Eckhard stared at her. I didn't wonder he did. She was pos-i-*tive*ly out of sight seated on a bench in Miss Tassie's garden."

Miss Tassie's garden? Something squeezed Myles's heart. Eckhard had asked permission to use Shore Acres garden for the sitting. Was Fran so angry with the owner that she had refused to go there?

"What frock was she wearing?" Gene's question broke in on his troubled reflections.

"One of her smart white spectator sports with the snappy green jade ring and choker to match. Nothing to write home about for a portrait, if you ask me. I wanted her to wear her lettuce green. I'll bet there are miles of net in the skirt, and wax beads. She's planning to wear it to Miss Tassie's waltz party tomorrow night. Jeepers, I wish the old girl would invite me to her blowouts."

"Wax beads! Don't you know Oriental pearls when you see them, kid?" Blake Sinclair demanded. "Clams coming up." He placed a huge wooden bowl full of steaming, partly opened shells in the middle of the white cloth. "Help yourselves, ladies and gents." Pat scowled at him belligerently.

"What if I don't know pearls when I see them, smarty —I know when people are nuts about Fran. I thought Mr. Eckhard never would get through telling her how to hold her head and her hands." She giggled. "I guess he liked to touch her hands. I don't wonder. They are out of this world."

"You're better than television, Pat. Did he do *any* painting?" Andrews inquired sarcastically, Myles stopped talking with Mrs. Sargent and looked at him.

"I shan't tell you, Hal Andrews. I guess from the way you hung round the Gallery a few mornings you'd be glad to paint her. She gave you the old heave-ho, she just babbled and babbled to get rid of you. I asked her why you beat it so fast and she said, 'I talked at exceeding length, Patricia, it worked like a charm.'"

"Do you mean that? Was she putting on an act—if she—"

"We'll end the discussion of Miss Phillips right here, Andrews." Myles was on his feet.

"Myles, sit down," Mrs. Sargent ordered peremptorily. "Hal, I didn't like the tone in which you spoke of Fran. You know that we are all devoted to her."

"Just as you say, if my simple remarks are to be censored, I'll leave." He picked up a tin plate which held a cracked lobster. "Just so there will be no misunderstanding, when I go I shall not come back." He ripped off the white apron and flung it down. With a stifled protest Matilde caught his sleeve.

"Don't be foolish, Hal. We'll take the rest of our

213

lunch out on the rocks till this unpleasantness blows over."

Myles dropped back on the sand as the two disappeared among the boulders. Morrison Grove, sitting cross-legged beside him, chuckled:

"As we were saying—by the way, what were we saying?"

"Pat, as usual, had the floor—she's being spoiled, Mother—she was treating us to a technicolor picture of her idol." The tone in which Gene spoke of the friend who had pulled her out of a financial hole infuriated Myles.

"What if she is my idol, Gene Sargent?" Pat brought up her guns of defense. "She's the kindest, nicest person in this town. I bet if you asked—"

"Don't take a poll now, Pat," Gene protested sharply. "Here comes Eckhard. The sitting must be over."

"Where is Fran, John? She said she would join us."

"It was so late when we finished the sitting, Mrs. Sargent, she decided she wouldn't have time to really enjoy the bake. She had promised her boss to be on hand at the Gallery this afternoon to help break in the new girl."

"But, this is her day off. You should be helping in her place, Gene."

"Fran planned it as she wanted it, Mother, I wouldn't interfere. Dad said she would have tomorrow afternoon free."

Luck was with him. He would have a showdown with Fran this afternoon, Myles decided. It was just one of the calls he had planned for the next twenty-four hours—Si, Betsy and one other. He patted the pocket of his shirt, thrust his hands into the pockets of his slacks. When he withdrew his right hand a newspaper clipping came with it and drifted to the beach.

"Hang it, I forgot I dropped my cigarette case overboard when I pushed the boat off the lighthouse reef. Brothers, can you spare a smoke?"

Mrs. Sargent, Gene, Grove and Sinclair promptly offered a package of their favorite brands. Feeling as he did that Sinclair richly deserved a licking it irked him to accept his offer, but there was more at stake than settling that score, he needed the cigarette.

"Thanks. I'll take one of each to prove I'm not playing favorites. I'll smoke all of them before I get the boat back to Shore Acres float. Sorry not to stay to help clear up but I have a heavy schedule for the afternoon. Join me, Morrie?"

"No. We three he-men are needed to carry the hampers to the house. Andrews seems to have reneged." As Gene, Sinclair and Eckhard joined Mrs. Sargent to collect the tin dishes to be rinsed, he added, *sotto voce:*

"Our artist friend picked up a newspaper clipping that dropped from your pocket. Looked as if he palmed it. Want it?"

"No. I have something to tell you. Meet me at the locker room at the Club at four, presumably for tennis. If I'm late stick around."

"I'll be there. I'll bet what you have to tell me isn't a patch on my piece of news. Sure, Gene, I'm coming to help, with bells on."

XXIV

Seated at the desk in her office Fran tried to concentrate on the memoranda slips she was preparing for the new assistant, but the beauty of the world outside lured her attention. Mr. Sargent had asked her to be here this afternoon that she might instruct the girl if she needed help. "Stay in your office," he had said. "You needn't appear in either gallery, just be on hand in case she wants to ask a question while I am busy with a patron. I've seen many a sale slip away because the psychological contact between buyer and seller was broken if only for a moment."

Perfect day, clear as a bell, must have been grand on the beach. Too bad to miss the clambake but John Eckhard had been so absorbed in his work she hadn't had the heart to remind him they had a date with the Sargents. She had suggested that the sitting be postponed, that a luridly scratched cheek was not an asset in an artist's model, but he had declared it made no difference so early in his work. She had suggested also that he use Miss Tassie's garden as a background, she preferred it to that of Shore Acres.

"It's up to you," he had agreed quickly, almost as if he suspected that she didn't want her life to touch Myles Jaffray's in any way.

A bug flew against the screen at the window and bounced off. A breeze stirred papers and scattered the pink petals of one of the Shirley poppies in a slim silver vase on the desk. Myles. Darn, he was back in her thoughts again. If she had decent pride she would keep him out of her mind as she had out of her life since their stormy midnight meeting in the garden. His detestable, "Is that a pajama leg I see dangling below your coat?" was unforgivable. Even after that she had tried to direct his attention to the bicycle against the hedge. Pretty noble of her after his dictatorial "Go back to the house and quick."

In her room she had had time only to strip off the cotton frock, kick off the white wedgies before Natalie had knocked. She had confessed to her that because of restlessness from the pain in her cheek she had fled to the garden, that to her stunned surprise Blake Sinclair appeared; that Myles had come while they were talking and had been furiously angry. Natalie had smiled.

"You are not telling your real reason for going to the garden or why Myles was there at midnight, are you, Fran? It's all right. I like and trust you enough to accept your explanation. Now let me plump up the pillows and smooth the sheets and I think you'll go to sleep." Surprisingly enough she had.

What had happened to Blake that night after her escape unattended by the master of Shore Acres? They had motored, sailed, played tennis together every late afternoon since but he had expertly side-stepped an explanation of his presence by the fountain. When in the few moments before Myles had descended on them with the suddenness of a lightning bolt she had asked him what he had flung into the pool, he had answered nonchalantly:

"A cigarette stub, what else?"

She had been so sure it wasn't true that she had hurried to the garden the next morning before breakfast but darting shadows of goldfish and stirring lily pads only were visible on the pebbly bottom of the pool. Had Myles found something that night?

"Come in," she responded to a tap on the repair-shop door.

"Thanks for the cordial invitation." Myles Jaffray entered and closed the door behind him. "Dropped in to inquire the size of the canvas of 'Country Lane.' Nat wants to know. Don't scream for help, lady, the galleries are full of maybe customers and your boss wouldn't relish a touch of melodrama; it might short-circuit sales."

"I had no intention of screaming. The canvas is 31 × 38. That question is an excuse. I don't know why you came when I have made it plain that I neither care to see nor hear you."

"You are about to find out why." As he walked toward her she had a creepy close-up of a tiger stalking its prey. "I don't like your attitude toward me, you blow warm and you blow cold, but before we take up that I want to know why you met Sinclair in my garden at midnight."

"Don't be mid-Victorian, from you it is funny. If what I've heard is true you have dated countless girls in countless gardens at midnight, and while we are on the subject of your line, don't call me 'darling' again." Unendurably hurt by the distrust in his voice, she slashed.

"I was advised the first evening I met you to 'beware the wolf,' to watch out for your one-woman-in-my-life line; that it is your sportive custom to love and leave."

"Say that again and say it slowly."

She had seen the same white line tighten his mouth when he saw Sergeant Bothwell leaning close to her in the wooded road. Now that she was the cause she was frightened. Her heart beating in her throat cut off her voice. She couldn't answer.

"I'm waiting for you to repeat that."

Why couldn't she think of a flippant reply? Time was ticking off the minutes, yet her voice wouldn't come. The silence magnified the sound of rapid footsteps, the opening and closing of the repair-shop door, of Gene's angry voice:

"I've come to have it out with you, Fran Phillips. You've taken Blake—"

The impetus of her furious protest swept her into the

room. Her angry color faded as Myles turned and looked at her. Fran's fright was for Gene now; she couldn't have entered at a more disastrous moment for herself. Perhaps it wasn't so bad. Myles didn't know who had given the advice she had quoted to him before the door opened.

"What's on your mind, Gene?" His query was smooth, too smooth, the flaming darkness of his eyes belied it. "Sit down in the large chair. I'm nicely primed for a showdown too."

"This doesn't concern you, Myles, but here it is." She flecked an imaginary speck of dust from the skirt of her carnation pink cotton frock and settled back in the chair. "Blake Sinclair has canceled dates for cards at Kitty Saunders's every evening this week. Fran is responsible, she urged him to play around with her. She's got to understand she can't do that to me."

"Gene, I—"

"I'll take care of this." Myles's curt interruption closed Fran's lips on her protest. "We'll go back, Gene, to the evening of the dinner at Rocky Point when you advised Fran to 'beware the wolf,' meaning me, to watch out for my 'one-woman-in-my-life line,' of my 'love and leave' technique. Don't waste your breath denying it. When you learned that I had been made trustee of Rebecca Harding's estate you flared at Fran, 'Why didn't you tell me when I was advising you a few minutes ago?' "

"Suppose I did warn her about you? You surprised everybody by your return here this summer, you dropped in at Shore Acres without a day's notice. Had I known you were coming, I wouldn't have suggested the job at the Gallery to her. She is unsophisticated enough to fall for your line. You had almost broken up Ben's home—"

"You *know* that isn't true." The line about his mouth wasn't noticeable now, his face was the same white. "You know who broke up your brother's home. Take that back and all the other rot you told Fran about my fickleness, and *quick*."

"How can I take it back when I believe it to be true?" Her pallor betrayed her brazen smile.

Into the tense silence broke the sound of something

218

heavy falling in another part of the house. Had the new assistant knocked over the bronze Buddha? The jar unlatched the door between the office and the entresol. Mr. Sargent will be furious if our voices seep into the galleries, Fran thought apprehensively and took a step forward to close it. Myles, sitting on a corner of her desk, back to the door, caught her arm.

"Don't go. I know this is damned unpleasant but I want you to hear Gene's retraction."

"She'll listen for a long, long time before she hears that."

"Will she, I wonder?" He rose. "I had intended to have this out with you alone, Gene, but you asked for it and plenty. Grip the arms of the chair, it is going to hurt."

"Sounds as if you were working up to a movie cut-in. Go on, I can take it." She smiled contemptuously but the knuckles of her hands showed white.

"Can you?" He regarded her as he might a curious specimen of human being he never before had seen. "Prove it—I know that you made up and delivered the fake message that sent the Digbys to Lem's mother." She started to rise in protest, sank back with a little gasp.

"Don't relax, that is only the beginning. The afternoon before the storm you stole the enamel box from the Louis XV cabinet, then used your friend's gold sandals to make a trail in the dust on the floor of the repair shop to where you hid the Apostle spoons to fasten the theft on her."

"Myles, you are the perfect answer to Hollywood's prayer. That is the most fantastic, screenable yarn I ever heard. Just to humor you, funny boy," her laugh was high, "why would I steal an enamel box from my own father? Steal was the word, you can't take it back. You can be sent to jail for that. It's dangerous. It's dynamite!"

It was, Fran agreed. Was he sure? When had he worked out this solution? Why hadn't he told her? It was what she had suspected, but—

"Not too dangerous, Gene." Myles stopped to light a cigarette with maddening deliberation. "I'm sure it will hold in court when I testify that you lost a thousand dollars at cards to your pals Kitty and Sinclair, that you had taken the box to sell as a last resort if the friend you have betrayed couldn't raise the money for you. I heard you whisper to her: 'I'm desperate, remember.' Sinclair is up to his neck in this; he found the key to the Louis XV cabinet in Fran's room so you could return the box *after* you received the money from the bonds she sold. The guy had threatened to go to your father if you didn't pay up quick, hadn't he?"

"Myles!" Fran implored frantically. The hand of Henry Sargent raised in quick authoritative protest silenced her. She was the only one who had seen him enter and softly close the door to the entresol behind him.

"Sorry, Fran, to disillusion you about your friend." Myles had misinterpreted her breathless interruption. "But it is time she was muzzled. No knowing what more harm she may do if she isn't."

"I believe you've gone stark staring mad, Myles Jaffray. Combat fatigue, perhaps. Fran has poisoned your mind because she's jealous of me. She—"

"Leave Miss Phillips out of this, Gene." Henry Sargent's voice, subdued by the remembrance of visitors in the galleries, broke into her angry recrimination. As he approached she cowered into the chair and stared at him with frightened eyes.

"I'm sorry, Mr. Sargent. I didn't intend to have you know—"

"Don't apologize, Myles, you have said what I suspected. Who else would know where to find the gold sandals? I have hoped against hope that I was wrong. You confessed the theft to your mother that same night, didn't you, Gene? I knew when I saw her the next morning that she was in deep trouble—nothing but the dishonor of a child brings that look to a woman's face."

It had been Gene to whom Mrs. Sargent had said softly that night in her room, "Come out. She's gone." Fran had time to think before Henry Sargent went on:

"I've known that you played cards for money, Gene. I haven't liked it but I banked on your good mind and sense of values to stop before it got too deep a grip on you. I will make good on your bonds, Miss Phillips, but every cent of the thousand dollars will be earned by my daughter." His implacable voice chilled Fran to the bone.

"Dad," Gene wailed, "why will you believe—?"

"Don't waste your voice arguing. Next winter you will take a job with me, a daily job until the debt is paid. Meanwhile you will leave tomorrow morning to stay with your grandmother until Miss Phillips has completed her contract here. It will be most unpleasant for her to see you every day, one of you must go. I can't spare her."

Unpleasant is an understatement if ever there was one, Fran thought. I can't even look at Gene now; it makes me sick to think how I have liked and trusted her.

"I won't go to that poky old place." Gene was on her feet, white, defiant.

"I think you will. If humanly possible I shall keep what happened here between us four. Now that is decided, where is the Constable, Gene?"

"The *Constable?* Do you mean a painting by the English artist Constable? Why should I know where it is? I didn't know you had one."

"Blake Sinclair left the picture with me. I intended to buy it. At the time you took the box the painting disappeared. Did you help him get it?"

"I did *not*. I didn't know he had a painting to sell. You've got me on the other. I did fake the call to the Digbys to get them out of the way—Betsy knows every article in this place, she would have missed the box and spoons five minutes after I left. Why all this fuss? They've been returned, haven't they? Why don't you ask teacher's pet, Miss Phillips, where the painting is? She's practically engaged to Blake. Perhaps she suggested to him before she came here that he unload the fake masterpiece on you."

"Gene!"

"Gene!"

Henry Sargent ignored Myles's sharp protest and Fran's horrified repetition of the name.

"Why do you say a fake masterpiece, Gene?"

"I'm psychic." How dare she be so flippant with her father? "Why is Eckhard here, an authority on bogus art, if not on the trail of a fake? Sure, he's exhibiting in the Gallery but with his work he would be hung anywhere. Ask Myles. I bet he knows."

"I do not know but—" Someone tapped on the door of the entresol. Blake Sinclair stepped into the room.

"Perfect timing," Myles said softly.

"I knocked twice but you were talking so hard I guess you didn't hear." Sinclair glanced quickly from face to face. "They told me I would find you here, Mr. Sargent. I hate to hound you, but I'd like your decision on the Constable. I have another customer—"

"It's gone."

"Gone? What do you mean, *gone?* Sold?"

"Disappeared. It has been suggested that you know something about it, Sinclair."

"I swear I don't, sir. I—"

"May I ask a few questions, Mr. Sargent?"

"Go ahead, Myles. We must find that painting."

"Damn it, Jaffray, are you insinuating by your 'ask a few questions' that I know where the Constable is?"

"No, but you were here in the late afternoon before Mr. Sargent discovered it was missing. You raced here in your car after you heard on the terrace at Shore Acres that Eckhard was an expert on old masters—"

"What do you mean—?"

"Don't interrupt, Sinclair." Henry Sargent forgot possible visitors in the galleries, rose on his toes, roared, "Go on, Myles."

"You found a key in the door of the ell, left wet footprints across the kitchen floor and began a hunt for the painting you had left that morning. You didn't find it. You were in this office when you heard Si Pond come upstairs. You had picked up a piece of firewood in case you needed a weapon of defense. Breaking and entering is a ticklish job. When Si appeared at this door and reached for the light button, you let him have it on top of his head, then dragged him into the repair shop and locked the door on this side."

Fran regarded him in wide-eyed amazement. When had he discovered all this? He hadn't dropped a hint to her. Days ago he had said, "Before we get through I bet there'll be some astounding crossing of wires." Was Blake's incredulous expression an act?

"This beats the Erle Stanley Gardner yarns I've read and I've read them all, Jaffray. Perhaps you'll go on with the story and tell me why you are so cocksure I was here?"

"That's an easy one. When Si came out of his daze he said that just before lightning struck him—that was his explanation of the blow—he smelled 'sort of sickish' cigarette smoke. His sense of smell is keen as a bloodhound's. Remember I borrowed one of yours at the clambake?"

"I remember you took three others as well."

"I tried them all on him. He recognized the smoke of yours as the brand he noticed before he passed out. After you had disposed of him you heard a key in the front door. You dashed to the kitchen, up the back stairs, hid on the seat on the landing and carelessly left a handkerchief there—probably used to mop your heated brow. You saw me take prints of your wet shoes, hide the blotters in the wood box outside the door. Later you dropped in the path the stick you had used on Si, knocked a man from a bike and trailed my roadster to Rocky Point; while I was inside the house you removed from the trunk the evidence that would incriminate you."

"Prove it, smart guy."

"You're a glutton for evidence against yourself, aren't you, Sinclair? Okay, I can do it. You were unlucky enough to sneeze, twice, while lurking in the shrubs waiting for a chance to get away. That sneeze was overheard. I discovered later that the following morning you were talking through your nose when you purchased aspirin from the local drug-store— Here's a pointer, if you continue your underworld tactics, avoid a local drugstore unless you want your moves checked. All is grist that comes to that mill. A week ago in Miss Tassie's garden you grabbed those same blotters and dropped them into the fountain pool at Shore Acres. How did you know they would be there? Answer. You read a note asking me to be at the summerhouse at midnight. That brings us almost up to date."

"If you know so much, smart fella, where is the Constable?"

"I don't know and I am sure you don't. My case rests, Mr. Sargent."

"And what a case, Myles. What is your defense, Sinclair?"

He hesitated, smoothed his already smooth hair, stroked his slight mustache. Why was he waiting? Why didn't he answer? Fran was in a fever of impatience. If he hadn't taken the painting why had he been prowling through this house? He thrust his nervous hands into his coat pockets as if he had reached a decision. Thank heaven for that.

"Jaffray has given you the low-down, Mr. Sargent. I'll admit it because except that I went haywire and bopped Si Pond, I can't see anything in the story to incriminate me. I didn't steal or destroy anything. I did take the blotters from Jaffray's roadster, I had seen him soak up the footprints from the kitchen floor, knew he would use them to frame me if he could—he has it in for me because Fran loves me, he'll get me in wrong if he can."

"Leave Miss Phillips out of it, Sinclair. Why were you in the Gallery after closing time?"

"I was looking for the painting which still belonged to me, Mr. Sargent. I knew that a Constable had been stolen months ago from an exhibition abroad. When I heard that Eckhard was an authority on old masters, I lost my head. Speaking of Eckhard, why not third-degree him as to why he was hanging round the Gallery?"

"Stick to your own story, Sinclair. I don't see how the stolen picture could affect you. You bought the one you offered me from an estate in the South, didn't you?"

"You misunderstood me, Mr. Sargent. I bought it from a man who claimed he had bought it from an estate." That wasn't true, he had said he had found the Constable in the attic of a Southern plantation, she had heard Mr. Sargent repeat it, Fran remembered. "I feared that if you offered it to Eckhard for examination he might hold it till he was sure it wasn't the stolen painting. I couldn't let that happen. Where is it? I had money in it. I want it. I still have money in it."

"And you're still a little uncertain as to its authenticity and of the honesty of the person for whom you're acting as middleman, aren't you? I don't know where it is. We'll close this meeting on that note, Sinclair. Take Gene to Rocky Point. Stay there until I come. I have something to say to both of you and it isn't about the Constable."

"Just a minute, Mr. Sargent," Myles protested. "Gene told Fran a lot of lies about me. I want her to retract them."

"I shan't."

"Understand, Gene, that I am not bound by your father's intention to keep the news of your theft and betrayal of your friend quiet. I'll give it front page coverage. It will make a choice tidbit for the scorpions at the Country Club. Retract or I talk."

"And can you talk. You win. I made up the yarn to keep you from falling for Myles, Fran, from personal experience I'd say Major Jaffray is about as responsive to the love light in a girl's eyes as Greenland's icy mountains. Pity I didn't save my breath, the whole world can see you're crazy about him."

Fran laughed. Nothing short of a miracle that she could, but miracles did happen.

"That's the funniest thing I ever heard, Gene. I couldn't fall in love with him if he were the only man in the world. He just isn't my type."

"How do you like that, Myles?" Gene's eyes and voice were tinged with malicious triumph. "Or don't you care?"

"No comment."

XXV

"Promise you'll marry me or I'll go straight to the devil." Blake Sinclair closed his wheedling argument with the threat. He brought both hands down on the desk in Fran's office with a force that scattered the petals of two yellow roses in the vase, the color of her cotton frock, and leaned across until his face almost touched hers. She rose hastily and backed away.

"I can't believe it is you, making such an out-of-date threat, Blake. Up-to-the-minute people don't go to the devil now, they just find someone else to love." The tinge of ridicule in her voice which she hoped might act as extinguisher to his anger merely added fuel to the flame.

"Will you marry me?"

"No. That is final, Blake."

"You don't care what happens to me?"

"Of course I care, but I have no intention of marrying a man to reform him."

"Gene is right, you have gone all out for Jaffray."

"I said," her voice caught in her throat but only for a split second, "all I had to say about that yesterday and said it rather well, I thought. Please go, Blake. Nothing will be gained if you stay and I have a lot of work to do."

"I'm going, but I'm not leaving this village till the Constable is found. I've had a tip where it is." The last words were a hushed whisper.

"Something about that 'tip' gives me the shivers. Be careful. There is a mysterious undercurrent here. Yesterday's revelations didn't explain all the curious things that have happened. Watch for a trap."

"Trap! Does this sound like a trap?" He flung a small sheet of paper to her desk. She clasped her hands behind her as she bent forward to read.

Want to locate something missing? Be at old radio station at three today. Don't appear till you hear whistle, 'Nita, Juanita.' It's a red-hot tip.

"Blake, be careful," she pleaded. "That note wasn't signed. I don't trust it."

"You wouldn't. Thanks to your aunt's restrictions you grew up afraid of your own shadow. I'll see you later—at Miss Tassie's waltz party—and report that I *have* the painting. Once again, will you marry me?"

"Once again, I will not."

He banged the door to the entresol behind him. Fran sank into her chair, flung her arms on the desk and rested her head on them. She was exhausted by his fury, by the tug of remembrance of years of affection and friendship, by the fear that he would carry out his threat. Would she be responsible? No. A man weak enough to make it wouldn't be held back from "going to the devil" by a woman.

Head down she lived over the unendurable hurt of the day before, of the knowledge of Gene's treachery, climaxed by Myles Jaffray's stony "No comment" after her amused declaration that she couldn't love him, that he wasn't her type. If she had told the truth she would have answered Gene's catty "The whole world can see you're crazy about him" with a fervent "I am. So what?"

Living over the past wasn't getting her anywhere. She raised her head. The anonymous note to Blake lay on the desk, forgotten in his angry departure. She reread the typewritten lines.

Could he trust the person who had written the note? If the man was honest he would come to him. Suppose the mysterious writer had the Constable? Suppose he produced it at the old radio station with no witness to prove that Blake had met him in good faith? A witness. She had this afternoon off in place of yesterday. That was an idea. She would be there. Because she didn't want to marry Blake didn't mean that she had lost all interest in his welfare. Three o'clock. She would be at the place of meeting first.

Several hours later, behind the wheel of her tan sedan with the sun bringing out the gold lights in her hair, Fran looked down at the little girl in a red and white striped play suit whose eyes were flooded with a moisture surprisingly like tears. The fox terrier squatting on his haunches beside her whined in sympathy with the mood of his mistress.

"Why won't you let me come?" Patricia asked for the second time.

"I told you, Pat, where I am going and you cross-my-heart and hope-to-die promised that you wouldn't tell anyone, remember? I'm off on a sort of treasure hunt, I don't know what I will find if anything. The road will be rough. I wouldn't dare take you along. If anything happened to hold me up, your grandmother would be frantic."

"If it is so dangerous you're nuts to go."

"I didn't say it was dangerous, just rough. Do you think I would take the chance of an accident with Miss Tassie's waltz party on tonight? Now that the scratch on my cheek has toned down I'm planning to wear the green evening frock you like so much."

"Jeepers, it's a honey with all those layers of different

tints in the skirt. Please take me along, Fran. Tweed and I would be a lot of company."

"No can do this time." She stepped on the starter. "Remember you're on honor not to tell where I've gone."

"I won't tell. What's the matter with this old world, anyway? Everybody's hiding something. After breakfast Gene got into her convertible just loaded with bags. She was mad. I asked where she was going and she snapped, 'Ask your grandmother, she knows.' She stepped into the car without a word to Gran and Gramp who were standing on the steps. Gran looked as if she had cried all night. Gramp's face was red as fire. Know where she went?"

"No." Fran let the engine die. Pat was telling this long story to detain her, but she did want to know the sequel to yesterday. "Don't you?"

"Nope. I guess Gene was ashamed for leaving like that for she backed the car, ran up the steps, hugged Gran and Gramp, mumbled, 'Forgive me,' then sort of choked and said, 'Tell Fran I'm sorry.' Then she beat it to the car and drove off as if answering a Red Cross call for first aid. What was she sorry about, Fran?"

"Grownups keep doing things they're sorry for, Pat, seems as if one never is too old to make mistakes." Who knew that better than Fran Phillips? "Tweed is too near the car. Hold onto his collar. I'm on my way."

"I'll bet after the treasure hunt you're going to the Country Club for tea. That light blue linen you've got on looks pretty special to me. Going to meet Hal Andrews, aren't you?"

"Meet *whom*?" In her surprise Fran let the engine die again. "Where did you pick up that crazy idea, Pat?"

"I get around. I told him at the clambake yesterday that you giggled when you told me that you talked at exceeding length to get rid of him. He sounded like Gramp when he roared, 'Was she putting on an act?' Gee, he was mad but not so mad as Myles. He jumped up, I thought he was going to hit Hal and he said, cold as ice, 'We'll end the discussion of Miss Phillips right here, Andrews.' His voice gave me the creeps."

"Then what happened?"

"Gran told Myles to sit down, and told Hal what she

thought of him, which wasn't much, then Mother buttered Hal and they took their tin dishes of lobster and went off. She's slushy about him, but I don't think she'll marry him. She told Gene she was fed-up going round with a man who squared his shoulders and straightened his tie every time he saw a skirt. Now, don't you think you'd better take us along? We'd be grand company and I know a lot more to tell you."

"No." With difficulty Fran resisted the wistful eyes, wheedling voice and the promise of more details to come. "I'll try not to be a minute later than four-thirty, I may get back earlier. Ask Mrs. Betsy to take a tea tray to my living room and we'll have a party. Won't that be exciting?"

"Huh, better than nothing. While you're gone I'll hitch-hike to the Inlet. Mr. Eckhard asked me to come and give the once-over to that sketch of you he made yesterday, said I would know if he had caught your spirit. What's your spirit?"

"Ask him. Back at four-thirty and where I have gone is hush-hush, remember."

She sent the car ahead to escape more questions and the sight of the child's wistful eyes. She checked the dashboard clock with the watch at her wrist. Abundance of time to make the top of the hill before Blake was due—that is, if the road was not too rough. When Gene had explained plans for the sunset supper there she had said to allow plenty of time, the road was full of holes.

Gene. All last night she had relived the scene in her office. When she had begun to doubt her friend's honesty the doubt had been a constant prick, now the surety of it was a dull ache.

Gene had gone, Pat had reported, leaving a "tell Fran I'm sorry" message. It had sounded genuinely repentant as Pat had told it, but it was hard to believe with her one-time friend's bitter voice still echoing in her memory. Why live over yesterday? Or the days before yesterday? At least the mental turmoil which had resulted from the Gallery theft had kept anxiety for Ken from wearing a rut in her mind. Weeks had passed since Myles had told her of his dangerous mission. She shivered. Was he—

She pulled in her imagination which was off on a

runaway. Why allow herself to be stampeded by fear when the world about her was so beautiful? Trees and wayside shrubs were vividly green. An ocean breeze was whipping the cobalt-blue sea into lacy ruffles. The sky was clear turquoise except on the horizon where it was violet. Haze? Did the haze mean fog? It had been like that yesterday. Mrs. Betsy had shaken her head when she looked at it. "You never can tell," she had said, "whether it will drop in or blow out to sea. It moves awful quick either way."

Better keep her attention on where she was going, the opening that indicated the road to the old radio station wasn't easy to see. She had driven on this highway along the base of the hills many times, had visualized what it had been like in the war years with armed guards to challenge a passing motorist.

It would be cheering to see even one armed guard, she decided as she turned into the road that wound to the top of the hill. Rough was an understatement to describe its condition, the holes suggested a professional application of dynamite. Had she been stark staring mad to come? What help could she be to Blake if his summons here proved to be a trap? Why think of that? She wouldn't welsh now that she had started, but the next time she had a crazy idea like this she'd throttle it. Meanwhile she would go on.

That was an easy decision, nothing else for her to do. No place to turn, backing down would be more perilous than the ascent which had bounced her up and dropped her back on the seat till she was hysterical with laughter. Her heart had bounced and dropped in sympathy. Pity a cardiograph couldn't be shot of its activity. The film would make medical history.

Something like a scarf, ethereal as pale gray malines, caught on the top of a pine, clung and swayed. Smoke? Had a fire been started in the old radio station or was it from a camper's fire? Nothing to do but go on. She glanced at the clock. She would be well ahead of Blake. It seemed hours that the small car had been plunging into holes that suggested Rocky Mountain canyons, lurching up and out, struggling forward like a bulldozer on high. For a gal who had been told what to do and what not to do for years she was certainly going places.

A sunny spot ahead. Thank heaven. Must be the clearing on which the radio building stood. She listened. Sounded as if a car behind her had begun the struggle up the hill. Was it Blake? He would be furious if he found her here. Pity she hadn't thought of that before. Another drift of gray malines swaying from a treetop. That wasn't chimney smoke. Were the woods on fire? She thought of the tragic holocaust of the year before, and had a vision of Pat waiting beside the tea tray for her return—suppose she didn't return?

"Don't be gooshy, Fran."

Memory reproduced the pitch and scorn of the child's voice to a vibration. It jolted her out of panic, brought up reserves of common sense. Why be so sure it was a forest fire? She sniffed. Didn't smell like smoke. The drone overhead meant that a plane was passing either to or from the airfield. If the woods were on fire the pilot would see it and radio an alarm at once, wouldn't he? She glanced back. No sign of flame visible, nothing but what looked like a gray ocean dotted with little dark islands. Treetops looming through fog. That distant, weird wail must be the foghorn blaring. Not so good but better, a whole lot better, than fire.

Another plunge, another lurch. She was on the edge of the sunny clearing. She had reached the top of the hill.

> A gal who bore mid snow and ice
> A banner with the strange device,
> Excelsior!

She chanted the lines. Her giggling appreciation of her adaptation of the classic frightened her. All that was needed to complete this nightmarish adventure was a touch of hysterics.

She stopped the roadster to regard a dark building which stared at her with dozens of glassy eyes and spooky sockets where glass had been. It had the haunted look. Icy chills slithered along her veins. The sound of a motor puffing in ascent like a porpoise—did a porpoise puff?—stopped her heart and then sent it thumping on. Suppose Blake didn't come? Suppose the other person did and found her here?

231

She mustn't be seen. She had come that she might serve as a witness later if needed. She would keep in the background. Where? The sunlight was beginning to be hazy but it was clear enough to see a shed among the trees. Had she time to make it? A second car was toiling up after the first. The engines had a different hum. She'd better get out of sight. While the two cars were making so much noise hers wouldn't be heard.

In the shed she gave thanks for the shelter from which vantage she could watch the arrival and departure of the other cars. Watch. Her mistake. Fog was rolling across the clearing as if it meant business. Her heart zoomed and grounded and resumed its beat. Why be scared? Wasn't this adventure, adventure in capital letters? What a story she would write to His Honor if ever she got out of this mix-up. *If*, that was a cheerful thought.

> Nita, Juanita,
> Ask thy soul if we should part.

The whistle was muted. Her eyes followed the sound. The two blurred lights must be on the car which had lumbered up after hers. Two more lurched on to the clearing, a bright spot in contrast to the surrounding trees. Two dark figures walking. Why stick around this shed? The men couldn't see her. If this conference wasn't about the theft of the Constable it was about something equally shady. Now that she was here why miss a trick? Blake wouldn't let anything happen to her.

She stepped cautiously forward. Curious, she had the feeling that she had left her body behind, that only her spirit was faring forth. "What's your spirit?" Pat had asked. "Something that casts aside fear like a discarded cloak," she could answer now. Moisture from the roof dripped on her head as she stole from the shed. The dark bulk of the building was at the right of the four blurred lights. Better edge toward that. Already her lashes were beaded with moisture; her linen frock damp.

"Who's moving? Bring anyone with you?" The low, hoarse voice was terrifyingly near. She shrank against the building. Would it show up her light blue frock?

"No."

"How can I tell in this soup if you are the person who wrote the note?"

"You wouldn't know any better if you could see me. I whistled 'Juanita,' didn't I?"

Though sounding hollow in the fog there was a familiar note in the last voice. Blake's? He wasn't the one who was to whistle the signal. If she were nearer she might be able to see the face. She took a quick step forward. Curious this sense of being a disembodied spirit as if she were floating—the toe of her human foot caught in a root and tripped her, disembodied spirit and all.

"Who was that?"

"Probably a fish hawk grounding, natives call them eagles. I'm much interested in fish hawks. There's a nest on top of this mountain. Let's talk business quick or we'll never find our way down."

Motionless where she had fallen Fran repeated to herself. "I'm much interested in fish hawks." Sounded familiar. "Much interested in crustaceans," the mysterious Barth had said. Barth! Barth had stepped into her life again. Holding her breath she strained her ears to hear.

"You're looking for a certain painting, aren't you?"

"That's what you think. Come across with your information and quick. You wrote, 'Want to locate something?' I do. Hand it over."

"I didn't say you would find it here. I have a party who is interested to know who stole it. I have found out."

"So that's the racket. A double cross. You won't get away with it."

"Put up that gun, you fool, this isn't an ar—"

Something like a very special current of air whirred by Fran's cheek. A bullet? She flung herself flat to the ground. Memory broadcast Betsy's voice, "I see a black cloud of danger, dearie." This must be the black cloud. Shadows merging, fighting. Fran struggled to her feet. Heavy breathing. Someone was being dragged.

"Get behind the wheel of your car and start down, you dumb heel!" a rough voice commanded.

Another shot? No, backfire. An engine purring. Whose, Blake's or the person's who had enticed him here? A second car starting. They were leaving her on the top

233

of the mountain in a fog which might last for days with only that grounded fish hawk and its family in the nest, horrible "eagles," for company. It was so thick now she couldn't see a foot ahead. She called:

"Blake! Blake! Don't leave me."

No answer but the drip, drip, drip from the eaves of the building, the drone of a plane overhead, and the diminishing sound of a laboring motor. Nothing for her now but to get back to her car. Where was it? Which way?

She took a cautious step forward with hand outstretched. Wood. The radio building. Step by slow step she followed the wall. A corner. Too thick to see another step ahead. Fog blanketed the clearing. Outlines were blurred. If she kept on she might get into the woods, wander until exhausted, fall and be forever lost. Better stay here until the fog lifted. It always did lift, didn't it? Only Pat knew where she had gone.

"Pat, Pat, never mind your promise. Tell someone where I am," she called.

Only drip, drip, drip, from the eaves in answer.

XXVI

Myles Jaffray stood at the window of John Eckhard's studio looking out at the colorful collection of boats moored in the Inlet and the equally colorful bungalows, shacks and cottages perched on its banks. Great day if one didn't know that the violet haze creeping forward on the ocean side meant fog and plenty of it. He tightened the silk scarf that carried out the tan of his shirt and the dark blue of his trousers and thrust his hands hard into the pockets of his white blazer. The interview ahead would prove darned uncomfortable, but it had to be. The best defense is a strong offense, carry the battle to the enemy, he reminded himself. Was Eckhard an enemy?

" 'The time has come, the walrus said,' " Morrison Grove, in white slacks and crimson pullover, declaimed theatrically as he turned from intensive study of an unframed painting hanging on the wall. Had there been

234

some curious telepathic communication between their two minds?

Eckhard, who was turning over a stack of canvases, looked up quickly and straightened. The rolled-up sleeves and turned-back collar of his blue shirt revealed vivid sunburn. He rapped his pipe clear of tobacco and thrust it into the pocket of his faded blue denim slacks.

"I had a hunch you two were here for a purpose. Sit down, if you can find anything to sit on, and get it out of your systems." He overturned a keg that had served as a wastepaper receptacle for a seat; Grove perched on a high stool.

"You're right, Eckhard," Myles admitted as he swung a camp chair away from the front of an easel. "I'll open the meeting. First, I want to know why you played me for a sucker with the mysterious summons to meet you in Miss Tassie's summerhouse? You left the note open on the desk in the Club writing room, knowing that Sinclair would read it, hoping that he would join us—as he did—didn't you? Second, why did you melt into thin air after he flashed that blinding light; third, what in thunder is the connection between you and the man who calls himself Barth, who, Grove told me yesterday, is a secret agent? Fourth, this isn't a question, it's a statement—you owe it to Miss Trent, whose guest you are, to tell what you know about the missing Constable."

Myles noticed the artist's furtive glance at the painting Morrie Grove had been studying. A lovely thing which showed a stretch of meadow with a shining stream crossed by a bridge, beyond which white cathedral towers rose against masses of soft gray clouds with silver edges. Eckhard started to fill his pipe, thought better of it and dropped it back into his pocket.

"I told you the other night, Major Jaffray, the underlying reason of my presence here. To explain 'Barth,' now it can be told. He is liaison man between the art experts along the coast."

"Did he have to act like a psycho, claiming to be proficient in a different job to each person he met?"

"I'm not wise to his methods. You'll have to take up that with him, Grove. He contacted me in New York, came here, found a job, and hired a room and boat from Si Pond. Following instructions, I arrived in this village a couple of days before my show opened. A day later he told me that a suspect had arrived, that he had a tip the guy would dine at Rocky Point that evening, that he had arranged with the caterer for whom he was working to deliver the ices at the house. He would be on the job after dinner. I was to sail Si Pond's boat along the shore, put a record, 'Nita, Juanita,' on the phonograph as a signal that I was on hand to take him off."

"For the love of Pete, does it take all that scheming to locate one stolen painting?"

"Not only the painting but the fence who had handled it was to be found. One false move and the gang would go underground. Of course there is a gang which passes a picture along from hand to hand like a water-bucket line at a fire.

"Our program went as agreed. I put on the record, the tenor sang 'Juanita' with a passion that stirred even my battered old heart, Barth came aboard, reported that kitchen gossip had it that his man was engaged to a girl dressed in amber satin, that when he saw a yellow gleam on a boulder in front of the terrace he had lingered among the rocks hoping to hear something he could use."

"A great and glorious profession for a he-man, that of listening at keyholes."

"Don't forget, Grove, that what you call listening at keyholes was a dangerous, heroic profession in the days just past, still is and will be in the future. Countries and armies have been saved by it."

"Right, my apologies to heroes past and to come. Did your man Barth get anything on the suspect?"

"No. He discovered that the man with the girl wasn't the suspect and beat it. The day after my show he was hunting crabs among the tide pools, it wasn't a coincidence that it was in front of the Gallery, when he heard Henry Sargent on a bench on top of the cliff, booming approval of a newly discovered Constable which was being offered him, by whom, Barth couldn't tell. The seller kept his voice low. A Constable had been taken from a frame at an exhibition a few months before."

"This is as good a time as any, Eckhard, for you to explain why a deleted account of the theft was sent to me and why you palmed the same when I pulled it from my pocket at the clambake."

"I don't know why it was sent to you unless someone thought it might incite you to more strenuous effort to find the painting. I palmed the clipping fearing that our suspect, who was at the picnic, might pick it up and take alarm."

"Ready to tell the name of the suspect?" Eckhard glanced at the watch on his wrist.

"Safe enough now, Grove. Barth has contacted him if he swallowed the bait and I am sure he did, bait, hook and sinker. A very, very nervous boy is Blake Sinclair."

Myles had known the name was coming but he winced. Would the truth hurt Fran unbearably?

"I made the midnight date with you, Major, left the open note, in which I asked you to come to Miss Tassie's summerhouse, on the desk when I heard Sinclair's voice in the lounge. I knew that if he read it and came, we were on the right trail. A mistake would be costly in more ways than one. I disappeared after he snitched the blotters and followed him to Shore Acres garden. What happened there, you know better than I, Major."

"You were about to tell me where you had found the blotters when that light flashed."

"Believe it or not, I was passing Sinclair's door at the Inn, not unintentionally, when the maid came out of the room carrying a waste-paper basket above the top of which stuck light blue blotting paper. I said, 'Throwing that away? Let me have it. I need a blotter.' Simple as that. By the way, the footprints were gone. Next question?"

"Why was Barth in chauffeur's livery driving a black limousine? Why did he have a note on the seat, 'Where would you hide what you had stolen?'"

"He was on another job, probably, didn't want you trailing him. That last is mere conjecture. I told you before I am not hep to his methods."

"Why the 'Nita, Juanita' whistle in the garden the night of Miss Tassie's party?"

"Barth, we'll call him that, it isn't his name, had made an appointment to bring your supper to the terrace, Major. Indirectly he intended to find out what happened at the Gallery the night of the storm. The

237

whistle was a signal for him to disappear. It had been observed that Sinclair, though apparently absorbed in his supper, had been watching him. There are likely to be two men on a job like this working together."

"Two? That means one beside yourself and the man called Barth?"

"That's right, not both necessarily agents, though."

"Do you know who it was?"

"Yes, but if I were to tell it might destroy the guy's usefulness in the future."

"Let's get back to the stolen painting. After the Digbys left the afternoon of the storm, your man Barth located the picture in the repair shop and slipped the information on to you?"

"Right again, Major."

"When you took one picture from the gallery to the repair shop with the explanation you wanted to replace it with another you had brought from the Inn, you carried off the Constable with the picture you had taken from the frame. You figured that it would not be noticed that you were carrying two canvases?"

"How did you guess?"

"It isn't a guess, I've been working this out as a problem for days. Something had to break. I'll be darned, though, if I understand why you didn't come out with the truth as soon as you found it and accuse Sinclair of handling stolen property."

"Not so simple as that. I told you we had to be very careful not to make a mistake, one false step and we'd lose the gang. I brought the picture here to study it, to determine if it were the missing masterpiece or a fake. No one but Barth, not even Henry Sargent, knows I have it. Sorry we couldn't spare him anxiety, but we couldn't. There it is." He waved his pipe toward the painting of white cathedral spires, of a stream and a bridge. Myles's eyes followed his, came back to his face.

"What's the verdict?"

"It is the stolen Constable. It is also a fake."

"Sure of that?"

Eckhard rose, took off his heavy-rimmed spectacles and nervously replaced them.

"Yes, I painted it."

"I'll be da—"

"Eckhard!"

Grove's expletive and Myles's exclamation collided. Both men were on their feet.

"Sit down again, please. Give me a chance to explain. During the years I studied abroad I was fascinated by the work of Constable. I liked his tones, his colors, his methods. Tried to paint as he did. A dealer, after seeing my canvases, suggested that I paint a Constable, that he would sell it as a work of one of the master's pupils for a good price. At first I was shocked by the proposition, then I began to think that the dealer had said he would sell it for the work of a pupil. I was a pupil, wasn't I? As I was living on practically nothing, the temptation was great. I fell for it. I worked as I never had worked before, studied Constable's canvases. As nearly as I could, discovered the paints, the oils, used by him. With the result that I got enough from the sales of four to be able to keep on living and working, though what I made from them was very little. Not until I went into the service did I learn that the tricky dealer had disposed of them as genuine Constables that recently had been discovered."

Eckhard was the first to break the tense silence which followed his confession.

"I don't wonder you are too shocked to speak. The ground rocked under me when I discovered what had happened. I have made it part of my job to track down and expose all those fakes. This is the fourth. It will go back to the owner."

"Do you think Sinclair knew it was a fake?"

"Yes, Major. Every Constable is known and catalogued. The unbelievable point with me is, how he could think for a moment that he could fool Henry Sargent with that yarn that it had been discovered in a Southern attic."

"What's so unbelievable about that? Masterpieces have been found that way, haven't they?"

"Sure, Grove, but we know that this painting came from Belgium."

"Belgium? Barth, a butler in a near palace in that country. I begin to see light."

"He was a secretary, not a butler, Major Jaffray. He had a list of the treasures that were stolen from his

239

employer. I'm not binding you to secrecy about my departure from the straight and narrow, though I had no idea at the time that my work was being sold for genuine Constables. Henry Sargent knows, I told Miss Tassie—I wouldn't accept her hospitality unless she knew—and of course, the commission that sent me here."

"As far as I'm concerned, I have forgotten. How about you, Morrie?"

"I know nothing about art, Myles, but I would say that Eckhard had settled it with the world and his conscience. He has corralled the fourth and last of his paintings, all of which doesn't alter the fact that Sinclair has offered for sale a painting he knew had been stolen. Who comes?"

Pat Sargent dashed into the studio, the fox terrier narrowly escaping decapitation as she slammed the door behind her. The seated men stared at her as if she were an apparition from another world.

"Hi, Myles. Hi, Morrie Grove. I've come to see the sketch of Fran, Mr. Eckhard." She looked from one to the other and shrugged.

"If I had a place to sit down I wouldn't keep you all standing, Gran says a lady should never keep gentlemen standing." As if motivated by the same spring, the men were on their feet. She couldn't see their broad grins, as Eckhard escorted her to the camp chair to the accompaniment of repressed chuckles. Grove slipped an unnecessary box under her feet and Myles asked with impressive formality:

"Is the lady comfortable?"

"Sure." She tried to spread her abbreviated red and white striped skirt. "Now may I see the picture, Mr. Eckhard?"

Myles felt as if he had been catapulted from a far country, a country of intrigue, imposture and mystery to a world of sea and sky where a child was asking to see the picture of the girl he loved, a girl who couldn't fall in love with him if he were the only man in the world, he reminded himself bitterly.

"In a moment, Miss Patricia," Eckhard assured with impressive formality. She sat demurely, hands in her lap, evidently relishing her importance. After one upward look at his mistress, the fox terrier crouched on his

240

haunches in dignified indifference beside her. Boy, the pup looks almost humanly intelligent, Myles thought as he dropped to the top of the overturned keg and clasped his hands about one knee. Grove perched on the high stool.

"Close your eyes, everybody," Eckhard suggested. "This is only a sketch. You'll get a better impression if you see it suddenly."

Before he closed his eyes, Myles glanced at Pat. In the process of shutting hers she had screwed her features into tortured lines, like a gutta-percha face which had been distorted by experimental fingers.

"Ready."

It might be a sketch only, but it was Fran, vital, beautiful, Myles thought with a quick contraction of his heart. If only—

"Jeepers! How I love that woman." A big tear rolled down Pat's face as, hands clasped, she leaned slightly forward gazing at the canvas. Myles cleared his throat of an uncomfortable lump. Morrison Grove followed a betraying sniff with a hollow cough.

"You've said everything, Miss Pat. I know now that I have caught her spirit," Eckhard declared.

"It's Fran, all right. Has she seen it?" the child asked eagerly.

"No, she doesn't want to see it until it is finished."

"What she says goes. I'm going to be just like her when I grow up—if I can. Gee, what's that drifting by the window? Smoke?"

"Fog, and it's rolling in fast. How did you get here, Pat?"

"Hitchhiked." She ran to a window. "Isn't it thick? Do you suppose it will reach the hill?" Her voice was shaky.

"What hill?" Eckhard and Grove demanded in unison.

"The old radio station."

"Why are you frightened about the fog on the hill, Pat?"

"Jeepers, Myles, don't yell. I—I promised Fran I wouldn't tell where she had gone."

"Fran!" Myles saw the startled eyes of Grove and Eckhard meet. "Has Fran gone to the old radio station, Pat? There are times when a promise should be broken

241

when—when perhaps a life is at stake. Tell me, quick, how, why did she go?"

"She left in her snappy tan sedan at about two o'clock, said she was going to the top of the hill, some foolishness about hunting for hidden treasure, as if I would believe that. I tried to get her to take me and Tweed for company. She wouldn't. Have I broken a solemn promise, Myles?"

"Only to save her, Pat." At a window he looked unseeingly out at the Inlet. She had gone to the top of the hill, in her car. "The road is full of shell holes and dark as Hades from overgrown trees," Gene had said. Suppose when Fran reached the top of the hill and it was blurred with fog and she began to wander—

"Major Jaffray, we must find her," Eckhard declared as he took the sketch from the easel and stood the canvas among others on the floor. "Barth wrote Sinclair that if he wanted to locate the missing painting he would get news of it at the old radio station. If the two men met there I'm not anticipating trouble, but you never can tell what a man will do when he's in wrong. We figured if Sinclair went it would clinch our evidence."

"Find her. I'll say we must find her. Morrie, start up the hill road in your car. Don't shout until I call from the top. It might confuse Fran."

"The top, Myles? Are you crazy? How will you get there?"

"This is a chance to test FIDO at the airfield. I'll have them take me above the soup. Ten to one the hilltop will be sticking through. I'll jump. Get going, Morrie. Take Pat along, phone the Gallery from Rocky Point to inquire if Fran has returned. I'll do the same at the field before I take off."

He didn't hear what the two men called after him. If Fran wandered into the woods—stop thinking of her. Concentrate. Lousy day. The airfield. Officials tense with excitement. FIDO to be tried out. Buckling a parachute harness, climbing into the plane. Two pilots. A great light burning a tunnel in the fog. Zooming. Voice from the tower. The pilot answering. He didn't listen, concentrated on the jump ahead. Up. Up. Out into dazzling sunshine. A dark hilltop below. The circling plane. Voice from the tower. Above the dark spot again. He opened the hatch. "Downstairs," he yelled and jumped.

Dropping through space. Down. Down. Down. A dark spot in the gray. The silk spread. Couldn't have taken many minutes to get this far. Grove shouting? No. Foghorn wailing. Damn those fish hawks. He beat off one. Must have brushed the nest as he dropped. Ground at last. He shed the parachute harness. Which way? Drew a powerful torch from his shirt. Still one foot of visibility. Conserve the light. He might need it for hours. The mist on his face came from the ocean. Keep facing it and he'd get downhill to the highway. The dark hulk must be the old building. If Fran had reached the top she might have taken refuge inside.

The muffled call must be Grove shouting below. Suppose she heard the sound and tried to reach it? She might collapse in the woods—

"Fran! Fran!" he shouted and turned on the torch. "I'm here! I'm here!"

She flung herself against him, his arms closed tight about a wet frock with a warm body beneath it.

"Blake, Blake, darling," she sobbed. "I knew you'd come. I knew—" The next word was smothered against his chest as she sagged in his arms.

XXVII

"What is the occasion of this grand party, Morrie? Miss Tassie has outdone herself," Fran said as they waltzed in the great drawing room at Sunnyside to the music of violins, poignant, ecstatic; horns gleeful and windy; a trumpet high and silvery. "This music sweeps every nerve and muscle of my body into rhythm."

"Says you. Miss Tassie announced that this blowout was to celebrate something she had wished for for years, she wouldn't say what. After your outing this afternoon on top of that fog-bound hill, you ought to be so stiff you couldn't move. I never saw anything wetter than the charming Miss Phillips. I don't wonder you collapsed in Myles's arms when he found you."

" 'Twas only for a minute, Morrie. Relief must have

243

made me woozy. It seemed years that I crouched on the steps of that building—fortunately I stumbled over them—not daring to leave for fear I might wander in the woods, thinking that at any minute those awful eagles might light on my back, begin to claw and carry me off to their nest."

"Eagles? Where do you get that eagle stuff? You mean the birds that nest on top of the hill? They are fish hawks. They would be scared to death of you."

"Pity I didn't know that. I've heard that a drowning person lives over his entire life while he goes down. I lived over mine, plus, and came out of it with a profound respect for Aunt Becky and her teachings. I haven't half appreciated what she did for me. That's enough about my reaction to danger—it was danger, wasn't it?"

"Danger, 'sdeath, gal. If you had wandered into the woods Myles and I stood one chance in ten of finding you in time—I won't say in time for what. I hope you've learned your lesson, not to go prowling off to rescue a boy friend. That's what you told me sent you on that wild trip."

"I have been fond of Blake for years, Morrie. I thought I might help him. Even though I know now from what you told me on the way home that he knew he was handling stolen goods, I feel tender toward him."

"It's more than the heel deserves."

"Let's forget him. How did you know where I was? Pat was the only person who knew where I was going and I swore her to secrecy. When that terrifying mist closed in I prayed she would tell someone where I had gone."

"She told. Sometime ask her about it. The afternoon just past has all the elements for a rip-roaring adventure story. Here come your boss and his missus. Mrs. Sargent is a push-over for purple frocks. Handsome woman, unusually pale, isn't she? They both look as if they'd had a knockout."

No wonder, their hearts must be raw when they remembered Gene's treachery, Fran thought.

"Quick, let's side-step them, Morrie," she suggested hurriedly. "If one more person asks me about my afternoon experience, I'll break. They're kind, but I know

244

they are thinking, 'How could the girl have been so silly?' "

On the terrace the air, clear as crystal, was scented with roses. The wind had changed and blown the fog out to sea. Stars were luminous.

"Lucky there's no dampness to take the pep out of your filmy skirt, Fran. Gosh, that green costume is sharp. It doesn't seem possible that this perfect night can be in the same twenty-four hours as the afternoon."

A plane thrummed overhead with lights twinkling.

"I heard two planes go over while I was wondering which way to turn, and decided that staying on the steps was my one hold on safety." She had purposefully led back to the hill. "Did you and Myles drive up that awful road together, Morrie?" He leaned against an upright trellis and stared down at her as she sat on the wall.

"Is that question straight goods?"

"Of course. Why not?"

"Don't tell me you haven't noticed that our Major has been the center of interest here this evening?"

She had. That wasn't all she had noticed. He had avoided her as he would the plague. Why not? It would take time for him to forget her flippant, "I couldn't love him if he were the only man in the world." Perhaps he never would.

"Why is he especially surrounded tonight, Morrie?"

"You're asking that. I guess you were more woozy than you realized. Don't you know that he took off from the airfield in the fog to find you, jumped when he was over the top of the hill?"

"*Morrie!* That's why Miss Tassie almost froze me stiff when I spoke to her. Her idol risked his life for me. She felt I was not worth the sacrifice."

"There was a whole long minute when I was in perfect accord with that statement. I drove up the road, if you can call that ascent driving. Myles was holding you in his arms. He handed you over to me pronto. You were limp as a wet sack with nothing in it. You had come out of your daze—partially. 'Take her home, Morrie,' he said in his stand-and-deliver voice—ever heard it?—'and I'll drive down her car.' I never saw Myles Jaffray hanging on the ropes before, he sure was this time. What had you said to him? He was white."

245

"Said to him? I can't remember. I thought he was Blake, whom I had heard talking a short time before, come back for me. When I heard a muffled call, 'Fran! Fran!' I flung myself on the voice, if one can fling oneself on a voice, and—"

"Miss Phillips, I've been looking for you." She glanced up and met Hal Andrews's challenging eyes. "I hear you've been bragging you fooled me. You did, all right. You owe me a dance to make amends."

"Lovely to Look at"—the ensemble leader's sugary crooning drifted from the house. Why not dance with him? Myles would neither speak nor look at her. Admiring Natalie as she did she felt like a traitor as she assented.

"That divine music has bewitched my sandals. Let's go."

Why had she accepted his invitation? Why was she doing all those foolish things like trekking up the hill to protect Blake, who had been proved dishonest, she wondered as they circled the hall. The silver sequins on Miss Tassie's frock shivered, her eyebrows went up, went down in angry disapproval, there was surprise in Mrs. Sargent's eyes, disappointment in her husband's, as they passed. Natalie in glimmering white smiled and nodded, but her friendliness didn't ease the smarting awareness of disloyalty.

"You're a divine dancer." Andrews's arm tightened. "Gone into the silence, haven't you? Okay with me. I prefer to have a woman silent. We'll do our getting acquainted on the terrace later and—"

"My dance." Myles Jaffray tapped his ex-brother-in-law authoritatively on the shoulder.

"Have a heart, Myles. I haven't had her but a minute. All right, all right. I suppose you'll stand here and make a scene till I give her up."

If looks could kill, Hal Andrews's ex-wife's brother would crumple to the floor, Fran thought. He didn't. He put his arm about her and adroitly whirled her free from a threatened collision. What could she say to him? What did a girl say to a man who had risked his life for her? She looked up. His face seemed more finely drawn than she remembered it. Her heart bailed out and dropped.

246

"Myles." Couldn't she do better than that husky whisper? She tried again. "Myles."

"Remembered who I am, have you?"

"Of course I remember. What do you mean by that?" Indignation cleared her voice.

"When you flung yourself into my arms on top of the hill, you called me, 'Blake, Blake, *darling.*'"

"I called you *what*?"

"I'll repeat that after I have spoken to Caesar. He's beckoning to me."

"A long distance call for you, Mr. Myles," the black butler whispered. "Take it in the library. I'll see that you're not disturbed."

"Come on, Fran. I'm expecting an important message and told the operator to switch it here."

"Why me? It is your call."

"That's right, but we have something to settle. If I let you go, I may not get you again." He closed the door of the room behind them, a book-lined room, a charming room with tall floor vases of scarlet glads each side of the fern-banked fireplace. Bowls of the same shade of sweet peas were on tables that held softly shaded lamps. A breeze stole in through the long open windows and gently stirred the beige hangings. She watched him as he picked up the receiver, he looked abnormally tall and straight in white dinner clothes.

"Myles Jaffray speaking." He was smiling. Only someone he liked immensely could bring that look to his face. "She's here. It's for you, Fran."

"Must be Judge Grimes, but why at this time of—" She spoke into the transmitter.

"Frances Phil—Ken! Ken, *Ken.*" She sank into the chair Myles pushed behind her.

"Ken! *Ken!* You're safe. . . . I won't cry— Why should I now? Back in Germany? . . . You are coming *home*? When? . . . September? Right, I'll be through here the fifteenth. Coming back for what? . . . A *wedding*? Whose? . . . Myles Jaffray's? No. He has not told me. Good-by. Good-by, Ken. I'm so happy—I—"

She cradled the receiver. Keeping her back turned didn't do much good. The huge gold-framed mirror above the mantel reflected both Myles and herself. She dropped her head on her bare arms outflung on the table. Into the room drifted the faint music of violins playing "It Had to Be You."

"Was the surprise too much for you?" Myles drew her up into his arms. He felt the tremor through her slim body as he held her close. "Steady, Fran, steady." He pressed his lips to the soft curls on top of her head, then to the faint welt on her cheek.

"I'll be all right in a min-ute." Her voice was muffled against his shoulder. "Surprise does this to me sometimes, I s-shake as if I had a ch-chill. I've been so troubled about Ken and then suddenly to hear his voice—" She raised her head and brushed a hand across her eyes. "Storm is over. Let's go back—" She freed herself from his arms, even as she thought passionately, I'd like to stay here forever.

"Not yet, we have a few matters to straighten out." He caught her hands and drew her toward him as he leaned against the desk.

"Miss Tassie won't like it if we—"

"Miss Tassie knows where we are. What I have to say to you has her enthusiastic endorsement. I told her several days ago. That's why she went the limit on this party, I hope it will prove the celebration she's counting on.

"Don't try to free your hands, I'll let them go—perhaps. She was waiting at Shore Acres when I came down from the hill. Someone had phoned her where I had gone. When I arrived we had a stormy session."

"She was furious because you had risked your life for me, wasn't she?"

"Risk my life in that jump? It was nothing more than practice stuff. She approves of you. She didn't like the idea of the jump but that is already ancient history. What did Ken say?"

"Not much. There wasn't time. He is coming home in September for your wedding. He was surprised that you hadn't told me."

"I couldn't tell anyone till I knew if the girl I loved loved me." He drew her close.

"Once you said, 'I hope sometime to meet *someone* who realizes that I am grown-up.' Here's my chance to prove *I* realize it. I love you. Will you marry me in September?"